LAST COPY

Roman Song

Brian Kennedy was born in Belfast in the mid-1960s. He is a singer-songwriter with numerous platinum-selling albums and he presents a TV show on the BBC, *Brian Kennedy on Song*.

Roman Song is his second novel, the sequel to *The Arrival of Fergal Flynn*.

BRIAN KENNEDY

Roman Song

HODDER
HEADLINE
IRELAND

First published in 2005 by Hodder Headline Ireland
A division of Hodder Headline

A CIP catalogue record for this title is available from the British Library.

ISBN 0 340 83231 2

Typeset in Plantin Light by Hodder Headline Ireland
Printed and bound in Great Britain by Clays Ltd, St Ives plc
Hodder Headline Ireland's policy is to use papers that are natural, renew-
able and recyclable products and made from wood grown in sustainable
forests. The logging and manufacturing processes are expected to
conform to the environmental regulations of the country of origin.

Hodder Headline Ireland
8 Castlecourt Centre
Castleknock
Dublin 15, Ireland
A division of Hodder Headline
338 Euston Road,
London NW1 3BH

www.hhireland.ie
www.briankennedy.co.uk

For Everyone, Everywhere

'love, the strongest poison and medicine of all'
Joni Mitchell, from 'A Strange Boy' (Hejira)

1

With his antique walking stick held firmly aloft, Alfredo Moretti, retired opera divo and world-renowned vocal teacher, looked as if he was about to conduct an unruly orchestra. Instead, he parted the waves of Da Vinci Airport's human sea of travellers like a better-dressed Moses. For counterbalance, he linked the arm of his newly arrived protégé, the very relieved and travel-weary Fergal Flynn.

Alfredo's legendary status was like an exquisite, exclusive perfume that infiltrated the airport's stale air, capturing the attention of the whirling throng. As teacher and pupil forged their way to the exit, they were studied, gawped at and, inevitably, halted by well-meaning autograph hunters who couldn't believe their luck. Fergal could only watch in bewilderment as the elderly, over-excited fans frantically mined every zipped pocket of their belongings for paper and a pen, finally and apologetically producing the back of a wrinkled receipt and a badly chewed Biro. All the while, they took pictures and hyperventilated some story from years gone by in breakneck Italian. Fergal didn't understand a word anybody said until he heard Alfredo saying his name and realised that he must have started telling his audience of two that Fergal had just arrived from Ireland to study singing under his wing. Suddenly, the same crumpled proof of purchase was thrust in Fergal's direction. Alfredo translated: they wanted him to sign too, because they were sure he was also going to be famous one day.

'What? Alfredo, I'm not sure. I mean, I've never...I'm not famous, for God's sake! Sure, I've never even been out of Ireland until this morning.'

Alfredo laughed. 'It's only polite to do as they wish. Without good people such as these, I would never have enjoyed such a privileged career. And this is an extraordinary moment, my boy. You haven't been in Rome for five minutes – discounting the hold-up at customs, of course – and already you've been asked for your first autograph! It's delightful – and an encouraging sign!'

It was enough to make Fergal laugh, albeit begrudgingly. He felt like a total fraud next to Alfredo. Blushing, he managed to write his name just under his teacher's broader, more confident stroke. Once the deed was done, the recipients reacted as if they had won the lottery. They threw their arms around Alfredo and kissed him on both cheeks, and before Fergal had time to breathe, they did the same to him. Then they trundled off as quickly as they had appeared, clutching their luggage-laden trolley and their freshly inked treasure. Alfredo raised his walking stick cum baton again, and they left the airport building.

Fergal's face was instantly caressed by a wave of warm, fresh air that brushed his skin like a velvet tide, as if to say, *You made it! It's all right now, you're safe*. After the greyness of Belfast, the sun's heat made him smile. Fergal undid another button of his shirt, and his winter coat, folded over his roasting arm, suddenly felt like a dead weight. The overcoat had been a last-minute present from

An enormous Bosendorfer grand piano had pride of place in the front room's bay window. Its lid was closed and a crystal vase of freshly cut white roses stood in the centre, surrounded by a carefully selected audience of framed photographs starring Alfredo and various luminaries of the opera world. The biggest and most opulent frame was reserved for his favourite, a picture of him with Maria Callas, who had signed it for him 'with love and respect'. Alfredo couldn't hide his disbelief when Fergal admitted he had never heard of her. Alfredo raised his eyebrows to the black-and-white legend as if to apologise for his protégé's innocence. Fergal, purple with embarrassment, quietly thought to himself that she looked like someone from *Star Trek*.

'This room is where I conduct most of my lessons,' Alfredo said. He looked at his watch and frowned. 'I planned to offer you a welcoming coffee and some delicious pastries, but the traffic has prevented that. I think it's best if we leave immediately, before it becomes even worse, to meet my sister in the family restaurant. That's where you will live and work.'

The traffic sounded not unlike the riots Fergal had thought he'd left behind. People were screaming obscenities at each other out of car windows and honking their horns repeatedly. Alfredo seemed no more bothered about the circus than about the increasing temperature outside, but Fergal thought he was seeing things – tiny cars and mopeds impatiently mounted the crowded pavements, nearly knocking down the pedestrians, who seemed to ignore the unlawful intrusion. Everyone was in a hurry to get somewhere.

Finally, like an unblocked drain, the traffic surged forward in awkward unison. Ten minutes later they pulled up in front of Bistro Moretti, as it announced in tiny white light bulbs above the entrance. At tables on the tiled pavement outside, customers of all ages were eating lunch, smoking, feeding fresh sticks of bread to children in prams and drinking coffee, so deep in conversation that they didn't appear to need to pause for breath. No one sat outside anywhere in Belfast.

Everyone acknowledged Alfredo's presence as he and Fergal entered. A group of men stood up from their table, calling him 'Maestro', and hugged and kissed him like a prodigal son. Alfredo introduced Fergal, hastily and proudly, as one by one the extended family, dressed in snow-white uniforms, began to appear from behind the swinging doors of the back kitchen. As they all stood looking at him, Fergal couldn't help feeling intimidated. Every one of them seemed to have a beautifully smooth, tanned complexion and pearly white teeth. He felt like an out-of-date bottle of milk beside them.

The last to appear was Alfredo's sister, Arianna, who single-handedly ran the successful business. She strode purposefully to her brother with open arms, her long blue-black hair shining. Fergal pictured the fanned feathers of a raven drying its glossy wings in the afternoon sun after a sudden rainfall. At first he thought she was much younger than Alfredo, but her youthfulness was momentarily betrayed by the occasional silver strand of hair that rose to the surface as she threw her head back to laugh at something her brother said.

Arianna turned to Fergal, took him by the shoulders and looked him in the eyes. 'So you are Mr Fergal Flynn, the one we've heard so much about, all the way from Ireland. My brother speaks highly of you, and we want you to know that you are most welcome here.' Then she pulled him close to her, in a motherly way, and kissed him on both cheeks.

Fergal felt his face redden, but he managed to thank her and acknowledge everyone shyly before Arianna clapped her hands and ushered her staff back to their duties. Then she and Alfredo led him around the back of the restaurant and up a flight of freshly bleached stairs to show him where he was going to live.

The brother and sister rattled away to each other as they ascended to the older part of the building. Fergal thought their language sounded more like singing than talking.

His room was small – just enough space for a bed, a wardrobe, a table and a chair that faced the window of his new world – but warm and bright and exacting in its neatness. Arianna had even made sure it had a fresh coat of white paint for his arrival. It was a far cry from the dilapidated room he used to share with his Granny Noreen.

'You should rest after your journey,' Arianna told him. 'If you're unsure of anything, you must ask me.'

'We would like you to begin working in the kitchen in a few days,' Alfredo said, 'if you're not too tired.'

'Of course, no problem. But when do I start singing lessons with you, Alfredo?'

Alfredo winked approval of his eagerness. 'There's no time to lose. We'll begin this evening. I'll return to collect you at six o'clock. For now, we leave you to settle in.'

As soon as his door was closed, Fergal lay back on the bed and stared at the white ceiling, imagining it was a blank page where his dreams were waiting to be written. He wondered about the people who had lived in this new room of his before him. If the walls could have talked, they would have gossiped like four old spinsters. They had outlived every coat of paint and every repair. They could tell him how many words of love had been whispered in the night air, how many angry insults had been flung in desperation, how many promises made and broken, how many lives had begun and ended here.

He got up again and paced the room slowly. Above the bed was a framed picture of Jesus, with a little red bulb flickering underneath. It made Fergal think of prostitutes for a split second, and he grinned at how quickly his mind could sink to the gutter.

His thoughts turned, once again, to sex, to Father Mac and the similar room that they had so often secretly shared. It struck him that over the time they had known each other, Father Mac had helped him forget what it was to be lonely. He couldn't believe that all those days and weeks and months had evaporated, and here he was, in a new country, surrounded by a language he couldn't understand, much less speak. He knew he was lucky to be in Rome, but at the same time he couldn't help feeling that he didn't deserve it. A mild panic rose in his chest.

Fergal shook his head in frustration and began unpacking his suitcase. He spread out his few belongings in the deep drawers and hung the second-hand winter coat up in the wardrobe, on its own. 'Sorry,' he said to it. 'I'll get another coat as soon as I'm rich and famous, then you'll have a bit of company.' He laughed at his own half-serious foolishness.

Before he closed the long mirrored door of the wardrobe, he ran his hand down one side of the coat and leaned his head closer to smell it, convinced that Father Mac's slight tobacco scent still lingered. He felt the little parcel in one of the inside pockets, a collection of secret poems about forbidden love. Father Mac had passed it to him as they'd said their final farewells at the security gate. It was the last time Fergal had touched his hand. Fergal took the parcel out, kissed the inscription and slid the tiny volume under his perfect white pillow. He hadn't the heart to read any more of it just yet.

The weight of the past was beginning to slow his heartbeat and tighten his head. He decided to go back down to the restaurant and offer to start work straight away if Arianna wanted him to. He looked at the picture of the Sacred Heart and said angrily, 'I haven't come all this way just to mope in my bedroom. Fuck that!'

The kitchen was another breed of motorway altogether, full of stainless steel, crockery and copper traffic. Arianna, surprised, reluctant, but delighted – she prized hard work above all else – gave Fergal an apron and an approving smile and sent him to the sinks to help with the endless washing-up and drying.

Fergal had never seen so many dirty dishes in one place. He thought of Walker Street back home and his poor mother's tiny kitchen (no one ever called it his father's kitchen, even though he quickly pointed out that it was his fucking house if anybody dared to change the TV channel). She was never done trying to cope with the chaos of four constantly hungry boys – or five, if you included her husband, as she often hissed when he was out of earshot. As Fergal scrubbed an enormous pot, he half-smiled to himself. No matter where he went, he always ended up doing dishes. But it was different this time – he knew he didn't have to, and in a few days he would be paid to do it and he wouldn't have to fight World War Three to get a clean cup. He washed and rinsed, his memory drifting back and forth across the sea, until Arianna came back and told him that the lunch crowd had finally left and they could take a well-earned break.

Fergal followed the rest of the kitchen staff to a circular table surrounded by chairs. It held a huge ceramic dish of steaming pasta, precarious towers of smaller bowls, a platter of perfectly cut loaves fresh from the oven and a small dish of olive oil and balsamic vinegar to dip the bread into. At first Fergal wasn't sure what to do, but after watching the staff, he helped himself to a generous portion of spaghetti with rich tomato sauce. It tasted nothing like the tinned hoops his mother used to heat up for lunch. He wasn't sure which he preferred, but he decided to keep that to himself.

The staff gathered in little groups, gossiping between mouthfuls and smoking out the side door. Arianna began handing out espresso in baby cups. One by one, the staff turned their attention to Fergal and reintroduced themselves, in very good

English. They were all members of the extended Moretti family – cousins, in-laws, nephews-of-cousins – and to Fergal all their names sounded extraordinary: Giacomo, Cecco…Try as he might, Fergal forgot them as soon as they were pronounced, but they laughed, telling him not to worry if he couldn't remember. After a Saturday night on the beer, they said, they couldn't remember their own names either.

Arianna smiled protectively. She was glad to see that Fergal was already settling in, and she hadn't seen her brother so genuinely excited for years. She picked up an empty wine glass and tapped the side of it with her fork until the little room fell silent. Then she cleared her throat and announced to the gathering, 'As you know, our newest member of staff, Fergal Flynn, is here to study singing with my dearest brother, who assures me he will be another star of the classical world. Now, if Alfredo has his way – and, if you know my brother like I do, you know he will have his way! – then we want to be the first to wish Fergal every success. If he sings as well as he washes dishes, he will have no problems!'

The staff roared their approval and slapped him good-naturedly on the back before heading back to their never-ending duties and the preparations for that evening's meal.

Arianna had noticed that Fergal was eating the bread but not dipping it into the oil. 'You don't like olive oil?'

'I wasn't sure what it was. I didn't want to be rude, but why is it dark in the middle like that?'

Arianna laughed. 'Olive oil is for Italy what potatoes are for Ireland. The dark one is balsamic vinegar, for contrast, to make the dip even more delicious.' She immersed the corner of a piece of bread in the mixture. 'Try it. If you don't like it, that's fine.'

Fergal thought he would hate it, but as the thick liquid oozed from the warm bread and down his throat, he thought it was the best thing he'd ever tasted. He'd always loved piles of salt and vinegar on his chips, but this was something else. To Arianna's delight, he swallowed every bit and instantly reached for another piece of bread.

She smiled and wiped some oil from the corner of his mouth with a napkin. 'Fergal, we'll make an Italian of you yet!'

3

Alfredo kept his promise. He returned to Bistro Moretti as the nearby church bells sounded six solemn times. Fergal was taking a much-needed shower, as the combination of the heat of the kitchen and the afternoon sun had made him sweat right through the back of his shirt. His hair was still wet when he came bounding down the stairs at Arianna's call.

At Alfredo's home the table was set for dinner, and Alfredo explained that some of his closest friends were coming to eat with them later. They were all dying to meet his new Irish protégé. Fergal liked the way Alfredo called him his 'protégé'. He wasn't really sure what it meant, but he could tell it was something good by the way Alfredo smiled proudly when he said it. Alfredo, catching the confusion on Fergal's face, explained how much he loved the word and indeed why it applied to him. It was as if he'd fitted a light bulb in a forgotten socket in Fergal's head – as soon as he flicked the switch, he managed to make him feel special and a little brighter on the inside.

Alfredo sat at the piano and began playing a slow, melancholy introduction. Then he burst forth, in full voice, with a dramatic melody in such a rich and impressive tone that Fergal nearly lost his balance. He thought Alfredo sounded incredible – and to think this man wanted to teach him! The piece came to an end with a note that Alfredo sustained for so long that Fergal felt breathless. He couldn't take his eyes off his teacher's mouth. In that moment, he understood why Alfredo's presence at the airport had created such a stir.

Fergal clapped awkwardly and quickly. Alfredo nodded modestly. 'Eventually,' he said, 'we will work on this piece for you.'

Fergal's heart sank – he felt like he would never be able to learn something so difficult – but Alfredo smiled at the worried look on his face. 'I felt the same way when my old teacher first played this song for me, more than twenty-five years ago. Fergal, do you know that I have been singing, and now teaching, for longer than you've been alive?'

They began with relaxation techniques, moved on to posture and then to scales. Over and over, Alfredo led Fergal up and down a staircase of notes, improving and polishing the sound of each step as they went. Every now and then Alfredo would stop and tell Fergal to pay attention to the shape of his mouth, or to imagine the different letters of the alphabet in different places in his mouth. Fergal didn't really understand all of it, but when he happened to make the sound that Alfredo was after, Alfredo would yell encouragement and get him to repeat it over and over until he understood what he was doing. Sometimes their concentration would unravel. Alfredo would playfully mimic Fergal's accent and they would both be in stitches laughing.

More than an hour later, the doorbell rang and Alfredo closed the piano, saying that their first lesson was at an end. Fergal wasn't sure how it had gone. He felt light-headed from the new way of breathing that Alfredo had insisted on, and he was glad of the rest.

Two men swept into the room carrying bunches of flowers and kissed Alfredo's cheeks as if their lives depended on it. Alfredo introduced them as Giovanni and Luigi, saying, 'We've been friends for more years than any of us care to guess or admit!' Giovanni was a set designer at the local opera house, and Luigi owned one of the largest flower shops in Rome.

When Alfredo introduced Fergal to them, Giovanni put the back of his hand to his mouth. 'Oh, Alfredo, if his voice is half as beautiful as his eyes, who knows what will happen in the classical world?'

Luigi clutched an imaginary string of pearls at his chest. 'Welcome to Rome. My poor heart is breaking just looking at you, young man. Oh, to be a youth again!'

Alfredo laughed. 'I'm not sure which of you should be on the stage after all.'

Alfredo's housekeeper, Daniela, was well used to her employer's 'unusual' friends, which was how she described them to her religious mother during secret phone calls if Alfredo was out and she got bored of dusting. She appeared from behind the door at just the right moment with a tray of drinks.

Alfredo was as much an expert on wine as he was on singing. He loved watching his guests' eyes light up as they recognised the vintage of the bottle, or the look on Fergal's pale face as he sipped nervously from a glass of Barollo for the first time. Fergal felt completely out of his depth. He'd tried altar wine a few times and Father Mac and he had shared the odd bottle of wine, but to his surprise, he liked the Barollo.

When they were all seated for dinner and had begun the first course of Parma ham, Luigi and Giovanni began asking Fergal about Ireland. They listened with interest as Fergal took them on a carefully edited journey around West Belfast. How could he explain what it was really like, the real images that came crashing into his head when he thought about Ireland? Like the time he had seen a local boy, not much older than him, shot dead by a bunch of foot-patrol soldiers, or the time he had stumbled upon a punishment beating, the victim screaming in an alleyway while one hooded man shot him through the side of his knee and another cut the word 'TOUT' – informer – into his bare chest with a rusted six-inch nail. His diet account concentrated on Father MacManus and their eventual trip to the monastery in Sligo where he had made a recording with Brother Vincent and his strict order of monks.

'Ohhh, strict monks? How strict were they?' Giovanni nudged Luigi and winked.

Alfredo cleared his throat and took over the story. Fergal was only too glad to be rescued. 'Brother Vincent was in charge of an extraordinary choir. They chant in Latin every morning before breakfast—'

'Oh my God,' Luigi broke in, 'before breakfast? If I don't have a cigarette in my mouth before the kettle boils, I'm no good to anyone before or after breakfast, am I, Vanni?'

Giovanni raised his eyebrows and nodded in agreement, and Fergal laughed. 'Brother Vincent is a character,' Alfredo finished. 'And if it weren't for that strange little holy man, I would never have heard Fergal's exquisite recording, nor been able to meet him and Father MacManus in Belfast, and Fergal wouldn't be sitting around the table with us now, after what I must say was a very promising first vocal lesson.'

They raised their glasses, and the food kept coming. Thankfully for Fergal's limited palate, the main course was roasted chicken and vegetables, and he couldn't get enough of it. Alfredo was delighted to see that he had a fairly healthy appetite, even though it paled in comparison to his own.

At the end of the meal, Fergal left the table to go to the toilet.

As he ascended the stairs, he looked at the pale cream walls adorned with framed posters of the operas and concerts that Alfredo had appeared in over many years. Outside the bathroom door was one from London's Covent Garden, signed by the rest of the cast of *The Barber of Seville*. He stood in the doorway and thought about all the places the posters were from and the life Alfredo must have led. He knew he wanted a life like that for himself. He felt a little rush of excitement as he fantasised about giving concerts in front of thousands of people and having his name on a proper poster. He looked around the perfect bathroom and wondered what it would be like to have his own big house one day, somewhere in Ireland or England or even America, maybe, with posters and artwork and books and a piano, of course – God, yeah, he'd have to have a piano.

On cue, an angry little voice with a strong Belfast accent started at the back of his head, getting louder and louder. *Wise up and stop dreaming. You'll never amount to nothing, because you are nothing. You're sick in the head, do you know that? You're a freak. God will never forgive your sins of the flesh with Father MacManus.* Fergal put his hands to the sides of his head in frustration. He threw some cold water on his face, trying to wash away the past. He looked at himself in the mirror and thought he didn't look that bad. He didn't look evil, did he?

When he came back down again, Daniela was serving rocket-fuel espresso to the little party who had settled by the fire in low, soft chairs to smoke thin, brightly coloured cigarettes and sip the Armagnac. When Fergal tried some, it burned the throat off him. He couldn't believe how strong everything tasted in Rome.

Alfredo put his glass down. 'Do you feel like singing, Fergal? It's absolutely no problem if you don't.' But Luigi and Giovanni had already begun clapping and positioned themselves near to the piano, and Fergal hadn't the heart to deny them.

'I don't know what to sing,' he said shyly.

'Do you know any Judy Garland? How about "The Man that Got Away"?' Luigi asked hopefully.

Fergal shook his head, and Alfredo laughed. 'No, Luigi, I'm afraid we haven't begun to study her – or Liza, before you ask!'

'Something Irish?' Giovanni asked.

Fergal thought for a second. He stood up, remembering to carefully adjust his posture to the new one he'd just learned that day, and said, 'This is an old one, one of the first I ever sang, and it's a County Down song.'

'And after this one, maybe a County Up song?' Giovanni quipped.

He and Luigi laughed and Alfredo made a face at them. 'What is it called, Fergal?'

'"The Flower of Magherally".'

The room fell silent. Fergal started singing, slowly and softly, drawing out the notes and sending them around the room with his eyes closed.

> *One pleasant summer's morning*
> *When all the flowers were springing-o,*
> *Nature was adorning*
> *And the wee birds sweetly singing-o,*
> *I met my love near Banbridge town,*
> *My charming blue-eyed Sally-o,*
> *She's the queen of the County Down,*
> *The flower of Magherally-o.*

By the second verse, his voice had grown stronger and more confident.

With admiration did I gaze
Upon this blue-eyed maiden-o,
Adam wasn't half so struck
When he met his Eve in Eden-o,
Her skin was like the lily white
That grows in yonder valley-o,
She's my queen and my heart's delight,
The flower of Magherally-o.

He sang the last verse almost in a whisper.

I hope the day will surely come
When we'll join hands together-o,
'Tis then I'll take my darling home,
In spite of wind and weather-o,
For let them all say what they will
And let them scowl and rally-o,
For I shall wed the one I love,
The flower of Magherally-o.

He held the last note as long as he could, and this time Alfredo was the one to stand up and clap. Luigi and Giovanni did the same, shouting, 'Bravo! Bravo! Encore!' Giovanni reached into one of the vases and threw a rose at Fergal. He caught it awkwardly, pricking himself on one of the thorns. He stuck his wounded thumb in his mouth, and Daniela, who had been watching from the hallway, returned with a plaster and helped him apply it. Luigi announced dramatically, 'Ladies and gentlemen, not only does he sing, but he bleeds for us!'

The room fell silent again all at once. 'A sign that an angel is passing overhead,' said Alfredo. 'You see, Fergal, even the angels have come to hear who was making such a sound.' Fergal loved the notion, even though he was mortified by the compliment.

It had been a very long day for him. When the clock struck ten he suddenly felt exhausted, and Alfredo suggested he go home to Moretti's. Giovanni and Luigi insisted on giving him a lift back to the restaurant, since they passed it on their way home, and Alfredo was glad of an excuse for an early night. Fergal felt nervous about travelling with them. He'd never met anyone like them before – they were so, well, so *girly*. All his life he'd been punished for being a bit girly himself, so Luigi and Giovanni made him uncomfortable and curious, all at once. But Alfredo obviously loved them. Fergal suddenly wondered if Giovanni and Luigi were gay, and then whether Alfredo might be, too, and whether he had some kind of quiet history – like Fergal's own history with Father Mac – with either of the two men.

Giovanni talked non-stop the whole way back to the restaurant, and although Fergal had enjoyed their company, he couldn't wait to get to the silence of his little room. They kissed his tired face and waited until he was safely inside before screeching off down the cobbled road, playing Madonna at full volume.

Arianna was still in the back of the restaurant, with her glasses propped on the tip of her nose, sipping a glass of wine and starting to go over the final receipts of the day. She asked Fergal how his night had been – she knew only too well what an incredible host her brother could be – and whether he wanted some wine, but he asked for a glass of water to take to bed. As he left, she asked if he still wanted to get up and work in the kitchen in the morning – the breakfast shift started at 8.30 am – and when he said he did, she promised to wake him.

Fergal wearily closed the door of his room behind him and looked at his neat bed. His thoughts turned naturally to Father Mac

– Dermot, as he called him in private. If he hadn't been called out to give someone the last rites, he would be about to go to bed in Belfast now.

He took off his clothes and folded them as neatly as he could on the chair by the window. The light had mostly left the Roman skyline, but the dying rays were still enough to cloak some of the buildings in orange and pink, and the whole town seemed to collect shadows. Fergal stood for a moment to study the view. He wondered whether his mother was looking out a window too, far away, whether she was safe, whether she was unhappy. Though she had hurt him so much over the years, he was surprised to realise that he worried about her still. He thought of his brothers and of his distant father, who he hadn't seen for a very long time. Fergal had been lying in St Bridget's House, battered and bruised from the beating John had given him, when his father had visited without warning, only to tell him never to darken his door again.

He turned from the window and opened the wardrobe door. There hung Father Mac's old, lonely coat, long and black and heavy. Fergal took it off its hanger and smelled the collar. He was convinced he could still detect the faintest hint of Father Mac. More than ever, Fergal could have done with his strong arms to hold him, his gentle voice to say that everything would work out all right in the end. Without thinking, he moved over to the bed and lay down, with the coat covering his whole body. He imagined it was Dermot himself on top of him, and he slipped into a deep memory of their last night together on the crisp, careful sheets of his new beginning.

The pillows crackled strangely as his head sank into them, and when Fergal closed his eyes he realised they must be filled with real feathers. He felt his chest tighten and he began to wheeze badly. He switched on the lamp, groped for the stash of inhalers that Father Mac had organised for him and sucked the trusted remedy deep into his struggling lungs.

He removed the pillows from the bed and got under the covers, using the coat as a pillow. At last he drifted into a well-earned, fragrant sleep, clutching the little volume of poems.

4

The next morning, when Arianna kept her word and tapped lightly on Fergal's door, it took a while for him to remember where he was. 'I'm awake!' he said at last.

'The coffee is nearly ready,' Arianna called. 'The other workers will arrive soon.'

Fergal slid out from under the warm sheets and hung up Father Mac's coat, then he shook himself, wobbled down the hallway for a shower and washed himself fully awake.

The kitchen had already swung into action, the staff's conversations clattering around the room while the air was filled with fresh bread baking – this was to become Fergal's favourite smell of all. Even at that time of the morning, the restaurant was popular enough that Fergal was needed. The staff were mostly friendly towards Fergal, although a few of the older waiters resented him slightly. Singers were very highly regarded. As far as Arianna was concerned they were gifts from God, especially those under the watchful gaze of her brother.

Gradually, as days turned into weeks, Fergal began to slip into a routine. After a month had passed, he stopped thinking about time altogether and often had to ask someone what day it was. Between voice training, the kitchen job and his Italian lessons, there was time for little else. Arianna soon treated him like one of her relatives. She helped him as much as she could with the language, but Fergal was amazed by the fact that everyone he met spoke English. It made him think how lazy Irish people were, in some ways. He had loved learning Irish at school, but it would have been good to be able to choose another language too, Spanish or Italian, maybe.

Like the food, the Italian language felt odd in Fergal's mouth at first when he tried to use it outside of his lessons. But after a while he found he had no choice – the rest of the staff spoke more and more Italian to him and waited for him to find the right words without prompting him too much. He loved the way Arianna answered the phone: '*Pronto?*' He also thought that the songs Alfredo was teaching him didn't sound nearly as good when they were translated into English so he would know what he was singing. As weeks turned into months, he eventually began to understand good chunks of the lightning chatter that flashed around the restaurant.

There was something about Maria Truvello, his language teacher, that reminded him of his own mother, Angela. Maria was short, like her, and sarcastic in her own way. She had never been married, though. She had worked as a local schoolteacher all her life until she was forced to retire at sixty, and then she had continued tutoring foreign students. Luckily she only lived up the road from Moretti's, so Fergal could walk there after the lunch-time rush had ended.

He loved window shopping as he made his way there in the sunshine. Everyone seemed to dress in their best, no matter where they were going. One day he watched in amazement as the local dry cleaner brought out a roll of the smoothest blank paper, wrapped a customer's clothes and stapled the parcel shut like a gift. As he neared Signora Truvello's house he saw a woman and her son having coffee in a tiny café and laughing at something in a magazine. It made him remember the day, just before he left Belfast, when he had said goodbye to his mother in a little café in the city centre. Her own mother, his dear Granny Noreen, had only just died. Even after all the bad, mad things that had happened, Fergal had just ended up feeling sorry for this little woman who had attached her heart and her life to the wheelless wagon of his whiskey-breathed father. She'd given birth to four boys in as many years, and Fergal knew he probably hadn't been the easiest of children himself – he was too different from the rest of them. Now, in those vulnerable late-night moments before he surrendered to sleep, he could allow himself to see more clearly how hard it must have been for his mother. Violently desperate, funny, clumsy and angry as all hell – and that was on a good day – she'd had to fight so many battles on her own, in her own way. Fergal was beginning to see how powerful a bit of distance could be.

And here he was, in front of another little woman, listening and learning. One day, when Signora Truvello reached over to pinch his lips, attempting to help him make the right shape for a word, Fergal recoiled as if she were about to slap him. When he was a little boy, his mother had hit him repeatedly on the mouth with the back of her hand for saying 'girly things'. Signora Truvello was a little taken aback, but she managed to brush it off and explain, stroking his head carefully to placate him. Over the next few months she put strange, beautiful new words into his mouth and into his heart, but she never hit him.

As time moved invisibly onwards, Fergal tried to write regularly to Father Mac, attempting to describe everything in minute detail. He wanted him to be able to picture exactly where he was, what his room looked like in the morning, what the kitchens were like. Most of all, he wrote about Alfredo's house, the challenge of the vocal lessons, Giovanni and Luigi and Signora Truvello. He used a bit of Italian at the end of each letter to show-off a little and to prove he was paying attention in his lessons. He even included a few petals from the lime tree in the garden that had found their way onto his window ledge and filled his room with their subtle perfume.

Father Mac replied carefully and with inevitable formality, saying that he and Mrs Mooney missed Fergal more than they could say and that the parishioners were like little flocks of hungry sparrows after the Sunday service, desperate for titbits of news from Fergal in Italy.

The letters were frequent enough, but sometimes Fergal felt that he didn't really have enough to say that he could say in safety. He knew he had to be careful about what he wrote. Belfast mail vans were sometimes robbed for possible cheques or cash, and the rest of the letters were left strewn around the road and trapped on car windscreens for the whole world to read. So he waited longer and longer each time before replying.

Moretti's restaurant had its own postcards, and one night after work Fergal set about writing a note to his mother on the back of one of them. He knew he couldn't mention how grateful he still was to her for signing his passport form – the postcard would be read by half the street before it even reached her home, and he could easily imagine the trouble that would get her into – so he simply told her how beautiful Rome was and how well everyone was treating him.

He didn't post it for another two weeks.

Everyone was expected to attend mass on Sundays, before the family lunch was prepared. Fergal would help to set up a few tables in the garden if the weather was kind enough, which it mostly was. It was at these gatherings that Fergal missed Father Mac the most. Everyone was either married or engaged, and he wondered whether there was anybody like him. It wasn't lost on Fergal that Italian men were much more demonstrative and affectionate with one another. He loved seeing the kitchen staff with their arms draped around one another during their breaks. Even the oldest, crankiest-looking men who played dominos or chess at the restaurant in the late afternoon always greeted one another with kisses. He couldn't help marvelling, too, at how cherished every single one of the children was. After much pleading, the various parents always relented and allowed the older ones to have little glasses of watered-down wine with the meal.

Alfredo seemed to sense Fergal's unease at these gatherings and paid special attention to him. Sometimes they would give a recital on the upright piano from the bistro, with the back doors wide open to the garden. Again, Fergal thought of the times he and Father Mac had spent in the chapel or in the front room of St Bridget's House, going through new music. The incense that had periodically clouded that faraway altar was like a heavily scented memory, floating towards him across the countless miles.

Arianna had noticed that any time she asked Fergal about his family, the very temperature seemed to drop. All the same, one day she asked him, 'Would you like to give your parents the telephone number of the restaurant?'

'I...' Fergal looked flustered and more vulnerable than ever. 'Thanks, Arianna. I'll write it down.' He hated the fact that the simplest enquiry about his family almost brought him out in a rash. It was his weak spot and made him lose all sense of his otherwise growing confidence. He knew he was learning fast, but in his heart of hearts he knew that the past was holding him back and that he would have to let it go completely in order to be truly free. But he just didn't know how.

Arianna could hold back no longer. 'Fergal, is something wrong?'

Fergal shook his head. 'We're just…we're not a very close family. They won't be ringing me.'

Arianna tried not to look as shocked as she felt. Alfredo had touched on the subject with her, although he and Fergal had yet to discuss it. She was devoted to Alfredo and had been equally devoted to their departed parents, and it was impossible for her to imagine what Fergal's family might be like. Privately, she realised that this certainly went some of the way towards explaining the melancholy in his voice, a melancholy that had made her eyes well-up the first time she had heard him sing.

Fergal's voice lessons inevitably got more and more difficult with each passing week. Alfredo Moretti was a demanding teacher. He knew from experience that if he dug deep enough, he would unearth the whole voice that was mostly buried under Fergal's inexperience and youth. At least Fergal didn't have many bad habits to unlearn, although there was the delicate issue of eroding the jagged edge of his Northern Irish accent.

Alfredo knew instinctively that all this would come, but he worried about how controlled Fergal was, how afraid of his own emotions. One day, when Fergal was unable to grasp a particular piece as well or as quickly as he wanted to, Alfredo lost his temper for a moment. 'You must try harder!' he shouted. 'Otherwise you should pack your things and go back home!'

He immediately saw from the look on Fergal's face that he'd gone too far. 'Fergal, it's all right. Surely you know I don't mean that? I believe in you! I was only being dramatic and trying to get some reaction from you. It's all right for you to get angry back at me! A bit of honest passion – negative or positive – is better for you, in the long run. You must not be so…controlled all the time.'

Fergal had never really thought of himself as controlled, and he felt very downhearted as he left the lesson. He went back to his room with the manuscript and almost drove himself mad going over and over the complicated melody in his head. Anything was preferable to facing the fact that he was holding so much in.

That night, Fergal dreamed that he was back at his lesson with Alfredo, except they weren't in his house, they were standing up to their waists in the fountain in the square, grand piano and all, with a crowd of people watching. He was supposed to be singing the Irish national anthem, but try as he might, he couldn't remember it. Suddenly, huge musical notes dropped out of the darkening sky with rifles, shooting for all they were worth, and the marble horses and riders came to life and chased him down the street like some nightmare cartoon.

He woke up with a dry mouth and went to the kitchen to get some water. As he stood at the sink, he saw the wrinkled calendar hanging beside it and was astounded to realise that he had been in Rome for just over six months.

5

For Father Dermot MacManus back in Belfast, those six months hadn't passed quite as quickly. He had taken on a lot of extra work to occupy himself, but even though he knew that Rome was the best place for Fergal, he couldn't shake the loss of him. Sometimes during Communion, if someone was playing the organ, he would picture him on the balcony singing for all he was worth and it made him smile, for a while. He had written to Fergal a few times in a row without expecting a reply, so any time he saw the Rome postmark on the breakfast table it cheered him. Mrs Mooney would hum away to herself – the letter was the next best thing to having Fergal back with them. Father Mac left the letter unopened, savouring the anticipation, until after the first mass. Then he would take his time over it, with a cup of Italian coffee in Fergal's honour. He would read the letter at least twice, in case he had missed a detail. If he had a free afternoon, he'd take a trip to the graveyard and read Fergal's words aloud to Granny Noreen's grave. Sometimes the rain came as he spoke to the soil, but he would always finish the letter before returning to the warmth of the hearth at St Bridget's House.

Night-times were often the hardest. When the front door was finally shut and no one rang or called him out for an emergency, Father Mac couldn't help remembering how he and Fergal used to attempt to put the world to rights while drinking tea and listening to music in front of the fire. When the colder weather came, his bed never seemed warm enough, and he had to admit to Mrs Mooney that he could do with an electric blanket. Often, too, if he'd had a few glasses of wine, he would put on the recording from Sligo Abbey and take some small comfort from the sound of his missing lover's voice floating from the speakers towards him. Then and only then could he face getting under the covers upstairs, knowing that he'd done the right thing in helping Fergal get to Italy. Fergal belonged to the world outside his parish now, and Father Mac's faith was strong enough to reassure him that it was all in God's plan.

Though he tried not to, he occasionally masturbated, revisiting the contours of Fergal's face and lips, but regret always followed close behind, so if he still couldn't sleep he would read and reread Fergal's letters. When he put them together he wondered if it was his imagination or if they seemed to be growing more hurried, less regular, more distant in their tone. He couldn't bear that thought for very long, so he managed to convince himself that he was a fool, that he was overreacting and reading too much into them. Fergal had to change sometime, he told himself, otherwise he wouldn't have learned anything.

One day, Father Mac had to visit a sick elderly man in Walker Street, a few doors down from Fergal's family. He resisted the temptation to call in to see them; he knew there was really nothing to say. Angela Flynn was just rehanging her freshly sponged net curtains when she saw a familiar frame coming out of a nearby door. She didn't have to reach for her glasses to know who it was, but she did know she had to be careful who saw her as she left the curtains half-hung and stepped out into the street.

It had meant a lot to her that Fergal had thanked her properly for helping him get his passport. That had been her own wee rebellion against her husband, and it hadn't been easy. She had managed to intercept Fergal's postcard before her husband rolled out of bed, and she kept it in her handbag, next to all her debt books and prayers and her mother Noreen's mass card. Angela had thought a lot about Fergal since he'd left, and between bouts of guilt about hitting him she secretly admired his bravery in leaving. She even felt jealous.

She focused on the back of Father Mac's head, took a deep breath and decided to be brave.

'Father MacManus? Is that you? God save us, it's been a brave while since we saw you on our wee street.'

Her voice stopped Father Mac in his tracks. 'Well, Mrs Flynn, how are you?'

Angela half-smiled, looked around and motioned for him to come closer. She ushered him into her hall and whispered, 'Father, I don't have much time. Do you have our Fergal's address?'

'Well, ah, I do, but not with me.'

'If I drop off a wee note, will you post it on to him for me? My handwriting's not the best – our Fergal used to do all that for me, you see. Anyway, look, my husband Paddy can't know about it, okay?'

'Drop it through my letterbox at St Bridget's when you have it, and I'll see it's posted.'

'Thank you, Father. Thanks.' Angela opened her front door just enough for him to back out into the street before she closed it behind him.

Father Mac was well used to the sometimes difficult burden of trust from his parishioners, and he knew he couldn't have done anything but agree to help. In truth, he was amazed that Mrs Flynn wanted to write to Fergal. He thought Fergal might appreciate the fact that someone in his family thought enough of him to write, even though he wasn't sure he trusted what she might say.

That same night, though, Father Mac had a dream. He was in an enormous bed and all of Fergal's letters were stacked in a neat pile on the bedside table, beside his Bible. He had left the window open and a gust of wind blew in from the street, scattering the precious sheets of paper onto the floor. Father Mac saw that they had landed in a perfect straight line, seven pages long, at the bottom of the bed. Then he saw that there was a huge capital letter on the back of each page, but their combination made no sense. When he got out of bed to look more closely, another gust of wind blew in and rearranged the pages, and this time he saw that they spelled the word 'goodbye'.

He woke in a sweat to the sound of Mrs Mooney scraping the downstairs fire to life with a poker, coughing repeatedly as the rising clouds of cremated coal flew in her tired face. Father Mac went into the bathroom and splashed himself with cold water, then went to his writing desk, took out several large sheets of blank paper and wrote without stopping.

My dearest Fergal,

I hope this letter finds you in the best of health. If I stop for a second, then I won't be able to finish writing what I need to say to you, so please excuse any mistakes.

Firstly, I bumped into your mother yesterday and she asked me if I'd post on a note to you when she drops it into St Bridget's sometime in the near future. I hope you don't mind, but I said I would, so look out for that – and I hope I did the right thing by agreeing. I know you've had the worst of times with her, but she looked really vulnerable when she said your name, and when all is said and done, she's your mother, for better or for worse. Forgiveness is a precious gift to give someone.

I've just woken up here, and as I write these words Mrs Mooney is humming away to herself in the kitchen. Fergal, what a dream I had last night. It was about you, of course – you weren't in it as such, but your letters were. When I woke up, it made me realise something very important, and I knew I had to write this.

Fergal, from this moment on, you must think of yourself as a free young man, in every sense of that word – that's if you don't already. I know you're probably working harder than you ever have in your life, but your new adventure in Rome should also be a time of incredible joy for you. You know how much I love you, and it's precisely because I love you so much that we need to let the past go. Forgive me, Fergal – the last thing I want is to make you angry in any way, or sad or hurt. But I would be angry with myself – furious – if I thought I'd held you back at this critical time in your life. Please don't be angry with me. Please don't try to change my mind, and please, please don't think you've done something wrong to make me write this. You have done nothing but make my life more worthwhile.

I love you now as much as I have since you first appeared, soaking wet and wheezing, at the back of the church. But the church and the fragile community here is where my full commitment must stay, and you mustn't – Fergal, this is so difficult – you mustn't 'save yourself' for me in any way. Do you understand? In one of your last letters, you were wondering when I would come to visit you, and I promise I'll do my best, but I have no idea when that will be and you mustn't wait for me. Do you understand? Rome is an incredibly beautiful and romantic city, you must be finding a world of new possibilities there, and I'd hate to think that you might limit your experiences because of me. Fergal, you are a beautiful and talented young man. You must let yourself be loved in whatever way feels natural to you – you know what I mean.

Remember this: we will always be friends, you can be one hundred per cent sure of that, and we will never lose touch. I will treasure our time together, and I realise how privileged I have been to go with you, at least a little of the way, on your incredible journey.

Please forgive me if these words wound you now. I promise they will all make more sense in time. I wish I was able to say all this to you in person, but I want you to be able to read and reread this letter on your own. Then throw it away and let the past be the past. There is only the future and all of the brightness it will bring. You know you have my heart, but you must go fully into the world now, as a free and single young man at the start of an incredible adventure.

Fergal, sing for me, sing for your Granny Noreen in heaven, sing for God and his angels, and try to forgive all those people who tried and failed to extinguish the flame that burns so brightly in your soul. Most importantly of all, Fergal, sing for yourself.

I look forward to the day when I can sit in an audience somewhere and see you at your best. Meanwhile, rest assured that you never feel too far away. Sure, I have the recordings from the Abbey to keep me company when I want to hear your voice. The other day I even caught Mrs Mooney playing them, with her eyes shut, while she was ironing away. Fergal, we miss you and we love you. Write back when you have something to write about, not because you think you should. One more thing: don't you dare come back for a long time!

All love,

D. x

Father Mac found some stamps in his drawer and put far too many on the envelope in the hope that it would somehow carry his letter to Italy faster. He ran out into the cold morning and reached the post box just as the van was pulling away, but the postman saw him in his rear-view mirror. He stopped and wound down his window.

'Good morning, Father MacManus. What have you for me? Must be very important, sure, you nearly broke into a sprint after me there.'

'Frank, thanks. It's very important that this letter goes right now. Thanks for stopping.'

The postman whistled when he saw the address. 'No problem. All the way to Rome, I see, Father.'

'Yes. Thanks, and good luck.'

Frank blessed himself automatically and drove off whistling, happy that he'd been able to assist in God's holy work. Father Mac turned and went slowly back inside to his breakfast, feeling as if a weight had been lifted from his heart. The decision to write that letter had been a difficult one, and he had been afraid that it would leave him with a constant and possibly overwhelming sense of loss, but the moment the bridge had been crossed and the letter put into Frank's hand, the storm in his heart had blown over completely, and all that was left was an extraordinary, unexpected calm.

6

As Fergal's Italian took hold of him, he found that he was able to move away from the edges of the conversations and closer to the banter with the kitchen staff. Two of the younger men, Antonio and Rocco, were always talking about the club they visited at the weekends – they always ended up getting laid, they claimed, or at least getting sucked off in their cars – and when they saw Fergal listening, they suggested that he come along the next weekend if he was free. He was a little taken aback, but he said he'd think about it. Antonio and Rocco looked at each other and laughed, asking him in amazement what there was to think about – what was more important than sex? They were miming the act when Arianna appeared to check an order and they automatically fell silent, spinning back to their jobs, before turning to wink at Fergal as she left through the swinging doors.

Fergal had masturbated a couple of times, in the shower, while replaying some scene from his and Father Mac's past. He'd even tried it one night in bed, but the old frame had creaked too much and he was convinced that the whole town had heard him, not to mention Arianna, who lived on the other side of the building. So he locked the bathroom door and relied on the sound of the running water to drown out his desire. One of the part-time waiters was called Riccardo, and Fergal had no trouble remembering his name because he was so handsome. Sometimes he allowed himself to picture Riccardo in the shower, soaping himself. Initially he felt guilty, as if he were betraying Father Mac, but as time moved on, Riccardo and a few of the other waiters became serious competition, albeit only in his fantasies.

One morning, when Fergal came back along the corridor from the bathroom, wrapped in an enormous towel, he found a letter from Father Mac waiting, wedged between his bedroom door and the frame. He instantly felt guilty all over again for fantasising about Riccardo as he masturbated in the shower. He took the letter gently and set it on the bedside table, instinctively making the contents wait a while longer, while he dried off properly and got dressed.

His eagerness for news turned sour as he read the pages over and over again, more slowly each time, to make sure he wasn't imagining things. He trembled suddenly, sitting on the edge of the bed in shock. He wanted to cry, but the stubborn tears refused to come. Instead, out of nowhere, he found himself hissing furiously at the only holy object in the room, the framed picture of Jesus on the cross, 'Dermot MacManus, you fucking bastard! You've met somebody else, haven't you? Jesus! Do you think I'm a complete fucking moron?'

Fergal sat on the side of the bed, hair dripping onto the carpet, unable to find any more words and staring into space.

Slowly but surely, the lava of his fury began to cool and set as Father Mac's words began to sink in. Somewhere in Fergal's own heart he had known this was inevitable, but he hadn't thought it would come so soon. He found himself remembering their last night of lovemaking before he'd left for Rome, and it dawned on him as he held the letter in his hand just how naïve he had been to think that Father Mac might consider following him to Italy.

He lay back on the bed and looked at the ceiling, suddenly angry again, but with himself this time. 'Fergal Flynn, what are you fucking like? You're a first-class idiot, that's what! Of course he was never going to – he was never…'

He brought the pages to his nose and smelled them. 'Ah, Dermot, I've lost you. I've fucking lost you.' Then he crumpled them into a ball and threw it against the wall. He got up and grabbed the crushed letter, wanting to rip it into a million pieces, like confetti, and send them back to Father Mac. He thought about writing an angry reply or phoning him, but right on cue, Arianna called from the bottom of the stairs that the kick-start coffee was ready. There wasn't much time to be upset in her restaurant, and Fergal knew that maybe that was a good thing.

That afternoon, during Fergal's lesson, Alfredo announced that his technique had grown much stronger and that it was time for them to begin preparing for his first vocal exam. It would take place in only a few weeks' time, three days after Fergal's eighteenth birthday. He also announced that they would begin attending the opera together once a month depending on what production was touring, as it was imperative for Fergal to see as many live operatic works as possible.

Fergal hardly seemed to care. Alfredo realised that although the melancholy in Fergal's voice was much more pronounced than usual, all day he had seemed incapable of connecting with the music. 'Is everything all right, Fergal?' he asked finally.

Fergal wanted to tell Alfredo everything, but he wasn't sure that he could tell him anything at all. No one knew that he and Father Mac had been lovers. 'I'm just tired,' he said. 'I couldn't sleep last night.'

Alfredo guessed that there was more to it, and he pushed carefully. 'Fergal, I hope you know that you can talk to me about anything – absolutely anything. I know I'm your teacher, but I'm a man of the world, and we're friends too, aren't we? Aren't we?'

Fergal wasn't sure what to say, so he just nodded.

'What is it? Tell me.'

Fergal suddenly felt angry again. 'It's nothing.'

'Nothing? Fergal, you look so tense. And you're here, yet you're not here. Your singing is progressing technically, but your heart is elsewhere. Where is it? If you're going to be like this, we should stop for the day. There's no point in wasting precious time when you're in this kind of mood.'

'I'm sorry, Alfredo. It's just…'

'Go on.'

'Maybe I'm not who you think I am. Oh, God, what am I saying? I don't even know who I am.'

'Fergal, shall I tell you what I see in front of me? I see someone who has had to grow up far too quickly in some ways, someone who has got used to carrying his burdens all on his own and who doesn't really know how to ask for help. I think you felt alone for a very long time before Father Mac came along. Am I right?'

Fergal's eyes began to fill up, and it was all the answer Alfredo needed. He reached over and put his arms around him. 'I'm your friend too, you know, Fergal, and perhaps we aren't as different as you think. Crying will make you feel better; you can't hold everything in. I know you miss Father MacManus. You may even miss your family, even though—'

Fergal was taken aback. 'My family? What the fuck – how much did Father Mac tell you?'

'Fergal, calm down. I know enough to see how disturbed you are if anyone mentions them. Father Mac told me a little, and I can see it in you now, although I wish you wouldn't swear at me.'

Fergal panicked even further. 'Alfredo, I'm sorry!'

'I can see that there are things you don't feel ready to talk about. So just know that I'm here, whenever you need me – and not just for our lessons. I care about the person as well as the voice. One would be no good without the other.'

'Thanks, Alfredo,' Fergal sighed. 'I do feel a wee bit better. My head feels tight, though.'

'Yes, that's pressure. I think you should take the rest of the day off. Go for a walk, or go and lie down – anything that will make you relax. And don't even think about wallowing in guilt! That would be detrimental.'

As Fergal headed back to the restaurant, he thought about his Granny Noreen. He took some comfort from the memory of the conversations they'd had towards the end of her life, when she had made him promise to go out into the world while he had the chance. Fergal knew that Father Mac was saying the same thing in his letter, but still, he couldn't help feeling as if he'd been abandoned in some way.

The only thing Fergal could do was throw himself even deeper into his studies and work like a demon at Moretti's. Anything was better than admitting that he was unhappy. At night, though, alone in his room, he tried to write back to Dermot time and time again, but when he read his words back to himself, he always thought they sounded too angry and needy. He crumpled the half-finished pages into snowballs and threw them into the bin. Then he worried that someone would read what he'd written, so he hid the discarded pages in his coat pocket. The next day, on the way to his lessons, he tore them to pieces and dumped them in a public waste bin. Once, driven half-mad with insomnia, he got up during the night and dialled the number of St Bridget's House in Belfast. It rang and rang and finally he had to hang up, knowing that Father Mac was probably out administering the last rites to someone. Fergal knew that the life he'd once known with Father Mac was well and truly dead.

The very next morning, a letter addressed in Father Mac's handwriting arrived. Fergal thought it might be an apology of some kind, but inside was another, smaller envelope, and his name was scrawled on the front in the unmistakable, unschooled hand of his mother.

Fergal thought there must be something wrong. He was amazed to read that she'd been thinking about him when Father Mac appeared in Walker Street, and she had taken it as a sign that she should write to him.

Fergal,

You know I'm no good at letters. Sure it's only bills I get with my name on them until your postcard came but I managed to hide that from your da. I thought our house was never ever going to be quiet after all my years of youse as babies and nappies and dinners and dishes and washing. At least you used to help with that. I don't know myself now. All of a sudden I have only your da and me to cook for most nights if he's not at the pub or the hurling. Paddy and John are both out working and sure they're never in now. I go to bed early and say my prayers and sometimes I hear their keys in the door and sometimes I don't. Even Ciaran is courting somebody but she's from Andersonstown so we daren't even ask him when we're going to meet her. He must be ashamed of us or something.

Fergal, I hope you don't mind me writing to you, you used to help me with my spelling and all. I passed by your granny's door the other day and there was a wee girl in the hallway with her ma. They'd just moved in I think. I felt so sad, Fergal. I have to go.

You're probably too busy to write back. I won't forget our wee cup
of tea before you left.
   From Mammy

Fergal wasn't sure what to think. He read the letter over and over.
Why was she writing to him? The few lines must have taken her
most of an afternoon, and he was amazed that she'd bothered. He
was mistrustful of any contact with his family – his mother was
like an old-fashioned tap that could spout hot and cold water at
the same time – but as he lay in bed that night, he couldn't help
feeling moved. She didn't sound angry at him, and maybe her
opinion of him, which he had always thought was bad, was
beginning to change.

Alfredo kept his promise and soon took Fergal to see his first
opera, *Tristan and Isolde*, at the Teatro degli Artisti. Fergal loved
the inside of the building, and although he didn't quite understand what was happening for most of the performance, he
enjoyed the singing. At the interval, Alfredo was less than
complimentary about the lead tenor's tone, but he was glad
Fergal had been so keen.
   The week before Fergal's eighteenth birthday and his first voice
exam, there was a birthday party for a customer in the restaurant.
Arianna carried in the cake and the entire staff followed, singing
'Happy Birthday'. The other diners joined in, clapping and
cheering. Back in the kitchen, one of the cooks mentioned that it
was his birthday soon, and naturally they eventually asked Fergal
when his was. When he told them, they thought he was joking.
They had assumed he was much older – he was so tall, for one
thing. Riccardo told him he looked at least twenty-five. Fergal
thought that was great. Antonio and Rocco urged him again to
come to the club with them (his right hand must be exhausted,

they said, and they knew a girl who loved musical men), but Fergal said he was too busy, what with the exam coming up.

It was true that Alfredo's lessons had intensified further, and Fergal ate, slept and drank all the music he could get. Alfredo had sensed a change in him, but he put it down to nerves. After a long session that Saturday afternoon, he asked him to stay for a special dinner of pasta with a sauce made from a very old family recipe that was believed to bring good luck and was only used on very specific occasions.

The sauce was incredible and singing always made Fergal hungry, but he ate slowly, pausing to sip the heavenly contents of the crystal glasses. He was surprised at how quickly he had grown accustomed to the strength of the wine. At first it had made him light-headed, but now he was able to enjoy it without feeling too sleepy too quickly.

'I appreciate the way you've thrown yourself so deeply into your studies,' Alfredo told him. 'Your Italian pronunciation has improved immeasurably, and you really are a different singer – and all this in less than a year. If you aren't ready for this exam, I'll eat a flower from my garden!'

Alfredo laughed, but Fergal didn't know how to reply.

'Oh, Fergal, why so serious? I'm joking with you a little. Listen, my faith in you is stronger than ever. Your natural ear for melody is wonderful – that's one of the hardest things to learn – and you like to work hard. You like a challenge. I knew that the moment I heard your voice at that monastery. I'm rarely wrong.'

This managed to make Fergal lower his tense shoulders for a second and attempt a smile.

Eventually, after dessert, he did begin to yawn and stretch out on the sofa, and Alfredo caught the bug and couldn't stop yawning himself. He suggested that Fergal stay the night in the spare room, which was always made up, and Fergal was too comfortable to argue.

'Believe me, Fergal,' Alfredo told him, 'everything will be fine. Just one thing, though. When were you going to tell me that tomorrow is your eighteenth birthday?'

'What…how…?' Fergal reddened with embarrassment. 'Sorry, Alfredo. It's just that, well, birthdays aren't really a big deal for me, you know?'

'What do you mean, not a big deal? That's what old people say! Eighteen is a very big deal.'

'Did someone at the restaurant tell you?'

'No, it was Father MacManus.'

Fergal was a bit taken aback.

'You know we talk from time to time about how things are going. I was speaking to him today, and he told me about your birthday. Fergal, you must celebrate the fact that you are in the world, with people who love you.'

'If you want.'

'If *I* want? Fergal Flynn, you are a strange one!'

All Fergal could do was nod in a half-hearted way.

'You know which room is yours, don't you? Up one flight of stairs. Sleep well.'

Alfredo opened his arms and hugged Fergal for all he was worth, then he kissed him on the forehead, playfully ruffling his hair. Fergal felt awkward about being touched by anyone other than Father Mac, and he wondered again if Alfredo was gay, but his teacher gave very little away.

The spare room was full of more framed memories of Alfredo's illustrious career and pictures of his favourite singers, Tito Scipa and Jussi Bjorling, looking into the black-and-white distance. Fergal surrendered to the warm, soft bed, but he couldn't sleep, his throat was too dry. Finally he stumbled out of bed, put on a T-shirt and made his way towards the kitchen in the darkness.

As he descended the thickly carpeted stairs, he began to make out the rhythm of Alfredo's lilting voice talking quickly behind his office door: he was on the phone. Fergal was about to move on when he heard his own name. He stopped in his tracks and listened, trying to translate what he heard.

Alfredo was laughing. 'Giovanni, you're outrageous! Just because Fergal's asleep upstairs doesn't mean I'm going to go up there and jump in beside him! I know he's officially eighteen now that it's after midnight, but keep your fantasies to yourself. I'm thirty years older than him – yes, I can hardly believe it either – and there's no way I would waste any more of my life being unrealistic about love. Of course I think he's gay…Yes, I do think he's sexy, but you know I prefer older men…Giovanni, stop it now…Of course I'll wish him a happy birthday, but not the way you want me to!'

The hallway floorboards creaked as Fergal leaned his weight on one leg to creep away and the conversation stopped dead. Fergal wasn't sure what to do, so he just carried on down to the kitchen, found a glass and filled it with water. Then he headed back up the stairs, pretending to be half-sleepwalking.

Alfredo opened his office door. 'Are you okay?'

Fergal blinked in an exaggerated display of exhaustion and showed him the glass of water. 'I was thirsty,' he mumbled, and continued his journey towards the sanctuary of the spare room.

'Happy birthday, Fergal!' Alfredo called after him.

'Thanks,' Fergal muttered sleepily. 'See you tomorrow.'

He closed the thickly painted door and leaned against the back of it. At least his question had been answered without having to be asked: Alfredo was definitely gay. That was what he'd meant when he'd said that they had more in common than Fergal thought. He wondered how Alfredo knew that he was gay, though. He had never told him, and Father Mac surely would have stayed as far away from that subject as he could. It also had never occurred to Fergal that Alfredo might find him fanciable, and it made him feel a little odd, because he could never fancy him back. He was glad that Alfredo seemed to be – what had he said? – realistic about love.

Fergal gulped down the cold water in one feverish swallow and tried his best to sleep. As he drifted off, he felt a little easier about being gay, although he wasn't sure why.

7

The sun rose early on another fine Italian Sunday morning, filling the spare room with warm light. Fergal sat up on the strange pillows, scratching his body awake. It was nearly ten minutes before he remembered it was his birthday. He was eighteen.

He dressed quickly, listening for any sound, but the house was quiet. He decided he must have overslept and everyone had gone to mass. He left Alfredo a note on the hall table before closing the front door behind him. It was a beautiful walk back to Moretti's, but when he got there Fergal was surprised to find the restaurant closed. For a second he thought something bad had happened, but then the chime from the city clock made him realise it was only half past six. He had thought it was much later. He didn't want to wake anyone up, so he rummaged about for the key to the side door that was kept in one of the hanging plant pots and managed to let himself in.

He took off his shoes at the bottom of the stairs and tried not to giggle as he stole silently to his room. Without thinking, he continued to undress and climbed under the undisturbed sheets.

As he began to drift off to sleep, he thought of his mother and wondered if she was remembering his birth. She had once told him that he had been born in the wee back room of their tiny house while Granny Noreen tried to keep the twins, who had just learned to run, from wrecking the place. Fergal remembered his mother's far-off expression as she told him how her sisters had roared at her to cry out, but she had been unable to make a sound; she had pushed him out of her swollen body in silent agony. It struck Fergal how strange it was that although he had been born in silence, it was his voice that had saved him, that had brought him to this very bed where he was drifting back into sleep.

The previous morning, Arianna had sighed with relief when she saw that the post included two letters for Fergal. She'd kept them in her bag overnight so he wouldn't get them until it was actually his birthday. She remembered her own mother pretending the postman had been if her birthday fell on a Sunday.

She couldn't help wanting to mother Fergal, on this day of all days, so she set about cooking him a special breakfast: an omelette, fresh toast and coffee. She loaded up a tray with the breakfast, the cards and a single flower in a tiny vase of water, then headed up the stairs, humming 'Happy Birthday', to put the tray on the end of Fergal's bed.

Fergal ate with one hand and opened the cards, a bit the worse for wear, with the other. He recognised the broad, old-fashioned sweep of Father Mac's favourite fountain pen immediately. Inside the stiff paper was a twenty-pound note and a card: *'I'm sorry I can't deliver this personally on your special day, but I'm thinking of you. All my love, D.'*

For a moment, Fergal thought he could see lip imprints as he held the paper up to the light of the window. In his mind he was instantly transported back exactly one year, to the night on Sligo strand when he and Dermot had first been truly intimate in the hollow of a sand dune. It had been the first time Fergal had ever felt so loved, and he hadn't wanted it to end. He closed his eyes, caressing the embossed insignia of St Bridget's official stationery as if it were Father Mac's secret mark.

He poured the rest of the coffee and stared at his mother's awkward handwriting on the second envelope. Fergal sliced it open with his greasy knife, and he was sure he got a whiff of rainy Belfast as he pulled out the card. As he opened it, something fell onto the floor: a tiny remembrance card with a faded picture of Granny Noreen, wearing her good coat and half a borrowed smile. His eyes began to water.

The printed card proclaimed, 'TO OUR DEAR SON…18 TODAY!' in loud gold letters on the front. Inside, his mother's tiny handwriting whispered, *'Happy birthday, our Fergal. You're a man now. You know it would have been my daddy's birthday too. Here's your Granny Noreen's mass card for you to keep. Rome sounds lovely but it's going to rain here. From Mammy.'*

There was a Child of Prague medal on the end of a red ribbon sellotaped in the corner. Fergal freed it and put it next to the mass card. He wasn't surprised that the card was only from his mother, not from his father or brothers, but he was genuinely touched that she had gone to the effort.

He put his birthday cards on the windowsill and headed downstairs. Alfredo had arrived and was just being handed a double espresso by his sister. When he saw Fergal, his face relaxed into a smile. He hugged him and kissed him gently. 'Happy birthday, dearest Fergal! I thought the Martians had landed and taken you up into their spaceship during the night! Or was that old bed too uncomfortable?'

Arianna laughed, and Fergal got a bit embarrassed. 'No, no, the bed was great. Sorry, Alfredo, I just woke up and thought it was much later than it was. It was very bright in that room. Sure, I left you a note.'

'Yes, I finally found it. I think my eyesight is getting worse. It's fine, I just wanted to give you your card.' Alfredo handed him a beautiful silver envelope with his name written on the front in wide black strokes, and Arianna handed him another.

'I didn't know what to get you,' Alfredo said as Fergal opened the cards, 'so I thought we might go shopping in town, after church? How about some shoes?'

'No, Alfredo, the card's enough, more than enough.'

'Don't be ridiculous. Look, Fergal, after singing, shopping – especially for other people – is my greatest passion. And you've been working so hard of late. Arianna has given you the day off – haven't you, my dear sister?'

Arianna nodded enthusiastically. She was glad to get them out of the way – she had a cake to make. After a bit of investigation she had managed to discover that Fergal was very partial to dark chocolate. Sometimes, if the chefs had any profiterole sauce left over, the craving got the better of him. Arianna had begun her preparations the night before and she had carefully hidden her efforts at the back of the enormous fridge.

'Well then, what are we waiting for? We go to mass, and then we go shopping!'

As they drove along the busy roads towards Alfredo's favourite shops, he was so excited that anyone would have thought it was his birthday, not Fergal's.

'You're eighteen now, my boy – I'm sorry: young *man*! And you're about to take your first step on the ladder of success. For that step, you need better shoes – Italian shoes, the best in the world. My gift to you.'

'Alfredo, you don't have to. You've given me so much already, and I've been saving a bit of money.'

Alfredo realised he would have to be careful not to embarrass his pupil. 'Fergal, please allow me to buy you your first handmade pair of shoes. If you treat them well, you may have them for the rest of your life. That is how good they will be.'

Fergal could only nod his head. He looked at Alfredo and remembered that he'd said on the phone that he was almost fifty. He could have been any age. His hair was expensively Elvis-black and slightly wavy, like a 1930s Broadway star's, and his skin looked almost tea-stained. It made Fergal think of a story his granny had told him of how during the war, when the women had no way of getting tights, they would rub used tea leaves on their bare legs and dry them by the fire. Then they would get a pen or a lump of coal and draw a line up the back of each leg, to just above the hemline of their skirts. Only then would they be ready to head out for the night. Everywhere they went was so badly lit, Granny Noreen had said, that nobody could tell the difference.

'What's occupying your mind so much?' Alfredo asked, breaking his reverie.

'I was just thinking about my grandmother.' Fergal looked out the window of the car. There seemed to be posters of Padre Pio everywhere; Granny Noreen would have approved of that. 'Alfredo,' he asked, 'how old were you when you took your first vocal exam?'

Alfredo smiled. 'Almost exactly the same age as you are now. And I passed – just as I'm sure you will.'

Fergal wished he hadn't asked the question. The old voice of doubt returned to his head, whispering that he just wasn't good enough.

Alfredo's walking stick tested the cobbled laneways, pausing every now and then outside the exquisite shoe shops near the Trevi Fountain. A few of them were closed because it was a Sunday, but this didn't seem to bother Alfredo – he simply asked Fergal to point at any pair he liked. Without warning, he turned up a tiny, dark side street, and Fergal followed him into a shop that sold nothing but handmade shoes. It only had a number above the door, no sign; its reputation was all it needed. It was the kind of place that spoke softly amid the noisier shops, drawing you to come closer.

Emilio, the manager, clearly knew Alfredo of old – they hugged and kissed before getting down to business. Alfredo motioned to Fergal, who was shifting his weight from foot to foot, and explained grandly that his Irish protégé had become a man that very day and needed a pair of shoes that would tell not only his vocal examiner but 'the entire world' that he meant business.

Emilio's young assistant gently removed Fergal's tired, cheap shoes and measured his feet. They turned out to be a size ten; he certainly had grown. Box after perfect shoebox was unearthed from a secret room. The legendary contents were tenderly unwrapped from their protective tissue paper and presented to him like some kind of award. Fergal imagined a legion of elves behind the scenes, tapping away all through the night with little hammers and nails, carefully stitching together pieces of leather, then passing them on to the younger elves to be polished to a spit-shine.

As he eased his foot into the mouth of the first shoe with the help of a shoehorn, he felt as if he was in a strange film, the kind he might have seen when he was off school sick. He was relieved that he was wearing his best socks, even though they were beginning to get thin at the heels. Emilio asked him to walk up and down the marble floor, which had long, thin mirrors instead of wooden skirting boards, to see how they fit. Fergal would have been happy with anything, but Emilio and Alfredo insisted that he try on ten different pairs. The list was then reduced to five, then three, and at last they settled on a dark brown leather pair that fit Fergal like gloves.

Alfredo handed over a considerable amount of money, which he made sure Fergal didn't see. As the shoes were returned to their box and expertly wrapped, Emilio explained how his family had been shoemakers for centuries and had shod many of the finest people in all of Italy, including some of its most famous tenors. He winked in Fergal's direction, and Fergal blushed like a bride.

Almost two hours after they had entered the shop, Emilio thanked them profusely and guided them out into the lane. Fergal was bursting with a mixture of pride and the inexplicable guilt that dogged him whenever anything good happened to him.

'Alfredo, thank you. They're so – so beautiful. I'm nearly afraid to wear them.'

Alfredo smiled. 'Think about how long you spend on your feet. Don't they deserve the best? It's my pleasure! Happy eighteenth birthday, my friend. When you're older, like me, I want you to think back on this day, the day you became a man and finally walked in a man's pair of shoes. Now, are you hungry? I think we might go back to Arianna for lunch?'

Fergal realised, suddenly, that he was ravenous.

8

Arianna appeared at the door of the restaurant, smoothing her skirt, to welcome them. She put her arm around Fergal's waist.

'Now, young man, close your eyes please.'

Fergal knew better than to argue. He did as she asked and was led blindly by the arm amongst the tables and stacked chairs, through the kitchen, to the back garden. He nearly fainted when a roar went up: 'Happy birthday, Fergal!'

He opened his eyes. Most of the staff were standing around the long tables that were packed with food and drinks. Alfredo and Arianna both said, 'Surprise!' at the same time, as if they had rehearsed it, and everybody laughed.

Fergal was overwhelmed that they had gone to so much effort. In the centre of the table was a massive dark chocolate cake that looked like the tyre off a cartoon tractor. The candles were lit, eighteen flames. 'Blow them out,' Arianna said, and as the whole gathering sang 'Happy Birthday', Fergal took a big gulp of air and extinguished every one.

There was a big cheer and Arianna weeded out the wax and began to cut up the cake and hand it out on paper plates. 'How does it feel to be eighteen?' Alfredo asked, hugging Fergal.

Fergal laughed and shrugged. 'I'm not sure. It doesn't feel any different, really.'

'What were you doing on your seventeenth birthday? Could you have imagined, then, where you would be only a year later?'

Fergal remembered exactly where he had been a year before. The Sligo monastery, the recordings that had led to Alfredo's interest and, of course, that night in Father Mac's arms under the blanket of sky and stars – waves and sand dunes and kisses, so many delicious kisses…

He looked around. Arianna had pulled a magnum of champagne from its nest of ice underneath the table. In only a year, he had come so far. He was under a new sky, surrounded by new friends and kind strangers. He missed Father Mac. He badly wanted to phone him, but he was too shy to ask. The Morettis had been so good to him already that he didn't want them to think he was taking them for granted. But the past was another place, out of reach now.

Arianna popped the champagne and filled the sparkling glasses to the brim, and Fergal blushed to burning point as she called for a toast.

'To Fergal Flynn!' Alfredo cried. 'We wish him many more years of happiness and music, and all the love and success the world can offer. He has an important exam in a few days, and we must all pray for him. To his success!'

The glasses were clinked to near breaking point. 'Speech!' someone called.

Fergal was mortified, but he knew he couldn't stay silent. His voice shook a little as he managed to thank Arianna, Alfredo, all the staff of Moretti's and his language coach, Signora Truvello, who raised her glass to him silently at the back of the throng.

Then someone shouted for a song, and Alfredo nodded approval as everyone clapped. So they quieted the children with bigger slices of cake, and Alfredo and Fergal put their heads together for a second and decided that Fergal would sing an old Italian song they had been working on.

The Italian words swam from his lips. He sang of a young farm girl who rebelled against her parents' choice of husband and left her family to be with the one she loved. Twenty years passed, and one day her family heard that she was living not far away, with her own brood of children; her husband had died two winters previously. Her father found her house and called on her, disguised as a beggar, and although she was poor, she took him in and shared what little she had. The 'beggar' asked about her family, and she grew sad and told him that she hadn't seen them in a very long time, but she had been in love, she said, and had followed her heart. Even if her parents were still alive, she said, she was sure they had forgotten her. With tears in his eyes, the beggar told her he was sure they thought of her and prayed for her every day. Then he started to sing a song she had loved as a tiny girl. Startled, she asked him how he knew the song. He took off his coat and hat to reveal his true identity, embraced his daughter and asked her to come home with him. As Fergal ended the song, there were a few tears among the older women – the song had been popular when they were girls, and their own fathers had sung it to them.

Antonio and Rocco congratulated Fergal on his growing command of Italian. 'We'll have to be more careful what we say about you now!' Rocco laughed.

'We're going to the club later,' Antonio said, 'and this time you *have* to come.'

'I'm not sure...'

'We'll all go!' Alfredo cried, a little merry from the champagne.

Rocco and Antonio thought this was a great idea, and coaxed Arianna to say she'd come too.

As the afternoon wore on and the guests began to take their children home, Fergal suddenly felt exhausted. He tried to stifle his yawns for fear of offending Arianna after all the work she'd gone to, but Alfredo, as ever, missed nothing. He suggested that Fergal, like many a fine tenor, should learn the benefits of a nap in the afternoon. He could sleep for a few hours, then get ready to go out and meet all the others at the club.

Fergal closed his bedroom door, glad of the half-light made by the filter of the curtains, and practically melted into the sheets. He dreamed that his Granny Noreen came to him with a glass of water. He was about to take it from her and drink it when she moved his hand away and knelt beside him. She dipped her fingers in the water and splashed the drops on his face, making the sign of the cross. All the time she was whispering a prayer to keep him strong and safe from the devil.

Fergal woke up with his face damp with sweat from the enclosed heat of the room. Noreen's remembrance card peeped out at him from where he'd tucked it behind the crucifix on the white wall. He wondered if she had really been in the room with him while he was asleep, whether she could see him, here in this better place, whether the dream had been her way of letting him know she was okay.

He undressed down to his underwear, wrapped himself in a huge towel and headed for the bathroom to take a shower. The door was locked. When he tried it a voice called, 'I'll be out in a minute!'

'It's okay,' Fergal shouted. 'I'll come back later.'

Suddenly the lock slid back and the same voice called, 'Come in if you want.'

Riccardo was naked and towelling himself dry. He smiled. 'I've left the water running.'

'Thanks,' Fergal said. He hung up his towel and stood there in his underpants. Riccardo continued to dry himself with broad, slow strokes of the towel. He was very fit, with the hairiest chest Fergal had ever seen, and Fergal dropped his gaze before he could stop himself. He was aroused in an instant and turned his back to try and hide it, but he heard Riccardo exhale a laugh. When he looked around, Riccardo was staring at him, with the towel pulled around his neck to allow him a full view. Fergal's heart felt like it was beating behind his front teeth.

Riccardo smiled and said quietly, 'It's okay.'

Fergal couldn't answer. Riccardo motioned for him to make sure the door was locked. When Fergal did as he was asked and turned around again, Riccardo was right beside him. He reached out and began stroking Fergal's chest, pushing his thickening penis towards him. They were both breathing harder now.

Fergal closed his eyes and attempted to kiss him, but Riccardo turned his head away, almost in disgust. Instead he grabbed Fergal's hand and pushed it between his strong legs. Fergal took hold of him, freeing himself from his underwear with his other hand. Riccardo watched him, then closed his eyes and ordered, as quietly as the running water would allow, 'Faster – faster …yes…now take it.'

Fergal wasn't sure what to do. Riccardo repeated, 'Take it!' and nodded down to his crotch. Then his big, hairy hand clamped the back of Fergal's neck and steered his head downwards. Fergal sank awkwardly to his knees. Before he had a chance to take a proper breath, Riccardo had plunged himself into Fergal's mouth. He cupped the back of Fergal's head with both hands, thrusting deeper and deeper into his throat. Fergal panicked for a second, almost gagging, then managed to catch a breath through his nose. Riccardo groaned in ecstasy. Suddenly his whole body stiffened, and he released his grip just in time to pull out and empty himself all down Fergal's chest.

It was over in less than three messy, loveless minutes. Riccardo turned away and washed his rapidly shrinking self in the sink. Fergal stood up, not knowing what to say. Riccardo didn't even look at him as he pulled on his clothes and unlocked the bathroom door. Before he opened it he put his ear to the wooden panels, listening for any sign of life, then, silently, he nodded to Fergal and left.

Fergal locked the door again and stepped under the shelter of the hot water. He stayed there for a long time, soaping his sticky chest over and over, until the evidence was washed away. Had that really happened, or had he just had some sort of daydream? Fergal had been attracted to Riccardo for months, but he had never thought they would end up doing what they had just done – and in the bathroom of Moretti's…He gargled mouthfuls of warm water until he couldn't taste Riccardo any more. He had imagined that sex with him would be brilliant, but it hadn't been. Fergal had to admit that he'd enjoyed the excitement of it, but at the same time it had seemed so one-sided and a bit violent. He hated the fact that Riccardo had refused to kiss him, and he felt used. Riccardo had had no interest in doing anything to him in return. It had been so different with Dermot…

Then, of course, the guilt reappeared, thundering over Fergal like Niagara Falls. He felt as if he had cheated on Father Mac. He knew Father Mac's letter had told him to spread his wings, but he couldn't help feeling that somehow he had let him down.

By the time Fergal ventured back to his room, it was growing dark. When he snapped on the light, the first thing he saw was a package on the chair by the window, a meticulously wrapped present tied with a huge red ribbon.

He began to panic – maybe someone had come up while he'd been in the shower room with Riccardo, maybe they had been heard. Then he realised that the present must have been there all along; he hadn't noticed it earlier because he'd been so tired. He dried himself and pulled on a clean T-shirt and pants, eyeing the package a bit warily. There was something about surprises he didn't trust. Then, putting the experience with Riccardo out of his mind, he undid the ribbon slowly and gingerly, as if he were defusing a bomb.

He freed the last knot and the package fell open. For a moment Fergal couldn't move. Then he carefully unfolded a beautiful chocolate brown linen suit, complete with a pale cream shirt, a dark brown tie and the softest pair of socks he'd ever felt.

His eyes filled up so quickly that he could hardly read the card. 'To our dearest Fergal – something to help you look more like the man you are now! Love from Arianna, Alfredo and everyone at Moretti's.'

Fergal dressed quickly, dying to see what the new clothes looked like on his freshly clean body. The linen felt incredible on his skin. He hadn't worn a tie since leaving school, but his fingers remembered how to tie it. He stood in front of the mirror to make sure the knot was straight. Someone he hardly recognised looked back at him. His hand stretched out to touch his reflection to prove that he wasn't dreaming. He hadn't realised what a difference a good suit could make.

He turned around as he heard someone coming up the stairs. Alfredo was in the doorway. Fergal hugged him fast, hoping his teacher didn't see his tears.

'Thank you, Alfredo, thank you – and Arianna too. Youse didn't have to, after the shoes and everything. It's too much. I don't know what to say. I'm not…I'm not…' Fergal turned his back.

'Fergal? You're not what?' Alfredo put a hand on his shoulder.

'I'm not…worth it.'

'What? What on earth are you saying, Fergal? Where did you get such a ridiculous notion? Not *worth* it? You're worth a thousand suits – and don't ever let anyone tell you anything else!'

Alfredo was purple in the face. 'Fergal, has someone upset you? Tell me who it is. Is it someone who works here? Or have those parents of yours been on the phone? This should be one of the happiest days of your life.'

Fergal was mortified. He wanted to tell Alfredo everything – about his family, about what had happened with Riccardo – but he was terrified that it would make Alfredo think less of him. 'No, no – no one's upset me. It's just all so *much* – the party and the cake and all those kind people...I've never had so much given to me in my whole life, never mind in one day. I'll be okay, I promise. Thank you so much, Alfredo. I'm just not used to, well, people being so good to me. It makes me feel...'

'What?' Alfredo gently prodded.

'It makes me feel bad about myself. I know it sounds stupid, but...oh, I can't explain it.'

Alfredo found a handkerchief and gave it to Fergal. 'Fergal, my childhood was wonderful, so I can't imagine what yours must have been like. But I do know that you can't move on in life unless you accept who you are and let the past, however painful, go. Do you understand?'

Fergal nodded, wiping his eyes.

'Good,' Alfredo said. He was glad that the storm had passed for now, but was well aware that Fergal hadn't even begun telling him the whole story. 'Now stand up straight so I can see you.'

Fergal started to thank him again, but Alfredo cut him off. 'Fergal, a hundred thank youse are enough. You are worth every stitch. Look how handsome you are! Let's get down those stairs and out into the city, to continue the celebrations as planned. Do you still feel up to it?'

'I do, Alfredo. I certainly do.' Fergal was glad of the change of subject, but somewhere in his heart he knew that Alfredo was right about facing up to his past.

When Fergal reached the bottom stair, the little gathering of staff clapped wildly, and Arianna attempted a whistle and hugged him tightly. She had helped her brother pick the suit after sneaking a look at Fergal's waist size when the laundry was being done. They had decided to go up a size, as he seemed to be outgrowing what little he had at an alarming rate. Fergal thanked them over and over again until they could take no more.

'Now,' Alfredo announced, 'we'll take a taxi to the club – now that you're old enough to do everything legally, Fergal!'

The room went mad again with whistles and applause. 'Who's going to be the lucky girl?' someone shouted. Out of the corner of his eye, Fergal noticed Riccardo sloping off to the kitchen.

9

Sofia Scapelli worked in a clothes shop near the city centre and dreamed of being an international model. She would never be tall enough for the catwalk, but she had no idea how beautiful she really was. Her heart-shaped face was framed with almond-coloured hair and she had huge, brown, traffic-stopping eyes.

She had first heard about Fergal Flynn when the famous Alfredo Moretti and his sister had come into the shop, looking for a suit for Fergal and perhaps an outfit for Arianna. They had described the young Irishman in detail – not just his waist and chest measurements, but his voice and their certainty that he was going to be a star. They had finally decided on a classic linen suit, which Sofia had assured them could be exchanged or altered if needed. By the time they left, satisfied, Sofia was mad with curiosity and determined to meet Fergal Flynn.

She had never been outside Rome in all of her twenty-one years. Most of her friends were married and on their second or third child, and her mother's desire for grandchildren was mounting with each baptism. Sofia had been single for over three years. She had always expected to marry her childhood sweetheart, but he'd had a tragic and fatal collision on his Vespa not long after his seventeenth birthday. Sofia had never really got over it.

After the Morettis' visit, Sofia had taken to phoning them on the excuse of alerting Arianna to newly arrived clothes that would be snapped up all too quickly. Arianna was delighted. She wasn't as keen a shopper as her brother, and Sofia's calls made it easier to purchase top-quality clothes without having to leave the business for any longer than necessary. She started to wonder, though, when Sofia's questions about Fergal multiplied beyond routine inquiries about whether the suit had been a success.

That night, a private table was reserved for the Moretti party at the exclusive Club Hollywood. Heads turned as Fergal, Alfredo and Arianna joined Antonio and Rocco and ordered a bottle of expensive champagne.

Sofia was sitting at the bar with her two friends, Dina and Luisa. She recognised Arianna immediately, and then her gaze turned to the new owner of the linen suit. 'That's him!' she hissed. 'The one I was telling you about!'

Fergal couldn't help noticing how different everyone looked now that they'd gone to the trouble of dressing up and given their uniform whites the night off. Arianna had decided on a pale pink silk two-piece suit with matching heels and everyone agreed that she looked stunning, but she was convinced she'd spill something on it. Inevitably, her prophecy came true. When she pushed her chair back to go to the toilet, she collided with a speeding waitress, upsetting a tray of beer and red wine that drenched her soft pink creation. The ensuing fuss was astronomical. The manager arranged for a taxi, on the club's account, to take Arianna home to change and promised that the champagne would be taken off their bill. She played her annoyance down for Fergal's sake, and it was agreed that Alfredo would accompany her home and then return in the waiting taxi.

'Will you be okay while I'm gone, Fergal?' Alfredo asked.

Antonio and Rocco threw their arms around Fergal, raising their glasses. 'Don't worry, we'll make sure he has a good time! You're only eighteen once, no?' Fergal laughed.

'I'll be back as quickly as I can,' Alfredo assured him, then left to join his damp sister in the taxi.

Sofia and her friends had taken to the dance floor. Sofia moved to the music with her back to the Moretti table so Dina could give her a running commentary on Fergal's activities. Antonio, Rocco and Fergal had ordered a round of shots and swallowed them in one gulp. Now they had their arms around one another and were singing along to Kool and the Gang.

'Come on,' Luisa called to Sofia, pulling her towards the toilets. Once inside, they reapplied their thick red lipstick and hatched a plan of action. On their way back to their table, they'd have to pass the handsome trio.

As soon as they were outside the toilet door, they formed a chain. Right on cue, 'Dancing in the Street' by Martha and the Vandellas came on. The girls almost ran Antonio over. He took the bait and clamped his hands around the tiny waist that was offered, shouting to Rocco and Fergal to join in. The chain grew and grew, travelling in circles around the tables and chairs and onto the dance floor, faster and faster. Fergal was drunk and the room was already rotating, but he felt great.

When the song ended, they were all soaking wet with sweat. They flopped down together at the nearest table, out of breath and light-headed, and introduced themselves.

The pace changed all of a sudden. Madonna's voice filled the smoky air with the opening bars of her romantic hit, 'Crazy for You'. Rocco and Antonio took their cue and stood up, offering their outstretched arms to Dina and Luisa, who accepted instantly. Antonio looked at Fergal, who looked at Rocco, who kicked him on the ankle, so Fergal stood up and offered his hand to Sofia, mimicking what they had done.

The dance floor was transformed into a windswept cornfield of swaying couples and they got lost in the tide of lovers and lovers-to-be. Sofia had to dance on her tiptoes to rest her head on Fergal's shoulder. He felt embarrassed and awkward at first – he had never really danced with anyone before – but he had a natural sense of rhythm.

Sofia had already decided not to admit that she knew anything about him. She stroked his back and said, 'Your suit is beautiful, Fergal.'

He laughed nervously. 'It was a birthday present.'

'Your accent is beautiful. Where are you from?'

Fergal was only too glad to talk about something he knew, so he set about describing Belfast and the church where he used to sing before Father Mac and Alfredo saved him.

'Oh, you're a singer? How exciting! But what do you mean when you say that these men saved you?'

'Just that there was a lot of danger on the streets, that's all.' Sofia was almost cross-eyed with the romance of it all, not to mention the drink. 'What do you do?' Fergal asked.

'Oh, I work in the fashion industry. And I do a bit of model-ling.' She thought that would impress him.

The song finished and one in Italian came on. Rocco and Antonio found a table and Fergal and Sofia joined them. The next thing Fergal knew, the two other couples were kissing as if their lives depended on it.

Fergal panicked. He was frantically trying to think of something to talk about when Sofia put her hand on his shoulder and planted her lips on his. Her breath was warm and sweet, and the first thing he thought was how soft her face was compared to Father Mac's rough, bearded touch.

She leaned towards him and he caught her. She grabbed him more tightly and pushed her tongue into his mouth. Fergal felt strange, as if he were watching himself from another part of the room. Sofia pushed her chest against his and squeezed his hand. Fergal was so drunk that he had no idea what to do. Somewhere inside himself, he decided to be a passenger and let Sofia do the driving. They opened their mouths wider and kissed more passionately. Fergal shot a glance at Rocco and saw that his hand was buried somewhere in the folds of Dina's outfit. He started to harden just watching Rocco's groin getting fuller in his tight black trousers.

Antonio knew that Alfredo would be back at any second. He whispered to Luisa, who consulted Dina; they nodded, giggling. The two girls grabbed Sofia as she was still kissing Fergal and made for the toilets, shrieking with laughter.

Rocco and Antonio leaned in on either side of Fergal, like a rugby squad discussing tactics. 'Listen,' Antonio said. 'My uncle has this house up in the hills and I look after it for him – he's always away on business. We're going there.'

'Dina and Luisa are asking Sofia if she wants to go,' Rocco said, grinning. 'Less crowded, more private…'

Fergal was still a little disorientated. 'Shouldn't we wait for Alfredo to get back?'

Antonio laughed and slapped him on the back. 'Alfredo isn't your fucking father, is he? There's nothing to worry about. Come on, Fergal, you're eighteen now. You're a fucking man, not some boy hanging off Alfredo's coat-tails. Do you do everything he tells you?'

'No, it's just…God, I'm drunk! We won't be long, will we?'

'I dunno; about seven and a half inches, on a good night!'

77

They burst out laughing.

Luisa gave Antonio a thumbs-up from the toilet door. They gathered up their coats and bags and bribed a taxi driver who was hovering near the entrance to take the six of them. Sofia was glad to claim Fergal's lap. She put her arm around his shoulders, silently praying that he didn't think she was too heavy, although she weighed almost nothing.

Fergal was too drunk to understand the directions Antonio gave the driver. He was dizzy and too warm. He opened the window, and the cold fresh air felt wonderful. They careered around a fountain and out to an unfamiliar road that led up into the hills. Rocco asked Fergal to sing something, but it was one of the rare moments when that was the last thing he felt like doing, so he refused, saying that he only knew laments and classical pieces. But the three girls needed no encouragement – they sang a song that they'd learned at school, and the chorus made them screech so hard with laughter that they were unable to finish it, much to the driver's relief.

The taxi wound its way higher and higher, off the main road, and finally halted outside a wooden house in complete darkness. Rocco paid the inflated fare and Antonio went to a hanging basket of flowers and began groping for the front door key in the moonlight.

The fire in the grate was set. They only had to touch a match to it and the room began to warm quickly. Antonio found one of his uncle's favourite Sinatra albums, *Songs for Swinging Lovers*, and Rocco went into the kitchen and found six glasses to hold the thick amaretto liqueur that was always kept in the top cupboard. Antonio poured more than double measures and began dancing with Luisa. Rocco kissed Dina as she sat side-saddle on his lap. Fergal looked at Sofia and she took his gaze as encouragement. She climbed on top of him, relieving him of his glass, and kissed him. Fergal couldn't find the right words to tell her to stop.

Antonio and Luisa moved out of the room and up the stairs, to the one bedroom. Rocco's shirt was undone and Dina's shoes were off. After another few songs they picked up a candle and retreated behind the closed door of the kitchen, leaving just the firelight for Fergal and Sofia.

Alfredo arrived back at the club later than he had expected. He had tried to convince Arianna to change her outfit and return to the party, but she had told him she was exhausted and made him stay for a nightcap.

They had ended up talking about Fergal, of course. They agreed that he seemed restless and tense, especially when the subject of his family arose.

Arianna shook her head. 'Alfredo, I can't imagine how awful it would be if we didn't get on with each other, or if we'd had a bad relationship with our parents. He told me his mother has written to him, though. At least that's something. But he seems so *sad* sometimes, and there's nothing I can do.'

'He's the same in his lessons. He's exceptional in some ways – his natural voice is extraordinary, and you heard for yourself today how well he's coming on technically – but I just can't help feeling that he's holding back so much. It must be exhausting for him. In some ways it's to be expected, when he's so young, but he must learn to let go. I'm teaching him as much as I can and he responds well to advice and criticism, but there's something missing, and I'm not sure I know what it is yet.'

'What about his exam? Will he be all right?'

'I'm not so worried about that. His technical ability is growing all the time. He needs to do some serious growing to really own his voice, but…it's his heart I'm talking about. He seems so unreachable sometimes.'

'Yes, that's what it is. Sometimes when I talk to him he

responds like he's listening, but there's a part of him that seems…impenetrable.'

'Exactly. That's a good word for it.'

Alfredo glanced at his watch and realised he had stayed longer than he'd meant to. He asked Arianna again to come back to the club in a fresh outfit, but she insisted on sending him on his way without her. Truth be told, she was glad to be back at home; she had felt old, all of a sudden, amongst so many young people.

When Alfredo didn't see Fergal anywhere in the club, he started to get worried. He called out Fergal's name again and again, but finally he had to concede defeat to the now-deafening music. He spotted the waiter who had been looking after their table and gladly hurried over to him.

'Have you seen my friend, the young Irishman?'

The waiter shrugged. 'He was here a few minutes ago. He was dancing with the other two young men and some girls. I think they left.'

Alfredo tried not to look too angry. 'They had better be taking good care of him,' he muttered. 'And he had better be protecting his voice.'

Sofia placed a bundle of sticks in the heart of the open fire and the flames ate them hungrily, throwing more light into the room. Then she turned around and opened the buttons of her blouse, one by one, to reveal her cleavage, almost bursting the banks of her tiny bra. Fergal tried to speak, but she quickly crossed the room and put her finger to her lips to hush him. She unhooked her bra with the other hand and her bare breasts hung inches from his puzzled face, like ripe fruit.

They could hear the low moans of Antonio and Luisa upstairs as the bed began to knock against the wall. Closer still, in the kitchen, Rocco's muffled voice repeated, '*Si, si,* Dina…*si,* baby.' It was like an epidemic.

Sofia pressed one of her breasts to Fergal's lips, and again he was struck by how soft her skin was. The soundtrack of what Rocco and Antonio were doing to the other girls was making him hard. He closed his eyes and imagined it was one of their nipples he was sucking on. Sofia's hand dropped suddenly to his trouser zip, and she giggled approval at the tent that had started to appear. Before he could say anything, she had unzipped him, taken hold of his hardness and started pulling at him, faster and faster.

'Did you bring…anything?' Sofia whispered.

Fergal shook his head.

She nodded. She began kissing him, all the way down to his belly button, opening his shirt buttons as she went. Fergal was distracted by Rocco's guttural moans in the next room, but when Sofia took the tip of his erection in her mouth, he gasped back to reality. Father Mac's face floated in front of him in the poor light of the fading flames. He wanted to tell her to stop, but he couldn't find the words to do it without hurting her.

When Sofia looked up at him, with his erection still in her mouth, she didn't expect to see such an unhappy face. She stopped. 'Are you okay?' she asked.

Fergal looked away. 'I – I'm just drunk.' He tried to stand up, but the room began to spin. Sofia put her arms around him, helping him regain his balance. Then she kissed his nipples, and Fergal felt powerless to do anything as she continued her tender journey downwards. His trousers fell to the floor in a heap. Sofia took him in her mouth again, more earnestly this time, and began sucking.

Fergal put his hand on her head and tried to move her away, but she held on to his buttocks and took him deeper still. He thought about the one-sided sex he'd had with Riccardo that very same day, and he started to hate himself even more.

He lost his balance and they tumbled to the floor. Sofia laughed drunkenly. When Fergal opened his eyes, he saw that she had taken her knickers off and was standing over him in the half-light. He could only stare at her in bewilderment. He could see that her naked body was beautiful, but in his heart of hearts he was somewhere else, with someone else.

She straddled his traitor erection in a single gymnastic movement and lowered herself onto it. Fergal gasped as she ground her hips wildly. He knew he didn't care about her, he shouldn't be inside her; he just wanted it to be over. He tried to sit up and lift her off, but she just moved faster and faster, moaning and calling his name, her eyes firmly shut. In sudden lucid desperation, Fergal heaved himself up and turned onto one side, making her fall off.

The silent room started to spin again. The Sinatra record was at the end of its vinyl groove, turning and hiccup-scratching pointlessly. Fergal felt sick.

Sofia, out of breath, thought he was being careful not to get her pregnant. 'It's okay,' she said. 'It'll be okay as long as you pull out of me before—'

Fergal shook his head, and Sofia saw that he looked terribly sad. 'It's okay if it's your first time,' she said gently. 'I'll take care of you.'

The fact that she was being so lovely made Fergal feel even worse. He looked at the floor. 'No, Sofia. It's not that.'

'What, then? You've had too much to drink?'

He couldn't find the words to answer. She turned away. 'You don't like me enough. That's it, isn't it? You think I'm ugly.'

Fergal clamped his eyes shut in frustration. 'Oh, for God's sake, Sofia! Sure, look at you – you're fucking gorgeous! Any man would…I mean, it's not you. It's me. It's just…'

She looked at him as his explanation evaporated, and then she finished the sentence for him. 'You don't like girls, do you, Fergal?'

He was shocked that she'd been brave enough to say it – braver than he was. He started to say something, but Sofia beat him to it. It had taken a lot for her to give herself to someone again, after years of mourning her lost love, and she was furious that Fergal had made a fool of her and her desire. 'I'm right, aren't I?' Her voice started to rise. 'Why the fuck didn't you say something before? Do you think I offer myself to just anyone? No wonder I had to do everything. I thought you were just nervous and shy, I thought you were a virgin…Oh my God, why did I pick you? You bastard, you let me make a fool of myself!'

She burst into tears of fury and embarrassment, slapping the dimly lit wall in search of the light switch. One of her bare feet came down on the sharp heel of her shoe and she screamed in shock. She started getting dressed as quickly as she could.

The other four had heard the commotion, and Dina stuck her head around the door. 'What's the matter?'

'I want to go home,' Sofia shouted through her sobs. 'Now!'

As Luisa helped Sofia find the remainder of her clothes and a bewildered Antonio phoned for a taxi, Fergal heard the low hum of a diesel engine cursing the climb of the hill. He thought he recognised the sound of Alfredo's car, but by the time he ran out onto the dirt road, the car had sped off, and all he could see was the embers of the taillights vanishing around a bend.

'Fuck, fuck, fuck!' he swore at himself. He was convinced that Sofia would tell everyone what she suspected. He hadn't confirmed it in words, but he had in his behaviour. On top of all that, Alfredo would be furious with him for leaving the club. Unsurprisingly, Fergal suddenly felt a lot more sober.

Rocco and Antonio weren't too pleased with him, either. They had both been at a fairly critical point when Luisa and Dina had gone to see what was wrong with Sofia. Sofia calmed down once the taxi had been telephoned, but she was still saying nothing, so

Rocco and Antonio went outside to have a cigarette and ask Fergal what was going on.

'What the hell happened there?' Antonio asked. Fergal shrugged.

Rocco said, 'From what I could hear, it sounded like it was going great – unless you moan your own name when you're fucking someone?'

He and Antonio sniggered, but they stopped when they saw Fergal's pained expression. Then a thought occurred to Antonio. 'Fergal, did you ask her to do something…you know, disgusting? You didn't try and park the train in the back tunnel, did you? A lot of girls hate that.'

The incredulous look on Fergal's face told them that wasn't the answer. 'It's natural to be nervous the first time,' Rocco tried, but Fergal stayed mute.

Finally two taxis arrived to take them home – the girls in one car, Fergal in the other. He was deeply relieved not to have to share a car with them. As the taxi pulled away, he felt a flash of jealousy that Antonio and Rocco had decided to stay the night in the house by themselves.

Moretti's was in total darkness when Fergal's taxi trembled to a stop outside. Luckily he still had some money left over from the club. He paid the driver and stood in the moonlight, looking at the sleeping restaurant.

Arianna was an insomniac at the best of times, and there was no way she could have slept when she knew Fergal was still out. Alfredo had come back from his fruitless search in Club Hollywood and had flown into a rage, cursing Antonio and Rocco, when his sister told him Fergal still hadn't come home. Arianna had tried to calm her brother, reminding him that they had all been young once, but Alfredo had insisted on taking his car out to look for Fergal again, even though he wasn't sure where to start. 'If one hair on his head has been harmed in any way, I'll kill Antonio and Rocco – I swear it, Arianna!' With that, he had sped off.

Arianna had been lying down, trying to distract herself with a book. She heard the taxi's engine and got up, thinking it was Alfredo returning with news, but when she looked out the window she saw Fergal's sorry silhouette. Although she wanted to go straight to him, she found herself watching him momentarily, almost like a mother learning to let go. He sat down on a bench with his head in his hands. For a moment Arianna thought he was praying, then she realised he was crying, and she pulled her dressing gown about her and ran to see what was wrong.

Fergal looked up when he heard the door open.

'Fergal, where have you been? Alfredo has been looking all over for you. Are you okay?' she said softly.

'Oh, God, I'm sorry. Has he?'

'Why are you crying?'

'I'm not,' he said pointlessly, wiping the tears off his wet face. 'I feel awful, Arianna. I didn't mean to upset you or anybody. You've all been so good to me, better than…well, better than my own family.'

He dropped his head again. Arianna put her arms around him. 'Come inside,' she said, leading him towards the restaurant. 'It's cold out here. Tell me, Fergal, what happened?'

Fergal shook his head. 'I don't…I just want to go to bed, Arianna. I'm so tired.'

Arianna poured him a large glass of water and helped him upstairs and into his room. As she closed his door, she said, 'Fergal, it's all right to let people be concerned about you. I'm not angry. I remember what it is to be young. Things happen, but I promise you this – whatever it is won't seem quite so bad in the morning. Or maybe it'll take a few mornings, who knows? You've had too much to drink, which is only natural on your eighteenth birthday. Drink as much of that water as you can, and sleep as long as you want, I won't wake you. Goodnight.'

Fergal managed a weary 'Thanks' before gulping down the cold water, sliding out of his shoes and clothes and pulling the blankets up over his head.

10

Alfredo had driven around the city, checking the haunts that he guessed Antonio and Rocco frequented to meet girls. Every club was getting ready to close and young people spilled out onto the streets, trying to wave down cabs and coax lifts from their mates, but there was no sign of Fergal. After half an hour Alfredo found himself taking the road that led out to the hills, just to calm down. Had he known that Fergal was only yards away, he would have stopped at Antonio's uncle's house, but he had no idea, and finally he forced himself to drive home, defeated, and tried his best to sleep, praying that Fergal had the sense not to get into anything too foolish.

Fergal woke the next morning to the sound of his bedroom door closing. A large glass of orange juice and a cup of steaming black coffee stood on the little bedside cabinet. He guessed that Arianna had been trying not to wake him.

He sat up to reach for the juice and his head almost rolled off his shoulders with dizziness. His mouth felt like someone had upholstered it with second-hand carpet and his head hurt so much that he almost panicked, convincing himself that he had somehow permanently damaged his brain with the unwise combination of drinks. The church bells insisted on telling him it was eleven o'clock – he couldn't remember the last time he'd slept so late. Slowly, the details of the previous evening returned like homing pigeons coming through fog, one by one, each carrying a snippet of vital information. Then, suddenly, a whole flock of images crashed on top of him, and he felt awful.

This time he made sure no one was in the bathroom. He stood under the shower, letting the cool jets of water massage his throbbing head. He couldn't help thinking about what had happened with Riccardo, and he began to get aroused – until Sofia's face floated into his mind's eye. He wanted more than anything to talk to Father Mac. He was sure that just hearing that calm voice would make him feel better.

Fergal hurried back to his room and dressed quickly. He had to get outside, into the fresh air. Out on the street, though, the sun was too much for his eyes. He kept having to shield them with his hand. He thought he might look for a cheap pair of sunglasses. Everyone else wore them, but he had always been too self-conscious – he didn't want anybody to think he was a poser. And then, too, they reminded him of the IRA men and women in Belfast who wore the darkest sunglasses invented, even in the worst weather – at marches, or at the graveside of dead volunteers as they tilted their rifles up to God and fired over the tricolour-draped coffin…Fergal suddenly shook all over, as if his body was trying to reclaim him back to Rome.

The bustling afternoon was just getting warmed up, to the usual symphony of mopeds and car horns. Fergal found himself outside the little Chapel of Regret. He stepped out of the current of tourists and shoppers and into the kinder, filtered light that soothed him immediately. Before his eyes had fully adjusted, he took the nearest seat. He only gradually realised that he had joined the growing queue for confession.

As he looked around, he saw that the building was much older than St Bridget's Church. There were ancient statues in every corner, their expressions almost worn away by the careless caresses of the centuries.

He heard the little wooden box open and realised it was his turn to go to confession. He almost changed his mind, but in the end he took a deep breath and went into the upright, oblong darkness.

When the grille slid back, Fergal started softly, 'Bless me, Father, for I have sinned…'

He hesitated, but the old priest reassured him. Fergal couldn't focus on anything except the purple darkness, broken now and again by the merest outline of the priest's head, and he found this strangely comforting. He told the priest how he had got drunk, how he had been with Sofia – he left out the details – how much he had worried Alfredo, how worried he was that everyone would find out the mortifying truth…There was no way he was going to tell the old priest about his encounter with Riccardo. 'How am I going to face Alfredo?' he asked the darkness. 'He's been so good to me.'

The old priest listened intently until the last echo of Fergal's story was gone from the confines of the box. Then he cleared his throat and said quietly, 'In God's eyes, confessing is the best thing you could have done. Say three Hail Marys and three Our Fathers every night this week, as penance. And go to your teacher, before the day is done. If he is truly your friend, which I believe he is, and he sees that you are genuinely sorry, then his heart will soften and he will forgive you. You will even find that, in time, your friendship will be stronger and deeper for this. Go now.'

Fergal sighed deeply. 'Yes, Father, I will. And thank you.'

*

Alfredo had telephoned his sister early that morning to find out whether Fergal had come home. When Arianna told him what state poor Fergal had appeared in he wanted to come over immediately, but she had managed to persuade him not to. 'Alfredo, the best thing we can do is let the boy sleep.'

Alfredo had barked angrily in reply, 'Oh, he's not a boy any longer, Arianna. I'm sure Antonio and Rocco have done their best to take care of that!'

'Don't talk that way,' Arianna had told him firmly, and Alfredo was instantly silenced. She sounded so much like their mother when she got impatient. 'I have to go, I've got a business to run. Come round later for coffee.'

It was almost one o'clock when she took Fergal up some food and a bottle of water. When he didn't answer her knock, she put the tray down and opened the door, expecting to see him still tangled up in the bedlinen. She was surprised to see that the room was empty. The bed had been roughly made and Fergal's suit was folded, albeit haphazardly, on the chair. She listened for any sound from the bathroom and called his name, but there was no answer. Not much got past Arianna's radar, and she was amazed and annoyed that Fergal had managed to leave the restaurant without her noticing.

Fergal knew he couldn't put off seeing Alfredo for much longer, but he wanted to keep walking. He had finally found a cheap pair of sunglasses that actually fit him, so the glare of the sunshine was more bearable. When he caught sight of himself in a shop window, he saw that his hair was a mess. He decided to visit the nearby barber for a decent cut. Maybe it would make his head feel cooler, too.

He felt about five years old as the barber put a nylon robe around him, whistling a tune through the gap between his front teeth. Fergal told him to clip it close, and shut his eyes as the barber sprayed his head with a water bottle like the one Arianna used for her hanging plants. Then he went to work with his scissors and comb. Finally he rubbed some kind of liniment into Fergal's head, and his scalp suddenly felt as if it had been in the fridge. It was exactly what he'd needed.

Just as he was paying and trying not to admire himself too much in the mirror, he froze. Behind his reflection in the mirrored wall was Riccardo, just opening the door, holding the hand of a little boy. Fergal thanked the barber and tried to leave as quickly as he could, but he had to pass Riccardo.

'Hello,' Fergal muttered. Riccardo nodded his head without looking at him.

At that moment the little boy started pulling at Riccardo's shirt, pointing at the selection of children's comics in a pile on the table. 'Papa, Papa, I want to look at the comics!'

Fergal couldn't get out of the shop quickly enough. Outside, he leaned against a wall, feeling dizzy. It had never occurred to him that Riccardo might be married – and with a child, too. He couldn't help wondering what, if anything, he would have done in the bathroom with Riccardo if he had known. Probably everything, he thought, but he promised himself that they could never do it again. He knew the promise wouldn't be difficult to keep. Judging by the look on Riccardo's face, he would be doing his best to avoid Fergal.

His self-loathing was heightened by his hangover – his whole body felt poisoned – but just being in the city, surrounded by so much energy, made him feel better. It was hard not to keep making comparisons with Belfast. He thought about how every-one in the streets of Belfast, even Dermot, looked worried all the time. They'd got used to it. Here, everyone looked happy, and

Fergal wondered if it was contagious. There seemed to be so many couples of all ages, sitting at tables and drinking and talking, so many groups of breathtakingly handsome fellas on mopeds, flying past hordes of girls and broadcasting high-speed details about next weekend's parties. Fergal couldn't help feeling jealous of the freedom they seemed to have compared to the life from which he had miraculously managed to escape. Their confidence was incredible and effortless, second nature. And every single one of them seemed to have a moped. At that moment, Fergal decided that the minute he made any money he was going to buy a shiny Vespa that he'd admired in the one of the local shops. He imagined driving it up the road to St Bridget's, and in spite of everything, the image made him smile.

As Fergal wandered along, daydreaming, he unwittingly passed the very clothes shop where Sofia worked. He nearly fainted when he glanced into the window and saw her. Luckily, she was so busy serving a group of women that he managed to back away undetected. Every disastrous detail of their evening flashed through his mind, no matter how hard he tried to distract himself. He felt sick with embarrassment. Why couldn't he have just pretended with Sofia for a bit longer? Then no one would know what he didn't completely understand himself. Fellas had one-night stands all the time; Antonio and Rocco certainly bragged about theirs often enough. Fergal wondered if Sofia had told her mates exactly what had happened. Surely they would have kept asking her till she told them every mortifying detail. He shuddered with embarrassment at the thought of the three girls going over every single clue to his gayness.

When he was a safe distance away, he sat down at a café and ordered coffee. He thought about how Sofia had given herself to him. He thought about Riccardo, and about how their clumsy sex had made him feel dirty and worthless and certainly unloved.

There had been no tenderness, as there had been with Dermot. Fergal suddenly understood that his bad experience with Riccardo had a lot to do with why he had allowed things to go so far with Sofia. He had just wanted someone to want him, to need him, to make him feel loved. He knew he had been lonely for a long time.

Suddenly, out of nowhere, he remembered something Alfredo had said to him, back in Father Mac's parlour, when Fergal sang for him for the first time. 'There are notes that you don't yet know exist, but they are only sleeping because you haven't woken them – and I feel I could...' Fergal hadn't really understood at the time, but now he began to realise how wise Alfredo was. And he came to the sobering conclusion that some deep part of him had wanted to see if Sofia could awaken new notes inside his soul, as Alfredo and Father Mac both had, in different ways, if she could awaken a new person, someone other than the Fergal he knew he truly was. He had never been with a girl before, and he had allowed himself to go along with Sofia because a part of him had wanted to see if it would mean something. But it hadn't. He couldn't have been surer about that.

The experience had been the only way to find out, but Fergal regretted hurting Sofia so much. He felt so bad about it that he almost retraced his steps back to her shop to say how sorry he was, but he was sure she must be exhausted and eager to forget he even existed.

He finished his coffee and strolled back to Moretti's, feeling much better able to take on the rest of the day.

11

Arianna had been watching the door like a hawk. When Fergal finally appeared, she was more relieved than anything. He looked much more like himself. He smiled shyly at her and she gave him a careful hug.

'Arianna, I'm so sorry. Thanks for taking care of me last night, and this morning, when you left the food and all, and let me sleep so late...'

'That's okay. You still look pale, though.'

'Ah, sure, my head was killing me for ages, and I felt so bad about everything – and sick, too. But I went for a really long walk and I feel better.'

'Good. You certainly seem better than you did last night, anyway. Where did you go?'

'I'm not sure. I walked for miles, and I even ended up in confession. Can I use the phone? I need to talk to Alfredo as soon as I can, and to Father MacManus in Belfast, if that's okay? He said I could reverse the charges or he'd call me straight back.'

'Of course you can. I know my brother is anxious to talk with you, so you might try him first, yes?'

'Yes, I promise. I need to see him and – and try to sort things out, if he'll let me.'

Arianna smiled. 'Fergal, don't worry so much. My brother will be only too glad to hear you're safe and feeling better.'

Alfredo was in the middle of a lesson with a butcher who sang in a booming, sonorous voice and paid a small fortune to learn the most popular love songs of the twentieth century. He was good, too. Normally Alfredo never took calls during lessons, but today Daniela was under strict instructions to answer the phone if it rang and to interrupt him if it was Fergal. When she rapped lightly on the door of his music room, Alfredo nearly pulled the door off its hinges. 'Is it him?' he demanded, rushing past her without waiting for an answer.

At the phone, he straightened his waistcoat to compose himself. 'Hello? Alfredo Moretti speaking.'

Fergal was unnerved by the formality. 'Alfredo? Look, it's me, Fergal.' Out of nowhere, he burst into a coughing fit.

Alfredo was horrified. 'Oh my God, Fergal, your voice! Are you all right? We have an exam in only a few days! What have those fucking waiters done to you? They didn't encourage you to smoke, did they? I'll fucking kill them.'

Fergal had never heard Alfredo swear so much, and it was enough to stop the coughing. 'No, Alfredo, no, of course I wasn't smoking – I'm not mad, I know I have an exam. I'm so sorry about last night. I don't really know what got into me. With all that champagne and all, I wasn't thinking. The fellas only wanted me to have a good time. Alfredo, I'm sorry I went off with them instead of waiting for you – it all happened so fast. I'm sorry. My birthday was great up until…up until…' Fergal burst into tears.

Alfredo's heart sank. 'Fergal – oh, Fergal, don't cry, we can fix everything. You'll make yourself more hoarse. Have you got a sore throat?'

Fergal's throat did still feel a bit raw, but he tried to play it down. 'No, no. I'm fine.'

Alfredo's anger was all but gone. He was just relieved that Fergal seemed unharmed. 'Listen to me, Fergal. I was worried out of my mind when I couldn't find you anywhere. But Antonio and Rocco took advantage of your drunken state. They dragged you off with those…girls.'

Fergal said nothing. He wondered how much Alfredo actually knew. He must have gone round to the restaurant and talked to Antonio and Rocco…

'Fergal, I take it you have no plans for this evening?'

'No, Alfredo, none at all. I wanted to come and see you and, well, explain.'

'Good. Come – but not for a lesson. You must rest that voice at all costs. The hoarseness should go if you stop talking for a few hours and give it a chance to heal. Giovanni and Luigi are coming over for supper, so come earlier – say seven o'clock? Then we can talk properly before they arrive. I want to hear every detail about last night, and then I'll tell you my plan.'

'Your plan? Okay,' Fergal said uncertainly. 'Do you need me to bring anything?'

'Only yourself, young man, and the truth. Don't bring anything but the truth. Drink gallons of water today and tomorrow, won't you? Hydrate your voice.'

'I will. See you at seven.'

Fergal put the receiver down, then he took a deep breath, lifted it again and dialled the number of St Bridget's House.

It rang and rang. Just when Fergal was about to give up, he heard a click and the old housekeeper, Mrs Mooney, said breathlessly, 'Hello, St Bridget's House?'

'Mrs Mooney, is that you?'

'Yes, it is. Who's speaking, please?'

'It's me, Fergal – Fergal Flynn. Mrs Mooney, do you not recognise my voice?'

Mrs Mooney went crimson with embarrassment. 'Ah God, Fergal, I'm sorry! You sound completely different. Tell us now, is the Pope all right? I've heard he hasn't been well. And if you remember, would you ever light a candle at the Vatican for my husband? His back's plaguing him.'

Fergal laughed. 'I will, Mrs Mooney. And the Pope's grand, as far as I know. Is Father Mac in?'

'I don't know where he is at all. He's busier than ever, God love him. Oh Fergal, he'll be so sorry to have missed your wee call. Will I get him to ring you back?'

'Please, Mrs Mooney. That would be great.'

'Oh, I nearly forgot – how was your birthday?'

'Ah sure, it was great, really great. Thanks for the card, too.'

Fergal heard the front doorbell of St Bridget's down the line. 'I've to go, Fergal. Your accent is lovely now, do you know that? So much softer. It suits you.'

It hadn't even occurred to Fergal that his accent might have altered.

He went upstairs to get ready. His suit was missing from where he'd left it on the chair, and for a second he almost panicked, but then he found it hanging in the wardrobe, next to the winter coat he hadn't worn since the day he'd arrived. Arianna had been to the rescue – she'd had the suit dry cleaned. Fergal wished he could do the same thing to the whole previous day, to his whole past. He settled for allowing himself the fantasy that the previous day hadn't happened at all, that he was starting afresh.

As he was leaving for Alfredo's that evening, Fergal made a point of showing himself to Arianna and thanking her for having the suit cleaned. She gave him some spare flowers left over from the delivery for that evening's tables to take to Alfredo, and Fergal, feeling a little less shaky, headed for the tram.

As the tram rattled across the river, its windows offered a perfectly framed, moving view of Rome by night. Fergal caught sight of his reflection in the window, and it occurred to him that he looked like he was going on a date, which made him laugh. He still hadn't fully adjusted to how different the new suit made him look and feel, but he loved it more and more.

Fergal felt that he owed Alfredo not only an apology but also a proper explanation. He wanted to tell him more about his childhood – how he worried about his mother, even after everything she'd done to him, how his father and brothers had treated him, how helpless he had always felt, how weighed down, how unlovable. But even the thought of telling Alfredo terrified him. He was sure that Alfredo would think he was mad ever to have taken him on.

Daniela answered the front door and ushered Fergal into the study. As he laid the flowers on top of the piano, Alfredo made his entrance, choosing his moment perfectly, as he had so many times on stage. Fergal couldn't move, but Alfredo went to him and they embraced each other tightly.

Daniela reappeared with two glasses of chilled white wine and they took them to the red velvet chaise longue. Alfredo studied every inch of Fergal's face, approved of his new haircut and then said, 'Now, Fergal, you must tell me everything about last night. You understand, I'm responsible for your well-being, especially the well-being of your voice. What else has all this work been for?'

'I know,' was all Fergal could manage.

'Fergal, how can I put this without sounding old-fashioned? You must be careful who you decide to associate with. I know

Rocco and Antonio are close to you in age, but they don't have their voices to consider. They're free to carouse around town, smoking and drinking too much and kissing God only knows how many pairs of lips. I know I sound like some old...fuddy-duddy? Is that what you say?'

Fergal shrugged uncomfortably.

'You must be especially careful who you're intimate with. The kind of things those boys get up to, the kind of girls they like...well, it's the easiest way to pick up germs. And it could set your training back weeks, even months, if you came down with a serious throat infection, for example.'

Before Alfredo could utter another word of his rehearsed lecture, Fergal blurted out, 'Oh God, Alfredo, I'm so embarrassed! It was a nightmare. I didn't realise how much I'd actually drunk. Everything was on fast-forward and then in slow motion...'

'My boy, it's all right. It's over now. Tell me what happened.'

'One minute we were in the club with you and Arianna, and the next thing I was dancing with this girl, Sofia, and Antonio and Rocco were dancing with her mates. Then they ordered a taxi, and before I knew it we were in some strange house in the hills some-where, I've no idea where. The fellas went off with the girls and left me and Sofia in the front room.'

Fergal's face had gone bright red and he took another sip of the wine. Alfredo nodded for him to continue.

'Then, well, things started to happen.'

'What things?'

'You know...sex. In the other rooms. Sofia wanted me to do the same thing to her, but – ah, Jesus, it was a disaster. We ended up on the floor, and she was trying to get me to, you know, do it, but I...I...I had other things on my mind. She got really angry and upset, and she wanted to go home. I went home too. Antonio and Rocco weren't very happy, I can tell you. Alfredo, I never meant to upset her, but it just wasn't me. I couldn't go through with it, I just couldn't…'

Fergal's voice trailed off. He said, almost in a whisper, 'It would've been a lie.'

Alfredo's kind eyes scrutinised him for a moment. 'Oh Fergal, poor Fergal. What do you mean when you say it would have been a lie?'

Fergal took a deep breath. 'I'm gay, Alfredo. Jesus. There, I've said it.' He looked away.

'Fergal Flynn, you brave, brave man.' Alfredo stood up and motioned for Fergal to do the same, and he hugged him even more tightly than before.

'I've never told anyone else, except Der— I mean Father MacManus.'

'He knows, does he? How did he react, seeing as the Catholic Church disapproves so deeply?'

Fergal hadn't meant to let that slip. 'I – I mean, he was…he was great about it…he was very understanding. Very supportive. But Alfredo, I'm really worried. Sofia kind of guessed, and I don't really want anyone else to know.'

'My goodness, Fergal, what a birthday you've had! It's not a good idea to broadcast this – you must know that. The world has a long way to come on that score.'

'I know, but it just sort of happened.'

'You've been very honest with me, so what would you say if I told you I was gay too?'

Fergal tried to look surprised. 'Really? God, Alfredo – thank you for telling me. When did you know?'

'For as long as I can remember. What about you? When did you first know?'

'Always. I don't remember feeling any other way. But in Belfast… well, it's not something you want to admit, even to yourself.'

'Does your family know? Is that why things are bad at home?'

'No – Jesus, no! I mean, they always slagged me about it, but I don't think they *know*, not really…Oh God, Alfredo, what if Sofia tells her mates and they tell Antonio and Rocco? It'll be all over the restaurant.'

'Fergal, calm down. I can't imagine that she would tell anybody. She's probably very embarrassed herself. You're both young. It's natural to make mistakes and misjudge situations that start out as fun, especially after so much alcohol. I had a bad feeling when I had to leave you there. Rocco and Antonio should have known better, though. They must have had at least some of that evening planned. How else would they know that the house would be free? Just wait till I see them…'

'Please, don't. I don't want them to get into any trouble with Arianna, or with you. You said it yourself – I'm a man now. I have to take more responsibility. I was thinking about that all the way over here on the tram. That's why I decided to tell you about me.'

'And I can't tell you how much I appreciate it,' Alfredo said gently. 'I know only too well how hard it is to reveal one's true self. Tell me something, if you don't mind me asking?'

'What? Anything.'

'Did you have a lover, a boyfriend, in Belfast?'

Fergal swallowed hard and absent-mindedly put his hand to his throat; it still felt raw. 'Well, ah…not really. In Belfast, it's pretty hard to do anything in secret.'

'Yes, I'm sure it is.'

'What about you? Do you have someone?'

Alfredo smiled. 'Goodness, no. I wish I did. No, it's been a very long time since I was in love with anyone – too long, in fact. Sometimes I think…'

'What?'

'That it's too late. I'm not far off fifty. I envy you, Fergal.'

Fergal was taken aback. 'You envy *me*? You must be joking!'

'No, not in the least. You have such an exciting journey ahead of you, if you'd only…Oh, never mind.' Alfredo exhaled in frustration and refilled their glasses.

'What? If I'd only what?'

'If you'd only get out of your own way, Fergal!'

Fergal shook his head. 'I don't know what you mean.'

'In a way, I'm glad this little crisis has happened. You have always seemed so impenetrable, and for the sake of your voice and your career, you must break past this barrier. Technically, you're gaining so much ground, but you must go deeper into yourself.'

Fergal felt as if he had been slapped in the face. 'Do you mean I'm not ready for the exam? Is that it?'

Alfredo sighed. 'No, I'm not saying that. I wouldn't let you take the exam if I didn't think you were ready. My reputation is on the line every bit as much as yours – more so, in fact, because I'm the one with a reputation. You don't have one – yet.'

Fergal's head began to hurt again and his eyes filled up before he could stop them.

'Fergal, I'm not saying any of this to hurt you. It needs to be said. At least you're starting to open up. I can't tell you how touched I am that you've told me you're gay. Certainly this can be a burden, but…'

'What?'

'I don't think that is all of your burden. Certainly it has been hard for you to be different, especially where you grew up, but I get the feeling there's something else much deeper. You need to dig, you need to uproot it. Only then will you be free to be who you really are – and what a singer you will be!'

For an instant, Fergal thought he understood, but in the next moment he felt more confused than ever. 'Alfredo, I can't…I don't …Look, I'm sorry for all this mess, I'm sorry I went off with

Antonio and Rocco. I won't do it again. And I'll work even harder for the exam, I promise. It's just that sometimes I feel like…like I'm not good enough.'

'Fergal, everyone has feelings of insecurity. For tonight, just concentrate on having a better time than you did last night! I won't ask you to sing – you sound a little hoarse, but it's nothing that sleep and plenty of water won't remedy, so you must not worry. I have to tell you, I expected you to look and sound much worse; this is why I was so upset. And that haircut makes you look even younger and more handsome, if that's possible!'

The laughter in his voice made Fergal feel better. When Alfredo asked if he wanted anything, he remembered – he needed to call Father Mac.

The phone was answered on the second ring.

'Hello, St Bridget's Parish House, Father MacManus here. How can I help?'

'Dermot? It's me, Fergal.'

Father Mac nearly dropped the phone. 'Fergal! I tried to call you on your birthday, but I couldn't get through for some reason. Happy birthday, fella. Did you get your cards and the money?'

'I did, yesterday. You're great to remember.'

'Sure, how could I forget? Eighteen, eh? How do you feel?'

Fergal lowered his voice. 'Ah, I've felt better. I won't lie to you – I was rotten drunk last night, and I made a complete eejit of myself.'

'Good man. Sure, that's what you're supposed to do on your birthday.'

'I suppose.' Fergal wanted to tell him everything, but the words wouldn't come.

'Fergal, are you okay?'

'I am, I am…Sorry, I'm just a bit, I don't know, disconnected today. Look, I'm at Alfredo's and I just told him…you know…that I'm gay.'

The line went very quiet. Finally Father Mac exhaled. 'I see. Well, that was very brave of you.'

'That's what he said. Dermot, I didn't say a word about – about us. I never would.'

'I know you wouldn't, Fergal.'

'But look, Dermot, how are you? It's been ages since I heard your voice. I've phoned you, but you're always out. Don't worry, I know how busy you get, but I'd love to see you. You know it's nearly a whole year now?'

'I was only thinking that myself. I can hardly believe you're gone a year.'

'Hey, Dermot,' Fergal said softly, 'do you remember where we were on my last birthday?'

There was a pause. The line crackled. In the Belfast distance, an ambulance siren wailed. Father Mac sighed heavily. 'Ah, Fergal, what do you think? That kind of night is like an eclipse – rare and completely unforgettable, but almost unreal at the same time.'

'I know. I dream about it sometimes. Do you?'

'I don't, Fergal. You know how I feel. I don't regret what happened between us for a moment, but I'm glad you're in Rome, where you should be, and I'm here, where I should be.'

Fergal's heart sank. Part of him still held onto the notion that Father Mac would change his mind and announce he was coming to Rome, to be with him.

'The thing about an eclipse, Fergal,' Father Mac said softly, 'is that sometimes it's never repeated in a lifetime. You know that, don't you?'

'Don't say that, Dermot. Look, I know you meant the best for me when you sent that letter, and I know what you're saying, but—'

'Fergal, don't—'

'I'm just saying, never say never.'

'You're young, free and single. You must have met someone in that gorgeous city.'

'What? Well, not really.' There was no way Fergal was going to tell him about his one-off with married Riccardo. 'Look, when are you coming for a visit? You have to see Alfredo's house.'

Father Mac laughed down the line, and the tension that had been building between them evaporated. 'You know I can't make any promises, but I might have some time coming up.'

'Seriously? Oh Dermot, that would be great! I bet you could stay here at Alfredo's – that would save money on a hotel. I'll ask him for you, will I?'

'No, don't do that. I haven't made up my mind, and even if I'm able to come I don't expect Alfredo to put me up. I'm sure he has enough on his plate. I might even bring my sister. She was asking for you, by the way.'

'But Dermot, this house is huge – it's about three times the size of St Bridget's! But I won't say anything if you don't want me to.'

'Look, let's see what happens. I do talk to Alfredo once a month or so, just to get updates, so I might mention it to him. It would be so good to see you too, fella. And a wee bit of sun wouldn't go amiss either, not to mention peace and quiet. There's been loads more riots, and the anniversaries are getting worse every year. If it's not internment, it's Bloody Sunday, and then the hunger strikes…Did you see anything about it on the news over there?'

'I did once. I even saw the bottom of the Falls Road – you know, where the massive Bobby Sands murals are – but when I turned up the sound it was gone. It was so weird to be here and see the Falls Road on the news. It made me think of you, and of my ma, too. Thanks for forwarding her card. Did you talk to her again?'

'No, it was on the hallway floor one day. I've only seen her once. I haven't talked to anyone else in your family since you left.

105

I've seen them from the altar a few times, but they never hang about after mass.'

'Oh, right.'

Father Mac hated to hear the subdued tone in Fergal's voice whenever his family came up in conversation. 'I do go and read your letters to Noreen, though, in the graveyard. Her grave looks very well kept – I think your mum goes there often – so don't worry about a thing.'

Alfredo's doorbell rang, and Fergal and Father Mac said their hasty goodbyes as Giovanni's and Luigi's laughter filled the hallway.

The rejuvenated atmosphere lifted everyone's spirits. Over dinner, Giovanni and Luigi admired Fergal's new suit and his new haircut. Giovanni said he had some potentially interesting news about the theatre where he worked, and Luigi told them all how the director of the coming production at the theatre had refused his suggestions of flower arrangements and opted for false ones. In the candlelight, Fergal couldn't help drifting back to his conversation with Father Mac. The sound of his voice had been like a love letter, like a thousand warm kisses. It would be so good to see him again, in Rome this time, but Fergal knew he would have to be careful or Father Mac wouldn't come. Alfredo spotted his far-off look and nudged him back to the conversation.

During dessert, Giovanni winked at Alfredo and announced, 'I have an interesting offer for Fergal to consider.'

Luigi nearly choked on his mouthful of ice cream in his efforts to make some arch comment, but Giovanni threw him a look that said, *Not now*. 'There's a job coming up at the theatre,' he said. 'As soon as I heard about it, I thought it might be perfect for a certain fledgling opera singer.' This time he winked at Fergal.

'Go on,' said Alfredo, leaning in earnestly.

'One of the dressers is leaving to work in London,' Giovanni said.

'At first, the job would be mainly helping with the costumes before and after the performances, and possibly running an errand or two if one of the visiting stars needs something. It would build up from there. The money's good enough, and Fergal could watch the performances every night. If he doesn't mind giving up his evenings, I can arrange an interview.'

Fergal's eyes widened. 'Alfredo? What do you think?'

Alfredo considered for a few moments. 'I think providence is smiling on you once again. It's a great idea. You could still work at Moretti's part-time to give Arianna time to find someone else if she needs to, and we can increase your study during the day. Yes, I think that would work, with a bit of rescheduling. At night you can go to the theatre and immerse yourself in the performances, and see first-hand exactly what is required of a leading man. Giovanni, this is great news! And it couldn't have come at a better time – providing, of course, that he gets the job.'

'I'll do my best,' Giovanni assured him. 'I don't think it'll be a problem.'

They refilled their glasses and toasted the future, but one worry was still niggling at Fergal – what would Arianna say? As if he could read Fergal's mind, Alfredo told him, 'Don't worry, Fergal – leave my sister to me. We all knew this day would come. You can't keep working at Moretti's forever.'

The dinner party lasted until well after midnight. As Giovanni and Luigi were leaving they offered Fergal a lift, but Alfredo said he needed to talk to him.

As soon as they were gone, Alfredo returned to the table. 'Fergal,' he said, 'I've been thinking about this for a long time. I didn't get a chance to mention it earlier, as we were talking about other things, but considering the possible changes that this job will bring, I want to offer you another change for the better.'

Fergal tilted his head, giving Alfredo his full attention.

'I want you to think about moving in here, into my spare room. Our lessons are going to become more and more intense, and with this new job on top of everything else, you'll be very busy and very tired. I know it seems strange to move again, but then, when you eventually join an opera company, you'll spend much of your life on the move. In our world, the only constant thing is change. Do you see what I mean?'

'Yes, I do.' Fergal was too tired and too confused – so much had been happening – to even know how he felt about the offer. 'Thank you, Alfredo.'

'Think it over. It's your decision, and you don't have to answer right away, but I think it would be better. By the way, this has nothing to do with last night's events.' Alfredo smiled. 'There are so many plans to be made, and so much incredible music to teach you. Don't forget about your exam in a few days. We start again in earnest tomorrow, after your shift at the restaurant. Now, go to bed. Daniela has the spare room ready for you.'

As Fergal floated up the stairs, he mentioned, 'Father MacManus said he might come to visit sometime.'

'Now that,' Alfredo said, smiling, 'is the icing on the cake.'

12

Fergal overslept the next morning, and Arianna was unusually unforgiving when he finally arrived at the restaurant ten minutes late, humming nervously. She'd been filled in by Alfredo the previous night. She had known that Fergal would have to go where his voice was leading him, but she felt like a mother whose first-born was leaving for university. At the same time, it stoked long-forgotten memories. Not long after she and Alfredo had lost their mother, he had started to travel for long periods with various opera companies and she had been left to run the family business. She had missed him and envied his freedom. In the same way, Arianna realised, she felt not only loss but a little jealous of Fergal.

By the time Fergal finished for the day, her bad mood had evaporated and she brought him a cup of coffee exactly how he liked it: no milk and one brown sugar. She smoothed his hair while he stirred the cup and gave her a smile that she knew she would miss. It was at times like these that Arianna thought about children, and her lack of them. Men had been few and far between, and she was past the age of conceiving. When Fergal had arrived, she had decided that he needed her to mother him. She'd noticed how ragged he was around the edges, and, most of all, how he mentioned his mother only rarely and his father not at all. There was also something about him, something apart from his love of singing, something she couldn't quite put her finger on, that reminded her of her brother when he had been around the same age.

Fergal, surrounded by the Italian culture, with its routine Sunday gatherings of generations of cousins and friends, was becoming more and more aware of how unusual it was to be so estranged from his family. It made him wonder how different his life could have been if he had got on better with his parents and brothers. If he hadn't been so afraid of them most of the time, would he have been in such a hurry to get away from Belfast? What if sport had come more naturally to him and he had been able to immerse himself in the deep-rooted friendships that came out of playing team games every week, come rain, shine or riot? What if he hadn't been gay? Where had that come from – and why to him, out of all the family?

He had drunk gallons of water as he worked and daydreamed through the day, and when he tested his voice the next morning he found that the temporary hoarseness was gone. He and Alfredo, relieved that his night of drinking had done so little harm, threw themselves back into the carefully devised programme of study for Fergal's coming exam.

The few days before the exam felt like weeks. Alfredo lost his temper more frequently if Fergal made silly mistakes. He still felt that Fergal was holding something back emotionally. Some of his performances, although note-perfect, left Alfredo cold.

'Fergal, you must give me more. I don't believe you!'

'I'm trying my best.'

'No! You must try harder. I want to believe you, but…'

'What?'

'You must get out of your own way. That's the best way I can say it.'

Fergal felt exasperated. He didn't really know what Alfredo meant, and he was too scared to admit it.

On the eve of the exam, Fergal stayed in the spare room again. He slept very badly. He thought his throat felt sore and he almost panicked, but as soon as he drank some water the soreness went away. He wondered whether Father Mac had phoned Alfredo about coming over, and whether he had changed, whether he would look any different, whether he would be cold towards him…His concentration was all over the place.

And then, all of a sudden, Daniela was calling him for breakfast. In no time, he and Alfredo were parked outside an enormous building with a shining brass plaque that proclaimed 'The Institute of Music'.

Fergal had never felt more nervous in his life. As they walked up the marble steps, every person they met seemed to stop and talk to Alfredo with excited recognition and questions about his shy pupil. They passed through mirrored corridors and stopped at a heavy door with a light bulb on each side, one green and one red. The red one was lit.

'They aren't ready for us yet.' Alfredo looked at his watch. 'We have time for a last little warm-up. Come.'

Fergal followed him down more corridors, and Alfredo opened a door. The room held only a grand piano and two seats under a stretch of windows that ran all the way along one wall, throwing light across the midnight-lake surface of the piano. Without a word, Alfredo struck the first chord of a familiar warm-up sequence and Fergal automatically took a deep breath and sent his voice into the stale air, searching the corners of the room for acceptance.

The scales got faster and faster, then slower again, until they sounded as if someone had poured syrup amongst the ivory keys. As the last chord vanished, Alfredo looked up at Fergal and managed a smile. 'We're as ready as we can be.'

Fergal wasn't sure how to take that, and he was too nervous to ask.

When they reached the first magnificent door again, the green bulb was glowing. Alfredo looked at Fergal and nodded. He pressed a button in the side panel. After a moment, the hinges began their slow grind and the door slid open, revealing the legendary examiner.

At first, Fergal, disorientated, thought he was looking at a child, then he noticed the examiner's white hair, combed obediently against his skull after a lifetime of grooming, and realised that he was a dwarf. He was skeletal and slightly stooped, but when he smiled up at them his entire face was transformed. The tiny man stood there with all the calmness of a king. Alfredo stepped forward and they bowed respectfully to each other. Alfredo announced formally, 'Signore Angelo Arnelli, may I present Fergal Flynn.'

The examiner stretched out his minute, bony hand. Fergal took it, wondering whether he was expected to kiss it, but Signore Arnelli, instead of shaking it, led Fergal over to the most ornate piano he'd ever seen. It looked as if it had been carved from meringue, glistening like an altar seen through a sugary winter window. Signore Arnelli fished for a little black case and took out his spectacles. Then he smiled at Fergal and asked quietly, 'Are you ready to begin?'

'Yes,' Fergal whispered. There was a decanter of water on a side table, so he took a sip.

Signore Arnelli's tiny hands leafed through a pile of manuscripts before settling on one. Then he nodded towards Alfredo, who took a seat at the piano and pushed the first rhythmic chords of the now-familiar 'Cavalleria Rusticana' into the warm room. The examiner settled himself on a chair with his arms folded solemnly. He watched as Fergal, his eyes shut tight, took a deep, silent breath, then the voice that had started this whole journey joined the music like a cold current of air, travelling around the room, pausing in every rehearsed place.

His pronunciation was better than it had ever been before, and Alfredo recognised that Fergal was trying his best to rise above his fear and meet the challenge he had worked so hard to face. There were certain passages where the voice was the only instrument. Fergal had to have complete control over his breathing so that his tuning would be perfect when the piano eventually rejoined him. But the old voice of doubt was rising in his head: *Who do you think you are, young fella? You're not able for this. You're nothing. Always were, always will be.* He forgot to breathe properly and began to sing flat, which was noticeable the moment the piano re-entered. Fergal tried to sing louder, to drown out the voice, but this was exactly the moment where he should have been singing most softly.

After six pieces of varying length, they took a break. Fergal went along the corridor and sat on the lid of the toilet, staring at his Granny Noreen's remembrance card, which he had pinned to the inside of his jacket. He wanted her to be with him, no matter what happened. 'I'm doing my best, Granny,' he whispered to her. 'I'm trying to make you proud.'

'Are you okay?' Alfredo asked through the cubicle door.

Fergal came out and washed his hands, saying nothing. Alfredo put his hands on his shoulders, helping them to relax a little. 'Open your eyes more,' he said gently. 'Concentrate, and let him see that you mean it.'

They entered the examination room again. In their absence, Signore Arnelli had lit a fragrant candle, and for a moment Fergal pictured Father Mac among the enormous wax columns of the Easter vigil mass. He took a deep breath and secretly dedicated the next piece to the first man, the only man, he had ever truly loved.

It was a mournful piece, and Fergal unconsciously pressed a hand to his heart, where the tiny picture of his dead granny was pinned on for dear life. At the closing note, he couldn't stop the tears from coming. He gave Alfredo a worried look, but Alfredo dismissed it with a quick shake of his head, signalling for him to take a deep breath and resume.

Fergal glided through the last piece without any hesitation. Faces floated repeatedly through his mind – his mother, his older brother John shaking his fist at him – but for once they seemed far away, outside of him. He ended the piece with a proud oak tree of a note that made his entire chest vibrate. Without moving, he waited until the sustain of the piano strings came to a final standstill.

Alfredo disengaged the pedal with one graceful movement of his whole body. Signore Arnelli removed his glasses and let the case snap shut, announcing the end of the exam. He stood up and crossed the polished floor, and Alfredo joined him at Fergal's side.

'I would like to speak to you alone,' Signore Arnelli told Alfredo. 'Thank you, Mr Flynn.'

Alfredo nodded. 'Wait in the car,' he said to Fergal, giving him the keys.

Fergal managed a 'Thank you', then he was heading back along the corridor and out into the street, away from the Institute of Music, as if he had never been there at all.

Ten excruciating minutes went by, then fifteen. Fergal watched the second hand moving on the clock inside the car and tried to distract himself. Any time anyone came out of the Institute, he nearly jumped out of his skin.

Exactly twenty-three minutes later, Alfredo's solid frame descended the stone steps. He opened the driver's door and got into the car, but he didn't start the engine. Instead, he turned and looked at Fergal in a way that made him frown with worry.

'So, Signor Flynn. How do you think you did?'

'I don't know. I don't know, Alfredo. I had a really hard time concentrating. I was dead nervous.'

'Well, yes, I could see – and, indeed, hear – that.'

'Oh God, I've failed, haven't I? After all your hard work, too. Oh God, I'm sorry, Alfredo.'

Fergal was beginning to panic, but Alfredo made an impatient gesture with his hand. 'Fergal, there's no need to be such a bloody drama queen! You would have failed completely, yes, if it hadn't been for those last two pieces.'

'What do you mean?'

'Fergal, then and only then did you sing with your heart and soul – for about ten minutes of the whole exam. Your performances in the first half were, well, there's no easy way to say this – they were boring and noncommittal.'

'Boring and…what? What do you mean? I sang all the right notes—'

'That's my point exactly. That's all you did. I didn't believe a word of it, not one word, and neither did Signore Arnelli. By the way, you didn't sing all the right notes, actually; your pitch went way off when the piano dropped out. You were flat, and you've never had that problem before. Your natural ear is normally extraordinary. What is going on with you?'

Fergal was shell-shocked. He hadn't realised he'd done quite so badly. He sank further into the passenger seat in silence, feeling like he'd just wasted the past year.

Alfredo looked at his ashen-faced pupil. 'You may as well know that you barely scraped a pass in your first preliminary exam.'

Fergal thought he was hearing things. '*What*? I thought you were saying I'd failed!'

115

'No. Signore Arnelli is one of the most difficult examiners in Italy, but he is very fair. He admired your tone, and as I said, the last few minutes were very moving. This is why he awarded you a pass. I was hoping for a distinction, of course – I know you are more than capable of achieving that – but...I thought you were ready for this, but now I see I was a little hasty.'

'I'm sorry – I'm so sorry. Oh God, I've let you down, Alfredo, and I don't know what to say.'

'Fergal, will you stop saying that! I won't pretend that I'm not disappointed, but you've only been here for a year, and you're still so young. I still believe in you, but you *must* shake yourself out of this...place you are in. I feel like I can't reach you, Fergal. What saved you was the fact that you gave Signore Arnelli the merest glimpse of how great you could be.'

'What do you mean?'

'Fergal, if he hadn't seen something special in you, he wouldn't have spent so long talking to me. He could hear your promise. He agrees with me that while there's a lot of work ahead, it will be worth it in the end – only, and I mean *only*, if you are prepared to work harder than ever.'

Fergal sat looking out the window for a moment. All kinds of scenes were playing themselves out in his head – going back to the airport with his return ticket, turning up on Father Mac's doorstep in a million pieces...

Alfredo started the engine. Fergal took a deep breath.

'Alfredo?'

'Yes?'

'You know how you asked me to think about moving into the spare room in your house?'

'Yes.'

'Well, does that offer still stand?'

'Of course, Fergal.'

'Right, then – when can I move in?'

Alfredo smiled at him. 'The sooner the better.'

By the time they reached the restaurant, a thick tear had begun to course down Fergal's cheek, but he wiped it away as soon as he saw Arianna. When she saw Alfredo's car pulling up, she signalled for their lunch to be brought out. She remembered how nervous Alfredo had been when he had started taking his exams, and after all of the birthday drama, she wanted good news for Fergal more than anything. When she saw his serious face, she hugged them both and began talking about the menu.

'Fergal passed,' Alfredo told her, 'but we still have a few mountains to climb.'

Arianna nodded, but she knew to play down her congratulations. She just ruffled Fergal's hair and said, 'I knew you would pass.'

After lunch, Alfredo insisted that Fergal should call Father Mac. Fergal's heart sank. Even though it was good news of a sort, he felt like a complete failure. He went into Arianna's office and dialled St Bridget's House, fully expecting Father Mac to be out, but he picked up on the second ring.

'Dermot? It's me, Fergal. I passed the exam.'

Father Mac knew by the sound of his voice that something wasn't right. 'Congratulations! Forgive me for saying so, but you don't sound very happy.'

'I know…'

'And? What happened?'

'I only just scraped a pass, Dermot. I was so nervous! And you should've seen the examiner, he was like something out of James Bond or something.'

Father Mac laughed.

'I'm serious. Do you remember that wee man from *Fantasy Island* – what was his name, Tattoo? He was as small as him, except he had white hair. I went to bits, Dermot. I don't know what happened.'

'You passed, Fergal. That's what matters. Don't forget, you've only been studying seriously for the guts of a year. Some people study their whole lives and never have your tone, or your ambition.'

Father Mac wanted to lift Fergal's spirits, but he knew he had to tell him the bad news. 'Fergal, I know the timing could be better, but I may as well tell you now.'

'What? What is it? What's wrong?'

'Nothing's wrong. It's just that I won't be coming to Rome after all – not this year, anyway. I'm really sorry, fella.'

'But why not?'

'Things aren't good here in Belfast. The parishioners really need me. The bishop just sent me a letter saying that holidays are restricted until further notice. I can have a day here and there – my sister has some leave coming up, so she's going to come and stay with me for a few days – but I can't go out of the country.'

'Ah no, Dermot, I was so looking forward to seeing you. It's not fair. I bet that oul' bishop gets to go away!'

'Now Fergal, you know it's beyond my control.' Fergal didn't know what to say. 'Fergal? Are you still there?'

'Yeah. But...'

'But what?'

'I need to see you, Dermot. I feel like things are getting on top of me.'

'You're living in Rome, you have the best teacher you could have, you're surrounded by great people and you're even earning money. You could be stuck on the dole in Belfast, fearing for your life every time you went out the door. What more do you want?'

'I miss you, and Granny Noreen. And I feel like I've let Alfredo down.'

'Fergal, you need to stop being so dramatic. The past is the past. You need to move on. We've been over this before.'

'I know, I know.'

'Don't keep saying you know, when you don't.'

'I'm sorry. My ma's been writing to me. She sounds so unhappy.'

Father Mac wanted to kick himself for forwarding her letters, but he knew he had no choice. 'Look, try and focus on the positive – you passed your first exam. I know you wanted to do better than you did, but sometimes expectations can be too high, and you're very hard on yourself. I think it's great you passed.'

'But the examiner said he didn't believe most of my performance.'

'Well, that will come in time. You're so young. You passed, and that's the end of it. Now move on.'

'I'm going to try, Dermot. Honestly, I am.'

But when they finished their phone call, Fergal couldn't find it in himself to feel much happier. He felt that Father Mac was getting further and further away, just when he needed him most. The voice of doubt had certainly won this round.

13

The day after the exam, Fergal got another letter from his mother. It was short, but as always, the contents stayed with him long after he finished reading. Angela poured out her heart to him. It was as if she found it easier to tell him things because he was so far away. She was worried because his father was drinking more than ever: *'He's hardly ever home for his dinner. Most of the time I have to throw it away. Honest to God, our Fergal, the local dogs have started drawing straws for it every night.'* She missed her mother and her father, Fergal's namesake, whom he had never met. *'My daddy would be so proud that you're in Rome learning to be a singer.'* It was her only way of saying that she was proud too.

Somewhere inside himself, Fergal was secretly beginning to look forward to her letters. He wrote back and told her he was moving into his teacher's house, writing the address very clearly on the top of the page so she wouldn't have to keep going to St Bridget's House.

Exactly one week later, Alfredo pulled up outside Moretti's to take Fergal to his new home. Fergal had packed up his belongings

– he didn't realise they had outgrown his suitcase until he tried to close it. Arianna kissed him on both cheeks and put a brave face on. At least he would be working part-time at the restaurant, so she would still see him.

As he unpacked his things in Alfredo's spare room, Fergal was bubbling over with excitement. Although he still felt that he had failed his teacher, he could feel a new chapter in his life beginning. He looked around his new room. It was much bigger than the one he'd had at Moretti's, with a huge double bed and an ancient wardrobe that housed a full-length mirror on the inside of the door. As he hung up his old clothes on the wooden hangers, he was sure he could still smell Belfast off some of them, and in some ways it was a comfort. He stared at his one good suit, hanging slightly apart from all his other clothes, like an overachieving child who could never belong to the family's inner circle. That was what Fergal felt like. It wasn't that he thought he was better than his family, but he was far too different to belong. Like the suit, he was just cut from a different cloth.

There was an old writing desk with a swivel chair in front of the window overlooking the courtyard. Fergal sat down and opened the drawers. They had been cleaned out except for a bit of blank stationery. He suddenly thought he should write to Father Mac and describe his new room, but once he'd written his new address in the top right-hand corner, he didn't know where to begin. He just sat there, staring at the blank sheet of paper.

He decided to reread his little collection letters from Father Mac. He was surprised at how little they had actually written to each other. Then, of course, there was *that* letter. The sentences circled him like long-tailed kites flapping in the wind. *It's precisely because I love you so much that we need to let the past go…You must be finding a world of new possibilities there, and I'd hate to think that you might limit your experiences…We will always be friends…You*

121

know you have my heart, but you must go fully into the world now, as a free and single young man at the start of an incredible adventure…

Fergal was surprised to find that the contents didn't hurt as much as they once had. Something had changed in him since the disastrous night of his birthday. He decided that if he truly had to let Dermot go forever, then he was determined at least to have one last night of love with him. Surely he wouldn't say no? But he knew it was probably impossible now that Dermot wasn't coming to Rome. He couldn't believe that they would never kiss again.

He sat down at the desk again and started to write.

Dear Dermot,

I'm sitting here in my new room on the first floor of Alfredo's house. What a shame you can't come over! I was so looking forward to it – it's been ages and ages since I've seen you. I was unpacking my stuff and I just reread your last letter again, and I think I'm beginning to understand what you mean.

I do think of you often. When I was in my exam I thought about you, and about Granny Noreen. It was like youse were with me for some of it. Maybe I was a bit distracted after all. I really thought I would do better.

Dermot, you should see my new room. I feel like a prince. I've also gone part-time at Moretti's, because I've got an interview for a new job at the Teatro degli Artisti tonight – working behind the scenes, of course, but I'll get to meet all the performers and watch the operas. I can't wait. I promise I'll keep working as hard as I can. I hope you're well and that you have a good time with your sister. Please remember me to her and to Mrs Mooney.

Yours,

FF

When he read it back to himself, he thought it sounded good. He searched for an envelope in the other drawer and quickly sealed it. Then Alfredo shouted from downstairs, 'You should take a bath soon, if you are going to look your best at the interview!'

Fergal had never taken baths at Moretti's – the shower was easier, and he usually didn't have much time – but Alfredo had insisted that he should begin a lifelong relationship with the claw-footed bath. It was the only thing that relaxed the Italian after a hard day, and he believed the heat was good for the voice.

Fergal locked the bathroom door behind him and began to smell the contents of all the brightly coloured bottles set on the window ledge and in the cabinets. He thought of a game he had played as a boy, where all the children in the neighbourhood had collected bottles of coloured liquids; they would have killed for some of these. He settled on a bottle of deep green liquid, and as he poured it under the running tap the room filled with clouds of lime-scented vapour, as if he were walking through an orchard. He took slow, deep breaths and watched as the water filled the old bath almost to the top.

When he eased himself into the scalding water it was almost too much to bear, but he found that if he didn't move a muscle he could endure it, and it made his whole body feel calm. After a while he began doing the little vocal exercises for which bathrooms seem to have been invented. He stayed in the water for a long time, happy in the liquid blanket of warmth, and for the first time in a long time he didn't think about anything.

When he got back to his room, there was a pile of unfamiliar black clothes neatly folded on his bed. On top of them was a note. '*You must look your best at all times. You can pay me back when you're famous. Welcome to my home, and I hope you will be as happy as I am that you're here. Love, Alfredo.*'

Fergal was overwhelmed by Alfredo's thoughtfulness, and by

that all-too-familiar hybrid of sadness and gladness. He didn't like the thought of owing anybody anything, but when he looked at what his wardrobe had to offer, he knew he had very little choice, and that it would be rude and pointless to argue. He tried on the clothes, a casual black cotton shirt and trousers. They fitted well, and they felt so good against his clean skin that he almost wanted to take them off again and save them for another occasion, but he knew they couldn't have come at a better moment.

He combed his damp, wavy hair as neatly as he could, decided he could wait one more day for a shave and went down to find Alfredo and thank him. As he neared the door of the music room, he could hear the singing butcher booming away: 'and Moon River…' Fergal always felt a little jealous when Alfredo was busy with other singers, and now, since his exam, he felt vulnerable too. The old voice of doubt surfaced in his head: *Not as shit-hot as you thought you were, are you? That exam proved it. You're wasting your time, trying to be some fancy singer…*Suddenly Fergal realised that the voice was a mixture of his father's and his brother John's. 'Fuck off,' he hissed under his breath, furious with himself for letting them get to him even though he was so far away from Belfast.

He had to leave or he would be late for the interview. Rather than disturbing Alfredo, he found a pad of manuscript paper and wrote in big letters, 'Alfredo, what are you like? You shouldn't have. How can I ever thank you enough? The new clothes fit perfectly. I didn't want to disturb your lesson, so I'll thank you properly later, in person. FF.'

He had been practising his autograph for weeks, but he couldn't decide on a style, so it was initials only for the time being.

The Teatro degli Artisti wasn't far away, and Fergal had a map and very clear directions from Giovanni and Alfredo. After only twenty minutes' walking he saw the dramatic sculptures on the front of the theatre, the awnings and the brightly lit posters. The current production was called *How Can I Keep from Singing: The Collected Arias*.

As arranged, he presented himself at the stage door. When Giovanni appeared, also dressed in black, he commented on Fergal's foresight in wearing the dark, casual uniform of the backstage staff – Alfredo to the rescue once again.

The 'interview' was much shorter than Fergal had expected. The theatre manager looked him up and down, then said, 'So you're Moretti's new protégé, eh, the one we've been hearing about? Yes, yes, you can have the job – a month's trial, and then we will re-evaluate the situation. You can start tonight. Giovanni will show you the ropes. Off you go, and be sure to give Alfredo my very best. We miss his performances here.'

As Giovanni led Fergal out of the office, he laughed at the startled look on Fergal's face. When they began to descend the old stairs, Fergal thought about all the hallowed, hurried footfalls that had slowly eroded the marble steps over the years and he wondered how many times Alfredo had rushed up those same stairs on the way to the stage. When he asked Giovanni why Alfredo had retired, the Italian rolled his eyes and told him to ask his teacher when he got home. He showed him his locker underneath the stage area, next to the orchestra pit. Fergal had never seen the pit before, and a strange tingle of excitement ran down the back of his neck. He wondered how Alfredo could have traded performing for teaching at all. Giovanni scribbled his name on a blank piece of card and placed it in the slot on the locker's grey metal door. When Fergal tried the key and opened it, there was a tiny bunch of violets inside with a welcome note from Giovanni and Luigi, wishing him every happiness.

As they were going back upstairs, they heard a sudden commotion. Giovanni pulled Fergal back against the wall as a man brushed past them in a flurry of velvet scarves. 'Lemon tea, please, to my dressing room,' he called over his shoulder, and Fergal heard his English accent. Then the man disappeared into his dressing room, leaving a trail of lavender fragrance that lingered in the ancient hallway.

Giovanni grinned at Fergal. 'Well, you may as well start as you mean to go on. Now is as good a time as any for you to meet our visiting star.'

Fergal looked a bit puzzled.

'That, Fergal, was none other than the great tenor Brendan Fiscetti, all the way from London – but you should refer to him as Mr or Signore Fiscetti. The kitchen is at the very bottom of the theatre. Make the tea very weak, with no milk but lots of lemon juice and honey – he should have a kettle in his room, but I think he prefers us to do it. Then knock on his door, but on no account enter until he responds. Be patient, he might take a while to answer. Then introduce yourself. Don't look so worried, he might even like you!'

Fergal ran down the stairs like a schoolboy on the last day of term. He found the kitchen easily, made a pot of the lemony concoction and put everything he could think of onto a tray. The sound of the orchestra rehearsing filled the stairway and swam around him in the air as he took two steps at a time.

The main dressing room had a huge '1' painted on the door in black, in the middle of a gold star. Directly underneath, in ornate calligraphy, was the leading man's name: 'Brendan Fiscetti'.

Fergal balanced the tray on one arm and knocked, almost dropping the whole thing. He stood still and waited as the scent of lemons filtered up from the pot. He was thinking of knocking once more when he started to hear groaning. Fergal was a bit worried – it sounded as if Signore Fiscetti was ill. He looked up and down the corridor, but it was empty.

Suddenly the door flew open and there stood Brendan Fiscetti in his shorts and vest. 'Ah, the tea. Come in, come in, young man. I'm not in the habit of parading around in a state of undress, I can assure you – unless it's called for on stage, of course! I hear you're new?'

Fergal nodded.

'I suppose you wondered what the noises were all about? I was in the middle of doing my daily stretches. My spine, sadly, isn't as supple as it used to be. Put the tea over there and tell me your name, otherwise I shall be forced to think that you're unfriendly, and that would never do, because without conversation we are lost.'

Fergal smiled. 'I'm Fergal Flynn, Mr Fiscetti.'

Signore Fiscetti nodded. 'An Irishman, if I'm not mistaken? A fine, fine country, with even finer singers and songs. I'm part Irish myself, you know.'

Fergal placed the tray on a low table. Signore Fiscetti looked at it and shook his head. 'Oh, it will never do, it simply will never do, Mr Flynn.' Fergal was mortified, thinking that he'd left out a vital ingredient, until Signore Fiscetti stopped teasing and said, 'You've only brought one cup, Mr Flynn. We won't have another word until you fetch one for yourself – so go, hurry!'

Fergal practically threw himself back down the stairs, dodging members of the chorus. He was a little out of breath when he returned. He knocked on the door again and Signore Fiscetti was waiting for him, this time fully clothed.

Fergal sat down at the little table and poured the lemon tea into two cups that bore the theatre's name. Signore Fiscetti was seated at an enormous mirror framed by tiny light bulbs. As far as Fergal could tell, in front of him was every kind of make-up ever invented. Fergal's predecessor had laid it out and checked it every day, and Giovanni had told Fergal to watch the tenor's routine as closely as he could so he would know if anything needed replacing.

Signore Fiscetti turned in his chair and picked up his steaming cup, blowing away the vapours and then sipping the contents noisily. He gestured for Fergal to do the same. 'Where in Ireland are you from? And how have you ended up at the Teatro in Rome?'

Fergal told him a careful version of his upbringing on the Falls Road – how all he had ever wanted to do was sing, and how Father MacManus had encouraged him, how the recording at the monastery in Sligo had led to Alfredo Moretti's visit, which had changed his entire life.

Brendan Fiscetti's eyes widened. 'Forgive me, Fergal – did you say Alfredo Moretti? Here in Rome?'

Fergal nodded. 'Yes, he's my teacher. So you've heard of him? He used to be a big star, like you.'

For a second Signore Fiscetti looked almost vulnerable, for such a big man. He turned to apply his make-up and said, in a quieter voice, 'My good God, this is amazing. I was only thinking about Alfredo Moretti recently, when I found out I was flying over to do these concerts. We used to know each other very well for a while, many years ago. We worked together on a production of…now what was it? Oh yes, *Tosca*. How could I forget? It must be twenty years…' His voice trailed off for a moment. 'He's about my age, wouldn't you say, Fergal?'

'I suppose so.'

'It must be him. Surely there's only one Alfredo Moretti who was an opera singer. I wonder why he doesn't sing any more. I mean, I'm busier than ever, and he was incredible, you know. What a bizarre coincidence! The angels are at work tonight, Fergal. Well, one thing I do know: if he's your teacher, then you must be very good. How is he doing?'

As Fergal was about to answer, the speaker on the wall announced loudly, 'One hour till curtain up. That's one hour till curtain up.'

Signore Fiscetti looked at his watch and furrowed his brow.

'Fergal, forgive me, but I must rest. We'll continue our chat tomorrow, of that you can be sure, but I always leave the theatre the second I come off, to avoid the public demands and to rest my voice. I'm sure it sounds a little precious, but one of these days you may understand the lengths you have to go to when you're doing six or eight performances a week and you're the leading man. Please leave the tray. And Fergal, as it is your first day, let me say welcome to the world of the theatre.'

Fergal sat at the side of the stage and watched that night's performance of classic arias in awe. There were so many incredible songs, so many lighting changes, and Fergal hadn't quite realised how much acting was required – not to mention how much volume. Signore Fiscetti's rich voice could be heard all the way to the back of the theatre, and there wasn't a microphone in sight. Signore Fiscetti was on stage a lot of the time. Sometimes he was joined by a young Greek soprano with a voice like a blackbird's. They sang a duet that Fergal remembered hearing on an advert on TV in Belfast, then Signore Fiscetti left her to sing two songs by herself and joined her again for the last selection of pieces before the interval. Fergal was at the ready with water and a fresh pot of tea, just the right temperature to drink.

The second half of the evening seemed to move a lot faster. One lament had some of the people in the nearby boxes in tears. Fergal thought Signore Fiscetti was magnificent. He started to clap in all the wrong places, purely because he was so moved, but luckily it was so dark that no one guessed it was him. There were three curtain calls and a standing ovation. As promised, Signore Fiscetti exited in the same confusion of scarves into a waiting car. Within fifteen minutes, the Teatro was completely empty.

Giovanni appeared and took Fergal through his various jobs, encouraging him to write things down in a little notepad so he would be able to carry them out to the letter every evening after the final curtain fell. 'So how was your first meeting with Signore Fiscetti?' he asked.

'He was nice. He made me get another cup and have tea with him.'

Giovanni looked incredulous. 'Seriously? I can't tell you how rare it is for a leading man to do that. Normally they're demanding old queens. Sorry, bitchy of me, I know. I wonder, is he…? Oh, never mind, we'll find out soon enough, I'm sure. Well, well, all this on your first day. Well done. So hang up his clothes and tidy his counter, then I'll meet you at the stage door to clock out, okay?'

Fergal had been about to tell him that Signore Fiscetti knew Alfredo, but the moment had passed.

He went back to the dressing room and stood there for a quiet moment, imagining that it was his name on the door. Inside, the room was in quite a state, with boots and clothes and make-up strewn everywhere. Fergal opened the window onto the street below to let fresh air in. He could hear people shouting for taxis and mopeds humming homewards in every direction, like bees.

Brendan had five different outfits thrown over the backs of chairs. Some were plain black suits with the shirts sewn into the waistcoats, for ease in changing, while others were ornately embroidered in silver and gold. They looked a bit ridiculous up close, but when the spotlights were on them they were impressive. Fergal caught sight of himself in the mirror and held one of the jackets up against himself to see what he looked like. Even though he knew Signore Fiscetti was much bigger than he was, he couldn't resist trying the jacket on. He burst out laughing when he saw how it hung on his shoulders, but then he closed his eyes and pictured himself on the stage. He could almost feel the curtains rising to explosive applause, almost hear his own voice steering the melody to the far corners of the Teatro until no ear was left uncaressed…

Giovanni's voice suddenly called up the hallway, breaking the spell. Fergal unwrapped himself from the jacket and the fantasy, finished tidying the dressing room and clicked off the light.

Giovanni offered Fergal a lift home, but he said he wanted to walk. His mind was racing with thoughts of being in a similar production one day, having a dressing room with a little daybed to rest on before performances...He started to sing quietly to himself as he got closer to Alfredo's road, and an old woman brushing away the petals of lime blossom that had covered her doorstep like heavy snow stopped and smiled at him. 'It's lovely to hear someone so happy with the world.'

Fergal smiled back. The old woman was small, like his Granny Noreen, and she was around the same age Noreen would have been. Sadness pulled at his heart. Sweet-smelling petals had never troubled his grandmother's Belfast doorway. Instead there had been litter and dog shite and soldiers' boot marks, and she had struggled to keep the passageway clean for decades until her tiny hands grew calloused and her spine weakened, and at last her whole body gave in.

Then, somewhere in his head he heard Father Mac's voice reminding him that he had promised his grandmother not to let his talent go to waste. As he closed Alfredo's gate and looked at his new lodgings, he suddenly realised just how far he had come towards keeping that promise. The rest was up to him. As he put the key in the front door, he smiled.

'Fergal?' Alfredo called from the front room. 'How did it go?'

He had been reading. He looked up over the half-moon of his glasses, smiling. 'I want to hear all about your evening. I assume you got the job, or you would have been home long ago. Did Giovanni look after you? Did you get time to see the production? I'm ashamed to say I don't even know what's playing. I haven't been there for quite a while.'

Fergal sat down on the bright blue sofa. 'It was great. I got the job; I'm on a month's trial. The manager was asking after you.'

Alfredo raised an eyebrow. 'A month's trial? I suppose they're being careful. One day they'll be telling anyone who will listen that you used to work backstage.'

Fergal looked at Alfredo so intensely that his teacher asked him what was the matter.

'Well, I was just wondering, why did you give it all up, you know, for teaching? Do you not miss the stage?'

Alfredo sighed as if the question weighed him down. 'Fergal, my dear young man, that was the hardest decision I ever had to make. But in the end, it was the right one for me.'

'What do you mean?'

'I'd worked too hard for too long. I was lucky that my international reputation was beginning to gather momentum, but I got to the point where I just couldn't face another long flight and months away from home. I was exhausted all the time. Life on the road can be very solitary when one has to put one's voice above everything and everyone else. My car accident was a blessing in disguise in many ways.'

Fergal's eyes widened.

'You see, Fergal, it literally made me stop and take stock, for a little while at least. I hadn't spent any time with Arianna in years and I virtually lived out of my suitcase. I know it's hard for you to understand what I'm saying, seeing as you have it all ahead of you, but I woke up one morning and realised that I just wanted to be here at home. If I'm honest, I never liked travelling very much. So I spent another year working through my commitments, but that's when I should've been resting, so my leg never healed properly, hence my slight limp, which is all my own stubborn fault. And that, my friend, is how I came to retire early from the world of performing. As you will find out yourself one day, the good times far outweigh the bad ones, and its rewards are plenty. But all great things have to end sometime, and I have no regrets.'

'And how did you get into teaching, Alfredo?' Fergal asked.

'That was an accident of a different kind. I was asked to quickly put a baritone through his paces here in Rome and suddenly I realised I could work here and still be surrounded by my passion, which of course is music. To answer your previous question, though, I don't miss the stage because it never really feels very far away from me. Tell me, who is singing there at the moment?'

'A tenor called Brendan Fiscetti. He's lovely, Alfredo.'

Alfredo nearly dropped his book.

'He says he knows you. He was really startled when I told him you were my teacher.'

Alfredo's breathing had gone a little odd, but he gathered himself. 'We did indeed know each other, but we lost contact decades ago...' He looked away. 'I haven't really thought about him since. The last I knew, he was living in England – London, I think – with a countess. They married very suddenly, after a whirl-wind romance while we were on tour in Venice. Was she there, by any chance?'

'I don't think so, but the Teatro was mad busy. What does she look like?'

'She had the most incredible red hair I've ever seen, curls like corkscrews. I suppose there may be some grey in it now – if they're still together. My goodness, it's been so long.'

'He was out of the theatre like a lightning bolt after the perfor-mance. To save his voice, he said.'

Alfredo burst out laughing. 'Oh Fergal, if only you'd seen him all those years ago! He used to try and get me to drink with him into the early hours every night, whether we had a performance or not. I was the one who finally put my foot down – my voice had started to suffer. What else did he say, Fergal? Did he seem pleased that I was teaching you? Did you mention that you were living here?'

Alfredo suddenly realised that he had asked too many questions too quickly. 'Wait a moment,' he said, trying to cover up his eagerness for information. He left his chair, opened one of the cupboards and searched through a pile of old scrapbooks. 'Here. Look, Fergal – Brendan Fiscetti and I weren't that much older than you are now.'

Fergal took the book carefully into his lap and marvelled at the sight of the two tenors, much younger and much thinner. They might have been the sons of the men he knew.

It was well after midnight when Alfredo stopped reminiscing and remembered they had to be up early for a vocal lesson. Many hours later, with scrapbooks littering his bed, Alfredo Moretti finally surrendered to sleep.

14

The next morning, during the voice lesson, Alfredo couldn't help asking Fergal what repertoire Signore Fiscetti was singing and whether he was in good voice. 'He's doing a collection of arias from different productions,' Fergal told him. 'Alfredo, I hadn't realised how much acting there is. I don't know if I can—'

Alfredo got up swiftly, tutting and shaking his head. 'Fergal, the more energy you spend on self-doubt, the less you will have for improvement. Remember that I have every faith in you. I wouldn't waste my precious time, or yours, if I didn't think you had what it takes. Your performance during the exam was a wake-up call, nothing more. Just wait until Brendan hears you!'

They started with the most difficult section of the aria that Alfredo had selected, then moved on to the less complicated parts as the day progressed. Alfredo still felt that Fergal was holding back, but not quite as much. He knew that Fergal was fragile and that it would do no good to roar and shout at him any more than was necessary. He needed time to work out whatever was blocking his progress.

Fergal certainly knew how to work, but he still felt outside the music. Sometimes he missed the buzz of Moretti's and Arianna's kindness, but he and Alfredo still attended the family lunches every Sunday, and Fergal always looked forward to them. And he was glad not to have to see Riccardo more than was necessary.

At the Teatro, Brendan Fiscetti began to rely on Fergal more and more as the days went by, and their chats continued over rivers of lemon tea. As Fergal talked about his studies, Brendan would suddenly interrupt him in mid-sentence to ask a question about Alfredo, like whether he had many pupils. When Fergal said, cautiously, that Alfredo did seem to be busy a lot of the time, Brendan nodded as if it was the answer he'd expected.

Brendan never mentioned his wife. When Fergal said one day, 'Why don't you try and meet up with Alfredo, Signore Fiscetti, while you're in Rome?', it was the only time he ever saw Brendan look truly vulnerable. He mumbled, 'Oh, I meant to arrange a lunch or something before the end of the run, but Alfredo is obviously a busy man or he would have rung me by now.'

Fergal didn't understand it at all. Alfredo was equally reluctant to call Brendan. Why were they both being so reticent? A week of performances came and went and the two men stopped asking Fergal about each other, but the silence reeked of sadness.

Fergal sang every day, working on his breathing technique and his sight-reading one morning and on his tone the next, alternating to keep things fresh. He also worked on his piano skills. Alfredo insisted that he needed to be able to play so he could figure out scores for himself. Fergal was intimidated at first, but after a few lessons he was amazed at how much sense the keyboard made. On alternate days he went up the road to Signora Truvello for a few hours of Italian tuition. After dinner every evening he went to the Teatro, where he stood at the side of the stage, riveted by the performances, drinking in every note and sometimes lip-synching along to the arias he and Alfredo were working on.

One night, when most people had gone home, Fergal went to the stage to collect a coat that Brendan had left behind. As he crossed the stage, he stared out into the empty auditorium. It was so quiet that it was almost unnerving. Fergal began humming to himself, softly at first, then more and more loudly. The acoustics were wonderful. He braved a few long round notes and shivered at the thought of what it must feel like to sing to a packed house.

With most of the lights out, the stage looked just as it did when Brendan sang his main aria: almost complete darkness, save for a moonlit wash. Fergal stood where he had watched Brendan take his position every evening. Then he started to sing.

His voice slowly rose through the empty theatre. He moved into the centre of the stage just as Brendan did, as if the weight of the world were on his shoulders. Fergal imagined the orchestra pit full of the ghosts of musicians past slowly joining him, each string a sympathy to his plight. He reached the edge of the pit and looked at the empty rows of seats, imagining that his Granny Noreen was seated there. With outstretched arms, he held the final note that was the climax of the aria. Each night, when that note ended, the house would fall into an abyss of blackness, giving Brendan just enough time to exit. It always left the audience breathless. Fergal listened as the theatre carried the echo of his own voice towards the carved roof and into the deep blue silence.

In the darkness, a single pair of hands clapped from the wings.

Fergal almost fell into the pit. For a moment of sheer panic, he thought it was one of the ghosts. Then he managed to steady himself. 'Who's there?' he called.

An unmistakable English accent answered, 'Well, well, young Flynn, I had no idea you sang so exquisitely.' Brendan Fiscetti moved out of the wings into the half-light at the side of the stage.

Fergal was speechless. Brendan continued, 'I came back from my hotel because I stupidly left my reading glasses behind. When I'm tired, reading a good book is the only way I can get to sleep after a performance. And on my way to the dressing room I heard a voice.'

Fergal glanced up for a second, still unable to say a word.

'Signor Flynn, you belong *on* the stage, not behind it. There can be no question about that.'

Fergal's mind was racing as he stood there, a little out of breath, holding Brendan's discarded gown. Brendan stepped forward and hugged him generously, instinctively, like a father. Then he placed his arm along Fergal's shoulders and they walked back to the dressing room.

'I want to write a note to Alfredo,' Brendan said, 'if only I can find my glasses.' Fergal found them under a newspaper and located some official Teatro stationery, and Brendan took out his antique fountain pen and wrote quickly, in large, sweeping motions, as if he were drawing.

'There,' he said with a sigh, sealing the envelope. 'Give that to Alfredo as soon as you see him. Now, may I offer you a lift home?'

As they set off, Fergal said, 'Signore Fiscetti, you know I have a room at Alfredo's house, don't you? That's where you're going to drop me. Would you like to give him the note yourself?'

Brendan hadn't seen that coming. 'I would prefer you to give it to him,' he said after a moment. 'I want to get back to my hotel – I need a proper night's sleep before the matinée tomorrow. And in any case…let's see how he reacts. I'll leave the ball in his court. The last time we spoke, you hadn't yet been born.'

As Fergal got out of the car, Brendan said, 'This has been a remarkable day, Fergal. Sleep well. Give Alfredo my best. Tell him…' He sighed. 'Just make sure he gets this note.'

The car pulled away into the warm evening and Fergal watched it disappear around the corner before he fished for his door key.

He found Alfredo snoring on the sofa beside an empty bottle of wine and one drained glass. Fergal was dying to wake him up to tell him what had happened, but he didn't have the heart. Alfredo looked too tired. He went to the piano and placed Brendan Fiscetti's note on top of the keys. He found a blanket and draped it around his unconscious teacher. Then, suddenly exhausted, he climbed the stairs and fell into bed as quickly as he could.

It was nearly three o'clock in the morning when Alfredo woke in the dark. His blanket had slipped off and he was freezing. He knew he was still drunk. His throat was parched, so he got up slowly and went to the little table where he always kept a decanter of water for his lessons.

He switched on the lamp and filled his glass. As he drained it, he saw that the piano was still open. He reached down to close it and saw the envelope. The hand that had written his name was oddly familiar.

He picked up the note and shut the lid over the piano keys. Then he sat down in his favourite leather chair by the unlit fire and studied the writing a little suspiciously, tracing the contours of his name with one stubby finger. He recognised the handwriting, and yet he couldn't place it. Carefully, he sliced open the envelope. As soon as he saw the official notepaper of the Teatro degli Artisti, he knew.

My dearest lost friend Alfredo,

I wonder how many years have passed since we were in the same city, never mind the same company. Too many.

Tonight I stumbled across your pupil, Fergal Flynn, singing on the empty stage after the show. He has without doubt one of the must exquisite voices I've heard in years. What a strange coincidence that he's assisting me and also studying with you. He has told me a good deal about how you met, and it is a credit to you that you recognised his potential and brought him all the way from Ireland.

And, somehow, seeing him tonight was the fuel I needed to make me put pen to paper. I realise your time must be heavily in demand, but if you have any free time at all, I would dearly love to see you. We could meet for lunch, or you could come to the show. There's so much to catch up on.

Always your friend,

Brendan Fiscetti

Alfredo read and reread the note. Every handwritten word burned deeper and deeper into his head, rekindling the painful, carefully archived embers of their buried past, the reasons why he and Brendan hadn't spoken in more than twenty years. Once the memories began, there was nothing he could do to stop himself from reliving them, even if he had wanted to.

15

Brendan Fiscetti was just twenty-four years old and Alfredo Moretti was a couple of months younger when they met for the first time. They had both secured lead roles in a new production of Puccini's *Tosca* in Cologne – Alfredo as Scarpia, Brendan as Cavaradossi – and neither of them spoke a word of German. At the company's introductory supper the evening before their first rehearsal, they were seated directly across from each other. The candlelight made the dining room feel very intimate, and Alfredo found he had to be careful not to stare too intently at his new co-star.

Brendan was London born. He had inherited his height – just over six feet – from his mother's Irish family and his smooth olive complexion from his Italian father. He was innately confident and a natural flirt, but a gentleman with it. It was second nature for him to be warm and friendly to everybody, male or female. After a few glasses of wine, he told risqué jokes and stories that he had learned from his legions of Irish uncles. The whole company was in stitches laughing, enraptured – especially Marla Davis, the soprano playing Tosca. She had made a pact with herself never to get involved with any cast member and until that moment she had been successful, but as she watched Brendan Fiscetti laughing in the candlelight, she realised that the little columns of wax weren't the only ones holding a flame for him. She knew she was going to find it all but impossible to keep her vow.

Over the course of the rehearsals, the three young singers, Alfredo, Brendan and Marla, became inseparable. They gave little gatherings with all the cast crowded around the piano, singing their hearts out. They stayed up all night together, playing cards and sipping brandy. Before they went to bed, Marla always asked Brendan to sing her an Irish song, and through the cigar smoke that hung stubbornly in the air, he would sing the songs that his grandfather used to belt out after much coaxing and just the right amount of whiskey. But for two of the three, at least, their happiness was a thin veneer compared to the constant shadow of pain that lurked beneath the surface. Neither Alfredo nor Marla wanted to admit, even to themselves, that they were both falling in love with Brendan.

The critics pronounced *Tosca* a tour de force. They singled out Alfredo's Baron Scarpia for his commanding voice and convincing cruelty, Marla's Floria Tosca for her breathtaking combination of intensity and vulnerability, and Brendan's Mario Cavaradossi for his perfect combination of strength and tenderness. Their personalities created an extraordinary cocktail of energy on stage. The audiences couldn't buy their tickets fast enough.

After almost a year of successful performances across Germany, America and England, the production reached the Teatro la Fenice, in the floating city of Venice. They would have nearly three weeks of performances in the magnificent old opera house. Marla, Alfredo and Brendan were staying in a stunning three-storey house that looked right onto the Grand Canal. The owner was their local promoter and a huge opera fan, and he considered it an honour to have the three stars staying there. The rooms were ornate and beautifully kept, each with its own unique chandelier and a balcony that overlooked the water. Marla took the top floor, while Alfredo and Brendan shared the second. It had two huge en-suite rooms with a connecting door and the longest floor-to-ceiling windows they had ever seen. Brendan and Marla had never been in Venice and Alfredo had been there only once, years previously. When they walked into St Mark's Square for the first time, they were overwhelmed by its ancient beauty. They found a table and sat sipping Prosecco while a fiddler and an accordion player sent their romantic soundtrack circling and spinning around their heads.

It wasn't uncommon for the trio to receive flowers, gifts and invitations to gatherings held by rich patrons. They knew it was always good for business to attend, even if they were tired, and sometimes it was even fun. The Mayor of Venice came to see *Tosca* on the opening night and again on the next night, and the next. Then he announced he was giving a celebration in the cast's honour at his official residence. It was there that all the trouble started.

By the time Countess Amelia Moore-Hampton was twenty-five, she was orphaned, widowed and childless. Her husband, Count Michael Moore-Hampton, had been twice her age and an old school friend of her father's. She had known him all her life, and when she turned twenty-one he asked her to marry him as he stared out the window at a skittering pheasant. She had no idea whether she wanted to marry him or not, but she didn't know how to say no.

They were married less than six months later. When Amelia arrived at Moore-Hampton House, the butler showed her to what she thought would be the marital bedroom, at the top of a winding walnut staircase. The lamps were lit and the natural evening light was retreating from the expansive surrounding land. She bathed, slid between the soft sheets and nervously awaited the moment when her new husband would come and visit her 'lady garden' and take her 'flower', as her grandmother had delicately but perplexingly put it.

But Count Moore-Hampton never came gardening, that night or any other. He and Amelia ate their meals together, she dutifully accompanied him on official engagements, as her position demanded, and he was always leaving her thoughtful gifts of one kind or another, but the subject of intimacy stayed firmly closed. She was like his mother, straightening his tie before he took the platform to make a speech, and in return he kissed her head gratefully, like a well-behaved child.

She grew accustomed to her new life simply because she had to. To the outside world she seemed to have it all, and she knew she was a very lucky woman indeed. She had heard horror stories about abusive husbands who beat their wives or treated them like sexual slaves. Although she felt something approaching love for her husband, she began to fall apart, very slowly, bursting into tears for no discernable reason in the middle of one stuffy dinner reception too many. The count was naturally concerned for her, but he was distracted by his governmental work. He spent the majority of his time travelling and had very little chance to realise what was happening to his wife.

Within three years, Amelia's father died from a heart attack and was buried next to the mother she hardly remembered. Only a few months later, Count Michael Moore-Hampton was out hunting early one morning when he became separated from the pack and his saddle girth loosened mid-chase. His horse tried to throw him off. His ankle got tangled in the stirrup and he was dragged mercilessly for miles. Hours later they found his broken, lifeless body in a ditch, almost unrecognisable save for the signet pinkie ring that had belonged to his own father.

For Countess Amelia, it was the final brittle straw. For weeks she wandered the beautiful, silent, empty house, crying helplessly. It was months before she found the courage to face the lawyer who took her carefully through the late Count Moore-Hampton's considerable will and testament. She could only stare at him over his desk, unblinking, as he told her that her husband – an only child, his parents long gone – had left her everything. She was richer than she could ever have imagined.

At that moment, something in Amelia changed. Like a starved, stunted sapling bought only for its beauty and with no thought for its welfare, now that she was free to grow and blossom she was turning tentatively, involuntarily, towards the light. Her life was beginning again, and on her own terms.

In the back of her favourite magazine, Amelia Moore-Hampton saw an advertisement for an expensive cruise around the world. She booked a place instantly, before she could change her mind. Her butler's final job was to drive her to the port of Southampton and see her safely installed aboard the magnificent cruise liner. Amelia was terrified – was she mad to be heading off for months on her own? – but she was determined. She was going to go out into the world and have an adventure.

Once aboard, Amelia sat on the little sofa in her sizable cabin and tried to take it all in. She carefully looked around the quarters that were going to be her home for the next few months. There was a living room section, tastefully but sparsely furnished in bright, hopeful colours, that opened onto a balcony big enough for a little table and two chairs. The double bedroom was off the living room and there was a decent-sized bathroom just off that. After years in draughty old mansions, she was glad of the compact nature of her new surroundings and the lack of fuss. The portholes opened just enough for the sea breeze to fill the air and she looked forward to watching the stars at night from her balcony.

As the world drifted by outside, though, Amelia's old restlessness began to resurface. There were some wonderful musical gatherings on board, the floating library was well stocked and she had met some nice people, but they all seemed to be married couples, and inevitably she began to feel out of place. She craved the company of someone who would challenge her, make her laugh, ignite a long-buried spark of passionate conversation. She wanted a friend.

The ship's captain's wife, Constance Westwater, had accompanied her husband on the journey, and she became increasingly drawn to Amelia's solitary sophistication. Initially she had thought it eccentric and suspicious behaviour in one so young, but gradually she realised that the young countess was simply shy. Constance set aside her misgivings and made it her mission to befriend her. One day, when Amelia returned from her walk on deck, she found an invitation to tea from Constance. Amelia was reluctant, but she thought it only good manners to go.

They hit it off straight away. Amelia was pleasantly surprised at how easy she felt in Constance's warm company, and Constance discovered to her delight that Amelia was highly intelligent and a great listener. The two women lost all track of time and talked the entire afternoon away. Amelia had found the friend she craved.

So when Captain Westwater told his wife of an exciting opportunity, she offered her new friend the chance to accompany a special party going off-ship to see a production of *Tosca* at the famous Teatro la Fenice. Amelia agreed in an instant. To add to the excitement, they had been invited to a post-performance party at the mayor's residence, and the cast was expected to be in attendance.

'This is more like it!' Amelia laughed, clutching the official invitation to her breasts. 'Oh, I can't remember the last time I was at the opera – or at a good party.'

That afternoon, she searched through her trunk until she came to a box she had packed reluctantly but instinctively. It contained a dress she had chosen years previously, for her honeymoon, but had never actually worn; her late husband had always been too busy to take any time off. It was still in its original wrapping, enfolded in the frailest white tissue paper that had kept the delicate fabric's pale green hue as fresh as the day it was finished. It fit her as if she had bought it that very afternoon.

The Venetian evening was a luscious, soft watercolour as the party – the Westwaters, Amelia, an elderly statesman and his nephew – descended the steps of the ship. The oarsman steered their river taxi forward with ease along the murky river, then they walked along narrow laneways and over miniature bridges until, in the fading light, they came to the Teatro.

As she ascended the steps, Amelia was glad that she had brought her grandmother's black velvet shawl. She unwrapped it from about her shoulders, unveiling her second precious heirloom: a stunning constellation of smouldering sapphires, the same colour as her own bright eyes. Her curly red hair had been sculpted tightly into a bun at the crown of her head; a few corkscrew strands had special permission to hang down at the sides. On her right hand she wore a sapphire ring and bracelet that her husband had given her as a clumsy but sweet attempt to lift her spirits shortly after her father had died. She had only recently stopped wearing her wedding ring.

They were shown to a pale blue leather box at stage level, just big enough for the five of them. Two ice buckets held perfectly chilled bottles of champagne. The Teatro la Fenice was magnificent in every detail. Amelia's eyes strayed to the ornately painted sky-blue ceiling, seemingly held up by its own audience of curious, frozen angels. Conversations buzzed as if they were inside a bees' nest. As Amelia took her first nervous sip of bubbles, she was reminded of the last time she had been to the opera, with her late husband in Covent Garden, but every sad approaching memory was silenced by the orchestra's booming opening chords, like a sudden thunderstorm. The curtain opened and the passionate, tragic story of *Tosca* began to unfold.

Amelia was entranced. She thought Marla Davis sounded like a nightingale – her voice pure and lonely one moment, inconsolable and angry the next – and looked like a lost Egyptian queen, with her heavily lined eyes and her regal splendour. She was amazed at the power and depth with which Alfredo Moretti sang the cruel Baron Scarpia. His voice, she thought, was like an oak tree. But from the moment Brendan Fiscetti came onstage, as the painter and republican Mario Cavaradossi, Amelia could hardly take her eyes off him. Their box was so near the stage that she could see every detail of his handsome, expressive face. His voice filled the theatre with ease, and for a moment Amelia let herself imagine that he was singing only to her. She thought her heart would burst.

The dark green velvet curtains announced the end of the second act and the lights came up. Amelia and Constance looked at each other with delight, but Amelia couldn't concentrate on what Constance was saying and she couldn't wait for the final act to begin. She was light-headed – from the music rather than from the champagne, which she had barely touched.

'Are you all right?' Constance asked. 'You look pale.'

Amelia was indeed pale, but her face was radiant. 'I'm having one of the best evenings of my life.'

In the ladies' room, she splashed her face with a little cold water before fixing her light make-up. Amelia studied her reflection for a moment and wondered silently if she was pretty or not, then laughed at herself for being so foolish and fixed a loose curl that had escaped its clip. She pictured the beautiful Tosca and decided that the soprano and the lead tenor must surely be lovers – or maybe the soprano's lover was the baritone who she had just stabbed to death onstage? They were all so talented, and they sang to each other every night… *What a romantic way to spend one's life,* Amelia thought. *They're so lucky.*

She found her seat again just as the curtains lifted like two enormous sleepy eyelids. As Cavaradossi, writing his last letter to Tosca, lost his nerve and broke down, Amelia stopped breathing. She fanned herself with her handkerchief. Little did she know that Brendan, seeing the white linen wafting like a dove taking flight in the corner of his eye, had just caught his first glimpse of her. He thought that she was the most beautiful woman he had ever seen. Tosca leaped to her death from the castle, and the curtains closed. The clapping was thunderous. Amelia could understand how Tosca's loss had literally pushed her over the edge. There was only one thought in her mind at that moment: Mario Cavaradossi was definitely worth dying for. In all the time she had known her husband, she had never once felt as excited as she did when she looked at the handsome stranger, Brendan Fiscetti.

As the curtains opened again and the cast began to take their bows, the audience jumped to their feet, cheering and calling for more, showering the singers with flowers. As Brendan took his final bow, he picked up one of the roses that had fallen at his feet and tossed it to the flame-haired young woman he had spotted earlier. It landed on the edge of the box.

Amelia thought her heart would surely stop. She looked around, almost expecting someone else to rush forward and claim the flower, but no one did. Brendan Fiscetti bowed ever so slightly, holding her gaze. Amelia picked up the long, barbed stem carefully and cupped its awakening petals as one would a baby's head, inhaling the perfume and closing her eyes.

When she opened her eyes again, the tenor was gone from the stage and the audience had started to leave. 'Well, well,' Constance whispered, 'it's a good thing we have those invitations to the mayor's party. That young tenor is obviously keen to make your acquaintance.'

The Lord Mayor of Venice was famous for his parties, and that night was one of the major events of the year. He'd invited just over one hundred guests, including the floating city's most influential lawyers, judges and politicians, and he received the cast of Tosca like a visiting royal family. There was a champagne reception in the vast hallway followed by a magnificent dinner, but Brendan, who was normally starving after a performance, found that his mind was elsewhere and he could only play with his fork. Alfredo was the only one who had spotted Amelia as he joined the mayor's entourage, but he had said nothing. He had seen the way Brendan had looked at her during the curtain call, and it had given him a deepened sense of unease.

It was only after the meal, as a string quartet began to play a waltz, that Brendan caught sight of Amelia. She had broken the long stem of the white rose and was trying to place the fragrant flower amongst the nest of bright curls on her head, where it would be safe. Their eyes met and locked. Brendan excused himself from the conversation, not caring whether he was rude or not, and set off across the ballroom floor as calmly and as quickly as possible.

Constance saw him approaching and nudged Amelia. By the time he reached them, the whole room seemed to be watching.

Captain Westwater stood up. 'Signor Fiscetti, allow me the honour of introducing my wife, Constance Westwater, our dear friends, Dr Bryant and his nephew Theodore, and—'

Constance couldn't contain herself for another second. 'This is our dear new friend, Countess Amelia Moore-Hampton, from England – our own English *rose*, if you will.' She giggled like a schoolgirl.

Amelia held out her hand and Brendan brought it to his lips and kissed her lightly on the knuckles, noticing with relief that her pale wedding finger was bare. 'May I have the first dance?' he asked.

Amelia blushed. He was even more handsome than she had remembered. She returned his gaze as confidently as she could. 'It would be my pleasure, Signor Fiscetti. I haven't danced for as long as I can remember.'

He bowed deeply. 'The pleasure is all mine,' he said, extending a hand to her.

Brendan Fiscetti was a wonderful dancer, and Amelia gradually relaxed in his arms as he steered her through the growing throng of swirling people. After a few moments, he said, 'Countess Moore-Hampton, I hope that when I threw that rose from the stage I didn't embarrass you – or indeed the count, if there is…'

She looked into his incredible green eyes. 'Signor Fiscetti, my husband, Count Moore-Hampton, died almost a year ago now, and it's been a very long time since anyone paid me that kind of spontaneous attention. I was surprised, naturally, and embarrassed, yes – but only in a good way.'

Her brow furrowed when she spoke of her dead husband, but then her smile returned and restored her beauty. With great relief, Brendan drew her closer. Amelia felt his easy strength as her tiny hand was completely enfolded in his large grip. She felt safer with every second. He was much taller than her – her head rested naturally against his broad shoulder, and they lost themselves in the spinning circles of the music. She shut her eyes and prayed it wasn't a dream.

Alfredo was surveying the whole thing from a busy corner of the room and his heart darkened with jealousy. He had broken into the kind of cold, clammy sweat normally associated with eating something that didn't agree with him, but he knew only too well what was wrong, and he was furious with himself for feeling the way he did.

Marla was also discreetly taking in the scene and trying not to fume as the mayor bored her half to death with a long account of his fencing prowess, but she was able to appear cool. Every now and then she stole a little look at her competition, studying the shape of her mouth, the milky sheen of her skin in the ballroom's soft light or her extraordinary hair. In her green silk gown, Amelia looked like a mysterious queen.

An older woman recognised Alfredo and pulled him onto the dance floor before he had a chance to protest. Once in the whirlpool of dancers, they were drawn ever closer to Brendan and Amelia. Alfredo's heart was in his mouth. His dancing partner was not a woman to miss an opportunity – she loosened her formidable grip on Alfredo and tapped Amelia on one exposed white shoulder, inquiring if she might cut in for one dance. Amelia was too polite to refuse. After a lightning introduction from Brendan, they swapped partners and she took Alfredo's sweaty palm.

On and on the couples spun around the room. Alfredo's aloofness was in stark contrast to Brendan's intoxicating confidence – he was as stiff as a board and he could hardly look at her – but Amelia recognised shyness when she saw it. She broke the silence. 'I can't tell you how much I enjoyed your performance as Baron Scarpia – even though you scared the life out of me!' At least that made him laugh a little. 'Your voice reminded me of an oak tree, somehow.'

Alfredo raised an eyebrow. 'No one has ever suggested that I was wooden before.' Amelia began to apologise, but he had thawed just enough to reassure her. 'No, I'm not offended. I'm flattered that you liked my tone so much.'

There was another silence. 'How long have you known Signor Fiscetti?' Amelia asked.

Alfredo didn't want to discuss Brendan with her, but at the same time he could see how sweet and friendly she was, and he wanted to kick himself for being so prickly. 'We met at the first rehearsal of *Tosca*, many months ago now.'

'Is that when you both met Marla too?' she asked cautiously.

Alfredo could see her vulnerability in all its fragile glory, but he didn't want to give anything away. 'Why yes, Countess. None of us knew each other before. But now we're closer than family. It's very strange how that can happen. It's fate of some kind, I suppose. We three are inseparable.'

They fell silent again. The waltz came to an end and the teeming dance floor emptied as quickly as it had filled. Brendan couldn't get back to Amelia quickly enough. Alfredo, seeing him approach, bowed solemnly to his dance partner and left the floor.

'Shall we go for a little walk in the gardens?' he asked. Amelia nodded.

As they descended the stairs, a constant stream of admirers kept approaching Brendan, asking him to sign their *Tosca* programmes. Finally they reached the stone steps to the private gardens, and Brendan offered Amelia his arm.

The evening air had grown thick with perfume from the magnolia trees. The gardens were scattered with candles set in open-topped glass jars to keep the breeze from snuffing them out. The little columns of white wax lit the way to a circular fountain. Amelia put her hand into the trickling water and touched a few drops to her forehead, and Brendan leaned forward so she could do the same to him. She let her fingers stray momentarily into his thick hair, then, suddenly shy, she turned away to look into the fountain.

'Are you all right, Countess Amelia?' he asked softly.

'I'm not sure, Tenor Brendan.' He laughed, and she went on,

'Brendan, if you don't mind, I'd rather you called me by my first name. I feel old when it's eclipsed by my title.'

'I'm sorry, Amelia. Of course I will.'

'I'm sure you've heard this a million times before, and no doubt you'll hear it again, but your voice…well, it's just sublime.'

'Thank you. I feel very privileged, to be honest, to do what I truly love for a living. I can hardly believe that I get invited to travel all over the world to sing – and they pay me, too!'

She laughed.

'So,' he asked, 'do you live here, or are you just passing through? I can hear your English accent, but it's not North London like mine.'

That made her laugh. 'My goodness, wouldn't it be nice to live here, without any cars or buses? No, I'm from Bath originally, and I've never been here until today. I'm taking a long cruise – alone. We've only just docked here, and the captain and his wife were kind enough to invite me to hear you sing.'

'What made you decide to take the cruise?'

'It's a bit of a story. Do you really want to know?'

'Of course I do, if you don't mind telling me.'

'After my husband was killed, I was all alone in the world. My parents died a long time ago and I don't have any brothers or sisters. I didn't know which way to turn. For a while I was unwell with grief. When I started to recover, I decided I needed an adventure, so here I am.'

'How long are you here for?'

'Just for a few weeks.'

Brendan rubbed his temples. A hundred thoughts were fighting for his attention. 'Amelia, if you'll permit me, I would love to go sightseeing with you. We could discover Venice properly together. Could we have lunch tomorrow, and maybe take a trip on a gondola, if you're not too tired of being afloat?'

She laughed with delight and looked straight into his eyes. 'That sounds perfect.'

A breeze blew up around them, and as Amelia pulled her grandmother's wrap more tightly around her shoulders, Brendan caught sight of her sweet vulnerability and his instinct took over. He put his arm gently around her shoulders and pulled her closer, warming her bare arms with long strokes of his hand. She breathed a little sigh of approval and leaned against him, sending her other arm around the small of his back.

People began to spill onto the steps of the house, lighting cigarettes and getting ready to leave, and Amelia saw Constance and the captain. 'I should go,' she said reluctantly. 'The captain and his wife must be looking for me.'

He turned and looked into her eyes. 'Before you go, Amelia, can I be bold and ask you something?'

Her heart began to beat faster than ever. 'Yes, anything.'

He looked around to make sure no one was near and asked softly, 'Can I kiss you goodnight?'

Amelia's whole face lit up and she laughed from pure excitement. She looked up at his hopeful expression and put her finger under his chin, as if to steer it down to her own. He moved his hand to the nape of her neck and stroked it gently as her silent permission answered his prayers and their lips joined for the very first time. Little images of her late husband floated in her mind, threatening the moment, but passion blocked them out. She heard the water trickling in the fountain and she felt as though the thorns of Brendan Fiscetti's rose had pricked her cold heart and all the years of sadness were finally ebbing away.

At last they returned to the surface of the moment, gasping for air. Amelia's curls were escaping from their clips and falling about her face. She felt as if she had drunk all the champagne in the world. They cuddled under Brendan's coat like two giddy teenagers and she noticed how wonderful he smelled at such close quarters. They walked, as slowly as possible, back towards the main house. At the bottom of the stone steps, he held her close and whispered, 'Sweet Amelia' as he let his chin rest on the soft skein of red curls.

As their gondola pulled away and Brendan waved them off, Constance huddled beside Amelia. 'Well, well, my dear! That was an evening that will go down in history, don't you think?'

'Oh Constance, my head is spinning! It's like an old movie or something. I'm so grateful that you invited me to join you, or I never would have met him.'

'I'm so happy for you. I know you two have just met, but, well, call me old-fashioned, but the instant I met my husband I knew he was the one for me. Nobody else would do.'

Amelia had no need of the water to feel like she was floating.

Back on the ship, Amelia paused at her door to look at the deep blue velvet night sky's choice of jewellery. The highest, most faraway solitaire winked at her with approval, as if it too knew how alone and unreachable someone could feel, regardless of how much they were admired. She wanted to shout out that for the first time in her life, she didn't feel lonely – Brendan Fiscetti had singled her out, he had asked to kiss her goodnight, and what a kiss it had been!

She winked back at the Venetian constellations and went into her cabin. As she surrendered to sleep, Brendan Fiscetti's tender kisses still felt fresh on her lips.

Brendan travelled home with Alfredo by river taxi, in complete silence. He was oblivious to the tense atmosphere at first – he was so caught up in the reverberations of Amelia's kiss – but when Alfredo cleared his throat pointedly, Brendan finally turned his attention to his friend.

'You look terrible,' he said, startled. 'What's wrong?'

'I'm exhausted,' Alfredo answered, trying to get the right balance of neediness and huffiness. 'I wish we'd never gone to that party. I think all that champagne has upset my stomach.'

'Sorry to hear that,' Brendan said, but his voice sounded absent. His thoughts were on Amelia Moore-Hampton, and Alfredo knew it. A little chill ran up his spine.

Marla was being chauffeured back in the mayor's private gondola, which was a far more elaborate and luxurious affair. The seats were upholstered in the finest pale blue silk and there was even a canopy that could fold out if need be. As she watched the prow of the boat slide across the dark water, she was struck by the sheer magic of the moment. She felt as if she were travelling in a huge slipper that had belonged to a giant wizard, its curved toe never touching the water. But as she wrapped her shawl more tightly around herself, her thoughts turned to Brendan and his countess. The memory of how attentive he had been to Amelia all through the party ruined the journey for her.

The house was barely lit as she entered the hallway. Glad not to have to talk to anyone, Marla went straight to bed. The two men had done the same. Alfredo had tried to tempt Brendan with a nightcap, but he had declined and headed to his room, where, like both Alfredo and Marla, he reran the evening again and again in his mind.

Over the next week, Brendan Fiscetti and Countess Amelia Moore-Hampton were inseparable. They walked along the milky green water to St Mark's Square, past the hundreds of little market stalls selling glass rosary beads, lace umbrellas and beautiful hand-painted masks, each one more flamboyant and feathery than the last. They heard the bells ring in the Basilica di San Marco and watched as hundreds of pigeons took to the air and every face in the square turned upwards to look at the magnificent structure. Like two and a half centuries of lovers before them, they sat in the famous Café Florian, drinking coffee and watching a black-tie ensemble play waltzes on a raised platform at the lip of the square.

They were nervous at first, but their nervousness trickled away, afternoon by afternoon, as their conversation came easily and the details of their individual lives began to unfurl. Amelia loved the way Brendan listened to her every word so intently, asking her questions about her childhood in Bath, wanting to know everything about her. She couldn't help recalling how different her late husband had been. Although they were surrounded by some of the most beautiful architecture in the world, all they could see was each other.

Late one night, as he walked her back to the ship after dinner, she invited him on board for a nightcap. The air was cool and clean, with a stiff breeze, as they made their way along the dimly lit waterways. It was just after one o'clock and the ship's lounge was heaving with people drinking and dancing. Brendan looked at Amelia, and she shook her head and led him by the hand towards her cabin, nervously ordering champagne as they passed a waiter.

As Amelia searched for her key in her bag, she found that she was trembling, and she knew the breeze wasn't to blame. Her room was in darkness except for the perfect circle of moonlight coming through the porthole. The cabin was warm, and she lit some candles and put on a collection of Mozart sonatas. The waiter arrived with the champagne. They slipped their shoes off and curled together on the sofa.

He stroked her hair and fed her more champagne. The piano music filled the room. Brendan's hands moved lower, and he bent his head and kissed his way down to Amelia's throat. She slid her hand easily into his shirt and found his chest had a thick covering of hair. He exhaled in appreciation as she touched it. He kissed her full on the mouth, and their tongues met. His hand found her breast. 'Yes, Brendan,' she whispered, 'yes, oh, yes…'

She put her hand behind her back to unhook her dress, kissing him all the while, until the hook was finally freed and the top of the dress fell away. Then she did the same to her bra, and he kissed his way down to her nakedness and slowly took one of her nipples in his mouth, playfully at first, then more passionately. Amelia had never experienced anything like it in her life; her whole body was on fire. When he kissed his way back up to her mouth, he looked into her eyes and said, 'Would you mind if we went somewhere more comfortable?'

She closed her eyes and heard herself say, 'Yes – yes, my darling. Take me into the bedroom.'

He picked her up easily in his arms and carried her into the barely lit bedroom. She stood up, stepping out of her dress, and Brendan marvelled at the way the moonlight fell on her back. He put his arms around her from behind, and she arched her back as he planted kisses on her neck, then down along her spine. No man had ever touched her in such a loving way, and she was close to tears. She turned around and pulled his loosened shirt over his head, revealing his broad chest. 'You're the most beautiful man I've ever seen,' she told him. He put his considerable hands on the small of her back and began massaging her in gentle circular strokes as she undid his belt and helped him take his trousers off. They stood in their underwear, holding each other and swaying to the music. His arousal was obvious, but it was past the time for shyness.

They moved to the bed. In one silent moment they both removed their last pieces of modesty and then lay down side by side, completely naked for the first time. She was fascinated by his hardness, and slowly but surely they began to explore each other's body while the stars, like their inhibitions, faded one by one.

It was almost morning by the time they finally stopped making love and the best sleep of their lives enfolded them both, without warning.

Alfredo had had a terrible week. One minute he felt fine, and the next he was close to tears at the thought of Brendan and Amelia wandering the beautiful city together. It was all he could do to stop himself from donning some disguise and following them, but he knew the sight of the two lovebirds would only make him feel worse. The fact that he was unable to control his own emotions was the most upsetting thing of all, compounded by the awful fact that, for the first time ever, he dreaded seeing his friend.

Their rooms were too close for comfort now. On the nights when Brendan and Amelia stayed in the house, Alfredo heard them laugh in a muffled way that made him realise they were under the bedcovers, and he had to get up, get dressed and escape his room as quietly as he could. Anywhere was better than listening to the sound of his own heart breaking. He ended up walking the length and breadth of the city, in a daze.

Marla was luckier. She couldn't hear anything from her top floor, even though, in desperation, she went as far as lying flat on the floor with her ear pressed to a water glass. She found she couldn't sleep either, so she sought the distraction of her balcony and her Henry James novel, trying not to think about what Brendan and Amelia were up to and wishing she were the one pinned to his bed under the weight of his body. She had known instantly when Brendan and Amelia started having sex. Brendan had come into the theatre that evening with an unmistakable glow about him. His very skin seemed to be singing.

The three of them saw one another very little during those

weeks in Venice. Their conversation had become slow and awkward, as if they were strangers meeting for the first time again. After the performance one night, they did discuss the subject of the future. *Tosca* was scheduled to take a break for an unknown amount of time straight after the Venetian run. The management had made no promises about the future of the company, even though they had done well wherever they went. Brendan mentioned that his agents were suggesting various auditions in London, but Alfredo said he was dying for a proper break. Marla decided not to be too specific about her hopes, but she insisted that they should meet up in London soon. They had become so close since that first company dinner, less than a year before. The thought that they would be parting in a few weeks hadn't really occurred to any of them until that moment.

That night, Alfredo, already very drunk, brought another bottle of wine to his room and drank three-quarters of it in bed. He was miserable at the thought of not seeing Brendan. He had even harboured thoughts of inviting him to stay at his new house in Rome, and he kept going over and over it in his head – how much fun they would have had as he showed Brendan all around the city where he had been born…Alfredo instinctively knew that Amelia's sudden presence spelled disaster for that plan.

Marla, too, had been hatching a plan. Once the run was over, when she and Brendan were back in England, she was going to make her feelings for him known. She was old-fashioned enough to believe he was worth waiting for, and she had never made an obvious move. She heard her mother's voice telling her that 'a lady never approaches a gentleman in matters of the heart'. Countess Amelia threatened to upset everything, but Marla was determined that Brendan was going to be hers, and no scheming stranger of a countess was going to stop her from becoming Mrs Marla Fiscetti. Marla was a romantic woman at heart, and she was convinced it would be one of the greatest love stories ever told: the tenor and the soprano, unable to resist each other.

Marla knew Alfredo was miserable, but she wasn't quite sure why. As much as she loved him, she sometimes felt as if he didn't want her around, as if a kind of boys' club mentality appeared late at night if Brendan produced a cigar and a pack of cards. Alfredo had noticed that Marla had been acting strangely, but they had never broached the subject. Brendan had noticed that something was wrong. One evening, as he and Marla met on their way into the theatre, he bent to kiss her cheek and said, 'My dear Marla, where have you been? I haven't seen you or Alfredo all day. I thought maybe you'd eloped together.'

Marla looked genuinely annoyed. 'Where on earth did you get that idea?'

Brendan followed her towards her dressing room, where her assistant was dutifully waiting with make-up and hairpieces to begin the transformation process. He caught up with Marla and held both her tiny arms. 'Marla, I was only joking! Forgive me if I was rude, but what's the matter with everyone? Surely you know I was only playing with you?'

'What do you mean, everyone?'

'Well, Alfredo has been acting strange too. He's hardly eating. What's got into him?'

Marla realised her mistake in overreacting, and the touch of his hands made her heart beat harder. She tilted her head and managed a smile. 'Oh, Brendan, don't pay any attention to me. I'm just on edge today because I slept badly last night. I don't know what's wrong with Alfredo. Normally nothing comes between him and his food. It must be a dip in energy. It's been a long tour, we've had a few full weeks in a row, and I think we've all had our fair share of alcohol.'

Brendan looked relieved. 'That must be it. I was just worried.

I've been spending so much time with Amelia, I might not notice if something was wrong. What do you think of her? Did you have a chance to talk to her, that night at the mayor's party?' Marla's heart felt as if it was speeding out of control at the mere mention of Amelia's name, but she managed to answer without her voice wobbling. 'The mayor took up most of my time. I hardly got to talk to anyone else, really. Amelia certainly seems quite charming – and so beautiful, too.'

Brendan, delighted that Marla was interested, began talking excitedly about how wonderful Amelia was and how he hoped that the others could get to know her too.

Marla's heart sank. 'You're obviously very taken with her,' she said, 'and by the sound of things, she's equally taken with you. But what are you going to do? Doesn't her ship leave just after our time here ends? That's less than two weeks away.'

She suddenly realised that she had given herself away by knowing when the cruise liner was leaving port, but Brendan didn't notice. He leaned against the wall by her dressing room door, dropping his gaze to the floor. He looked confused and lost in thought. 'I know she's leaving, and to be honest I'm not sure what to do. I know it sounds insane, but I feel like I've known her all my life. She really is extraordinary. You'll all love her when you get the chance to spend a bit of time in her company. Will you have a drink with us tonight, after the show?'

'I'm not sure, Brendan. I feel particularly drained today, and I'll be even more tired after the performance—'

'Oh please, Marla. Please.'

He looked at her with such hopeful eyes that she couldn't stand it. 'Well, all right. Maybe a glass of something in your dressing room.'

Marla's dresser coughed amongst the hairpieces, and she was grateful of the excuse to end the conversation. As she was closing the door, Brendan said in a quieter voice, 'Marla, you and Alfredo are like family to me. I do so want you both to like her.'

She stroked his shoulder affectionately, hiding her horror. 'Yes, like family...lovely. A drink, then, in your dressing room after the show. Alfredo will stay too. We're sharing a lift home.'

Brendan skipped down the stairs to get ready, and Marla closed her door and leaned against it with her eyes tightly shut, not wanting to see her own devastated face in the brightly lit mirrors.

The growing tension hadn't harmed their performances. Indeed, they all were singing better than ever. For Marla, it was even easier to be in love with Mario Cavaradossi on stage because she had finally admitted to herself – too late – that she was in love with Brendan Fiscetti off stage. It was safe to open her heart on stage because she was playing someone else. Admittedly, Brendan was too, but a little part of her had always hoped that he might feel the same way as his character. She had pinned her hopes on their romance blossoming gradually, as the tour progressed; it had never occurred to her that Brendan might meet someone else.

She also had no idea that her main rival, up until that point, hadn't been female. As Brendan moved gradually further and further away from his co-stars, Alfredo had fallen more deeply in love than ever.

Suddenly, there were only two days before Amelia's ship left Venice. Brendan knew he had to do something. He knew Amelia had grown anxious too. Although they made love at every opportunity, he felt her growing unease and unhappiness as much as his own.

When that evening's performance ended, he took Amelia back to Café Florian, the first place they had visited together. They were shown to a large private booth at the back. She was about to speak when he put his finger to her lips.

'Amelia, I've spent all day plucking up the courage to say this. I don't want you to answer until I've finished, okay?'

He was more serious than she had ever seen him in the fortnight they'd known each other, and she nodded nervously.

Brendan began slowly, 'You and I have known each other just a little over a week and a half, but I feel like I've known you for years. And I can't bear the thought of you leaving on that ship – of not being with you. I need to know if you feel the same way about me.'

She nodded again.

'Amelia, my love…' He cleared his throat and fumbled in his pocket. 'I bought this for you today because I've never been so sure of anything in my life. Amelia, darling, will you be my wife?'

All at once everything seemed to fall into slow motion. Amelia had known she loved him within hours of their first meeting, but nothing could have prepared her for this moment. There he was, the most handsome man she had ever seen, seated across from her, nervously opening a dark blue velvet box, offering her a sparkling solitaire diamond ring and a new future. She felt like pinching herself to see if she would wake up back in her husband's empty mansion. But it was all real, and she burst out crying.

Brendan panicked, thinking that he had upset her. He pulled her closer, stuttering, 'Oh Amelia, I'm so sorry – it was stupid of me—'

She reached up and caught his shoulders. 'Yes,' she said while he was still talking a mile a minute. 'Yes.' He stopped in his tracks.

'What?'

'Yes, I'll marry you.'

'You will?' he said incredulously. 'Oh, my God in heaven!'

They kissed until they were both out of breath. Brendan helped the ring onto her finger and kissed her neck, laughing like a schoolboy. 'My darling,' Amelia said, wiping her eyes, 'I can't believe it. I've never been so happy in my life.'

'I decided yesterday that I just couldn't bear the thought of letting you go. If you'd left on that ship, I think I would have jumped into the water and swum after you. Are you sure you like the ring? We can change it if you're not happy.'

Amelia looked at the precious stone and wept again. 'I couldn't love it more.'

'Oh God, I want the whole world to know that I'm the luckiest man alive! Shall we go and tell Alfredo and Marla?'

'Darling Brendan, can we wait until tomorrow? I need to let it sink in. I just want to be with you tonight, on our own. Is that all right?'

She smiled at him and Brendan smiled back, his hands on hers. At that moment he would have done anything for her.

That night they looked into each other's eyes as they made slow love. Afterwards they held each other in contented warmth, whispering conversation. He hummed a melody to her while she rested her head on his chest, but they never reached the end of the song: exhaustion swept over them and they surrendered to it like babies, legs and fingers entangled as if they had been born that way.

Alfredo thought he was going out of his mind. He and Marla had hardly seen Brendan at all that final week, aside from onstage. If the lovebirds, as they'd both taken to calling Brendan and Amelia, came back to the house at all, they were always either in Brendan's room or down at the bottom of the garden, kissing or snoozing. Alfredo, like Marla, managed to reassure himself with the misguided thought that once Amelia's ship had sailed with her on it, things would return to normal.

That morning, Alfredo had overslept and was feeling particularly fragile at the breakfast table. The army of empty wine bottles on the kitchen dresser made him feel even worse. He knew his drinking had got out of control, and he blamed it on the stress.

Marla breezed into the room in satin pyjamas, a headscarf and perfect eyeliner, making straight for the coffee. 'Why are you so pale?' she asked.

Alfredo exhaled and pointed to the queue of empty bottles. Marla was about to suggest a cure when they were interrupted by the now-familiar laughter that always announced Brendan and Amelia. The lovebirds had obviously been up for hours, looking fresh and pristine. Even Marla looked a bit jaded next to them, and they made Alfredo feel worse than ever. He began pouring coffee into two more cups, but Brendan produced a bottle of champagne. 'I'd like you to join me and Amelia in a toast.'

Marla raised her eyebrows. 'What's the special occasion?' she asked carefully. Privately, both she and Alfredo were hoping that it was a send-off for Amelia.

Brendan laughed as he popped the cork and began filling the glasses. Then he composed himself and declared, in his best voice, 'My dear, dear friends, we wanted you to be the first to know. Last night I asked Amelia to be my wife, and she has done me the honour of accepting.'

He raised his glass in the air, and Amelia followed. 'We're getting married on the ship,' Brendan said triumphantly, 'the day after our last performance of *Tosca* – this weekend! We asked the captain at breakfast, and it's all being arranged as we speak.'

Marla stood stock-still, like a rabbit caught in headlights, unable to speak or move. Alfredo swallowed hard and reached for his glass too quickly, knocking it over. He grabbed a cloth and began to wipe everything in sight.

Amelia looked mortified, but Marla snapped out of her trance and began attempting congratulations, pulling Alfredo to his feet. His glass was refilled, they clinked their glasses together and drained the contents, hugged Amelia and Brendan and admired the ring. Then, when the moment had passed, Alfredo and Marla went back to their beds, pulling the covers over their heads to blot out the day.

The fact that they were upset wasn't lost on Brendan, but he was sure that, given time, they would come around to the idea. He couldn't imagine anyone not loving Amelia. They were just in shock, he told himself. They were concerned that it was all moving a bit fast, but that was because they were such good friends. One day they'd all laugh about it together.

The news spread quickly through the theatre that evening. Members of the cast kept coming up to Brendan and Amelia, congratulating them and marvelling at the romance of it all – in Venice, of all places, too! Brendan was walking on air, and Amelia couldn't contain her joy as she showed off her ring. The theatre manager arranged an after-show party. Though Marla and Alfredo were united in their lack of enthusiasm, they knew they couldn't opt out. They cheered and applauded and drank champagne with the rest of the cast and crew, avoiding Brendan's eye, until they found chances to slip away. Marla went to an after-hours club with some of the chorus – normally she never even spoke to them – and Alfredo went home.

He found the house dark except for the embers of the fire. He didn't bother turning any of the lights on, but instead headed straight for the kitchen, found a bottle of brandy and drank glass after potent glass in the frail moonlight. Then he staggered up the stairs to his room, taking the brandy with him. He stopped at Brendan's door and leaned against it to steady himself. It opened under his weight and he fell into the dark room, landing awkwardly on his side. He managed to sit up, miraculously still holding the bottle in one hand and the glass in the other. 'Typical,' he muttered. 'For most people the glass is either half full or half empty. Mine is completely fucking empty.'

He stood up, and the room began to spin. He cushioned his fall on the side of Brendan's enormous, undisturbed bed and struggled under the blankets. The brandy bottle and the glass had crashed to the floor, but Alfredo was too far gone to care. He caught the familiar scent of his friend's cologne on the pillows, and he called Brendan's name until the world was no longer recognisable. He hugged the overstuffed cotton pillow as if it were the man himself, and it was finally enough of a comfort to allow him to sleep.

Half an hour later, the gate rattled as Brendan asked his taxi to wait – 'I only want to pick up some clean clothes, I'll be back in a moment' – and walked up the path, fishing for his key in the dark. He had expected to see some sign of life, and when he didn't, he decided that Alfredo and Marla must still be out drinking some-where. He ran up the stairs and flicked on the light in his room.

His bed was occupied. Someone was under the covers, snoring like a hibernating bear. For a second Brendan wasn't sure what to do, then he called out, 'Hello? Hello? Who's there?'

When he got no answer, he pulled back the blankets and recoiled. Alfredo was curled up in a foetal position, unconscious beside a pile of thick, dark vomit.

Brendan shook his shoulder and Alfredo gave a muffled groan. Brendan pulled him off the bed and tried to get him to stand up, but his legs had turned to jelly and he collapsed awkwardly into his friend's arms. Brendan dragged him towards the bathroom, turned on the cold tap and splashed some water on his face, and Alfredo began to open his eyes.

He thought he was still dreaming. The last thing he remembered was wrapping himself around a pillow, wishing it were Brendan, and now he was waking up in his arms for real. Brendan began to wipe the dried vomit away from his face with the wetted corner of a towel. 'Good God, Alfredo, look at the state of you! What's wrong? And why were you in my bed? You've been sick all over the place, and there's broken glass on the floor.'

169

Alfredo tried to focus on him, but he was still extremely drunk. Their faces were closer than they had ever been off stage. Before he knew what he was doing, he tried to kiss Brendan on the lips, but Brendan turned his head away and Alfredo's lips met his cheek.

'What are you doing?' Brendan shouted, dropping him onto the lid of the toilet.

Alfredo's words were very badly slurred. 'I love you, Brendan, I always have. I can't bear it any more – it hurts too much. Please don't leave me for her.' He hugged Brendan clumsily around the waist, sobbing into his stomach.

Brendan couldn't believe what he was hearing. He pushed Alfredo away roughly. 'What the fuck are you talking about, Alfredo? You're drunk, you idiot. Stop it before you say any more nonsense you'll regret tomorrow.'

Alfredo's sobs rose, and the anger left Brendan's voice. He knelt down beside his friend, one hand steadying his shoulders, and said more quietly, 'Alfredo, I can't believe this. I love you like a brother – but I just got engaged to Amelia, for Christ's sake. We're about to be married. I even thought you might consider being…well, I didn't want to ask you like this, but I thought you might consider being my best man. I just don't understand where this has all come from.'

Alfredo was crying into his hands, too embarrassed to look up, but he managed to reply, 'I can't help the way I feel…for you. Oh God, I've been in love with you from the second we met. I didn't plan it, you know. Who plans these things? Did you plan to fall in love with that…that…that fucking ginger bitch?'

Brendan punched him in the face. 'Don't you ever speak about Amelia that way again!' he shouted.

Alfredo slumped on the toilet seat, clutching his eye, half hysterical. 'I didn't mean it – I'm sorry – Jesus, you didn't have to attack me!' He pushed Brendan out of the way with a sudden burst of strength and fled to his room, locking the door.

Brendan chased after him and pounded on the door. 'Alfredo, let me in! I'm sorry, I didn't mean to hit you so hard. Please, let me in!'

'Leave me alone!' Alfredo shouted. 'Just get out and leave me alone!'

Brendan sat on the floor outside Alfredo's room, not knowing what to do next. The gondolier, who he had completely forgotten, shouted up the stairs, 'Everything all right?'

'Sorry,' Brendan called. 'I'll only be another minute.'

He got up off the floor and tried one more time, speaking quietly through the crack where the door met the frame. 'Alfredo, will you please let me in? I'm sorry I lost my temper. I haven't hit anyone since I was in school, but you were so rude about Amelia… Alfredo, Jesus, I had no idea you were so unhappy about…about all of that. I'm sorry. Look, I know everything has changed, but you said it yourself: it's not like anyone planned any of this.'

All Alfredo would say in response was, 'Go away, you bastard. Leave me alone.'

'Ah, Alfredo, don't be like that. How many times can I apologise? We're going to have to talk sooner or later. I'm so sorry that I hit you, okay? Believe me, I'm sorry.'

Alfredo wouldn't reply. After a long time, he heard the front door shut. He put his head in his hands. He didn't know what time it was when he finally fell asleep.

When Alfredo woke the next morning, in his own room, he almost managed to convince himself that the whole episode with Brendan had been a bad dream – until he found the soiled sheets in the bathroom and almost vomited again. He didn't know what he was going to do. He would have to face Brendan sometime; there was a show that night. Their awful exchange replayed itself over and over in Alfredo's head. He couldn't believe he'd let those words leave his mouth. He was normally so careful, even when drunk. His face still hurt, his throat was raw and he saw that the skin under his left eye had begun to bruise badly.

He forced himself under a cold shower as a kind of punishment for his stupid behaviour, especially for what he'd said about Amelia. After the cold water had shocked his skin as much as he could bear, his head gradually began to clear, although the dread was still firmly parked in the pit of his stomach.

As he started down the stairs, he could hear Marla humming away to herself. He took a deep breath and found her on the porch at a table that was laid with enough food for half the cast.

She looked up from her newspaper and then threw it down dramatically. 'Oh my God, Alfredo, what happened to your eye? You look terrible.'

He had momentarily forgotten about his black eye, but he managed an instant lie. 'I was so drunk after that party that I tripped on the steps. I hit my face on the door handle.'

Marla gave him a suspicious look. 'Well, it's a miracle you didn't lose an eye. Let me get you some of my special ointment.'

Before he could argue, she had gathered herself up and was gone. Alfredo poured himself some strong coffee and flinched as the hot liquid travelled down his raw throat. He tried singing a single long, deep note. Although it had a rough edge, he knew it would be in better shape in time for that evening's performance.

Marla returned with her ointment and got him to lean his head back while she applied the thick cream to the area below his eye. 'Here,' she said, placing the tube in his palm. 'Put it on every hour or so. And don't worry about the performance. I'll get my make-up artist to work her magic on you.'

They sat in silence for a while. 'Why is there so much food, Marla?' Alfredo asked finally. 'We're the only ones who'll be here for lunch, aren't we?'

'Brendan phoned earlier. He and Amelia are due to arrive here – any minute, actually – for a special lunch of some kind. He says he has something he wants to ask us. Obviously it can't wait until tonight. Do you have any idea what it might be?'

'None.'

'I mean, what else could they possibly spring on us?'

The blurred scene in the bathroom replayed itself in Alfredo's mind like a bad film on fast-forward, and he remembered that Brendan had said something about a best man. He broke into a cold sweat. 'I have no idea what Brendan is up to,' he said as calmly as he could. 'If only I'd known earlier, I would have stayed for lunch, but I already have plans. I'm meeting someone in town, and I have no way of contacting them to cancel.'

Marla eyed him again. 'My goodness, Alfredo, what a lot of intrigue there is in the air today.'

He stretched his sore back as he stood up. 'Oh Marla, it's really nothing to worry about. I'll see you all tonight. Have a pleasant lunch, won't you? Apologise for me, if you would be so kind.'

She knew from his determined, polite tone not to press him. She watched him drain the coffee cup too quickly before practically running out the door. He took an elaborate route to the city centre, avoiding the main street, where Brendan and Amelia nervously travelled towards the house.

Brendan hadn't intended to lie to Amelia, but he couldn't bring himself to tell her what had happened. He simply said that someone had poached his taxi while he was getting his clothes from the house and that it had taken him a while to find another. He convinced himself that everything would be better in the light of day.

When they arrived at the house and Marla offered the excuse that Alfredo had given her, Brendan knew the real reason for

Alfredo's absence, but he put it out of his mind. He would have to deal with it later. 'Well, Marla, my dear, I wanted to ask you both together, but our friend seems otherwise occupied. So, Amelia and I have something to ask you.'

'Marla,' Amelia said tentatively, 'I know we've just met, really, and I know you're busy with the opera, but...' She glanced at Brendan for an extra bit of courage. 'Well, I – I mean, we – would be thrilled if you would consider being my maid of honour. You see, I don't have any family. You don't have to answer now, and of course we'll understand if you feel you can't...'

Marla hadn't seen that one coming, and she suddenly envied and understood Alfredo's distance. *He must have known*, she thought. She felt as if someone else was controlling her brain as she heard herself say, 'I'd be delighted.'

'Can I ask you one more favour?' Brendan said. 'I promise it'll be the last thing I ask. Please?'

Marla tried to smile. 'Of course.'

'We were wondering if you might consider wearing your final *Tosca* outfit at the service.'

Marla did a double take and half-snorted a laugh. 'What? Are you serious?'

'I know it sounds a bit odd, but it symbolises so strongly how Amelia and I met. Will you think about it?'

'Well, it'll have to be cleared by the wardrobe department, and you know what they're like.'

Brendan grabbed her and swung her around, laughing. 'It's all coming together – it's all coming together, Marla!' He put her back down on her feet. She was dizzy and furious with herself for agreeing to further humiliation.

When Brendan left Amelia and Marla in the garden and climbed the stairs, he discovered that his room had been cleaned to perfection, leaving no trace of the ugliness of the night before. He only wished the situation with Alfredo could have been fixed as easily.

Alfredo had found himself outside a church at the edge of the oldest part of Venice. He had walked aimlessly for what seemed like hours and his head still throbbed. He entered the church and sat in the damp silence at the back of the tiny congregation. He pictured himself going back to the house, packing his things and then leaving the city without a word of goodbye to anyone. Then he wanted to kick himself for being so dramatic. He knew perfectly well that he couldn't be so unprofessional. He wondered how he was ever going to look Brendan in the face again.

Slowly but surely, the panic and the hangover began to leave him as a small choir started to sing from the altar and a tiny priest hurled clouds of incense in his direction. The old man kept his eyes shut, praying over and over for the long list of the dead. When Alfredo looked at his watch, he was surprised to see that it was nearly time to face the music. He had sat at the back of the church, in a kind of trance, for nearly two hours.

As he walked back towards the house, he felt a sudden calm take him over. He would stay for the end of the run, only two days away, then leave Venice as quickly as he could.

Marla was waiting in the river taxi, and he immediately knew from her face that something had happened. 'Why didn't you tell me, Alfredo,' she demanded, 'before you conveniently disappeared and left me to face them both on my own? You could have at least warned me!'

Alfredo, assuming that she was talking about the fight with Brendan, could hardly breathe. How much had Brendan told her – how much had he told Amelia? Probably everything. 'I'm sorry for the mess upstairs,' he stammered. 'I didn't plan to get so drunk. Oh God, Marla, it's a fucking nightmare. I'm sure he didn't mean to black my eye. It was my fault. If only I hadn't insulted Amelia – if only I hadn't tried to kiss him...' Alfredo covered his face as the tears began to pour out of his eyes. He wiped them away with the sleeve of his jacket. When he looked up at Marla he was half-expecting some sort of compassion, but her horrified, bewildered expression told him she had absolutely no idea what he was talking about. He dropped his gaze to his shoes, suddenly mortified. The driver had probably heard every word.

Marla came to her senses and took his hand. 'Alfredo, oh my God,' she said softly. 'I don't know what to say. I was angry because they came to lunch to ask if I would be their maid of honour – can you believe it? A *maid*, me? – and I thought you knew. I thought you hadn't told me on purpose. Oh, my poor friend – I had no idea you were so unhappy, or that you felt...that way towards Brendan.'

Alfredo didn't know where to look. He managed a weak smile. 'Oh Marla, I'm so sorry. I didn't know they wanted you to be the maid of honour. I don't know how I'm going to face them. He must have told Amelia what I said, and what I tried to...do.'

Marla squeezed his hand. 'We'll face them together. Look, we're nearly there. Come straight to make-up; no one must see those bruises. What a beast to do that to you.'

'Well, I was very rude about her.'

'I'll tell you one thing. I'll bet you he hasn't told her a single word about your argument. Why would he? There wasn't a single mention of it over lunch. Mark my words: even though he's been a stranger to us lately, he'll be very glad to see you tonight.'

Brendan and Amelia had spent that afternoon going through the wedding preparations with Constance, who was so overheated with excitement that she had to keep fanning herself. Brendan was glad of the chance to stop thinking about what had happened with

Alfredo, but his friend's vulnerable face floated before his mind's eye, over and over. *I love you, Brendan, I always have…I can't help the way I feel…Oh God, I've been in love with you from the second we met…*Amelia asked what was troubling him, but he smiled when he saw her worried face and assured her that he was just tired and that nothing was the matter.

When he kissed her goodbye, she whispered in his ear, 'Don't forget to ask Alfredo to be your best man, will you?'

Brendan laughed. 'Of course not, my love. I'll have to pick my moment, though. He's been so tired lately.'

There was a river taxi waiting near the ship, and he reached the stage door with five minutes to spare before the vocal warm-up began.

Marla's make-up woman had done a good job on Alfredo. As he headed back down the stairs, with his bruise temporarily camouflaged, he was surprised at how much better he felt – until he almost collided with Brendan on the landing. Brendan instinctively caught him by the arm and laughed nervously. Alfredo looked at the floor, but when Brendan saw the obvious make-up, he moved his hand towards the swelling.

Alfredo pulled away. 'You're not going to hit me again, are you?'

Brendan looked up and down the hallway in desperation. 'Oh Alfredo, my dearest friend, I never meant to hurt you like that. You just shocked me and made me angry, and I lashed out. I'm not proud of myself, and I've thought of nothing else since it happened. Please forgive me, Alfredo. I'm truly sorry.'

He reached for his friend again and stroked the side of his head. Alfredo closed his eyes, too late, as one Judas tear escaped and ran down his lowered face. His heart was racing. The two men both tried to speak at once, tripping over each other's thoughts. Then Brendan raised his voice. 'Alfredo, please, let me finish.'

'If you must.'

'I'm in love with Amelia, Alfredo, and I know you know what that feels like. I can never share the feelings you have for me – not ever. It's just not who I am. I've always thought you were the brother I never had, and that's love, even if it's not the love you want. I'm sorry, but that's the truth. I'm flattered, if that means anything.'

Sadness overtook Alfredo. He looked away and swallowed hard.

'Alfredo, please. Oh God, this is so hard. We missed you at lunch today – we came over specially to ask you…we would like you to consider being my best man. That's how much you mean to us.'

All Alfredo could hear was *We, we, we…*

'Will you even consider it? Can we let what happened between us stay between us? It's no one else's business – I haven't said a word to Amelia.'

Alfredo managed to hold his gaze for a second. 'Marla knows everything. It came out by accident.'

'What? Oh, shit. I'd better have a word with her then. She's agreed to be Amelia's maid of honour. That's why it would be so perfect if you were at my side too, do you see? Will you think about it? Don't say anything now, just let me know when you're ready, will you?'

Alfredo was thinking how clueless and insensitive Brendan could be, but he heard himself say, 'I'll think it over.' All he wanted to do was end the conversation.

Brendan reached across and hugged him quickly. The call for the vocal warm-up came through the tannoy system, breaking the moment. As Brendan ran down the stairs, Alfredo stayed in the same position for a moment, as if he were still being hugged by an invisible force. His heart felt far more badly bruised than his eye.

★

The show only seemed to benefit from all of the high drama backstage. Alfredo was glad to be the cruel Scarpia – having Brendan arrested and pulling his hair back roughly gave him a kind of thrill – and the audience was particularly responsive to his dark, threatening performance. He avoided Brendan's eyes at all costs.

After the performance, Alfredo got changed at lightning speed and told the river taxi just to wait for Marla, as he had other plans. The abandoned tourist gondolas were his only audience as he moved slowly through the quiet Venetian laneways. He wandered the floating city, every window shuttered above the now-silent shops and cafés. The quiet was eerie. The very buildings seemed to halt their creaking gossip, waiting for him to leave. The canal trickled, the hollow gondolas nudged each other, even the legions of tiny dogs that wandered freely during the day knew that the barking hour was over.

On and on he walked, feeling like some kind of vampire, damned to wander the watery world alone. He stopped to look up the canal from the great wooden bridge. The night-varnished surface of the water was only momentarily unsettled by the occasional police boat moving up and down. When Alfredo looked upwards, there wasn't a star in the sky, but there was a certain ship silhouetted on the horizon. His legs wobbled, and a few tears tried to escape his eyes without being noticed. He found a step and sat down to rest.

There was a heaviness in his heart, and he unconsciously placed his hand over it to check that it was still beating. As he did, he felt another weight in his breast pocket and suddenly remembered that he had brought his silver brandy flask. As he unearthed it and took a comforting sip, he imagined some other poor creature, somewhere in the world, doing and feeling exactly the same thing. He raised his flask in a toast of unrequited solidarity, and drank the rest of the brandy in one swallow.

When he finally reached the house, it was in darkness. Alfredo went upstairs and slipped into the best sleep he had had for weeks. He had made a final decision about what to do next.

The next morning, Alfredo went into a travel agency and changed his ticket. He would leave for Rome at six o'clock in the morning, the day after the final performance of *Tosca*.

The Teatro la Fenice was full to capacity for the final performance. Flowers were arriving from all over the city. Backstage was like a Christmas celebration, with decorations adorning every possible surface and various members of the cast passing around programmes to be signed and treasured for decades to come. Alfredo had bought special last-night gifts for all his favourite people, as was the custom. He gave Marla and Brendan exquisite sets of Venetian crystal champagne glasses, which he had his dresser place in their respective dressing rooms. In his own, he found similar packages from his co-stars: crystal candlesticks from Marla and an ornate bejewelled mask from Brendan and Amelia. Brendan had also wanted to buy Alfredo something to make up for the fight, but he hadn't been able to find him. He had no way of knowing that he had walked right past the travel agency where Alfredo was booking his escape.

Brendan tried to talk to Alfredo in private that last evening, but Alfredo made sure he was never on his own before the curtain came up. Brendan did find a little bit of comfort in the fact that Alfredo seemed to be in better spirits, smiling broadly and even laughing with the house manager. Marla had also noticed that Alfredo seemed more at ease with himself, but she attributed it to the coming end of their long, exhausting run. Brendan simply thought that it meant he had put everything into perspective and was going to be his best man after all.

Their final performance of *Tosca* was electrifying, and they received ovation after ovation, plaudit after plaudit, from the seemingly insatiable audience. Amelia and Constance sat in the same private box where they had been only weeks before, when all their lives had been so different. Brendan couldn't help himself: when he came out for his curtain call, he plucked a pink rose from one of Marla's bouquets and threw it to his wife-to-be, amidst roars of approval from audience, cast and crew – all except Marla and Alfredo, who rolled their eyes at each other while Amelia kissed the crown of petals and placed it in her hair.

Compared to the opening celebrations at the mayor's official residence, the *Tosca* farewell party was a bit more restrained. It was held at the very top of the Teatro. The manager presented each of the principal singers with an engraved silver goblet in thanks for a very successful and entirely sold-out run. Alfredo put on a smile, but his secret itinerary was going round and round in his head. His bags were packed, and a river taxi was booked to pick him up at four o'clock that morning.

Constance was adamant that it was bad luck for Amelia to spend the night before her wedding with her future husband, so the two women left discreetly for a light supper back at the ship and an early night. The mayor insisted that the rest of them continue the party at his house. Brendan protested that they couldn't possibly put him to any more trouble, but the mayor wouldn't take no for an answer, especially when he heard that Brendan's family was unable to attend the wedding on such short notice.

'I need to go back to the house for something,' Alfredo said. 'I might see you later on.' Without waiting for a reply, he turned away and hurried down the steps. Brendan tried to follow him, but the increasingly drunk mayor was having none of it. He ordered more champagne, and three chorus singers cornered Brendan to joke about his last night of freedom.

When Alfredo got back to the house that he and his friends had called home for a little under a month, he went to his bedroom and began writing what he considered the easier of his two farewell notes.

My dear Marla,

I'm no good at goodbyes, so I hope you'll understand that I can't stay any longer, and that it has nothing to do with you. I can't thank you enough for your friendship and your professionalism over the past year. I wish you all the success in the world, and I hope our paths will cross again in the future.

With love,

Alfredo

He sealed it and placed it under Marla's pillow. Then he went back to his room to write his letter to Brendan, but every time he tried to write down how he felt, it sounded all wrong. After ripping several frustrated attempts to shreds, he sat on the edge of the bed with the heel of his hand pressed to his good eye to stop the tears. When he looked up, he realised there was only one sheet of paper left, and he finally let his heart speak instead of his head.

Dearest Brendan,

This is the hardest letter I've ever had to write. By the time you read this, I will be long gone. I can't stay. There are too many reasons to fit on this page, but you know most of them already. Only know that I wish you and Amelia everything you hope for in the future. Thank you for asking me to be your best man, but I just cannot do it. I'm sure you'll find a better man for the job. I'm so sorry if I've made things difficult on your most special day. I will never forget this time in Venice. Forgive me if you can.

Your friend,

Alfredo Moretti

He kissed and sealed the envelope, resisting the urge to crush it into his coat pocket with the rest of the torn paper. Instead, he carefully placed it under Brendan's perfect white pillows.

There was a knock at the door and Alfredo jumped, but to his relief it was only the driver of the water taxi he had booked. The old man was early, so he agreed to take Alfredo around the city one more time before they headed for the airport.

By the time the extremely intoxicated Marla and Brendan escaped the suffocating hospitality of the mayor, it was almost morning. As they crept upstairs with their shoes in their hands, Marla whispered, 'I'm so glad you and Amelia had the sense to make the wedding service late in the afternoon, so we can have a lie-in!'

'Shh!' Brendan hissed. 'Don't wake Alfredo. At least someone had the sense to try and have a good night's sleep. I hope he's written his speech.' With that they parted, stifling giggles, and passed out as soon as their heads hit the pillows.

Hours later, Brendan woke suddenly from a blurred dream, convinced he could hear someone shouting, but it was only the good-humoured gondoliers vying for business. He pushed his fragile head under his pillow for cover, and it was then that he found the letter.

16

A quarter of a century later, Alfredo Moretti stood in his living room staring at Brendan Fiscetti's letter like a waxwork dummy, frozen by the sheer weight of memory, loss and regret.

He slowly realised he had been standing in the same spot for so long that the sky had completely changed colour and the hungry sparrows had begun arguing with each other outside his window. His left leg had gone numb. When he moved he stumbled, in more need of his walking stick than usual. He cursed under his breath as the blood returned to his heavy foot and the pins and needles kicked in, coursing up to his thigh as if thousands of fireflies were trapped under his skin. He held his breath and stamped his foot on the floor, over and over, until their tide began to break. Then he switched off the light and headed awkwardly up to bed, clutching the letter from his long-lost friend in sheer bewilderment.

Fergal was the first to wake and come downstairs the next morning. He saw that the letter from Brendan was gone and looked towards the ceiling, wondering what Alfredo's reaction had been. He didn't have to wait long to find out. Alfredo descended the stairs, grumpy after a terrible night's sleep, and headed for the kitchen and coffee. The doorbell rang. Alfredo was so preoccupied with Brendan's letter that he had forgotten he had a ten o'clock lesson with the singing butcher. Fergal welcomed him in and went to alert Alfredo, who thanked him abruptly, downed a full glass of water in one go and began apologising profusely to the burly figure in the music room.

During the day's lessons, Alfredo found himself drifting off, then getting angry with himself for letting the past distract him. By the end of his day, he was sure of one thing – he wanted to see Brendan Fiscetti before he left Rome. But he was terrified and embarrassed when he thought of how he had behaved all those years ago. He knew it had partly been the fault of his own youth. He thought of Fergal, trying to reach for some kind of sophistication and wearing it like an ill-fitting uniform, at the cost of not being himself. Alfredo knew he had to strike a fine balance between guiding Fergal and allowing him to make mistakes, and that he had a responsibility to lead by example. He was going to start by meeting Brendan and apologising properly for the past.

Fergal's day was full, as usual – an Italian lesson in the morning, then the post-lunch shift at the restaurant – but all he could think about was Father Mac's abandoned visit and the letter from Signore Fiscetti. When he brought the lemon tea to Brendan's dressing room, Brendan noticed that he looked downhearted.

'What's wrong, Fergal?' he asked.

Fergal seized on the first excuse he could think of. 'I was…I was thinking about my exam. I had my first preliminary vocal exam not long ago. I only just passed. I'm still ashamed of myself.'

'Don't be ridiculous,' Brendan said forcefully. Fergal was taken aback. 'It's admirable that you set yourself high standards, of course, but everyone is allowed to have a bad day. It's just unfortunate that an examiner was in the room when you had yours. And he passed you in the end, didn't he?'

'Yes, I suppose so.'

'There's no supposing about it. Tell me, what do you think singing is?'

'What do you mean?'

'What do you think singing is?'

Fergal wasn't really sure what he meant; he shook his head. 'It's just something I've just always been able to do.'

'Yes, I know that. You're what they call a natural. But singing is more than that. Do you want to know what I think? Singing, Fergal, is truth and beauty. Singing is honesty, even if that honesty is the hardest thing to achieve. How can you possibly move any-one if you are not moved yourself? Singing can be an immense responsibility, almost like being one of the soothsayers of years gone by. Emotionally, you must be as honest as you can, regardless of what the words are, whether they're Italian or English or what have you. As long as the feeling is truthful, that's an international language. Do you understand?'

'I think so.'

'Try not to think about it too much. I'm sure Alfredo has it all planned out for you. And try not to beat yourself up so much, young man. Have a little holiday from yourself.'

Fergal did feel a little better.

The half-hour curtain call came across the tannoy. 'Did...' Suddenly Brendan looked a little less certain. 'Did Alfredo get my note?'

'I didn't really see him last night or this morning,' Fergal said, 'but he definitely must have got the note, because I left it on the piano and this morning it was gone.'

Brendan didn't know what to think.

Over the next few days, Alfredo picked up the phone to dial

Brendan's hotel more than once, but as soon as the number rang, his nerve gave way and he hung up on the hotel receptionist. Any time the phone in Brendan's room rang, his first thought was that it might be his old friend, and he grew increasingly upset when it was always housekeeping asking him if he had enough towels. Every evening, when Fergal came to his dressing room, Brendan couldn't help dropping his gaze in the vague hope that there would be an envelope in his hand, and then tutting at himself in annoyance when there was none.

Finally, Alfredo knew he had to do something; precious time was running out. He scribbled a note asking if Brendan would join him for lunch one afternoon, or for a late supper after one of his performances if he preferred – Alfredo remembered what a night-owl he had always been. He put his phone number at the top of the page, sealed the envelope and gave it to Fergal to deliver. Fergal smiled broadly as the pale blue envelope was placed in his hand as carefully as a Holy Communion wafer.

When he closed the door behind him, Alfredo found that his heart was racing. He went into the front room and poured himself a large glass of red wine.

At the Teatro, Fergal handed Brendan the note and saw his face cloud over for a moment. 'Thank you, Fergal,' he said. 'Give me a moment alone, would you?'

Once the door was closed, Brendan put on his glasses and sat staring at his name on the front of the perfect blue envelope, remembering the last time Alfredo had written to him, all those watery years ago. He laughed a little at himself when he saw his nervous expression in the mirror. He opened the note too quickly with his big hands, almost tearing the folded invitation.

'Well, well, Mr Moretti, my lost friend,' he said as he read the contents over and over, 'I see you still like to do things at the last minute!'

Fergal, running down the stairs of the Teatro, had no way of knowing just how much the contents of the innocent-looking envelope would influence his own life.

Father Mac had had a hard year, filled with broken people in broken situations who he could only try to put together again with his particular brand of Catholic glue. He couldn't remember the last time he'd had an unbroken night of sleep, without some needy parishioner on his doorstep or making him jump when the telephone by his bed rang. But that morning's frantic knock on the door of St Bridget's meant he would see Fergal a lot sooner than he had expected.

Paddy Flynn Sr, Fergal's father, had been born at the wrong time in history. Career prospects for men of his generation and religious persuasion were all but non-existent, as was his confidence. In his head, he should have been an all-Ireland hurling champion turned coach, but his temper, among other things, had held him back. He had recently started working as a part-time security man in a box like an upright coffin in a car park near the city centre. The only thing that made it bearable was the bottle of whiskey that he hid in his coat and drank from throughout the night.

Paddy had spent the evening fuming in the pub. His sons' hurling team had lost badly, and he felt the referee had been biased in favour of the other team. More than a few times Paddy had cursed him from the sidelines, calling him a 'dozy culchie cunt', mortifying his three sons. If his other son Fergal entered his mind at all, he felt nothing but a secret spark of jealousy that Fergal had been able to escape.

For some reason, when he was due to head down the road to start his shift, he dreaded it even more then usual. He had been to the doctor on the quiet the previous week and had been told in no uncertain terms that if he didn't stop smoking and drinking then he risked serious heart disease. As usual, Paddy paid the doctor not one blind bit of heed. If anything, the advice had made him drink and smoke even more.

When the little Hitler of a supervisor made his round of the car park early the next morning, he thought he'd caught Paddy Flynn asleep: he was slumped against the inside of the security box. The supervisor booted the side of it, calling him all the lazy bastards under the sun, but when there was no reaction he stopped the abuse and looked into Paddy's purple, oddly peaceful face. When the ambulance came, he was pronounced dead on the scene from a massive heart attack. He wasn't even fifty.

When the police arrived at Angela's door in Walker Street, she assumed one of her boys was in trouble. When they told her Paddy was dead, she thought they meant her eldest son, named after her husband, and she almost fell to the ground in shock. A policewoman helped her up and managed to explain that it was her husband, not her son, who was dead.

Angela screamed. All the neighbours came out and someone called the doctor, who offered her a Valium, but for the first time in her life she refused. She felt as if she had taken about ten already. Someone called her sister Jeannie, who came round right away, and someone else found the twins. Ciaran, the youngest, had been in a deep sleep upstairs. When a huge policeman woke him up, he nearly wet himself.

Angela suddenly spoke to the policewoman. 'How the fuck are we gonna tell our Fergal? He's in Rome.'

'Is he on holiday?'

'Holiday, my arse!'

'Do you have a number for him?'

'No, but Father MacManus will know. He's at St Bridget's. Will somebody go over and tell him our Fergal has to come home?'

189

'Do you feel up to identifying your husband at the morgue?' the policewoman asked gently.

Angela started to cry, but she nodded her head. 'I don't want him lying there on his own. Can we go and get the priest first?'

And so it was a policeman who knocked heavily on the door of St Bridget's House while Angela sat in the backseat of the car. Although Father Mac was shocked, he swung into action. He accompanied Angela to the morgue, where she identified her husband's lifeless body and then threw up into her hand with shock. He drove her back to Walker Street and only agreed to leave her once her sons and her sister had all gathered to look after her. He promised to phone Fergal and arrange for him to come home as soon as possible. It was the last phone call in the world he wanted to make.

Fergal woke up just after ten o'clock, safe in the knowledge that he had the whole day off until his shift at the Teatro that evening. He stretched and yawned, and suddenly remembered he had been dreaming. He had been swimming with Father Mac in a clear stream, but then the water had started to get muddier and muddier, until they couldn't see each other. That was when he had woken up.

He went into the bathroom and turned on the shower. As he was walking back to his room, wrapped in a towel, the phone rang in the hallway. He waited to see if anyone stirred. When it kept ringing, he realised that Daniela must have left and that Alfredo must be out too. He ran down the stairs two-by-two, suddenly wide awake, shouting, 'Hang on, hang on, I'm coming!'

When he heard Father Mac's voice, he thought for a selfish second that his plans had changed and he was coming to Rome after all. But then the terrible details unravelled, as did the large bath towel, but Fergal was too shell-shocked to notice that he was sitting on the stairs naked as the day he was born, on the day that his father had died.

'Fergal, are you okay? Say something. I'm so sorry to have such awful news.'

Fergal was freezing all of a sudden, even though the house was more than warm, and he shivered from head to toe. He tried to hear his father's voice in his mind. It was ironic – when he was growing up, he had wanted nothing more than for his father to be dead, but now that it was real he felt almost poisoned by the news. His blood felt as if it didn't belong to him. He pinched himself angrily on the leg to make sure he wasn't still dreaming.

Finally he was able to speak. 'Where's my ma?'

'She's in Walker Street, I think, or maybe with your aunt. She asked me to ring you and see about you coming home. I take it you want to come home, for the wake and all?'

Fergal was numb. The thought of having to go back to his old life made him feel sick, but he heard himself say, 'Yeah. I'll come back.'

'Don't worry about a thing, Fergal. I'll arrange everything. Oh fella, I wish I was there with you to give you a hug. Is anybody there? Where's Alfredo?'

'I don't know. I think I'm the only one in.'

'You shouldn't be alone on a day like this. Promise me you won't be on your own. What about Alfredo's sister?'

At that moment Alfredo put his key in the front door and Fergal fumbled with the towel and covered himself up. Alfredo had only to look at his face to see that something was wrong. It was all Fergal could do to hand him the receiver; it seemed to weigh a ton.

Alfredo caught his breath and put his hand to his mouth in shock. 'Yes, call back later…Yes, I'll take good care of him. I promise.' He hung up.

'Oh my God, you poor, poor boy. Come here.' Alfredo hugged Fergal as tightly as he could. They moved into the living room and sat together on the sofa. 'What do you want to do?' Alfredo asked, but Fergal couldn't even think straight.

Alfredo called Giovanni and told him the terrible news so he could inform the theatre manager that Fergal would need at least a week off. Then he made some coffee and put brandy in it, but Fergal could only manage a few sips. He was lost in a vacuum of shock.

'I'll come to Ireland with you,' Alfredo said. 'Tonight, if we can get a flight.'

'You don't have to,' Fergal told him, but Alfredo was insistent and Fergal was calmed by the fact that he wouldn't have to go alone.

Father Mac rang again. He had been to see Angela, and she was resting at her sister's. With each digit that Fergal pressed on Alfredo's phone, his dread grew. When his Aunt Jeannie answered, she didn't recognise his voice at first. 'Who's this?'

'It's me, Jeannie. It's Fergal.'

'Fergal? Jesus, you sound so…different.' Then she burst into tears. 'Your mother's taken a wee tablet,' she told him through her sobs, 'and she's asleep up on her bed, away from all the neighbours. They mean well, sure, but they're that nosy.'

'Make sure and let her know I'll be home as soon as I can,' Fergal said, 'probably in the next few days – as soon as I can get a flight.' As soon as he hung up, the phone rang again. It was Father Mac, saying that he'd got them the last two seats on a flight later that night.

The flight went by in a blur. Fergal sat in the window seat and didn't even blink when the plane touched down in the lashing rain of his hometown. They'd only packed carry-on luggage, so they were able to walk right past the queue at the carousel. Fergal was instantly struck by the accents all around him – the security guard making a joke to two of the cleaners, one old man telling a story to another, a little boy asking his mother for money to buy sweets…Everyone had the same familiar accent, and he hadn't heard it for so long.

And then he saw Father Mac, standing by the payphones, transferring his weight from foot to foot and craning his neck to spot them. Fergal did a double take. He'd gained a serious amount of weight on Mrs Mooney's cooking and it made him look a lot older. When Fergal stopped in front of him, Father Mac thought he was a tourist trying to use the payphone. He was moving out of the way when Fergal said, 'Dermot, do you not know me?'

17

Father Mac's mouth fell open and he shook his head in utter disbelief at the tall, broad-shouldered, sallow-skinned man in front of him.

'Fergal?' he gasped. 'Fergal Flynn, is that you? It can't be!'

Their eyes filled up and they flung their arms around each other. Fergal buried his face in Father Mac's neck, but it was clear that he'd grown a good few inches taller. Even when they regained their composure and Father Mac was greeting Alfredo, he still couldn't take his eyes off Fergal. Fergal had no idea how much he had changed physically in the past year. He had gained weight too – mainly because of the quality, and indeed the quantity, of Italian food – but in all the right ways. 'Oh my goodness, Fergal Flynn!' Father Mac said softly. 'Look at you!'

'Look at me? Look at *you*, Der— Father.'

'Well, as you can see, I'm fading away to the size of a mountain. Nobody can accuse Mrs Mooney of not looking after me.' He patted his impressive stomach self-consciously and put his arm

194

around Fergal's shoulders. 'It's good to see you again, fella. I'm only sorry it had to be like this. How are you holding up?'

'It's just so weird – you know, that he's…dead. I don't know how I feel, to be honest.'

'That's to be expected.'

They headed out to the car park. Father Mac ran off into the heavy shower and returned moments later in the car, pulling up beside them with his damp hair stuck to his head. The boot held their bags easily, and Alfredo sat in the back while Fergal automatically sat up front. The windshield wipers struggled as they headed down the motorway. Father Mac kept looking over at Fergal every few seconds, saying, 'I just can't believe how much you've changed. You're a big man now.' He noticed, too, that Fergal's accent had been eroded around the edges into a softer, slower and more confident rhythm.

They were stopped at a checkpoint, and although Father Mac did his best to explain the sad situation, they were kept waiting for quite a while: passports had to be checked and the boot had to be searched before they were allowed to go on. 'Welcome back to Belfast, eh?' Fergal said to Alfredo when they were far enough away.

The car went quiet again. 'How did he…?' Fergal asked. 'How exactly did he die?' Father Mac told him. 'Where's he now?'

'He's in the morgue, at the Royal Vic.'

It was well after eleven o'clock at night. St Bridget's House was only partially lit, but once they were settled in the front parlour, the fire didn't take long to wake up again from its premature sleep. Fergal couldn't help wandering over to the piano and touching the keys. He felt as if he had been away for a lifetime. Father Mac had gotten bigger, but St Bridget's House seemed to have gotten smaller, and this made Fergal feel all the more disconnected. He could still hardly believe that he was home to bury his father – and unearth only God knew what.

Mrs Mooney had prepared loaded plates of food before she left, but understandably, no one had much of an appetite. As they tried to eat, they had to move their chairs further and further away from the hearth. The heat filled the room and steam began to rise off their damp jackets, which were stretched ambitiously on the radiators. Father Mac vanished into the kitchen again, this time returning with a jug filled with a strong concoction of whiskey, hot water, lemons, cloves and sugar. Fergal thought of Brendan Fiscetti, and he missed his routine. So much had changed in only twenty-four hours.

The drink had the desired effect – Fergal's mood defrosted enough to loosen his tongue. 'You know, it's so strange to be in Rome one minute and then back here the next – and for my da's wake. The last time I ever saw him was here, you know, upstairs – do you remember, Father? It was after John attacked me. I was recovering, and you were saying mass in the chapel, and Da barged in and told me to stop disgracing the family...some fucking family!'

The two men looked at each other and then at him, not knowing what they should say.

'You know how badly I wished he was dead then?' Fergal's voice shook a little. 'And now he is...but...oh God, I don't know. It's just too weird.'

Father Mac took another sip. 'Fergal, you have every right to have mixed feelings. I can't say I was a fan of the man, especially after the way he treated you, but he's in God's house now, and there are different rules there.' Alfredo nodded in agreement, at a loss for words.

They drank the jug dry, but when Father Mac offered to make another, they refused; they were all exhausted. Fergal was given his old room and Alfredo had the tiny box room, which looked onto the entrance to the hospital. Father Mac thought it might be too upsetting for Fergal to sleep there. He hugged Fergal more tightly than ever as they said goodnight.

For the two older men, the hot whiskey did the trick – they fell asleep not long after their heads hit their respective pillows. Fergal, however, lay awake for hours. Now that it was dark and he could be truthful with himself, he felt lonely and a bit scared. Pictures of his father's face floated in his mind's eye, and their last bitter, angry exchange replayed itself in his memory, growing more distorted each time. It struck him that he would never hear his father speak badly of him again, and he felt relieved – and, at the same time, desperately sad. He knew his poor mother had spent her hardest years being married to that man, but he also knew she had loved him, in her own way. Fergal wondered why it was easier to work things out at night, in the pitch black of his room. He decided it was because of confession. He'd grown up learning to tell the truth and shame the devil in little dark boxes, so it made sense that truth would come to him more easily when he was in the dark, surrounded by four walls.

There was a loud creaking sound on the landing, and for a second Fergal thought it was Dermot, unable to stay away from his kisses and his heat. More than anything, he wanted to be in someone's arms, but he wanted Dermot to make the first move. He lay still, not breathing, but it was only the house finding a more comfortable position for the night. He stayed where he was, under the blankets, making do with the embrace of the past, until sleep finally won.

As Fergal was on his way to the bathroom the next morning, Mrs Mooney popped her head out of the sitting room door. When she saw him on the landing, she crumpled her dishcloth against her chest. 'Holy Mary, Mother of God – Fergal? I would never have recognised you in a month of Sundays! What have they done to you?

I'm so sorry to hear about your daddy, son.'

Fergal ran down the stairs and she tried to put her arms around him, but her head only reached his chest. 'Thanks, Mrs Mooney,' he said. 'That's very kind. At least you recognised me – not like Father Mac.'

'I'm not surprised he didn't, son. What do they feed you on over there? Fergal Flynn, it's a pure miracle, that's what it is. You put me in mind of the time Father MacManus arrived here from the missions in Africa – do you remember how dark his skin was? And you've got so tall, too.'

'Thanks, Mrs Mooney. The Italians certainly know how to eat.'

'Ah, I'm sorry it's not for a better reason that you're back, son. You must've got an awful shock. You speak so lovely, too. Your own mother wouldn't know you, I'd say.'

'I haven't seen her yet,' Fergal said, with a flutter of nerves in his stomach. 'I'd better get dressed.'

As he finished getting ready, Alfredo appeared at his door. 'How are you feeling?' he asked.

The question was getting on Fergal's nerves already. 'I'm okay. Did you sleep all right? That bed is very small.'

'Oh, it was fine. Don't worry about me. I could sleep standing up!' Alfredo had been all but crippled by the sponge of a mattress. He looked at Fergal intently and cleared his throat. 'Fergal, forgive me for prying at a time like this – and tell me to be quiet if you choose – but what did you mean when you said last night that the last time you saw your father you were recovering from your brother John's attack?'

Fergal looked at his teacher and realised he had to tell him. He sat down on the edge of the bed and took a deep breath, as if he were about to dive under water for as long as he could bear it. That was what the past felt like – a place where he couldn't breathe.

By the time he'd finished telling the story, Alfredo couldn't find a single word. He gently reached across, steered Fergal's head to the hollow of his neck and hugged him. Finally he said softly, stroking the back of his head, 'It is a miracle, Fergal – *you* are a miracle. No wonder you've been so impenetrable. You know that I'm here for you, don't you? We will keep you safe. Don't worry.'

Fergal wanted to cry, but the tears wouldn't come. He and Alfredo sat there, not moving, until they heard Father Mac calling them for breakfast.

Mrs Mooney had fried spectacular amounts of bacon and eggs, and they made decent inroads on them. She had even remembered to buy coffee, for which Alfredo went out of his way to thank her. He hated the instant granules, but he was too well-mannered to say so, and he drank two revolting cups in a row.

'Your father's body will arrive at Walker Street this afternoon for the wake,' Father Mac said gently. 'Then he'll be transferred here, to St Bridget's Church, for the service tomorrow morning. He'll be buried at Milltown tomorrow afternoon.'

'My God,' Fergal said, dazed. 'It's all so quick.'

'That can be a good thing. Do you want to go to the wake or not?'

Fergal took a deep breath. 'I have to see them sometime.'

'Yes, I suppose you do. What about your mother? How about trying to see her first, at her sister's?'

'Okay.'

Angela's sister Jeannie answered the door, and Alfredo and Father Mac waited downstairs as she brought her nephew upstairs to see his mother. The whole house looked as if a bomb had hit it. They had to step carefully over the toys and clothes strewn across every surface.

Jeannie opened the bedroom door and there was Angela, curled up like a stray kitten under the blankets, half drowned in medication and brandy and the shock of her sudden widowhood. The room was half-lit and Fergal was dressed in black. 'Are you new to the parish, Father? ' Angela murmured weakly.

'Angela, Jesus,' Jeannie broke in, 'do you not know your own son? It's Fergal, back from Rome!'

Angela shook her head and fished for her glasses. It was all Fergal could do not to cry – she looked so much like Granny Noreen. 'Fergal? Is that really you?'

She began to cry uncontrollably, and when he went to her she clung to him like a wee girl. 'Fergal, what am I going to do? Your da's gone, and he was only young. I know he was a handful, but… What am I going to do?'

Jeannie tutted loudly. 'A handful? That bastard gave you a right few handfuls over the years, Angela. The number of black eyes you had to cover up because of that cunt!'

'Stop it, Jeannie. Stop it.'

'Yes, Jeannie,' Fergal said firmly, 'stop it, will you? Now's not the time. Mammy, it's all right. Everything will be all right.'

Jeannie sniffed. 'Oh, listen to fucking snooty-voice! What would you know, Fergal? You fucked off as quick as you could! Mind you, I wish more of us had your bloody sense. Look at you – you look fucking loaded. I hope you brought money home for your poor ma.'

Fergal got angry. 'I'm only in the door! And what do I *know*? I know plenty, Jeannie! I used to live there, remember?'

Jeannie went quiet. 'Would you ever make me a cup of tea?' Angela asked her.

Jeannie shrugged. 'Okay, but there's two priests downstairs and I've nothing to give them but toast. I've to go and get my family allowance. Are you coming down?'

Fergal was beginning to calm down again. 'Actually, there's only one priest – you know Father Mac, Mammy? The other fella is my vocal coach from Italy.'

'Vocal coach!' Jeannie mouthed behind his back, making a face as she left the room.

Fergal hadn't a clue what to say to his mother. He was shocked at how much smaller she seemed to have become.

'Jesus, Fergal, we got an awful shock yesterday. The police came to the door, and I thought it was one of your brothers in trouble. I never dreamed your da would be dead.'

'I know. It's hard to believe.'

'Let me look at you properly.'

He got off the side of the bed and stood up, his head almost touching the ceiling of the small room.

Angela blessed herself. 'You're not the same fella that went away.'

'I know, Mammy. I know.' It was the first time she had ever said anything that made him feel good about himself.

Father MacManus appeared at the door – he had heard the raised voices from downstairs – and they both were glad to see him. 'The funeral's all arranged, Mrs Flynn.'

'Father, I don't know how we're going to even start to pay for it all. I've a bit put by in the credit union, but I'm not sure—'

'It'll be grand, Mrs Flynn. Don't worry.' Father Mac was well used to these conversations. Fergal was mortified. He wished he were as loaded as Jeannie thought, just so he could pay for the funeral. He hated the fact that, even in death, his father had managed to make his mother worry.

'I had to go to the morgue and identify his body,' Angela murmured. 'I thought I was going to fall down dead beside him. It was horrible. His poor oul' face was all twisted from the heart attack, all big and purple...I hardly recognised him. Oh, Jesus and his holy mother, him stuck in an oul' fridge like bloody Frankenstein – he always hated being cold. They might have to keep the coffin closed at the wake; that's what the wee doctor said.' Her voice trailed off and she lay back on the pillows, exhausted.

Jeannie reappeared with the tea. 'The twins are after ringing,' she told Angela. 'They'll be over at Walker Street in an hour, to meet the hearse.'

'John and Paddy live up the road now, with a few of their mates,' Angela told Fergal and Father Mac carefully. 'They were over last night to get the house ready, with Jeannie.'

Jeannie held her tongue because the priest was in the room. What she wanted to say was that she had done all the cleaning, while Paddy and John and Ciaran drank a bottle of whiskey they had found at the back of a cupboard.

'Will you sing at the service, our Fergal?' Angela asked.

It was the very last thing he felt like doing, but all he could say was, 'Yes...yes, of course.'

As he was leaving, she said feebly, 'I'm glad you're home, son.'

'Thanks, Mammy.'

Fergal almost lost it at that point.

They drove over to Walker Street after the early evening mass. Alfredo was mute for most of the journey, trying to take it all in, but he was genuinely scared when he saw the policemen with their rifles on the corner. As they parked outside the house where he had grown up, Fergal suddenly felt ashamed and embarrassed. Alfredo was about to see just where he came from and how different it was from the mansion in Rome. Experience told him that Alfredo wouldn't care – he had a bigger heart than that – but still, Fergal blushed scarlet through his tan as they got out of the car.

There was a large black ribbon tied in a bow on the front door. Fergal realised he hadn't seen his brothers in almost two years, since he'd moved into St Bridget's House. The old dread suddenly reappeared, and he looked at Father Mac for reassurance. 'I'll be beside you the whole time,' Father Mac murmured.

When Fergal walked through the front door, he was again struck by how small everything was. He hadn't had time to get used to the fact that he had outgrown his past. The tiny room where he'd spent so much of his childhood was packed full of people, most of whom he didn't recognise, but they parted a little when they saw that the Church had arrived. There, in front of the unlit gas fire, was the body of Patrick Flynn, stretched out in his coffin. To their surprise, the lid was open after all, and Fergal looked into his dead father's face.

Somehow the morticians had managed to smooth away the expression that Angela had described, and Paddy Flynn looked like he was sleeping. The make-up made Fergal catch his breath; it was almost exactly the same shade that Brendan Fiscetti wore at the Teatro. Fergal could hardly take it in. This man had repeatedly beaten him and finally disowned him for being too 'girly', and yet here he was, lying in his coffin with his Sunday suit on and his face covered in foundation. There was even a slight touch of blusher, to give his cheeks a bit of healthy colour. It was so perverse that Fergal wanted to laugh out loud.

At that moment, he heard the unmistakable voice of his brother John. 'Hello, Father MacManus. Would you like a drink, or a cup of tea? Will the other priests take something?'

Fergal turned around and looked John in the eye. He couldn't believe it – he'd outgrown him by a good few inches. John's eyes widened, but all he said was 'Fuck' before two old women scolded him for using that language in the presence of the dead.

His twin, Paddy, came in behind him with a tray of sandwiches, followed by their youngest brother, Ciaran, who had obviously been crying, with another pot of tea. John backed towards them instinctively. 'Look at the state of our Fergal,' he said. 'He's turned into a nigger.' A few of the older women gasped and blessed themselves.

'That's enough of that talk, John Flynn. God rest your poor father,' Father Mac said calmly but firmly, with an arm around Fergal's shoulders.

Now that Alfredo knew Fergal's history, he had been expecting to see two great hulks of men, but the twins were more like their father's people, wiry and small. Alfredo introduced himself, to get a better look at them. The twins' girlfriends, who also happened to be sisters, nudged each other and stood up, smoothing their black mini-skirts, to say hello, but John shot his girlfriend a withering furnace of a look and she sat down again, telling Fergal she was sorry for his trouble. Fergal already felt sorry for hers.

Paddy uncomfortably nodded recognition to Fergal. 'When did you get here?'

'Late last night.'

Paddy had already assumed the position of man of the house, and when he felt that John was about to say something sarcastic again, he shot him a glare that made him keep his mouth shut. 'Have you seen Mammy?'

'I have.'

Paddy didn't know what else to say. He went back to handing out sandwiches, but he glanced over at Fergal when he was sure he wasn't looking back. He couldn't get over Fergal's tan and how fit he seemed. It was ironic, Paddy thought – Fergal had turned out to be the tallest of them all.

Ciaran nodded to Alfredo, looking confused, and smiled tentatively at Fergal. 'Do you want a cup of tea?' he asked. Fergal wanted to cry then and there. How the tables had turned.

'What's Rome like?' Ciaran asked.

'It's brilliant,' Fergal told him. 'You look well, Ciaran.'

'So do you. What happened to your accent?'

'Ach, I dunno. It just happens when you live in another country, I suppose.'

John, who was keeping well away from Fergal, called over, 'Ciaran, we need more tea. Come on into the kitchen with me.' Fergal was glad that Ciaran had tried to be friendly, but it was clear that John had no such intentions.

Father Mac announced to the room that the memorial service would be at ten o'clock the following morning at St Bridget's Church, and then the remains would be taken to the cemetery before lunch. Someone started a round of prayers. When that ended, Father Mac took Fergal by the arm and guided him back out the door and into the street.

When they were safely in the car on the way back to St Bridget's, Alfredo asked, 'Are you all right?

Fergal nodded.

'Are you sure you're related to the twins, Fergal? You look nothing like them, nor even like the youngest one.'

'I know. I'm more like my grandfather, apparently.'

'Well, forgive me for saying this, but thank heavens for that.'

Father Mac stopped at the chip shop and bought three fish suppers, and when they got back to the parish house Mrs Mooney buttered an entire white pan loaf and made pots of tea before she left them to it. Fergal could see why Father Mac had expanded to the size he was – he and Alfredo swallowed four chip-packed sandwiches each in addition to the enormous battered fish without even breaking a sweat. The chip sandwiches did taste gorgeous, but after a couple Fergal felt as if he had eaten a brick.

On and on the rain fell. They tried watching a bit of TV, but the news was as depressing as ever, so they switched it off. Fergal's emotions were all over the place. One minute he was trying to make jokes, and the next he wanted to cry like a baby and be held tightly. He wanted to go back and talk to his mother, but he knew that his brothers would be around, so he thought better of it.

'Have you thought about what you're going to sing at the service?' Father Mac asked.

Fergal hadn't forgotten his promise to his mother, but he still felt resentful. His father had never come to hear him sing.

'If you don't feel up to it,' Father Mac reminded him, 'nobody could fail to understand.'

All of a sudden, Fergal was angry. 'I promised my mother,' he said forcefully, 'so that's that.' Angela had snuck into his fundraiser concert to stand at the back and listen, all those months ago. He would sing for her.

'An Irish song, perhaps?' Alfredo suggested calmly. 'Instead of something religious?'

Father Mac and Fergal looked at each other and said, in unison, '"Danny Boy."' Once they agreed on a key, it was settled.

Alfredo yawned and asked if anyone minded him having an early night. Although he had no idea just how well Fergal and Father Mac knew each other, he realised that it was important for Fergal to have some time alone with his old friend. Fergal was secretly delighted. Alfredo drained his glass and climbed the stairs, and they were finally alone. The temperature in the room seemed to rise.

Suddenly Fergal felt overwhelmed. He needed a moment by himself, to clear his head. 'Dermot, can I go and have a quick shower?'

'Yes, of course. You must be exhausted too. Do you want to have an early night as well?'

'No, I don't think I'd sleep at all if I went to bed now. Will you open that bottle of wine? I'll be down in ten minutes.'

'If you're sure.'

'Yeah, I'm sure.'

Under the water of the shower, Fergal reran the mental footage of his fleeting visit to his father's wake. There were two things that stood out – his father had been stretched out wearing make-up for the whole street to see, and John had backed away from him, where Fergal had always been the one to shrink away from his older brother's fury. As he dried himself, he thought about his mother and how she would cope without a husband. He wondered whether some part of her was glad, or whether it was too early – or even too late – for that. Then he thought about Father Mac, waiting downstairs.

Fergal pulled on his shorts and Father Mac's old bathrobe. When he re-entered the parlour, he saw that Father Mac had taken his collar off and was sipping the red wine. Fergal sat on the sofa and stretched, rubbing his hair with the towel in front of the roaring fire. He took a few sips of wine, then boldly undid his robe and stood up, letting it drop to the floor, leaving him in only his underwear.

Father Mac was doing his best not to stare, but as Fergal dried himself more thoroughly, Father Mac couldn't help noticing that his body had lost its Belfast pastiness and that his chest and shoulders were muscular where once they had been softer and less defined. His chest hair had grown and darkened. A thick trail of it led down across his stomach and into his shorts…Father Mac dry-swallowed in quiet panic.

Fergal smiled in the way that Father Mac had never been able to resist, but when he moved towards him, the priest felt rooted to the spot. It was as if he was seeing Fergal for the first time, and in a way, he was – he was seeing this new, more confident Fergal, who was more beautiful than ever. Out of nowhere, tears began to fill his eyes. He turned quickly away, lifting his hand to try and stop them, but it was too late.

Fergal's eyes widened. 'Dermot, what's wrong? What's the matter?'

Father Mac kept his back to him, trying to gather his thoughts. 'Oh Fergal, I don't know. I'm not sure if I can even find the right words. I'm a bit overwhelmed, I think.'

'What do you mean?'

'I can't tell you how many times I…well, how many times I pictured this moment, when we would see each other again.'

'I know. Me too…me too.'

'I never imagined that it would take your father's death to bring you back. Do you know how many nights I wished you were here, at St Bridget's, even though I knew it was the last place you should be? I missed you more than I thought I could miss anyone, but…I coped, you know? I learned to cope. What we had was…well, it was rare enough, and I knew it couldn't last. That's why it was so incredible. Neither of us was the same person after we met. Do you understand?'

'I think so.'

At last Father Mac turned back to him. 'Fergal, look at you! Do you see yourself the way I see you now? I don't suppose that's possible. I see a transformation that takes my breath away. Your accent, even – I still hear Belfast, of course, but it's a Belfast after a storm has washed every inch of the city and it gleams like it was always meant to. You know what I'm saying, don't you?'

'But Dermot, why are you crying?'

'I'm crying because…because we got you out in time. I see so many young people from my window, and indeed from the altar, and it's too late for them. I can't help them. Sometimes it just gets to me. I'm so glad that Brother Vincent, Alfredo and I – and your hard work, and your voice – managed to propel you to this point in your life. Fergal, just looking at you makes my heart want to burst. I can't wait to hear you sing again.'

They hugged each other as closely as they could. Smelling Father Mac again at such close range was enough to make Fergal braver, and he bent his head to kiss his neck gently, remembering the bedroom upstairs where Father Mac had taught him what love really was. He could feel himself hardening as they pressed against each other, and slowly he began to kiss his way down Father Mac's neck. Father Mac gasped and moaned in momentary defeat. Fergal opened the buttons of his shirt and kissed his way down to his chest.

'No, Fergal – stop. Don't…please don't.'

They both froze. Fergal tried to kiss him again, but Father Mac grabbed him by the arm and started doing up his shirt buttons with a shaking hand.

'But Dermot, I thought—'

'Fergal, please. It's taking all my willpower to do the right thing here.'

'What do you mean?'

'I meant what I said in that letter. I really did. I thought you would understand.'

Fergal was suddenly embarrassed. Father Mac was still fully clothed, and his own erection was poking out of his shorts. He reached for the dressing gown and pulled it on again, in a huff. 'I *don't* understand. I thought you…oh, forget it.'

'What, Fergal? You thought I what?'

Fergal lowered his voice. 'I thought you loved me. You said it enough times.'

'Fergal, it's precisely because I love you so much that we need this…this barricade. No, that's a bad choice of word, Lord knows we've seen enough barricades around here. I mean a boundary, I suppose. A line we mustn't cross again.'

'But Dermot—'

'"But Dermot" nothing, Fergal. We're not going back – only forward. Look at how you've changed.'

'I haven't changed how I feel about you, Dermot. I haven't.'

'Fergal, I don't want to argue with you. You're tired and upset. Your father is lying dead over in Walker Street. He'll be delivered to the chapel in the morning, just a few feet from here.'

It was enough to kill the moment stone-dead, but Fergal was angry. 'My fucking father...' His eyes filled up and he turned away from Father Mac, embarrassed.

'Fergal, it's okay. It's good to cry.'

Suddenly Fergal thought of Riccardo in the bathroom at Moretti's, of Sofia in front of the fire...He shook his head to get rid of the images. 'Dermot, what am I supposed to do with how I feel?'

'I'm not asking you to do anything. You know how much I treasure our past, but that's just what it is – the past. I told you that on that phone, too.'

The tears in Fergal's eyes spilled over. Father Mac's voice wobbled badly as he tried to comfort him. 'Ah, now, come on, Fergal, please. You'll break my heart.'

Fergal felt completely stupid. He instantly regretted trying to make a move on Father Mac so soon, but being back at Walker Street had made him feel lonelier than ever, and it had been so long since they had seen each other, he hadn't been able to help himself. He cursed himself for not waiting a bit longer. *Nice one, you idiot,* he thought. *What are you, some kind of bloody nympho?*

'I'm all right,' he said at last. 'I understand. I'm fine.'

Father Mac cleared his throat. 'Fergal, we should both really go to bed.'

'Okay,' Fergal said. 'See you in the morning.'

18

The next morning, the Belfast sky pretended it was going to be a better day, like a child promising to be good for the babysitter, but as the funeral service drew nearer, uninvited clouds gathered and the rain poured down relentlessly. Mrs Mooney had arrived early and cooked yet another gigantic breakfast. The house was so busy that there was no time for Fergal and Father Mac to be awkward with each other. From the seclusion of the upstairs window, Fergal was able to watch people arriving through the chapel gates. He hoped that his mother would arrive with no one but Jeannie so he could invite her into the parlour, but his stomach knotted when he saw his three brothers and their girlfriends flanking Angela on her way into the chapel.

At five minutes to ten, Alfredo accompanied Fergal into the chapel. The coffin was decorated with a wreath from the local GAA and someone was playing the organ, very badly, from the gallery. Fergal thought it was ironic – his da had always occupied one of the furthest stalls at the back of the chapel, leaving at Holy

Communion most of the time, and now he was centre stage, right at the front, facing the altar. He and Alfredo sat opposite the row reserved for the immediate family. He managed to catch his mother's eye and gave her a little wave, but she barely reacted. He could see that Jeannie had made sure she was on another planet. Suddenly Fergal wanted to be back in Rome, practising his Italian or working at Moretti's. He felt as if he had accidentally stumbled into somebody else's life.

It was time for the readings. His brother Paddy squeezed past the row of mourners and read the gospel in a nervous monotone. Fergal noticed, now that he got a better look, that Paddy too had a swollen belly and a few double chins. John stared straight ahead, though Ciaran managed a weak smile when Fergal glanced over again.

Father Mac suspended his disapproval where Patrick Flynn Sr was concerned. He talked about how Paddy had been a sporting man, much revered by his old teammates, but when he looked down at Fergal he couldn't say much more. He finished by saying, 'Patrick Flynn is survived by his loving wife Angela and their four sons, Paddy Jr, John, Ciaran and Fergal, who has flown all the way from Rome to be with us today.' Fergal felt light-headed. He looked over at his family again and met his mother's vacant eyes, partially framed by her black widow's mantilla.

When Father Mac announced Communion, it was Fergal's cue to sing. As he walked past his father's coffin, he let his hand rest on it for a brief second. Then he took his position on the altar while a few people formed an orderly queue in the aisle.

Fergal's heart was pounding in his chest. When he looked at what was left of his family, he saw that the twins were leaning against their girlfriends and staring into space. Even Ciaran's girlfriend was holding his hand and rubbing his arm gently. Jeannie had her arm around Angela, but she seemed lost to the world.

All of the people who had ever hurt him were right in front of him, like some kind of judge and jury, and for a second he was afraid that he wasn't going to be able to get through the song. The first few words left his mouth like birds that had been trapped in a cage for a long time, suspicious of their sudden freedom. Then Fergal closed his eyes and sang from the deepest place he could find.

When he got to the second verse, he couldn't help opening his eyes and looking directly at the coffin.

And if you come, and all the flowers are dying,
And I am dead, as dead I well may be,
You'll come and find the place where I am lying
And kneel and say an Ave there for me.
And I shall hear, though soft you tread above me,
And all my grave will warmer, sweeter be,
For you will bend and tell me that you love me,
And I shall sleep in peace until you come to me.

When he finished holding the last, longest note, a few people in the congregation forgot where they were and started clapping. Father Mac was wiping his eyes with an overstarched cloth, and Alfredo was even worse – he had his head in his hands when Fergal went to take his seat, and he spent the last bit of the service rubbing Fergal's shoulders in appreciation and drying his own eyes on his sleeve.

Something powerful had happened to Fergal in that moment; perhaps the most difficult moment of his life. For the first time, he was no longer afraid of his family. He thought of his poor father and realised that he had spent his whole life in a kind of box. All Fergal could do was feel sorry for him; he suddenly seemed like a lost child. Fergal let a single tear fall down his cheek.

The mass came to an end, and Fergal waited in his seat as the congregation filed out. It was customary for the women to stay behind until the men were ready to carry the coffin along the main road on their shoulders, so Angela was still in her seat with Jeannie. But when Fergal went to hug her, she was so doped up with Valium that she could hardly respond. 'Father...' she said, looking into his eyes.

Jeannie blessed herself repeatedly. 'That's Fergal, Angela!'

His mother looked around, getting more and more distressed. 'Fergal – our Fergal? Where?'

'Mammy, it's me. Right in front of you.'

She looked at him, doing her best to focus without her glasses, and eventually she saw traces of her child. She started to weep. 'His mother ruined him and his father beat him because he hated him so much. How could he help himself? Sure, it was all he knew...'

Fergal thought for a second that she was talking about him, but then he realised she meant her husband. He got a glimpse of a part of his father he had never known, but then it was gone and Angela was incoherent again, thanks to Jeannie's well-meaning intervention.

Fergal and Alfredo accompanied his mother and aunt as they walked the length of the Falls Road. The coffin-bearers were relieved every few hundred yards by four fresh shoulders, and soon enough he and Alfredo ended up taking a corner each, with the milkman and one of Paddy Flynn's old friends. Fergal wanted to avoid any drama at all costs, so he made sure that he kept one eye on John. The rain seemed to fall harder and harder as they got closer to the graveyard gates, and the hearse took over the rest of Patrick Flynn's final, muck-logged journey to the deeply dug grave.

Father Mac prayed loudly as the gravediggers, struggling to keep their balance, lowered the coffin on ropes into the watery darkness. Angela slumped against Jeannie, heaving soundlessly with sobs under her umbrella. Fergal's brothers held onto their girlfriends, and it was difficult to tell rain from tears on their drenched faces. Alfredo tried to shield Fergal with an umbrella, but a gust of wind that had been playing hide-and-seek amongst the graves turned it inside out and sent it flying, carrying it like an empty crisp bag towards the motorway in the distance.

Father Mac invited Mrs Flynn forward to throw the first fistful of dirt onto her husband's coffin. At the edge of the grave, she lost her balance and nearly fell in. Fergal gave Jeannie a filthy look for doping her so much, and she dropped her guilty gaze. One by one, the Flynn boys dropped handfuls of earth onto their father's coffin. Then the gravediggers filled in the hole as Father Mac finished the prayers, and the mourners practically ran back to the few cars that were parked nearby.

Fergal wasn't sure what to do next. His mother was whisked away to Walker Street, where there would be tea and sandwiches and no doubt far too much whiskey, but Father Mac advised him not to attend, knowing what his brother John was capable of even when he wasn't under the influence. 'Instead, I think you should invite your mother over to St Bridget's before you decide when you want to go back to Rome.'

There was a part of Fergal that would have gladly gone to the airport that very second, but he knew he wanted to see his mother first. And, before anything else, he wanted to visit his Granny Noreen's grave.

When they found it, Fergal knelt down on the ground and blessed himself, rain saturating his back. Father Mac and Alfredo huddled a respectful distance away under the priest's umbrella, hoping he wouldn't be too long.

Fergal looked at the gravestone and whispered, 'Granny, it's me, Fergal. I told you I'd come back. Mammy's in an awful state now Da is dead. I thought about you when I sang "Danny Boy" – I know you love that one. I'm going back to Rome. I'm doing okay, but I could do better. I didn't do that well in my first exam, but that's going to change. I'll make you proud. I promise, Granny, I will. I miss you. See you.'

He blew her a kiss and joined the two men, and they found Father Mac's car and headed back to the warmth of St Bridget's.

The three of them were soaked to the skin. They had to peel their clothes off in their rooms, wrap themselves in sheets and towels and take turns in the shower. Mrs Mooney had made loads of coffee and toast, and they practically sat on top of the fire to get warm.

Fergal still couldn't cry properly. He felt under pressure, as if Father Mac and Alfredo were waiting for him to break down properly. Although he had come close when he sang on the altar, he realised it was because he was relieved that his father was dead. It was an awful thing to admit, but it was true. Fergal wondered if he and his father would ever have been able to be friendly, when a few more years had taken a few layers off each of them. Slowly, the sadness of the question began to dog him, because he would never find out the answer. One thing was sure, though – he wasn't going to give up on his mother.

'I only wish Signore Arnelli had been in the chapel to hear you sing today,' Alfredo said. 'Fergal, I know your father was buried today, but I must tell you – your performance on the altar was the bravest I've ever seen. It had exactly the kind of feeling I've been talking about. It was exceptional, truly. Your heart was so open.'

'I agree,' Father Mac said, drying his thinning hair with a towel. 'Do you need anything, Fergal?'

All Fergal wanted at that moment was to be under the blankets with him, like the old times, but instead he said, 'Ah, no. I feel a bit numb from it all. I just have to work out the best way to see my mother. It would be good to see her, at least once, when she wasn't out of her head on Valium.'

'At least the worst part is over,' Alfredo said. 'In years to come, you'll be glad that you were present when they buried your father.' He looked at Fergal for an intense second and said, 'Fergal, forgive me for interfering, but it seems almost impossible for you to see your mother safely here. So why don't you invite her to visit us in Rome, at my house – maybe for a long weekend or something like that? I'm sure she could do with a change of pace and scenery. I have a friend at a travel agent's, and it would cost very little, I can assure you.'

Fergal's eyes filled up at his thoughtfulness. 'Oh Alfredo, thanks for even thinking of it! But I'm not sure she'd come – and you've been so good already…'

'Nonsense. This is the time when your friends come together. You should at least ask her.'

Father Mac chipped in, 'Yes, Fergal, ask her. At the very least, I'm sure she'd appreciate the thought.'

'I will. But I'm not sure where she is. She might be at Jeannie's, but I don't want to go there in case, you know, John and everyone are there. They'll have been drinking for the past couple of days, and it'll be a nightmare.'

The chapel bells sounded the half-hour, and Father Mac had to leave for an hour or so to meet some parishioners before that evening's service. When Fergal climbed the stairs to the toilet, Father Mac asked Alfredo to keep a close eye on Fergal and to dissuade him from going out if he could.

They needn't have worried. Ever since Fergal had hurried back to Belfast, he'd been afraid that his hometown had some kind of paralysing power over him, that he would never be able to leave again. But as he sat in the bathroom on the closed toilet seat, he felt as if he was beginning to shed a layer of skin, like a snake, leaving a perfect, hollow shape of his previous self behind.

It was his mother he was most anxious about. After everything they'd been through, he felt responsible for her, and he wondered how she would cope. It had come as a shock to see how small she was. He wondered why he'd been so afraid of her for years. It made him want to laugh – and cry. He breathed in and out deeply, and he vowed to help his mother as much as he could.

He thought about his father's lifeless body, buried under the earth, and all he could feel was pity. His father would never see him sing, would never come and visit him at Alfredo's amazing house in Rome and hear Brendan Fiscetti sing in the Teatro…At that moment, Fergal wanted to see Brendan Fiscetti more than anything, just to sit and drink tea and have someone talk to him like he was a human being, not the piece of dirt his father had always treated him as.

The dammed-up tears came crashing down, flooding his face. He wept so loudly that Alfredo heard him and came to the bathroom door, calling for him to open it. At first Fergal wouldn't let him in.

'Fergal, don't be so unwilling to accept help. This is exactly what I'm talking about in my lessons with you. I know you had to learn to rely on no one, but you must stop pushing people away. You're allowed to fall apart. In fact, it's vitally important for your soul. How else do we learn to put ourselves back together? Let me in, please.'

When the door was unlatched, Alfredo held him without saying another word. Fergal's whole body shook as if he were being electrocuted. He cried and cried, and Alfredo unconsciously rocked him from side to side like a baby as wave after wave of grief soaked his face.

At last the tide of tears began to subside. Fergal felt light-headed, out of breath and suddenly embarrassed again, but Alfredo rubbed the side of his head, as if to remind him there was no need to feel anything other than relief, and said that he'd go and make some tea.

He turned at the top of the stairs as Fergal began to wash his face. 'Fergal Flynn, I am proud to know you. Come down when you're ready.'

19

After the evening mass, Father Mac was in a hurry to get back to his visitors. The last person he expected to see was Angela Flynn, waiting by the sacristy door, smoking. When she saw him she stubbed out the cigarette against the wall like a teenager caught by her daddy.

'Father, I'm sorry to bother you. My sister thinks I'm asleep up her stairs, but I snuck out when she went to the shop for more drink. They've all had a skinful, they won't even notice I'm gone for ages.'

'Mrs Flynn, my goodness! Come over to the house. Fergal wanted to see you – he was only talking to me about it earlier – but he wasn't sure where you were.'

'Oh…right. Well, I took a few wee tablets to help me sleep, you see, so I wasn't myself. This whole thing's been like one long nightmare. Where is he now?'

'He's at my house, with Alfredo. Please come in.'

Father Mac left her in the front room and found her son lying down upstairs. He could see that Fergal looked exhausted.

'Fergal, your mother's downstairs. She just showed up at the church on her own. I hope I've done the right thing?'

'Of course – of course…'

'Have you been crying?'

'I have, but I feel much better for it.'

Fergal pushed his feet into his shoes and followed Father Mac down the stairs. Angela was sitting by the fire, smoking a fresh cigarette and rubbing her hands. She turned around in her seat when the door clicked open.

'Fergal! Jesus, I keep thinking you're going to look like you did before you left, but you don't.'

'Mammy, what has you out? I thought you'd be resting, that's why I didn't come to Jeannie's. Are you all right?'

He wanted to kick himself, because he knew she wasn't all right. He sat beside her, and her eyes filled up.

'Jesus, Fergal, you're the image of my daddy, so you are.'

'Am I?'

'The photos from the day he married your granny. You even have the short haircut he always liked. Mind you, your skin is darker.'

Alfredo, coming slowly downstairs from the box room – the cold and the rain made his bad leg even stiffer – was taken aback to see Angela in the front room, but he was as warm as ever. Then he and Father Mac retreated to the kitchen, where they took longer than usual to make tea.

Silence fell between Angela and Fergal, and he felt a little helpless. She looked so tiny next to him, and she rarely took her eyes off the fire.

He took a deep breath and said, 'Mammy, I was talking to Alfredo, and we want you to think about coming to Rome soon – you know, for a wee break. Sure, it would do you good.'

Fergal's old accent resurfaced just enough for her to hear the kindness in his voice. 'Ah, Fergal, I don't know. Sure, the boys need me. I know they'll be married and all soon enough, if them girlfriends have anything to do with it, but they're still my boys. Your brothers have taken your daddy's death very badly – sure, we all have.'

All of a sudden, Fergal felt furious with her. 'For God's sake, Mammy, would you think about yourself for once? Just once? I want you to come to Rome and stay at Alfredo's gorgeous house for a weekend or something, that's all. The plane journey is quicker than you think. Surely my brothers can cope for a few days without you? Look, I know Da has just been buried and all, but you need a holiday or something! You look exhausted.'

It was true – Angela didn't know how to think about herself first. Women of her generation seldom had the chance to learn.

Father Mac and Alfredo braved the front room again with a tray of tea and biscuits, and it seemed to revive Angela. She took little sugary sips and began to warm to the idea of a wee trip away. Alfredo chose his moment and invited her officially. She looked at him and then at Father Mac, saying, 'Sure, I don't even have a passport or nothing.'

Father Mac leaned towards her. 'I seem to remember you helping Fergal with his first passport, so the least we can do is help you get yours. It won't be a problem, I promise – just a few forms, and I'll help you with those.'

All Angela could do was try her best to smile. It was the first time that Fergal had ever felt he'd been able to do something really good for her.

'You are welcome to visit as soon as you like,' Alfredo said, 'once we have got back home and settled into our routine of work.'

'When are you going back, Fergal?' Angela asked.

Fergal looked at Alfredo and said, 'Well, nothing's been booked, but now you've agreed to come over, I think we might fly back as soon as we can get a flight. Then you should try and visit as soon as you feel up to it.'

Father Mac added that he'd be calling over to see her soon, to start the ball rolling with her passport forms. She looked genuinely relieved.

Angela wanted to ask Fergal if he was going to see any of his brothers, but she remembered waking up at Jeannie's, out of her Valium stupor, and hearing John and his girlfriend arguing downstairs. His girlfriend was saying that he should have at least talked to Fergal, seeing as he'd travelled all the way from Rome and given the day that was in it, but John had flared up drunkenly: 'Fuck him and his fucking gay tan. He's lucky I didn't stick one on him.' So Angela wisely decided to leave things as tightly wound as they were. As John had got older, he had got more and more like her late husband, and she had grown afraid of him too.

She looked at the clock. 'I've to go back to Jeannie's before they send out a search party.' She stood up, and Fergal towered above her when they hugged awkwardly. She felt like a little girl to him. He repeated that she was to come to Rome as soon as she could.

Father Mac insisted on driving Angela back over to Jeannie's; he wouldn't take no for an answer. When they were gone, Alfredo looked at Fergal and saw some of the old bad weather resurfacing in his eyes.

'Don't worry, Fergal, everything will get better. I'm sure it will. Your mother really appreciated the invitation.'

'I hope so. I just want to do the best I can, you know? I don't want to fail again.'

'What do you mean?'

'You know…the exam.'

'Fergal, for goodness' sake! Put it out of your head. We'll get you back to Rome and then make a plan.'

'What do you mean? I always get nervous when you say that.'

'I think it's time you gave a little recital, somewhere special in Rome, with a specially invited audience. Nothing too grand.'

'Really?' Fergal was excited for the first time since the exam.

'It's just that something happens to you when you're in front of an audience – or, indeed, a congregation. It really struck me. You're more – how can I put it? – alive. I'm sorry to put it this way, with your father…'

'No, no, it's okay. But I thought I wasn't nearly ready for that, Alfredo. I don't want to mess it up.'

'Fergal, let's change the subject. I'm sorry. There should be no more pressure on you today. Shall I get us on an early flight back to Rome in the morning, or do you need to stay longer?'

'Ah, no. I want to get back to Rome and my job and my lessons. Please, Alfredo, that would be great, just great.'

Alfredo went straight to the hallway phone, and when he returned ten minutes later their escape was booked.

When Father Mac returned, he told them that Angela was safely back at Jeannie's and that she seemed a little happier, even though it was still early days after such a shock. 'Fergal, that was a great thing you did, inviting her to Rome. She said she's always wanted to go.'

'Has she? God, I never knew.'

'I'd say there's lots of things you might not know about that wee woman.'

It was hard for Fergal to think about Angela as anyone but his mother, and he wished he could have known what she was like when she was younger. He wondered how she truly felt about the prospect of being on her own again.

When Alfredo announced that they were leaving the next morning, Father Mac looked surprised, but he agreed it was probably best. They set about cooking pork chops, baked potatoes and beans for dinner, and the mood seemed to lighten for the first time since Fergal's arrival. Father Mac apologised for the lack of good wine, saying that their local off-licence really only sold spirits and beer. Alfredo excused himself and went to fetch the two bottles of red wine he had packed as a present for Father Mac at the last moment before they'd left for the airport. Father Mac insisted that they drink them immediately. They even managed a dessert of chocolate cake, and then Father Mac suggested they get comfortable in the front room.

Alfredo poured more wine, and Father Mac pulled out the little piano stool and laid one hand on the keys, as if he were touching the undisturbed surface of an early-morning lake. Without thinking, he played the first few bars of a Gershwin song, but when he realised which one it was, he stopped, pretending that he couldn't remember the rest of it.

'What's that song?' Fergal asked. 'It's gorgeous.'

'It's a lovely but profoundly sad song by the famous Gershwin brothers. It's called "Our Love Is Here to Stay". George Gershwin wrote the music, and Ira Gershwin wrote the words. They knew Ira was dying when they wrote it. These were the last words he ever finished, and they were about his brother George. Isn't that beautiful?'

'It is. But Ira's a funny name, isn't it? Is it Italian?'

'Jewish, I think.'

'How do you spell it?'

'Just like it sounds. I-R-A.'

Fergal's old grin found his face again for a second. 'Hey, can you imagine having that on your passport coming from Belfast?'

Father Mac grinned. 'Oh Fergal, only you would think of that!'

He slid off the piano stool and offered it to Alfredo, who pretended he couldn't possibly, all the while putting his drink down and moving to the piano. Father Mac looked at Fergal and

225

said, 'Well, Fergal, seeing as this is such a fleeting visit, you can't leave without one more song for me.'

Fergal couldn't have refused, even if he'd wanted to.

Alfredo played the first few bars of 'Cavalleria Rusticana', and Fergal's eyes widened. 'Alfredo, I don't think I'll be able to remember it.'

'Don't worry,' Alfredo said. 'I'll join in if you lose your way.'

Fergal accepted the challenge. He took a deep breath, and his voice took flight. Father Mac was so moved by how much Fergal had progressed, especially in his pronunciation and command of Italian, that he nearly dropped his glass. When the mournful piece came to a close, Alfredo looked down, head heavy with pride, and Father Mac stood up and clapped. Fergal knew that something new had happened, but he wasn't completely sure what.

'Oh my goodness, Fergal,' Father Mac gasped. 'Either this wine is stronger than I think, or that's the best I've ever heard you sing!'

Alfredo had to agree. He was sure the change had to do with Belfast, Father Mac and, of course, the death of Fergal's father. He quietly thought that this had forced Fergal to confront some things that might otherwise have taken much longer to surface. The results were already impressive. Although Fergal still had work to do, Alfredo could hear that he was singing from a deeper place altogether.

They drank on into the night, until Alfredo finally bade them both goodnight. He badly wanted to lie down, as his leg was beginning to bother him. They made loose arrangements for the morning – they had to order a taxi to the airport because Father Mac was saying early mass – and Alfredo made every stair complain on his way up to bed.

When he was gone, Father Mac reiterated that he was amazed at Fergal's progress. 'Alfredo is like Michelangelo himself. It's like he's gone into your throat and carefully sanded off the rough edges of Belfast and sculpted out even higher notes for you to reach. And your voice has so much more power now, too. You'd never need a microphone if we were back in St Bridget's. Fergal, it's only been a year, but I've never heard you sing better.'

'Thanks, Dermot. That really means a lot.'

They had nearly finished both bottles of wine, but they were enjoying each other's company too much to think about their early start the next morning. Father Mac refilled their glasses. 'I'm also so glad to see how much Alfredo cares about you. It sounds like his sister practically adopted you when you were living at her restaurant.'

'Yeah, they've been so good to me. I can't believe it, really.'

'What do you mean, you can't believe it? I'm not surprised that so many people love you.'

The last sentence hung in the air, and Fergal downed another mouthful of strong wine. 'Dermot, can I ask you something?'

'Anything.'

'It's very personal.'

Father Mac looked worried, but he nodded his head. Fergal lowered his voice.

'Have you met someone else – you know, since I left?'

Father Mac closed his eyes and exhaled as if the question had punctured him. Then he lowered his voice too. 'For goodness' sake, Fergal! Absolutely not!'

'I'm sorry. I was just curious – you know, after your letter and all...'

'I wrote that letter because I came to a decision never to stray into those waters again – with you or anybody else. I told you all that in my letter, and I meant what I said. I'm sorry if you were expecting...you know...'

'No, no. I wasn't.'

'I want to stop talking about this stuff, especially with Alfredo upstairs. The last thing I want to do is make you feel bad, because

I actually feel as close to you as I ever did. Aren't we having fun now, after such a difficult few days?'

'Yes, yes, of course. I just thought that maybe there was someone else, that's all.'

'Well, rest assured, there's not. I've been celibate, and I will remain so. You, however, must promise me that you'll move on. It's been over a year. Surely you've met someone you like?'

Fergal went bright red – he hadn't bargained for his question being thrown back at him – and he lied with a shake of his head. When he looked at the side of Father Mac's face, he saw a loneliness that he hadn't seen before. His instinct told him that Father Mac was telling the truth, though, and that he didn't have some new secret lover tucked away. By the time they cleared up and headed to bed, Fergal really felt that their old closeness seemed restored – with one essential ingredient missing, of course.

Fergal lay in bed in his shorts. It felt strange to think that Father Mac was only down the hallway. Even though he was exhausted, he knew there was no way he was going to be able to fall asleep. After about twenty minutes of staring at the ceiling, he decided to get up and pretend he needed a drink of water from the kitchen. As he opened his door, he could just hear Alfredo snoring from the top room, and that made him feel a bit braver – his teacher wouldn't be able to hear anything. He walked along the dark landing, as calmly as he could, towards the room that he and Father Mac used to share.

'Dermot? Dermot?' he whispered.

No answer.

'Dermot, it's me.'

When he got no answer again, he knocked lightly on the door and then opened it, just in time to see Father Mac getting out from under his blankets in only his shorts. His belly looked even bigger with no shirt to cover it.

'Fergal, what is it? Is something the matter?'

'No, I was just getting some water and I wondered if you were still awake. Would you like some?'

When Fergal came back with two full glasses, Father Mac was back in bed, with the covers pulled up around his neck. Fergal set the water down on the little table beside him, and they drank in awkward silence.

The darkened room was getting colder, and Fergal started to shiver. Father Mac looked at him in the half light. 'You'd be better off in bed,' he said. 'I'll see you in the morning, before you go.'

Fergal looked crestfallen. 'I can't sleep,' he whispered. 'Can I not get in with you for a while? I won't stay long, I promise.'

'Fergal...'

'Come on, just for a minute. Please? I promise I won't stay all night. I just want—'

'Fergal, Alfredo is only upstairs.'

It was all the green light that he needed. 'Alfredo's snoring like a bear,' he said, pulling back the blankets and squeezing in beside Father Mac. 'A bomb wouldn't wake him.'

As they lay there motionless, Fergal's heart pumped so hard in his chest that it felt like a sledgehammer was excavating his ribcage. There wasn't an inch of each other's body that they hadn't visited and explored, but they were acting as if it was the first time they had ever shared a bed. Finally, Fergal turned on his side and gingerly put his hand on Father Mac's chest, fully expecting him to refuse it, but Father Mac just caught his breath and exhaled nosily. He turned towards Fergal, and their faces were right next to each other.

The lost, whispered language in their bones came back to the surface of their skin, and they closed their eyes as their lips touched, almost as if suspiciously tasting the moment to see if it was real.

'Fergal, I—'

'Dermot, it's all right.'

'I promised myself I wouldn't—'

'Dermot, one more night before I go…to say goodbye.' Fergal kissed him gently, in between words. 'Please. I promise I won't ever ask again. I promise.'

'I…'

Gradually Father Mac's inebriated protest evaporated as the heat of their desire rose. They retraced the long-abandoned trail of their lovemaking. No matter how overgrown with neglect it had become, they knew their bodies would instinctively remember the way. Not another word was spoken as they kissed, more and more deeply, their tongues exploring each other's mouth. Then, as if it was preordained, they sat up momentarily and hugged tightly, and then Fergal lay down on top of Father Mac's body. He began to travel south with his kisses, along the hairy chest that he had missed so much, stopping to taste each nipple. Down and down he travelled, but just when he was about to take Father Mac's waiting thickness into his mouth, Father Mac suddenly turned his body away.

'No – stop. I'm sorry, Fergal. No.'

'What?' Fergal lifted his head. 'What's wrong, Dermot?'

'Everything's wrong. I'm sorry, I'm drunk – but I don't want this.'

'But you said—'

'Fergal, we have to stop. I mean it. I'm sorry for letting you into my bed. Forgive me. We can't do this. Please go back to your room…please. We made a promise.'

'I know, I know we made a promise – but for old times' sake, I thought…'

'Stop saying that! Oh, God, I shouldn't have drunk so much. Please, go.'

'Dermot, I don't want to.'

'I'll go and sleep on the sofa, then. We can't stay here like this.'

Fergal sat up and flung himself out of the bed. 'All right, I'll go back to my room. You stay here. I'm fucking going.'

'Fergal, don't be angry! I—'

But Fergal was gone, without even a goodnight kiss. He slipped back across the landing, feeling rotten and angry and foolish. He wished he hadn't bothered going to Father Mac's room in the first place.

As he lay in his own bed again, alone and frustrated, he understood only too well that everything had changed. He remembered how alive he used to feel, well over a year ago, after he and Father Mac had made love, but now, in the dark, he admitted to himself that he just felt empty.

20

The next thing Fergal knew, Alfredo was rapping on his door, saying that breakfast was ready if he could face it. Fergal was hungover, but not too much to remember every excruciating detail of his failed attempt to seduce Father Mac.

'Yeah, okay, I'm up,' he lied. He washed his face, drank as much tap water as he could and joined the two men downstairs, where Mrs Mooney was in full swing with toast and bacon and coffee.

Father Mac was scanning the headlines of the paper, trying to look relaxed. 'Morning, Mr Flynn,' he said brightly. 'Why on earth did we drink so much wine last night? Alfredo, it's all your fault, you know. If it hadn't been so delicious, we'd all be fine!'

Fergal felt relieved that at least there was no tension, but he thought Father Mac was trying just a bit too hard.

No sooner had they cleared away the breakfast things than the taxi driver rang the bell. Mrs Mooney kissed Fergal and told him not to worry about his mother, as if she'd read his mind. They checked the rooms once more in case they'd forgotten anything, and Fergal looked at his empty old room and knew that his old life with Father Mac was over, once and for all. To him, in some ways, two men had died: his father, and Dermot – the old Dermot, at least.

Alfredo packed their bags in the boot and planted kisses on Father Mac's and Mrs Mooney's cheeks. Father Mac smiled at Fergal, and somewhere in his face was a plea for forgiveness. As they hugged, he whispered, 'Travel safely. I'll look after Angela and you look after yourself, okay?'

'Okay. Good—'

'No – no, we don't say goodbye twice, fella. Farewell for now. See you when I see you.'

'Okay. See you when I see you.'

Fergal instantly felt better about the night before, even though his head didn't.

They left the graffitied streets behind and passed the cemetery where Paddy Flynn lay newly in the ground. As the big wooden gates came into view, Fergal blessed himself and whispered, 'See ya, Da.' He felt so sad that he had never been able to mend his relationship with his father. If there was any comfort, it was that Angela had come to find him the night before, and that meant she had wanted to see him. It felt odd to think that she might actually care about him. At least he hadn't lost her completely, too. As Belfast evaporated behind him, a shadow of a smile crossed Fergal's face.

Daniela was waiting for them at Alfredo's door. She hugged Fergal and even cried a little for his father. Fergal thanked her, touched, but all he could think about was getting to his room, where he could sit and think about everything that had happened.

He got under the clean white sheets and thought about the past few days. He had buried both his father and his past with Father Mac. Everything seemed to be changing so quickly, and he had never felt happier to be under Alfredo's roof. It was no coincidence, he thought, that 'Rome' rhymed with 'home'. As he drifted off to sleep, he wondered when he would be able to go back to work at the Teatro.

Alfredo spent the rest of his day trying not to think about Brendan, but he couldn't help wondering what his old friend might look like after all these years. What expression had occupied his face as he read the note that Fergal had delivered? He rang Giovanni to tell him that he and Fergal were back.

'Brendan Fiscetti asked about Fergal every day,' Giovanni said. 'He was wondering when he'd be back.'

'Vanni, if I know Fergal, he'd be happy to come back to work tonight if he could!'

'Do you think? Is he not too devastated?'

'Well, he is, in his own way, but I think being around the Teatro would be good for him.'

'Great! We'll expect him tonight.'

What Alfredo didn't say was that he had decided to attend the Teatro himself that night. He didn't want anyone to know – not Giovanni, not Fergal and especially not Brendan.

By the afternoon, Fergal felt more rested and indeed restless. When he came downstairs, Alfredo told him he'd been talking to Giovanni. Before he could finish his sentence, Fergal jumped in.

'Alfredo, I'm dying to go back to work. Do you think I can go to the Teatro tonight?'

'Are you sure you're ready?'

'I'm positive. Why don't you come with me? It's nearly the end of Brendan's run, and you two haven't even met again yet.'

'Well, I'm not sure I—'

'Ah, Alfredo, why don't you just meet him? He's lovely.'

'Yes, I know that, Fergal. But...' Alfredo looked off into the distance for a long moment.

'Can I ask you something?'

'Yes, what is it?'

'Well, it might be a bit, you know, personal.'

'In light of what has happened in the past few days, you have my permission to ask me anything you like.'

'Why are you and Brendan so afraid to meet each other again?'

Alfredo looked at the young man who was growing up faster than he had realised, and sighed. 'It's a very long story…but here's the shortened version.'

Half an hour later, Fergal had a greater understanding not only of Alfredo's reluctance, but also of the man himself – and of the fact that they had more in common than he had ever thought possible.

'It's called unrequited love, Fergal, and I hope you never have to suffer it. It's such a waste of life.'

Fergal shook his head. 'I'm so sorry, Alfredo. I had no idea. And there was me going on and on about him…'

'No, Fergal, don't be sorry. You may well be the miracle that was needed to bring about some kind of reconciliation. I wouldn't, and probably couldn't, have done it on my own. I need you to promise me something.'

'Anything.'

'Don't mention a word of this to Brendan.'

'I won't. I promise.'

'Giovanni is expecting you back at work tonight at the usual time. You're sure you want to go in?'

'Oh God, yeah – I couldn't be more sure!'

After Daniela and Fergal left, Alfredo went upstairs and looked out his window to see if the sky was giving any clues as to what temperature it might bring the city that evening. He thought he might change into a lighter suit so he could walk into town and not bother taking his car.

He looked at himself in his full-length mirror and wondered if Brendan would be shocked at his appearance. Would he think he had changed for the worse over the years? He knew in his heart that both of them must have altered in twenty-five years. He moved closer to the mirror and let his finger trace the outlines of his eyes, where the skin was darker and sagging. As the years had evaporated, Alfredo's youth had retreated behind the face of a much older, lonelier man. He grabbed the loose skin under his chin, making his jowls more pronounced, and frowned, vowing to eat less and maybe drink a little less wine in the future. Then he placed his hands at the sides of his face and pulled the skin back, wondering if he should have surgery...

He snorted. *Don't be ridiculous,* he told himself. There he was, in his late forties, acting like a nervous teenager before a first date. He finished dressing, gave his hair a final brush, sprayed a few clouds of lime cologne into the air and then walked through the citrus-flavoured mist as it fell.

As he drew closer to the Teatro that evening, Alfredo began to feel calmer. He was glad that he'd decided not to drive. He sat at a café opposite and waited until the last moment before he approached the box office. He bought a ticket and slipped into the back row just as the house lights were beginning to fade.

Even though more than a quarter of a century of silence had passed between the two men, Alfredo was unprepared for the well of feeling that awoke in the pit of his stomach when Brendan Fiscetti stepped from the dark into the spotlight. As soon as his voice entered the air, it was as if they had never been apart at all. Alfredo studied him from the safety of the darkness and saw that time had been kind to him. His hair was snow-white at the temples and his chest had grown even bigger, but if anything, he only looked more distinguished and handsome for it. Just before the intermission, Brendan paused before his closing song and said to the rapt audience, 'Ladies and gentlemen, I want to sing a song that I haven't performed for longer than I care to remember. This is for two special men: firstly, a new friend, Fergal Flynn, an extraordinary singer who recently suffered a bereavement, and secondly, an old friend – a more local man. I received a note from someone with whom I had lost contact for far too many years. We first met, long ago, in a production of Puccini's *Tosca*. I don't sing this piece out of context very often, but tonight I want to dedicate it to Alfredo Moretti.'

The audience cheered and clapped, and for a second Alfredo thought that someone must have alerted Brendan to his presence, but his heart sank from his mouth as the moment passed and no spotlight singled him out. Brendan closed his eyes to sing, and the audience instinctively quieted again.

When Brendan started his lament from *Tosca*, Alfredo had to close his eyes too, but it wasn't enough to stop the warm tears that trickled silently down his face. He was glad that he had sat right at the back, in the last seat. When Brendan finished and left the stage, Alfredo was able to dart out the side door as quickly and discreetly as he had entered.

He went back to the café and found a table in the corner, where he sat staring into his glass of water. He didn't go back into the theatre for the second half of the performance; he knew that he couldn't handle being there for a moment longer. At last, after a long time, he headed back home.

Brendan Fiscetti had welcomed Fergal back with open arms and given him a beautiful condolence card. He had been very moved to hear that Alfredo had accompanied Fergal to Ireland at such short notice, dropping everything, so after rereading Alfredo's note, he had decided to dedicate his lament to his old and new friends. Fergal had been watching from the wings, as always, and he couldn't wait to get home to tell his teacher. When he did, Alfredo feigned ignorance. He said that naturally he was very flattered, as Fergal should be, and then changed the subject.

That night, when Brendan got back to his hotel room, he took his usual hot shower, poured a brandy and sat by the phone in his bathrobe. Alfredo's note was folded neatly in the pocket of his jacket. He took it out and placed it on the table by the phone. He picked up the receiver, paused in thought for a second and then dialled the code for England.

Amelia's phone rang just as she was getting ready to settle down for the night with a good book. She knew it was Brendan; no one else called her at this time.

'Hello, my dearest. What news?'

She listened, in her careful way, as the line crackled and Brendan told her about Alfredo's new note. 'Well, my love,' she offered eventually, 'you must do what you think is right. And don't forget to remember me to him, will you? My goodness…I wonder if he's changed much.'

They said their goodnights. As always, Brendan waited until she hung up first, then he lay back on the bed, finally exhausted, and resolved to meet Alfredo.

Early the next morning, the phone rang in the Moretti household. Daniela answered: '*Pronto?*'

Brendan, thinking it might be Alfredo's wife, asked a little awkwardly if her husband, Mr Moretti, was available. Daniela giggled and explained that she had been Mr Moretti's housekeeper for many years, and that he had gone for his usual walk to buy the papers before breakfast. Brendan gave her the hotel's phone number, and she assured him that her employer would return his call as soon as possible.

Sure enough, no sooner had she hung up than she heard

Alfredo whistling as he opened the front door. When she told him he had just missed Signore Fiscetti's call, she could tell he was annoyed. But he decided not to phone straight away. He needed time to think. He made up his mind to phone after his mid-morning lesson with Fergal. When the phone rang again, he thought it might be Brendan and he grabbed it, beating Daniela to it. He was disappointed, and a little relieved, when it wasn't.

Fergal didn't know whether it was his imagination, but Alfredo seemed to be much harder on him than usual in that morning's lesson. They warmed up with scales and breathing exercises, but after that it was like an assault course. Fergal felt as if he had never been worked so hard, vocally, in all his life. Alfredo got him to sing the same phrases over and over again, and lost his temper wildly if he made a stupid mistake.

'Come on, Mr Flynn! You can and you must do better than that!'

'I'm doing my best.'

'Well, today your best is not good enough. You're relying on your natural ability too much. I need you to dig deeper. I know you have it in you, I've heard it more than once in the past week. *That* is the sound we're after!'

On and on he pushed him, higher and higher. 'More full voice!' he shouted. 'Less falsetto! You're being lazy now, Mr Flynn. I will only accept chest voice for those notes!'

At the end of the lesson, the two men were exhausted. Alfredo knew he had pushed Fergal a little harder than he had meant to. He was nervous about phoning Brendan and he had taken it out on his young pupil. He relented and made a point of complimenting Fergal, saying that he had risen to the challenges like a true professional and that he was proud of him for not losing his nerve, but that his old habits were still circling and he had to prevent them from ever landing again. Sometimes Fergal didn't really get Alfredo's metaphors.

Alfredo climbed the two flights of stairs to the top of his house, where he could use the phone beside his bed in privacy. By the time he reached the top, he was breathless, nervous and angry at himself for being so childish. He grabbed the phone and dialled the number of Brendan's hotel.

The receptionist connected him to Signore Fiscetti's room, but the phone just rang and rang. Then, as Alfredo was about to give up, the receiver was picked up and a sleepy English accent said, 'Hello?'

Alfredo started talking, nervously, at high speed. 'My goodness, it's so good to hear your voice again, after all this time! You sound so young—'

'Hello? Who is this, please? I asked not to be disturbed.'

'Oh, I'm so sorry – it's Alfredo, Alfredo Moretti. I'm sorry we kept missing each other, but, as you know, I was busy with Fergal and Ireland and so on. I didn't mean to disturb your rest. I hope I didn't wake you up?'

'Well, actually, you did, but—'

'Oh, Brendan, forgive me. I should have waited until later, but since you rang so early this morning, I thought—'

'Hang on, hang on, hold your horses. I'm not Brendan. Who's this again?'

Alfredo stopped babbling.

'What? Not Brendan? But I specifically asked to be put through to Signore Fiscetti's suite. Forgive me, sir, for—'

'No, no, I'm Mr Fiscetti as well, but I think you want my father, Brendan. Who is this?'

Alfredo nearly dropped dead on the spot, but he dropped the phone instead. '*Cazzo!* Sorry – ah, sorry…'

When he managed to pick up the phone again, he tried to rein in his confusion. 'Forgive me. This is Alfredo Moretti. I knew your father many years ago, and we were trying to arrange a meeting here in Rome before he goes home again. Are you really his son? What's your name?'

'Yes, I'm Fintan Fiscetti. Look, forgive me if I sounded rude. I've just flown in and I'm exhausted, but my own room's not ready, so my dad gave me his bed. Wait a minute, Alfredo – he did mention that you might phone, and I see a note here...yes, he wrote down where he was going, and he says I'm to ask you to meet him there.'

'He did? I have a pen, go ahead.'

'It's a café called the Meeting Place – not far from this hotel, actually. You'll find him there if you leave soon. He was very excited about seeing you, Mr Moretti, that much I do know.'

'Thank you. I'll let you get back to sleep. Goodbye – and I hope to meet you too, perhaps?'

'Oh, I'm sure we'll meet! Bye, then.'

Alfredo hung up and sat on the side of his bed, feeling as if someone had just slapped him hard across the face. He wasn't sure whether he should go or not, but when he caught sight of himself in the mirror over his little fireplace, his reflection said, 'Go and meet him, you imbecile.'

21

Alfredo left the house and walked at a fast pace, unable to believe that he had just talked to Brendan's son. He wondered if Amelia was Fintan's mother. He certainly sounded as if he had grown up in England. He reached the corner of the piazza and picked out the awning of the café. He'd driven past it a few times since it had opened – it had once been a bookshop, but the insatiable tourist industry meant that cafés had been multiplying – but he had yet to go inside. Indeed, family loyalty would have prevented him from ever eating there of his own choice. But he hadn't chosen the venue for this meeting, and he was glad of the relative privacy.

A broad-shouldered man wearing a cap was sitting at a corner table with his back to the street, and as Alfredo got closer he saw that he was reading an English newspaper. Alfredo stopped for a moment and stared at the nape of his neck, where the hair, now turning white, dipped into a V shape. It was one of the details that he had first found attractive about Brendan.

Brendan Fiscetti turned around, tilting his head to make his reading glasses slide down his nose, then he stood up, dropping his paper.

'Alfredo? Alfredo Moretti, is that you?'

Alfredo could only nod and smile. Brendan stepped towards him and pulled him to his chest like a long-lost brother. He stroked the back of his head, and the two men stood there, embracing silently, in the mild heat of the late morning.

Alfredo was overcome by how wonderful Brendan smelled. Memories came crashing back, unlocked by the secret key that could only be turned by fragrance. He was unable to stop the tears from blurring his sight as they finally let go of each other. Brendan reached for a tissue and wiped his own eyes unashamedly, simultaneously offering one to his old friend.

A waitress came over, and Alfredo was glad of the large laminated menu to hide behind for a second or two. They ordered omelettes, bruschetta and cappuccino. When the waitress was gone, Brendan was the first to speak.

'So you talked to Fintan, then?'

'I did. I thought he was you at first. I woke him up, I'm afraid.'

'It'll do that sleepy-head no harm to be woken up.' Brendan tilted his head to look at Alfredo more closely. 'You know, you haven't changed a bit in all this time – still as handsome as the day we met! And no grey hair, unlike myself. It's not fair.' They broke into a shy duet of laughter as Brendan tugged at his white sideburns.

'Brendan Fiscetti, I see you still have the – what do you call it? – the gift of the gab! You look very distinguished indeed. I think you may look even better than you did twenty-five years ago, though I never would have guessed that was possible. How could time be so untruthful?'

Brendan grinned. 'I know one thing, Alfredo, my friend: I couldn't be happier to see you again at last.' He put his big hand over Alfredo's and squeezed it tightly, as if to prove to himself that his mind wasn't playing tricks.

As the day progressed, they talked easily and constantly. Alfredo felt that a great weight was lifting from his heart, a weight that he had never fully realised was there. He was so happy that he felt almost drunk, although they had sipped nothing but coffee and water.

When a little gap appeared in the conversation, Alfredo braced himself and said, 'I have to say something, Brendan, before we go on any further.'

'Of course. Go ahead.'

'I never apologised to you or Amelia in person for leaving you without a best man. I hope you can accept my sincere apology now. I was young and selfish, and I didn't see the bigger picture – you and your bride, and the whirlwind romance of it all. Can you forgive me for fleeing and not coming to your wedding?'

Brendan looked at his long-lost friend for a mute moment. 'Alfredo, I'd be lying if I said we weren't disappointed and upset. Everyone was. But it's water long gone under a Venetian bridge. Of course I forgive you – and, indeed, thank you for being man enough to bring it up. I'm just happy that you're here now.'

Their eyes filled up once more, and they sat silently. The traffic was beginning to build up on the nearby street. Someone was trying to park in a space that was much too small for his car, causing a cacophony of car horns and abuse.

Alfredo's confidence was boosted enough to ask, 'So how is Amelia these days? Did she not travel with you?'

Brendan cleared his throat. 'Amelia is very well. She's not here, no, but we speak on the phone every evening. Oh, Alfredo, where do I start? At the beginning, I suppose.'

They ordered more coffee. When they were alone again, Brendan began.

'After we were married on the ship, we went back to England and found a wonderful house in Highgate village, in North London. That first year was bliss, Alfredo. We had the best time making the house into our home, trawling the markets for interesting furniture – Amelia has a wonderful eye for detail. We thought of you often. I almost went to Rome for work a few times, but it always fell through at the last moment and I ended up doing better in America or Germany – you know what our business can be like, so unpredictable. Time has that awful habit of slipping by when one's back is turned. Amelia used to come everywhere with me at first, but then she became pregnant. Initially we were overjoyed.'

'That's when Fintan came along? I'm so looking forward to meeting him, Brendan.'

'Well, no. Amelia isn't strong, you know. She miscarried – twice, actually. But the third time was lucky: she managed to reach full term, and our beautiful son Fintan was born – a whopping eleven pounds, and I'm sure you remember how tiny Amelia is!'

'My goodness, Brendan! The poor girl.'

'Well, without going into too many details – otherwise we'd be here for weeks – she was very ill and had to stay in the hospital for quite a while after the birth. And when she finally came home, she couldn't get Fintan to feed, and on top of that, he was a terrible sleeper – not like nowadays, when he can sleep standing up – and a real screamer. My God, what a pair of lungs he had on him. I always joked that he'd be a singer like his father. Anyway, Amelia's health only got worse as the months went by. Of course, they didn't call it post-natal depression then, but that was what it was.'

Alfredo shook his head.

'And she did her utmost to hide it from me. She felt that she would hold back my career somehow if I was worried about her – which was ridiculous, of course. We were trying for a sister or brother for Fintan, but with no success. We had every test imaginable. Amelia was more despondent than ever. Alfredo, it was breaking my heart. Just when we thought things couldn't get any worse, she suddenly got very sick. The end result was that we would never be able to have any more children. It was the cruellest possible blow, and that was the worst time in our lives. We talked about adopting, but because my job took me away so much, it was unlikely that we would have made good candidates. And, to be honest, she struggled enough with the one child we did have. No matter what we did, she just became more and more withdrawn.'

'Oh Brendan, how awful! I'm so sorry that I wasn't there for you – for both of you.'

'As I said, water under the bridge.' Brendan took a sip of cold coffee. 'Anyway, I don't know if you knew this, but Amelia's first husband died tragically, not long before we all met her in Venice, and he left her a huge house in the countryside. The only time we saw Amelia smile properly was when she was in that garden, tending the flowers. We all went down there as often as we could. The difference that place made to her was like night and day. She regained some of her old confidence – for a while, at least – but as soon as she returned to London she would start to feel low again. So it made sense that she began to spend more and more time down there. And I had to base myself in London, because I was travelling so much.'

'Brendan, I don't know what to say.'

'I was the thoroughly modern father and took Fintan away with me on trips, to give her a decent break. He was one of those children who are fiercely independent from the second they can walk, and he didn't seem to mind all the upheaval. I suppose he really didn't know anything else. When it came time for him to go to school, Amelia insisted he be enrolled in a private nursery near her, and I could hardly argue because I was away so much. She said she couldn't live with herself if I ever stopped singing, so I just kept accepting work in the vain hope that she might get bored of being in the same place all the time and start travelling with me. I really thought we could get back on track, be together again, but the situation never changed. A few years ago, Amelia turned her first husband's house into a convalescent home. She spends her time running it.'

Alfredo could hardly take it all in. 'And what happened then? Did you divorce?'

'Good God, no – heaven forbid! That was never an option. We're still married. Like I said, we talk on the phone every night, and I see her as much as I can, especially at Christmas. It's unconventional, I suppose, but it genuinely works for us. By the way, she knew we were going to be meeting, and she asked me to give you her fond regards.'

Alfredo didn't know what to say. He tried to make sense of it all. It was so strange, hearing Brendan's condensed life in fast-forward. Finally he found his tongue.

'Brendan, I'm speechless. It's so sad, but it touches me greatly that you feel you can trust me with such intimate details of your life with Amelia. I want to ask you so many questions...'

'Ask me anything you like, Alfredo. Our bridges were never burned.'

'How old is your son now? And what does he do?'

'Fintan's nineteen. He'll be twenty tomorrow, on my closing night in the Teatro. That's why he came over.'

'Does he look like you or like his mother?'

'Oh, he's a healthy mixture of us both. Wait till you meet him. He's grown into a fine man, very bright, and very artistic too. He's been studying painting in Paris for the last two years.'

'That's wonderful. And tell me, what about you?'

'What about me?'

'Tell me if I've gone too far – but do you have a new partner now?'

'No, no. I've had a few interesting offers over the years, but I could never act on them. Amelia and I are still married, and I've never loved anyone as much as I still love her.'

'I understand. How could any of us forget how smitten you two were with each other, all those years ago in Venice? Will you please send my love to her when you talk tonight?'

'Of course.'

'I'm so glad you two forgave me.' Alfredo was lost in thought for a second. 'Brendan, if you'll permit me – and, indeed, if you and your son have no other plans – I would love the honour of giving both a closing-night supper for you and a birthday cele-bration for Fintan at my house. Nothing too fancy, not too many people. Please, say you'll let me. To me, that would mean you've truly forgiven me. No pressure, of course!'

Brendan was surprised, but genuinely delighted. 'That's a fantastic idea! I would love it, and I'm sure Fintan would too. Are you sure it wouldn't be too much trouble at such short notice?'

'My housekeeper and I would relish the challenge.'

'Oh, yes, your housekeeper. I must admit I was a little surprised when she answered the phone. I mistook her for your wife. And it's my turn to ask you a personal question.'

'Of course.'

'I presume no wife ever materialised?'

Alfredo laughed and shook his head. 'No.'

'Well, then, tell me about you, Alfredo! You've been listening to me rattle on for ages, but I don't know a thing about your life. Is there someone special to you, someone I'll meet at this party at yours?'

Alfredo looked at him for a long moment. 'Unfortunately, no one special just now, no. Brendan, I was crazy with jealousy when you and Amelia became engaged. I still wince when I think of it – how childish I was. I never gave her a chance, and her only crime was falling in love with you. I think that, when I settled back in Rome, I was too afraid of being so badly hurt again. I did go to London a few times to sing, and I hoped I might bump into you somewhere, but I was much too embarrassed to try and find you. To answer your question, there have certainly been a few dalliances over the years, but – like you, I suppose – I buried my heart in my work. Even after I was in a bad car accident, which is why I need my walking stick, I just ploughed on, so it never healed properly. I suppose I'm talking about my heart as much as my leg. I had to give up touring altogether, and slowly I replaced performing with teaching. But do you know what I think?'

'What, my friend?'

'I think those lonely days are at an end. Something extra-ordinary is at work here today. I can call you my friend again. Oh, Brendan—'

They clasped each other's hands, and their eyes were wet again.

'Alfredo, I knew our friendship would never be over for good. We just got lost. And I'm so glad to hear you feel the same way I do – friends again.'

They sat wordless for a few minutes as the last of their tears dried on their faces. Then Brendan looked at his watch and realised that they had been talking for most of the day, and he was due at the theatre in a little over an hour. They reluctantly parted, promising to make more concrete plans by phone the next day. Alfredo said he would definitely come and hear Brendan sing the following night, the last night of the run. Brendan hugged the breath out of him as they parted, and Alfredo was amazed that he was still so strong.

As he walked back home alone, Alfredo felt as light as a cloud.

In one day, two and a half decades of invisible heartbreak had been mended and he had his friend back. He was afraid that the anaesthetic of their reconciliation might gradually wear off and the dull ache might return, but it didn't. He knew that Brendan could never have loved him as he had so badly wanted him to, but this knowledge no longer hurt. It was nothing short of a miracle.

22

When Fergal got to the theatre for his shift and knocked on the door of Brendan's dressing room with their tea, he couldn't believe how different Brendan was. He practically pulled the door off its hinges, helped Fergal put the tray down and hugged him tightly.

'Fergal Flynn, it's so good to see you! How are you feeling?'

'I'm okay, I think; thanks. You know, one day at a time and all that.'

Brendan was humming away to himself, with his stage make-up already applied. Fergal wasn't sure whether to ask him the reason for his high spirits – he thought they might be because the end of the run was near – but Brendan suddenly explained. 'I've just spent the entire day with your elusive teacher, Alfredo Moretti. Did you know it had been twenty-five years since we last spoke?'

Fergal nodded.

'I want to thank you for being instrumental – or should I say vocal? – in bringing us together again. If you hadn't mentioned that he was your teacher, I probably would have finished this run and gone home, and that would have been that. The icing on the cake is that my son arrived from London this morning, so I couldn't be happier.'

'Your son?'

'Why, yes, did I not mention him before? He's not much older than you, and about the same height, I'd say – although I haven't seen him for a while. It's his birthday tomorrow, on my closing night, so it will be a double celebration – and Alfredo has offered to host a supper party at his house after the show.'

'Right.' Fergal was instantly curious about Brendan's son. He thought of his own da. He couldn't imagine how different it must be to have someone like Brendan for a father.

The half-hour call put an end to the conversation. That evening, Brendan seemed to take the music to new heights. By the end of the show, his last outfit was soaked through with sweat from working so hard. Before he had even finished holding the last note of the night, the audience was on its feet and calling for an encore. Fergal noticed that this time he didn't run away from the stage door, but instead stood chatting and signing everything he was offered until the very last person was satisfied.

When Fergal got back home, he found Alfredo in a similar state of bliss. He was at the piano, surrounded by old sheet music and singing at the top of his voice, stopping only to drink from a glass of expensive wine that was balanced precariously on the edge of one of his rare books. When he saw Fergal, he jumped up and hugged him, proclaiming drunkenly, 'I just want to say that the Lord works in mysterious ways. Don't you think so, Fergal?'

'I suppose so.'

Alfredo hiccupped. 'When I first heard your voice in that damp old monastery, little did I know that you would be the one to lead me back to my old friend Brendan Fiscetti. I can't begin to tell you what a miracle it is. How can I thank you?'

Fergal went bright red. 'Alfredo, what do you mean? You and Father Mac saved my life – first him in Belfast, and now you here in Rome. I don't know how *I'll* ever thank *youse* enough.'

Alfredo looked drunkenly touched. Suddenly he made for the record player, put on a record and grabbed Fergal to dance around the room, shouting, 'We're going to have a party, we're going to have a party!'

Fergal was a bit taken aback, but Alfredo was laughing so hard that it became infectious as they spun around the room. It was sheer luck that they didn't collide with anything priceless before the music finished and they stood still, sweating and gasping for breath.

Alfredo was exhausted after a day he would never forget, but he regained control of himself. 'I almost forgot – Father MacManus phoned. Your mother's passport is being worked on, and he hopes it will be ready in a few weeks.'

'Oh? When did you talk to him?'

'Earlier this evening. He called to see how you were, and I told him you had gone back to work, which he thought was probably a good idea.'

'Right.' Fergal felt a bit put out that he hadn't spoken to Father Mac himself.

'You do feel sure about being back at work, don't you? You would say if it was too much?'

'Yes, of course. I love being at the Teatro, and Brendan is so nice to me. Hey, did he tell you he has a son? My age?'

'Yes, he did. Just when one thinks things can't get any stranger… Are you sure you're okay? You're sure you want your mother to come? If you don't, then just tell me.'

'No, Alfredo, I do. I think she deserves to come and see how beautiful it is here.'

'Well done, Fergal. It's the right thing to do. I can't tell you how much I'd love to see my own mother again. She'd have loved your voice, too.'

Fergal went red and thanked him, and they said goodnight. As Alfredo slipped into a deep sleep, he was already planning every detail of the imminent party.

The next morning, Fergal was in the middle of a dream when the doorbell rang. He turned over, hoping somebody else would answer it, but when it rang again, he reluctantly dragged himself from under the sheets.

'I'll get it,' he called to no one as he pulled on his dressing gown and half-sulked down the stairs, rolling his eyes at the cornicing. When he unlocked the front door, he was just in time to catch Luigi cursing his way back down the path, hugging so many tall bunches of flowers that he looked like a peacock. Fergal shouted after him.

Luigi turned back, delighted at the sight of the sleepy young Irishman in only his loosely tied bathrobe. He begged forgiveness dramatically. 'Oh, I didn't want to wake you, my dear. I wasn't due to make the delivery until a little later, but I ended up with another order in the next square, so I thought I'd try my luck.' He pushed past Fergal and went straight to the kitchen. 'I'd better get these into water, before we all wilt!'

Fergal couldn't believe how many bunches of white orchids and lilies Luigi unloaded into the sink. 'See you tonight, handsome,' he called as he headed back to the front door. '*Ciao!*'

When Daniela got back, laden down with endless bags of shopping, and saw the sink full of flowers, she exclaimed, 'Signore Moretti has gone crazy! Is the Pope himself coming to this party?'

The phone didn't stop ringing all day with more and more preparations for the party, and Fergal was glad of the distraction of his Italian lesson with Signora Truvello. More than a few times, though, she had to tap her desk and demand his full concentration as he sat staring into space. He was glad she couldn't read his thoughts – they were full of the rain-soaked graveyard, his dead father's face in its ghoulish make-up, Father Mac's nakedness and his rejection.

He returned to Alfredo's just in time to meet Arianna, arriving in her little van with two of her kitchen staff. They unloaded the buffet equipment that Alfredo had asked for and Fergal helped them carry in armfuls of stainless steel receptacles. He hadn't seen Arianna since returning from Belfast. She squeezed his arm and exclaimed, 'Fergal, you are fast becoming a man! How are you doing, after…Ireland?'

He smiled weakly. 'I'm doing okay. Thanks, Arianna.' Then he flexed his arm, to break the moment. 'Yeah, I'm getting muscles, amn't I? It's down to all the work I'm doing at the Teatro.'

As he said the word, he looked at his watch and realised he would be late if he didn't leave right away. He kissed Arianna goodbye and ran off down the street. As she watched him go, she said to his wake, 'Something is changing, but I don't know what.'

Backstage, the theatre was packed with closing-night flowers, baskets of fruit and champagne, and the excitement was palpable in every room. Fergal clocked in and headed automatically towards the basement kitchen, but Giovanni shouted down the stairs, 'Bring an extra cup to Signore Fiscetti's dressing room – he has a visitor.' Fergal knew it must be someone important – Brendan usually refused all demands on his time before the performance; his ritual was sacred. He wondered if it might be Alfredo.

When Fergal rapped on the door, he wasn't prepared for the vision that opened it. There stood the handsomest red-haired young man he had ever seen. Brendan called out from the little bathroom, 'Fintan, that'll be Fergal Flynn. Remember I was telling you about him? Will you let him in?'

'Of course, Dad. I already have,' the young man answered in a soft English accent. He smiled and stepped aside to let Fergal put down the tray.

'Hello,' Fergal offered, a little shyly.

'Hi. We meet at last!' Fintan said warmly, and shook his hand.

Brendan came out of the bathroom and put his arm around his tall son. 'Fergal, meet my son and heir, Fintan Fiscetti – born exactly twenty years ago today!' He kissed his son's forehead and ruffled his hair.

'Dad, get off!'

Fergal wished Fintan a happy birthday and began to back out of the room, thinking they would want some privacy. 'Where are you going?' Brendan demanded.

'I thought you might want to be on your own since you haven't seen each other in a while, and it's Fintan's birthday and all.'

'No, no, not at all, my dear boy! I've had the pleasure of being with my handsome son all day. And anyway, I've been telling him all about you, and I'm glad you're finally getting to meet.'

So they poured tea, and Fergal listened wide-eyed to Fintan's stories of trips to London and studies in Paris. As he talked, Fergal tried not to stare too obviously, but he couldn't help taking in the details of this beautiful young man, the incredible green eyes that shone under his thick mop of dark-red curls. Fergal kept looking back and forth between father and son, trying to find physical similarities. At first he couldn't see any, but gradually he began to see the resemblances in their mannerisms – the identical way they held their cups, the way they both threw their heads back and laughed, pushing each other and closing their eyes.

Fergal could only think of his own father, lying dead in the cemetery. He couldn't imagine what it would be like if they could be in the same room together. It struck him, harder than ever, that he would never get the chance to laugh with his father about anything. There had never been any joy between them; it simply hadn't been allowed. The temperature in Fergal's heart dropped and he felt intensely jealous of Fintan Fiscetti.

The half-hour call came too soon, and Brendan asked Fergal if he would bring Fintan up to the guest box closest to the front of the stage. Fergal was only too delighted, of course, and after Fintan kissed his father on the cheek, he led the way through a maze of corridors under the stage towards the box.

'Are you coming to the supper party later?' Fintan asked him.

Fergal laughed. 'Well, I hope so. It's at Alfredo Moretti's house, and that's where I live too.'

They laughed together this time. Fergal opened the velvet door of the box and Alfredo stood up, hand outstretched to welcome Brendan's son. 'Signore Fiscetti Junior, I take it?'

'Yes, how do you know my…Wait a minute, are you Mr Moretti, who I spoke to on the phone yesterday morning?'

'I am, well done. I see you've met Fergal Flynn.'

'Yes. My dad says he's the best he's heard in a very long time.'

Fergal blushed and Alfredo smiled, saying, 'Your father is right about that.'

Fergal left them to it and went backstage. That night's show was completely sold out, and Brendan found he was unusually nervous. He laughed to himself when he realised it was because Alfredo was in the house. But he needn't have worried. There was magic in the air, and the evening went perfectly.

At the interval, Alfredo and Fintan went to the little bar for a drink.

'So, Fintan – that's an unusual name for an English boy.'

'Yes, I know, but Brendan and Amelia had this thing about Irish names, especially after they saw my little red head.'

'Yes,' Alfredo said, noticing that he called his parents by their first names. 'Your father tells me you're a brilliant painter.'

'Does he now? Well, I'm still studying, of course, but I've come to the end of my term in Paris and I'm eager to move on, you know?'

'Of course. For a young man like you, the world is your canvas. Where are you planning to go next? London again, perhaps?'

'Oh God, no, Signore Moretti. I've spent so much of my life in England, and I do love it, of course, but I want to see the world. I think you and Fergal are so lucky to live here in Italy. I'm already blown away by what little architecture I've seen. So who knows?'

'I must say I feel privileged to have been born here. Why don't you think about Italy? Surely you could study here?'

'I'd love to. That's one of the reasons why I jumped at the chance to come and see Dad singing here. I have an obsession about Italian architecture, but there's so much I need to see up close. Is the Sistine Chapel as beautiful as they say?'

'You mean you've never seen it?'

'Not yet, but ever since I started painting at boarding school I've been a particular fan of Michelangelo.'

'Well, young man, your timing couldn't be worse. The *Cappella Sistina* is closed for renovations, so you'll just have to make a return visit when they officially unveil their cleaning work. The rumour is that they're doing a stunning job, so it'll be worth it, I'm sure.'

'Typical – just my bloody luck!'

'Not to worry. San Pietro is still worth seeing. If you need me to show you around at all, don't hesitate to ask. I'm sure your time with your father is precious, but he has my number and I'm not far from the city centre. You'll see later, when you come to supper.'

The bell rang for them to take their seats for the second half. Alfredo had to admit that Brendan's voice had only got better with age, more lived in. He looked over at Brendan and Amelia's son and allowed himself to imagine, for a moment, that Fintan was his own child. How different his life would have been if he'd married...He smiled to himself, knowing that it would have been the most dishonest thing he could ever have done. Fintan felt his stare and glanced over, and Alfredo's intense gaze melted into a kind smile. He reached over and rubbed the young man's arm, nodding towards his father on stage as if to say how proud he was.

Fergal couldn't help himself – he borrowed a pair of house binoculars and watched Fintan from a gap between the curtains at stage left. He studied his hairline and the way his fingers strayed to his lips every now and then as he bit his thumbnail and then thought better of it. Fergal loved the way his smile completely altered his face. He thought that Fintan probably had a string of girlfriends. Why wouldn't he? He was obviously rich, certainly handsome, and so confident for someone who was only a year older than Fergal himself. Fergal felt intimidated by Fintan, but he couldn't take his eyes off him.

For the final encore of the night, Brendan looked in the direction of the box where he knew his son and his guest were sitting. 'Ladies and gentlemen, I need your help. I want to dedicate these last two pieces to three very important people. The first piece is for my son, who I love very much. He has flown in especially to be with me on my last night in this exquisite Teatro – and he is twenty years old today! Please join me as I sing...Happy birthday to you...'

The crowd went wild. As they all joined in, Alfredo got Fintan to stand and take a bow, mortifying and delighting him to the core.

'The second piece,' Brendan said, 'and the final one tonight, is one I want to dedicate to a future singing star, Fergal Flynn, who also happens to be my assistant backstage. I predict great things for Fergal, not only because I've heard him sing, but also because he is under the guidance of the third man I want to acknowledge, one of Italy's finest...Signore Alfredo Moretti.'

This time the spotlight did pick out Alfredo in the box. He stood up as gracefully as he could without his walking stick and the audience whooped and cheered.

Finally, when they quietened enough, Brendan continued, 'I want to sing this song for them and for all of you here tonight. Perhaps my friend Alfredo might recognise the tune?'

It was his signature song from *Tosca*, which Alfredo had always loved. He closed his eyes in the dark box and drank in every note, and for a moment he was transported back to the side of that stage in Venice, all those years ago. He opened his eyes. Brendan was staring at him, nodding and beckoning, so Alfredo stood up and joined him in harmony.

The audience gasped, and as they finished the last note together the whole theatre burst into rapturous applause. Fergal and Giovanni were jumping up and down in the wings. When Brendan finally bowed and left the stage, Fintan rubbed Alfredo's arm as he saw that his father's old friend's eyes were full of tears.

23

Alfredo's magnificent house looked even more incredible than usual. There were extraordinary flower arrangements in every room, a buffet of fragrant chicken with rosemary and roasted potatoes, and Arianna had sent over dessert from the restaurant while everyone was at the theatre. She had also allowed one of her staff to go to Alfredo's and help Daniela serve the buffet. She had noticed the dramatic upswing in her brother's mood, and she knew how important the evening was to him.

The patio doors were opened and the evening sky was unstained with clouds, leaving the garden starlit as Alfredo got home. By a quarter past eleven, the house was alive with his carefully chosen guests, and not much later Fergal opened the door, followed by Brendan and Fintan. The room erupted into applause, and champagne was handed out to toast the two Fiscettis. Brendan was overcome with the obvious effort to which Alfredo had gone in their honour. He hugged him and thanked him over and over until his host banned him from saying it again.

Everyone helped themselves to the delicious buffet. As usual, there was enough food to feed the guests twice over.

As Alfredo and Brendan settled into a corner, Alfredo said, 'I never got to ask you – what news of the great Marla Davis, our Tosca all those decades ago?'

'Funny you should ask. I performed with her again, many years after Venice, quite by accident. It was *The Barber of Seville*, in New York, and I was drafted into the production at the last moment. The lead tenor and his understudy had both come down with the flu – they were sleeping together, but that's another story. Marla was in the production. She asked after you, but I still had no idea where you were. I had hoped that she might. She was friendly enough, but it wasn't the same. Too much time had passed, the old closeness wasn't there. It was a lot to expect, I suppose.'

'It's strange – I was worried about seeing you again – I wasn't sure you would remember me kindly – but now it's as if you had never been away at all.'

'Alfredo, I'm so glad you feel that way. You remember I always thought of you as the brother I never had. I still do, even though a whole lifetime has gone by. My baby son is a man now – how did that happen?'

'I can't believe it. I was looking at him watching you onstage. He was so proud, and he has your smile. I don't know where he could have got his charm, though – not to mention that accent!'

They laughed again, and clinked their glasses together.

Fergal had managed to slip upstairs and change his clothes. He put on some cologne, regretted it and looked doubtfully at himself in the long wardrobe mirror. He could hear the revellers downstairs through the floorboards, but he could think only of Fintan Fiscetti. After combing his hair for the fourth time, he finally allowed himself to go back downstairs, where, to his surprise and delight, he found Fintan standing at the bottom of the stairway, with two glasses of champagne.

'Fergal, there you are! My God, that room is full of geriatrics. I thought you might like some of this.' He handed Fergal one of the glasses. 'Cheers, then.'

'Yeah, cheers – and happy birthday again.'

They stood looking at each other for what seemed like an eternity. 'Could I have a tour of the house?' Fintan asked.

'Of course, yes. Follow me.'

They climbed to the very top of the house, and Fintan stopped and studied every painting and framed poster on the walls. Alfredo had spent his money wisely; he had an impressive collection of modern Italian works. They stopped outside Fergal's room, but he made embarrassed excuses. 'It's in a bit of a state…'

Fintan laughed. 'You should see mine in London, at my dad's place. It looks like a bloody bomb hit it…oh, sorry.'

'What for?'

'You know, Belfast and all that. It must have been very hard for you.'

'Ah, you don't really want to hear about all that.'

'Of course I do, if you're willing to tell.'

Fergal began to panic slightly. He could tell simply by looking at Fintan that their lives couldn't have been more different. 'Ah…do you want to see the garden, Fintan? It's a lovely clear night.'

'Great, I'm dying for a cigarette! But don't tell my dad, he goes mad. I blame bloody Paris. If you don't smoke there, then you don't breathe.'

They descended the stairs again and went out through the kitchen. Fintan grabbed a bottle of champagne from a loaded tray and followed Fergal down to the back of the garden, where it was a bit more secluded. Fergal was struck by his sheer bold confidence, and he loved it.

At the bottom of the garden was a hanging sofa. Alfredo sometimes reclined on it when he napped in the afternoon, if it was warm enough. 'Brendan won't be able to see you here,' Fergal said, 'not unless he comes down. Have you smoked for long?'

'I only smoke when I drink. It's a filthy habit, I know, but fuck it! I don't have to mind my voice like you and Dad. Did you never smoke, Fergal? Not even at school?'

Fergal loved the way Fintan always looked him straight in the eyes, whether he was talking or listening. 'Jesus, no. Asthmatic, you see, but it's much better these days. And anyway, only the coolest of the cool fellas smoked at my school.'

'So tell me, how did you end up here? My dad told me a bit, but I want to hear it from you. Do you mind?'

'No, it's fine. I'll tell you, if you're sure you won't be bored to death.'

'Ah, now, no need to play so hard to get! I'm all ears – but not till I've opened this champagne. Here, hold your glass out. Shall we get pissed?'

It had been a very long time since Fergal had spent any time with someone his own age, and he loved it. As Fintan poured with one hand and sucked on a cigarette with the other, Fergal wondered if he had heard him right – was he really playing hard to get? Was he really starting to flirt? So, after a swig of bubbles, he told Fintan the edited highlights of his story: his Granny Noreen, meeting Father Mac, Brother Vincent, Sligo Abbey and then Alfredo. Fintan was genuinely fascinated. He kept refilling their flutes until the bottle was empty. The sofa gently swayed under their weight.

'What about you, Fintan? It must've been amazing, growing up with an opera star for a father.'

Fintan laughed. 'Well, amazing is one of the many things that it was. I mean, it's great now, and I wouldn't change him for the world, but he was always away, you know?' Suddenly he dropped his gaze. 'Oh Fergal, how thoughtless of me. I'm so sorry.'

'What do you mean?'

'Your just lost your dad, and here's me waffling on about mine. I'm so sorry '

'No, it's okay. We weren't anything like you and your da. We never got on.'

'You didn't? God, Fergal, that's awful. You poor thing.'

Fergal was mortified. The last thing he wanted was Fintan's pity. 'No, no, it's fine. I don't really want to think about him just now. Tell me about Brendan. What's it like to have him as your father?'

'Don't get me wrong, I love him to bits and I know he loves me and would do anything for me. And I've never had to worry about money – my mum was independently wealthy before they even met. But it would've been nice to have him around more, you know? I hated having to share him with so many fucking people. There's always someone who just has to talk to him, while I stand there like some invisible prat. God, Fergal, I didn't mean to get so serious. Am I boring you?'

'No, no. I never thought about it like that. Go on.'

'It's a privilege to have him as a dad, hand on heart. He can't help being so gifted. And God, does he work hard at it. I don't know how he does it. I suppose you're probably the same, right? You feel like you have to give everything to your singing, without compromise?'

'Yeah, I suppose I do.'

'You left Ireland, didn't you?'

'Yes, that's true.'

'What I'm saying is that when I've finished a painting and I'm happy with it, then that's it – it's done and dusted, and I move on. I don't have to keep repeating myself. And when Dad – or Alfredo, or you – goes to a party, you can bet someone will want him to sing, but no one would ever think of asking me if I wouldn't mind just knocking off a landscape before the coffee arrives.'

Fergal laughed. 'I see what you mean.'

'I've met a lot of singers through Dad, and they're very driven people – the good ones, anyway.'

'So you're a painter? I'd love to see some of your stuff – not that I know anything about it, mind you. What kind of paintings do you do?'

Fintan laughed again, simply because he was drunk and he loved Fergal's accent, but Fergal got embarrassed, thinking he had said something stupid. Fintan realised this and leaned towards him on the seat, to explain, but he tipped his glass too far and the contents soaked the sleeve of Fergal's jacket.

'Oh shit, look what I've done! God, I'm pissed. I'm sorry, Fergal. When I saw that look on your face, I was worried that I'd offended you. It's just that I could listen to your accent all day. Here, let me try and dry it off a little.'

Fergal was fairly drunk too, and he couldn't think of what to say as Fintan took out a perfectly ironed handkerchief and started dabbing his sleeve, where the damp was spreading. They were right up against each other, their faces almost touching. Fergal could smell the cigarette on Fintan's breath, and for a moment he thought of Father Mac. 'Ah, Fintan,' he started, 'don't worry, sure, it'll—'

He never got to finish the sentence. His lips were stopped with a kiss.

All he could hear was the thudding of his heart and his own deafening breathing – or Fintan's breathing, he could hardly tell whose was whose. Fintan moved away and started to say, 'I'm sorry—', but Fergal kissed him back. This time the kiss was longer; they knew it was too dark for anyone to see them. Fergal leaned back, and Fintan moved on top of him.

Just as they were losing themselves, Alfredo's familiar voice cut through the air like a firework.

'Fergal! Fergal, wherever you are, there's some singing about to start.'

Fergal and Fintan opened their eyes and stared silently at each other, a little panicked, then laughed under their breath. They waited, frozen. When there were no footsteps on the garden path, they breathed a sigh of relief. Slowly, Fintan moved off Fergal and they sat up, fixing their clothes.

'Jesus, that was close. We'd better go in, eh, Fintan?' Fergal almost whispered.

Fintan got up and steadied himself, offering Fergal his hand to help him off the swinging sofa. 'You have beautiful hands, Fergal.'

'Have I?'

Fintan laughed again, but this time Fergal understood. He pulled his jacket down to cover his erection. When they got back to the patio doors, Fintan gave him his handkerchief and walked on ahead. Fergal opened it out to find a dry section, and saw the twin letters 'FF' in the unused corner.

'We have the same initials,' he said to the champagne stain on his jacket.

Inside the music room, everyone had gathered around the grand piano where Alfredo was seated, ready to play. When Brendan saw Fintan come in, he nodded his head. Alfredo struck up the first chord of 'Happy Birthday' and the entire room joined in. The lights were dimmed and Daniela carried in a huge chocolate cake covered in candles. Brendan called his mortified son to the front, holding a brandy in one hand, and told him not to forget to make a wish. Fintan closed his eyes, took a huge breath and managed to blow out every candle in a puff of smoke and loud clapping. He winked quickly at Fergal as the lights went back up.

Brendan started searching through a pile of old music for something that he and his son could sing together, but Fintan was backing off. 'Dad, you always do this! You know I can't sing. I'd much rather hear you – how about you and Fergal? Go on, please – for me?'

Alfredo looked at Fergal and suddenly remembered. 'What about all that Irish stuff you used to sing? I bet Fergal would know some of it too.'

Brendan put the sheet music down and called Fergal over. He whispered into his ear and then said to the room, 'Let's see who knows this one!' Then, in a loud voice he began to sing 'Dirty Old Town', and Fergal joined in.

Song after song followed. Alfredo and Brendan alternated on the piano as they went along, and the guests picked up the choruses. Finally Brendan asked Fergal if he could sing something from Belfast.

He thought for a moment. 'This song was originally called "The Belfast Maid",' he said, 'but it's turned into "My Lagan Love", after the River Lagan that runs through Belfast.' He closed his eyes and started to sing, unaccompanied.

The very temperature in the room changed. Alfredo had never heard the song, so he turned away from the piano, but he held the pedals down so that every now and then one of Fergal's stronger high notes made the strings vibrate, adding to the ghostlike, melancholy quality of the melody. Fintan had initially stayed at the back of the gathering, but as Fergal sent the song around the room the notes seemed to pull him to the front of the crowd with quiet ease. Their eyes met, and neither of them could look away.

Her welcome, like her love for me, is from the heart within;
Her warm kiss is felicity that knows no taint of sin.
And when I stir my foot to go, 'tis leaving love and light
To feel the wind of longing blow from out the dark of night.

As he finished, the whole room exhaled as one and clapped. Alfredo and Brendan couldn't help noticing the way that Fergal had delivered the lines in Fintan's direction – nor, indeed, the way Fintan had received them.

There were calls for the host to sing. Alfredo playfully rejected them at first, but at last he loosened his shirt collar dramatically, saying, 'Well, if you insist.' Once the laughter had settled down, he thanked them all for coming and then turned his attention to Brendan. 'Dear friends, I can't tell you what it means to me to have the great Brendan Fiscetti in my home. I was privileged enough to share a stage with him very early in my career, and I'm so happy we can share our friendship again today – and hopefully into the future. I thank him for bringing his son Fintan here, and I look forward to getting to know him too. Fate works in strange ways. If I hadn't met Fergal Flynn in Ireland, then none of us would be celebrating here now – and we also wouldn't have heard Fergal sing so beautifully. I wonder who his teacher is?'

Again, the room burst out laughing, and Alfredo smiled. 'And if Giovanni hadn't worked at the Teatro and put in a good word for Fergal, then Brendan and I would never have found each other again. So I'll get to the point, before you all fall asleep. I want to sing a song that I love, by Carole King. It sums up how I feel tonight. Join in the chorus if you can.'

He struck the first chord dramatically, then began to sing 'You've Got a Friend'.

The whole gathering became a choir, and when Alfredo finished there was hardly a dry eye in the room. Brendan went to hug him. When they turned to smile at Fergal, they were just in time to see Fintan rub his back and then quickly take his hand away.

It was after two in the morning when the guests left and Fergal stood with Alfredo at the front door, waving off the last taxi. Brendan and Fintan, somewhat the worse for wear, were in the backseat.

The Fiscettis weren't due to fly back to London for another few days. Fintan wanted to soak up as much of the art and architecture as he could, and Brendan looked forward to having a bit of time with his son and to seeing the city at night instead of worrying about a performance. As Alfredo and Brendan agreed to have dinner in a day or so, Fintan had managed to slip Fergal a note with the hotel's phone number and whisper, 'Promise we'll meet as soon as we can.' Fergal was bowled over.

As the taxi disappeared and before Alfredo had a chance to say anything, Fergal went upstairs as quickly as he could, which, of course, said everything. He closed his bedroom door, his heart flying. He looked out his window at the back garden and the swinging seat where he and Fintan had kissed. He closed his eyes for a second and let the moment replay in his mind, remembering how good his lips had tasted.

As he got undressed, he couldn't believe it had happened at all. Fintan was so handsome and tall and lovely. Fergal couldn't help feeling paranoid as he wondered why someone like Fintan would be interested in him at all. What did he have to offer someone who was rich, someone who had grown up in the countryside and gone to boarding school? But he was too exhausted to worry for long. He fell asleep almost as soon as his head hit the pillow. As he drifted off, it struck him again just how far he had travelled from his family – and not only in miles.

24

It was all Fergal could do to stay away from the Fiscettis' hotel the next day. He thought about phoning Fintan, but whenever he even looked at the phone in the hall, Daniela seemed to be there, practising for the hoovering Olympics. He would have given anything for an excuse to visit Fintan.

Instead, he went for a long walk before going into the theatre. He thought about his mother, and decided to ask Alfredo to invite her for the coming recital. She would be able to hear him sing then. Fergal realised that it was important to him that she should see how hard he was working to make something of himself.

When he clocked in backstage, it was strange to find the place so empty. The next production was a few weeks away. Brendan's dressing room was bereft of his belongings and his name had already been removed from the door, as if it had never been there.

The tannoy clicked, and Fergal looked up at the speaker. 'Telephone call for Fergal Flynn. Fergal Flynn, please pick up at the stage door extension.'

Fergal had never heard his name over the tannoy before, and he ran to the stage door as fast as he could, thinking that it might be bad news of some kind. He needn't have worried. When he took the receiver from the stage doorkeeper, a soft English voice asked, 'Fergal, is that you? My Italian is crap, but obviously they understood me. I hope it's all right to call you at work?'

Fergal's heart started doing somersaults. 'Fintan? Yeah, it's me. Of course it's all right to call me here.' He actually had no idea what the Teatro policy was on personal calls, but the stage door-keeper just continued reading his paper, unconcerned. 'Ah, how are you today? How's Brendan?'

'Oh, he's fine. Look, I called you there because I didn't want to ask him for Alfredo's number. Alfredo did offer to show me around the city, but I kind of thought it might be more fun to see a bit of Rome with you. Are you doing anything after work tonight?'

'Nothing, just heading home.'

'Why don't we get a drink somewhere? What do you say?'

Fergal could hardly breathe. 'I'd love to. I'm off around ten, I think. Is that too late?'

'Too late? That's when I start to wake up! Where should we meet?'

'How about the Café degli Artisti, just across from the stage door here?'

'Right, see you then. Oh yeah – Fergal?' Fintan lowered his voice. 'You're a great kisser. See you at ten.'

As Fergal put the receiver down, Giovanni appeared from nowhere, saying archly, 'Well, someone's looking very pleased with himself, I must say!' Fergal disappeared down to Wardrobe as fast as he could so Giovanni wouldn't see his red, flustered face.

As the chimes of the city clocks sounded ten, Fergal clocked out of the theatre and left by the stage door.

Fintan was sitting at a table just outside the Café degli Artisti, with a lit candle and two beers in front of him. When he saw Fergal coming, he beamed. 'Hey, Fergal! I got a couple of beers, is that okay?'

'Yeah, great.' Fergal hardly ever drank beer, but it was cold and refreshing after the heat of the Teatro, and he finished his too quickly.

'You were thirsty, eh? Do you want another one?'

'No, not right now. Jesus, it's strong, isn't it?'

Fintan laughed, and Fergal wanted to kiss him then and there.

They were both nervous in their different ways, but they managed to keep the conversation going. They decided to go for a walk. They left the main road for cobbled laneways and sleeping shops and turned into a quiet piazza, completely empty except for a young woman crouched on the ground, unpacking a plastic bag in the middle of the square. They watched as she took out a small battery-powered tape recorder and set it at her feet. She uncoiled her waist-length black hair and shook it out, opened her coat and did little stretches, then bent down and pushed the play button on her tape recorder. Suddenly, a familiar piano part began floating from the tiny speaker, and she took a deep breath and began to sing.

'*Ave Maria, grazia plena…*' floated into the evening air. She was magnificent. Fergal and Fintan couldn't believe it. They leaned against a wall to listen. Slowly but surely, shutters began to open above their heads all the way around the square as the residents left whatever they had been doing and leaned out, arms folded, to listen to this young woman's exquisite voice. It was like a dream.

When she came to the end of the song, she took the applause as graciously as if she were on stage at the Teatro. Then she straightened her skirt, and the piano began again. This time she sang something unfamiliar to them, but no less beautiful. Fintan had moved into a shop doorway and lit a cigarette. Fergal squeezed in beside him and they pressed against each other, transfixed.

The mysterious girl finished on a quiet, crystal-clear high note, bowed and then packed up as her elevated audience clapped. Some people threw down money. She picked it up as quickly as she could, grabbed her things and was gone before Fergal and Fintan could speak to her or give her anything. One by one, in their own rhythm, the shutters closed above them and silence was restored in the piazza.

'Fintan, wasn't that pure magic? Jesus, you wouldn't see that in Belfast. People would've bounced shoes and bricks off her head, not coins.'

Fintan nearly choked on his cigarette with laughter. 'You're not serious, are you?'

'Well, not really – but almost. Wait till I tell Alfredo. I'm glad you're here, or he might think I made it up.'

Fintan nodded in agreement and then whispered into Fergal's ear, 'I'm dying to kiss you again. Will you let me?'

'What? Here?'

'Why not? There's nobody about.'

Fergal smiled slow, nervous permission, and Fintan dropped his cigarette as they tasted each other's lips in the doorway of the closed shop. Fergal could feel himself thickening, and as they pressed against each other he was glad to feel that he wasn't the only one. They stopped dead for a moment, convinced that someone was coming, but it only turned out to be an old lopsided dog. They whispered and kissed, and slowly grew braver. Fintan's hand went to the front of Fergal's trousers, feeling him through the material, and they tried not to groan too loudly.

At last the piazza's clock told them it was almost midnight. 'Shit, look at the time!' Fergal said. 'I should get back. Alfredo waits up for me.'

'Does he? He really cares about you, doesn't he?'

'Yeah, and I'd hate him to think I take it for granted.'

'I know, I know…but I don't want you to go. Flynn, what are you doing to me?'

'Look who's talking!'

They unfurled themselves from the darkened corner and found a taxi rank. As they sat in the back seat of the car, Fergal looked at the side of Fintan's face and thought it was the kindest he'd ever seen. Fintan turned and smiled. He took Fergal's hand and held it as they drove the rest of the way.

The taxi dropped Fergal at Alfredo's before going on to Fintan's hotel. Just as they arrived, Fintan leaned towards him. 'Fergal, how about you come to my hotel after work another night? Is that too forward of me?'

Fergal stared into his eyes. 'No, it's not. I'd love to.'

They squeezed hands, and Fergal got out. He stayed there, watching the taxi, until it rounded the corner and disappeared.

Alfredo was still up and in good form. The house was more or less back to normal after the previous night's party, and he had started to put together a plan for Fergal's recital. He had even found a possible venue, a music space on the other side of the city that was part of a Catholic seminary that boasted a wonderful choir, and the rector had given Alfredo the go-ahead to start making preparations.

They took glasses of wine into the sitting room, and Alfredo told Fergal the good news. Then he could resist no longer. As casually as he could, he said, 'Tell me, Fergal, what did you make of Brendan's son, Fintan? You two seemed to be getting on very well. It must have been nice to have someone close to your own age to talk to for a change, instead of all us old men going on about the past.'

Fergal was unprepared for the question, and he wondered if

Alfredo had seen Fintan dropping him off in the taxi. 'Ah, yeah, I thought he was a lovely fella, and really easy to talk to. He doesn't look like Brendan, though, does he? I mean, he's big and tall and all, but he's got that red hair, and his da's so dark.'

'Yes, that's true. He has his mother's colouring.'

'Does he? Well, he's really friendly. He asked me if I wanted to meet up and go see a museum or something.' Fergal tried to make it sound as casual as possible, although his lips were still a little raw from Fintan's kisses.

'If you both want an experienced companion, then you have only to ask me. I know this city inside out. He's only here for a little less than a week, no?'

'Yes, I think so.'

'Well, that should give him enough time to make up his mind.'

Fergal was confused and a little panicked, but he wasn't sure why. 'Make up his mind about what?'

'About Rome, of course. He tells me that his time in Paris is over and that he feels like moving on, and where better for a young aspiring artist to study than in Italy, the country that gave the world Da Vinci and Michelangelo? I think we should try and convince him to make Rome his next home for a while, don't you agree? I mean, you love it here, don't you?'

Fergal's face lit up like a Christmas tree, and it wasn't lost on Alfredo. 'Of course I love it here. In fact, I can't imagine not being here. You know, it's funny. I thought I might miss Belfast, but I don't, especially not since my da's funeral. I did miss seeing Der— I mean Father Mac, at the start, but not so much now.'

'That's good to hear. We must call him to see how the passport for your mother is coming along, and then we should set a date for your recital. I needn't tell you how much work is ahead. I think you should have an hour's repertoire – nothing too dark, but the kind of pieces that show your flexibility and range of tone.'

Fergal swallowed hard at the thought.

'Now, now, Fergal. Remember, we have only to locate that temperature in your voice that you revealed in Belfast. I'm not saying you have to go around heartbroken all the time, but, well, we need to find a way to unearth that sorrow. I can never say it enough – it's one thing to have all the notes, but it's quite another to move someone with them.'

'I know, I know—'

'Fergal, stop. People usually say "I know" when in fact they don't know.'

'I'll do my best. It's just…'

'What?'

'Well, I dream about the day when I can repay you. I think it's great that you're going to let my mother stay here, but I wish I could help her myself.'

Alfredo smiled. 'Fergal, you can repay me by giving me the best seat in the house at your opening night in a major production. This is the only debt you owe me. And we have an early and quite long lesson tomorrow, so I think we should say good night.'

He leaned over and kissed Fergal on the head, noticing the faint cigarette smoke that still clung to his hair. 'Fergal, you haven't started smoking, have you? You reek of tobacco smoke.'

'No, no.' Fergal almost panicked. 'That's just from…from working beside Giovanni.'

'Oh, yes, of course. Goodnight, then.'

Fergal gave him a little hug and almost ran up the stairs, rubbing his hair and smelling his fingers the whole way.

25

By the end of the lesson the next day, Fergal was exhausted. Alfredo was pleased that he had been able to keep up the fairly punishing pace, and he complimented his sight-reading and his natural ability to remember a difficult melody. But there was still that feeling that Fergal was holding back, and it drove Alfredo mad.

'Fergal, you're making me sound like a broken record. You're trying too hard to sound emotional, do you understand? And it's not moving at all. Just how badly do you want to become an international tenor?'

'More than anything. I—'

'It's not enough. What you have learned is how to mimic sophistication, and it will not do. Do you hear? Where is your own soul? Stop trying to sound like an opera singer! I even hear a bit of Brendan Fiscetti in there. Of course one must have influences, but one day, if you work hard enough and find your *own* voice, people will say that such-and-such a singer is trying to sound like you! That's how good you are. So stop this charade.'

Fergal felt miserable. He understood what Alfredo was saying, but he just didn't know how to put it into practice. He knew that if he apologised it would only anger Alfredo more, so he stayed tight-lipped and nodded his head to show that he understood.

Alfredo finally calmed down enough to ask him, 'Are you working late? Surely you and Giovanni can't have too much to do, now that the show is down.'

'I won't be sure until I get there. We have to paint the entire set black for the new production, and I haven't a clue how long that will take.'

'If you finish early, give me a call and I'll save you some food.'

'Okay, but I think I'll be late again. I don't mind, and sure, I have that key you gave me just in case.'

'You think you might be as late as that?'

'Ah, well, I'm not sure. Fintan was talking about trying to meet for a drink, because Brendan's going to bed early now that he doesn't have the show.'

'He's obviously exhausted. Well, if you want me to come and join you two, you know where I'll be.'

Fergal smiled and nodded. Although he felt guilty for thinking it, he could think of nothing he wanted to do less than share his precious time with Fintan with anyone. Although he loved him, Alfredo could be overbearing, and Fergal wanted to get away from him for a while. He knew his teacher was trying to get the best out of him, but sometimes it all got a bit too much and he needed to talk to someone his own age.

When Alfredo went upstairs, Fergal grabbed the phone and dialled Fintan's room at the hotel.

'Hey, can I come over after work and see you?'

'God, yes! Perfect.'

Fergal took a warm bath and got ready carefully, making sure to shave his rough chin slowly. He ironed his clothes to perfection, even though Daniela was always telling him, 'Are you trying to get me fired, Signor Flynn? I will do it! This is my work!' He thought about his mother and all the washing and ironing she had always had to do – and was probably still doing. At least his father's absence meant one less load of laundry.

Fergal kept changing his mind about which shirt to wear, but finally he settled on a new light blue one that the woman in the shop had said matched his eyes. When he eventually came downstairs, Daniela looked up from her work and cried, 'Whoa! Going somewhere special, Fergal?'

Mortified, he mumbled something and was out the door before she could ask any more questions. Daniela gave Fergal's back a wry look and wondered who the lucky girl was.

At the theatre, Fergal hung up his clothes carefully in his locker and put on the painting overalls that Giovanni had left out for him. They painted the entire set black, finally stopping at half past nine. Fergal and Giovanni got on well, and they often had a cup of coffee in the basement after their shift. Giovanni brought in little treats, like chocolates, so he was surprised that night when Fergal refused them in his hurry to leave. He changed into his ordinary clothes and almost ran out the stage door.

The hotel's reception area was a blaze of lights and mirrors, and the biggest, most attention-seeking chandelier Fergal had ever seen hung from the ceiling. *Jesus, I'm glad I don't have to clean that,* he thought as he approached the reception desk and asked for Fintan's room. The receptionist looked sceptically at his paint-splashed hands, but he rang Fintan and then told Fergal to go up to the room.

Fergal travelled up in the lift, nervously checking his hair in the mirror. Little did he know that Fintan was doing the same thing, trying to make his mop of red curls behave for at least a little while. He found the room – he couldn't help checking up and down the corridor for any sign of Brendan making an unannounced visit – and knocked quietly, saying, 'Room service!'

Fintan opened the door. 'The porters in this place are getting more handsome by the second.'

Fintan's room was huge, with an enormous blue sofa big enough for at least four people. 'Hi there,' Fintan said. 'Hey, what's up with your hands?'

'Oh, yeah – I had to paint the set at the Teatro with Giovanni. God, it was boring, but we got it done.'

'Hey, I'm the painter around here! Do you want to go and scrub them while I order a bottle of wine?'

'Great, I'd love a glass.'

While Fintan was on the phone to room service, Fergal scrubbed the stubborn paint away and looked at his reflection in the bathroom mirror. He marvelled at the thought that only a few years previously, he had been living in Belfast, wild with excitement about being able to make himself toast in his granny's rancid kitchen, sneaking in lumps of coal from her postage stamp-sized yard in an effort to keep the downstairs room warm without her finding out and shouting at him for costing her money…It felt so long ago.

Now here he was, in a beautiful hotel room, ordering wine. Fintan shouted out the list from the room service menu and asked him which he wanted, but Fergal hadn't a clue, so he said he didn't mind. He felt completely intimidated by Fintan's ease, even in something as simple as ordering over the phone. Even though there was only a year or so between them, Fintan's confidence seemed to be miles ahead of his.

Fintan opened the curtains. The window looked out onto a little piazza, empty apart from a trickle of a fountain in the centre. The wine arrived quickly. Fergal tried to pay, but Fintan insisted on signing for it. 'Look, it's on Dad, really, he's the one paying for me to be here, room service and all.'

'Wow.'

'I know.'

The waiter asked them where he should put the tray, and Fintan suggested the little balcony. There was a breeze so they kept their coats on, but Fergal felt warm on the inside and he tingled all over. Fintan looked at him silently as they sipped the wine, then he said, 'May I hold your hand, Fergal Flynn?'

'You may, Fintan Fiscetti.'

As their fingers nervously interlocked, Fintan laughed. 'I've just realised our initials are the same.'

'And there was me thinking you had that handkerchief especially made for me!' Fergal teased.

'Oh, yes. Actually, that was a present from my mother. I have lots.' Fintan lit a cigarette. 'You don't mind, do you? I promise I'm giving up…soon.'

'It's fine,' Fergal said. 'Hey, what's she like, Fintan? I know that's where you get your red hair.'

'She's very delicate. She's a bit like her roses – she loves roses. She spends half her waking hours looking after them, and she probably does it in her sleep too.'

'So you grew up with an opera singer and a gardener? What a mixture!'

'What about you – what does your mother do? I know your dad just passed away. God, that must be one of the hardest things in the world to cope with. I don't know what I'd do if anything happened to either of mine. Are you doing okay?'

'Yeah. It's not easy.'

'So was your dad a singer too? Or your mum?'

Fergal realised that it was completely natural for him to be curious. 'Ah, no, he wasn't a singer. Neither is Ma. He was into sport.'

He was beginning to get flustered, and Fintan knew he'd steered into troubled waters. 'So where does your voice come from, then? Grandparents? Or are you the only one in the family, like my dad?'

A knot of panic had risen into Fergal's stomach. How could he tell this young man about his past? He almost wished he hadn't come. Fintan appeared to have everything, including a wonderful father. What would he think when he found out the violent details of Fergal's past? Maybe it would put him off altogether.

'Fintan, I'm sorry to be so…it's just that, well, things were very bad at home for a long time, and I just got used to it. I thought it was normal. The more I meet people like you, though, the more I see that it wasn't normal. That's all.'

'Oh Fergal, I'm sorry I brought it up. We don't have to talk about it now. Let's just enjoy the wine, eh?'

'No, you see, that's just it. You *should* be able to ask me. The fact that you can't – that's what's not normal, or natural, or whatever is the best word.'

The atmosphere had grown tense, and Fintan thought carefully before he continued. 'Look, we can't know everything about each other in one evening, can we? Fuck it, Fergal – shut up and kiss me.'

Fergal put his glass down, almost laughing with relief and wishing he had said it first. They clung to each other on the little balcony and kissed hungrily, more and more deeply as they got braver. Fergal thought his heart had grown to the same size as his chest; it beat wildly and deafeningly. He realised that Fintan was the first person he'd kissed this way since Dermot and a little wave of guilt came over him, but it was quickly blown away by a real kiss, blind and full of love, that robbed him of his breath.

They parted for a second and leaned awkwardly against each other. It had grown colder. They went back inside, to the sofa, and

Fintan dimmed the lights. He found a radio station that played old jazz ballads, with a soft, hoarse DJ who dedicated each song to all the lovers out there, new and old.

They continued kissing, and slowly undid each other's shirt buttons. Fergal loved the way their mouths seemed to fit perfectly together, and they laughed as desire took hold of their reins and the rest of their clothes ended up on the floor. Fintan loved kissing Fergal. He tasted wonderful, and the very smell of him was enough to get him hard. He moved his mouth down to Fergal's nipples and played with them with his tongue. Fergal's chest had sprouted hair since the previous summer, but he was still shy about his body in a way that Fintan found irresistible.

Fergal climbed on top of Fintan, and they could feel each other's hardness against their stomachs. Fintan slid his hands down the back of Fergal's underwear, kissing him all the while. Then, slowly, he moved his hand around to the front, and Fergal gasped.

Fintan grinned. 'Oh, Fergal, you brought me a present – and it's my favourite flavour.'

Fergal could only laugh helplessly as Fintan left a trail of kisses from his chin to his belly. Then he pulled off Fergal's underwear and took him into his mouth. Fergal thought he would burst right then and there, but he just managed to hold himself back. Fintan looked up at him and smiled, then he began sucking, gently and lovingly, and Fergal threw his head back with a sudden unstoppable moan.

He wanted to do the same thing to Fintan at the same time, so he twisted around on the sofa, managed to get Fintan's underwear down around his thighs and took him into his throat as deeply as he could. They came up for air only when they both knew they wouldn't last.

They lay side by side and continued kissing. Fergal stroked Fintan's hair, and again Father Mac flashed through his mind. He didn't want to think about him. He climbed on top of Fintan, and they rubbed their entire bodies against each other. The motion grew wilder. Fintan's legs widened and he bucked against Fergal, thighs clasped around his waist, and then there was no turning back, and one final heave left them both exhausted and soaking.

Involuntarily, they drifted into sleep. When they woke, Fintan went to the bathroom to take a shower. Fergal sat up, rubbing his eyes. He remembered Father Mac's letter telling him to go into the world as a single, free young man. At the time, that had sounded impossible, but then Fintan had appeared out of the blue...

Fintan came back wearing a bathrobe that should have belonged to a sumo wrestler and handed him a huge bath towel. 'The shower's still running if you want a quick rinse.' Fergal stood up and they kissed again before reluctantly parting, and he stepped under the warm running water. As he turned off the shower and stepped out onto the mat, he picked up a bottle of French cologne from the sink and unscrewed the top. Sure enough, it smelled just like Fintan.

Fintan was still in his bathrobe. He had flicked on the TV and was channel surfing, and it struck Fergal that he hadn't seen any TV in ages. Even though he had just shared his body with this young man, he suddenly felt self-conscious as he saw his underpants on the floor. He pulled them back on under his towel, as if he were at the beach, and his timidity made Fintan like him all the more.

'Do you want to stay the night, Fergal?'

'I'd love to, but I think I should probably go. What time is it? I've got an early lesson in the morning.'

They couldn't believe it when the hotel clock told them it was almost two o'clock. 'My God,' Fergal said, 'are you sure that thing is right? Fuck – how long were we asleep? I should ring for a cab.'

'There's no need, there's always one at the front door. Do you want me to get dressed and leave you down?'

'No, no, sure, you look far too comfortable there. Hey, where's my other sock?'

When Fergal was finally dressed, they kissed again on the sofa, and Fintan played with his hair in the way he was beginning to love.

'I always used to want dark hair like yours.'

'Really? But yours is incredible. I've never seen hair so red before.'

Fintan opened his bathrobe and looked down. 'You weren't put off by my ginger pubes?'

They exploded laughing, and Fergal shook his head. 'The opposite, actually.'

'I'm glad. You know they used to call me Fanta-Pants at school?'

They collapsed with laughter on the sofa again, and Fintan wrapped his open robe around them both. They lay there, listening to the fountain, until somewhere in the city a bell told them it was half past two. Fergal wrote down Alfredo's home number on the hotel pad and told Fergal he didn't usually leave for the theatre till after five o'clock.

They said goodbye at the door of Fintan's room. One more kiss, and Fergal was gone.

Sure enough, there were a few taxis waiting, and he was back home in no time. He opened and closed the front door soundlessly and he was about to head up the stairs when Alfredo appeared from the kitchen in his nightclothes, holding a glass of milk.

'My goodness, Fergal! Did you end up painting the outside of the theatre as well?'

It took Fergal a second to figure out what he meant. He managed to quell his panic. 'No, I bumped into Fintan, and we ended up going for a walk and a drink and stuff.'

'That was a long walk. It's nearly three o'clock.'

Fergal wanted to tell him everything. He needed to tell someone, to help himself make sense of it all, so why not Alfredo? There wasn't much his teacher didn't already know about him.

But what could he tell him? That he and Fintan had had sex? How good it had made him feel? Maybe it hadn't meant as much to Fintan as it had to him…'Ah, we had some food and talked a lot, and then we ended up back at his hotel, watching TV. You should see his room, it's like an apartment or something, with its own wee living room and balcony.'

Alfredo noticed that Fergal didn't meet his eyes, and he dropped it. 'A phone call to say you were going to be this late would have been appreciated. I don't want to sound like some dreadful governess, but I worry, Fergal, it's my nature. Father MacManus was on the phone. He's worried about you too, since the funeral. He did say that he took your mother to get her passport photos, so things are moving along. He was sorry not to speak to you.'

'Right…Look, I'm sorry, Alfredo. We just lost all track of time.'

'Well, you're young – and you're home now, and you're safe, and that's the main thing. You look exhausted, though. Get some sleep.'

But Fergal couldn't sleep. His heart was racing, and he wanted to kick himself for being caught coming in so late.

'Fintan Fiscetti is leaving in less than a week,' he whispered to the ceiling. 'Maybe he'll decide to study in Italy, but it might not be Rome. Maybe he won't come back at all. What am I doing? He can't be that interested in me. Maybe he's got another fella in London or Paris, or…'

On and on the questions rattled around in his head, and the church bells sounded six before he was finally able to drift off for a few hours of sleep.

26

It was just after half past ten when Fergal made it downstairs. Daniela was in full swing, dusting and polishing, so he hid in the kitchen, making coffee and looking out at the swinging sofa at the bottom of the garden, remembering his and Fintan's first kiss. Just then the phone rang, and to his surprise Daniela called out, saying that it was for him.

Father Mac's voice was a nice surprise. 'Fergal, you sound completely exhausted. Are you sure you didn't go back to work too soon?'

'No, no. I'm fine.'

'Maybe you're doing too much. I know how hard you work – the lessons with Alfredo, the Italian lessons and the Teatro job... Do you want me to have a word? If it's about money, I'm sure we can come to some kind of agreement.'

'No, it's not that. I just didn't sleep well, that's all. My lesson doesn't start till noon.'

'At least that's something. Alfredo seems in good enough form about your recital. I was thinking maybe that would be a good time for Angela to arrive – unless it would be too much extra pressure?'

'It's funny you say that, I was thinking the same thing. Do you think she'll still come, Father Mac?' Instinctively, now that they were officially ex-lovers, Fergal had stopped calling him by his first name.

'She'll go to Rome, all right. I think she's told the whole street she's going to meet the Pope himself!' Fergal felt a sudden little pang. Somehow, he had hoped that he himself might be enough of a reason for his mother to visit Rome. 'Listen, Alfredo was worried because you weren't home. Did he wait up for you?'

'Yes, he did. I was much later than I thought, but he told me you'd phoned.'

Father Mac sighed heavily. 'Fergal, I'm not stupid. Are you going to tell me about it?'

Fergal knew he had to tell someone, and Father Mac was the person he trusted most in the world. So he told him everything that had happened between him and Fintan. Father Mac listened, almost forgetting to breathe as he heard how alive Fergal sounded, how his voice lit up at the mere mention of Fintan's name. In that moment, he knew he had lost that part of him forever.

'But I'm worried that I'm not good enough for him, Father Mac. We come from such different backgrounds, and Fintan's so much more sophisticated – he's travelled all over the place, and he knows all about art and books…'

The silence was long enough that Fergal started to worry about what Father Mac's reaction would be, but finally he said softly, 'Fergal, you shouldn't worry about things like that. I'm sure your very difference is exactly what attracts him to you – and maybe you to him. When will you learn to value yourself? I know you had a hard start in life, but it's not who you love that matters. Rearrange those three little letters: it's *how* you love that's important. Anyway, I think it's brilliant news. Thank you for trusting me. And please, be careful.'

'Oh, I will, I will.' Fergal sighed with relief. He had told the truth to the only other man in the world who he had ever truly loved. He also knew that their intimate days were over, once and for all. He only wanted Fintan now, but he was still scared that Fintan might not want him as much.

'Is he not going back to England with his father?' Father Mac asked.

Fergal explained that, in fact, Fintan was thinking of staying in Rome, but he didn't know what was going to happen. He was too scared to even think about it much. When Alfredo called out that he was willing to start the lesson early and Fergal said goodbye, he was actually glad of the distraction.

The lessons were growing more and more intense as they concentrated on building the right repertoire for Fergal's forthcoming recital. Alfredo reminded him that it never hurt anyone to be over-prepared. They also listened to a few recordings by Tito Schipa and Jussi Bjorling while Alfredo discussed tone, but Fergal found it hard to concentrate. He wondered what Fintan was doing at that very moment, what he was feeling about the previous night. Did he have a friend he could call, to talk to about it? Was he thinking about it at all? Fergal got more and more paranoid as the day progressed. Finally Alfredo slammed his hand down on top of the piano in frustration.

'Fergal Flynn, is there somewhere else you'd rather be?'

'What? No, of course not.'

'Your concentration is all over the place. I'm not surprised, given how little sleep you must have had.'

'I'm sorry. I'm just tired. And Father Mac rang. My mother is telling anyone who'll listen that she's going to Rome to meet the Pope.'

'And?'

'I was just…oh, never mind.'

'No, come on. Better out than in. What we need from you, Fergal, is what's in your soul, and that will inform your singing at the deepest level. So out with it, don't be embarrassed. Tell me what you're feeling.'

'I was kind of hoping that I was a good enough reason for her to visit Rome. Don't get me wrong, I'm not trying to compete with the Pope or anything, I was just hoping she might be…well, you know…proud of me. I know I've not really done much yet, but…'

'Let me stop you there. Firstly, you have done an incredible amount so far. Your voice has improved immeasurably. You must believe that. And if your mother isn't proud of you by now, then the recital is the perfect opportunity to blow her away. Fergal, I only wish you would stop placing so much store in what other people think of you. Never mind trying to impress your mother, you're not an infant learning how to talk. All this hard work is about being the best you can be, for yourself and for the music. So stop feeling so sorry for yourself, it's a waste of energy.'

When they broke for lunch, Alfredo told Fergal that he was thinking of inviting Brendan and Fintan for dinner the night before they left for London in two days' time. At that moment the phone rang, and Alfredo answered. 'Synchronicity is alive and well. Fintan Fiscetti, we were just talking about you and your father. I'm having a dinner party – much smaller this time – the night before you both leave. I was going to call Brendan this afternoon.'

Fergal was dying to know where Fintan was, and if he was lying around in his hotel bed with only his robe on.

'Yes, of course, Fergal's just here. See you then.'

Fergal took the receiver. He was flushed in the face and couldn't stop smiling.

'Hey, you,' Fintan said. 'What are you doing this afternoon?'

'Nothing. I'm free.'

'Want to meet in Café degli Artisti in about an hour?'

Alfredo and Daniela were discussing possible menu ideas, trying to hear what Fergal was saying without being too obvious.

'I'll meet you there. Great…no problem. See ya.'

'Well, well,' said Alfredo, 'you two seem to have hit it off.'

'Yeah,' was all Fergal could manage.

Fintan met his father for a late breakfast on the balcony of Brendan's suite. Brendan noticed immediately how excited he was for someone who wasn't normally a morning person – the one thing he had definitely inherited from the Fiscetti side of the family.

'Fintan, how much coffee have you had already? If you're not careful, you'll sprout wings and take flight – or knock over something that will go on the bill.'

'I'm sorry. I was up late, that's all. I'm feeling wired today.'

'Why didn't you give your old dad a call if you couldn't sleep? We could've played chess or cards. I woke a few times myself and ended up reading. Actually, I nearly rang you.'

'I'm glad you didn't.'

'Why?'

'I…I had some company.'

'You did? At that hour? But surely you don't know anybody here…Hang on a minute.' Brendan started laughing. 'It wasn't a certain Irishman, was it?'

Fintan blushed, which was all the answer his father needed.

'Look at the state of you, Fintan, you've gone purple. That can only mean one thing.'

'Oh stop, Dad.'

Brendan's voice softened. 'I hope you know what you're doing. It's none of my business, I know, but Fergal is incredibly fragile right now. He's just lost his father, and they were estranged. Alfredo was telling me.'

'I really, really like him. It's only been a few days, but I do.'

'Well, I'm the last person to tell anybody to take it slowly. You know your mother and I were married after only a few weeks, and I don't regret it for a second. In fact, I'd do it all again in the morning. I know you're not about to go rushing off down the aisle, but you will be careful, won't you? We go home in a few days, and then you've got to think about where to study next.'

'I know, I know, I know. I'm meeting Fergal later.'

'Oh. I thought we might take the train to Florence for the night.'

'When did you decide that? That's typical of you, Dad, just like when I was a kid. I only saw you when it fit into your schedule, and then you expected me to drop everything. You can't keep doing that.'

Brendan felt as if he had been slapped across the face. 'Fintan, that's a monstrous thing to say. You were always our first priority. We don't have to go to Florence at all – I haven't bought the tickets – but I was actually thinking of you, and your need to see as much art and architecture as possible. Where did this all come from?'

'Oh Dad, sorry. It's just that I didn't expect to feel this way about Fergal. I can't stop thinking about him.'

'Fintan, do you really think I treated you like that when you were a child? Honestly?'

'It would've been nice to see you a bit more.'

'But I saw you as often as I could. And I wrote to you, wherever I was.'

'Oh for fuck's sake, that's hardly the same thing. You can't tell a postcard that you've got a sore ear, or that you're frightened of thunder during the night in a boarding school in the middle of nowhere.' Fintan saw the stricken look on his father's face and his heart sank. He wished he hadn't said anything. 'I'm sorry, Dad,' he whispered.

Brendan reached over and enfolded him in his arms. 'Don't be sorry for being honest. And I'm sorry, too. You know I love you, don't you?'

'I do. I just feel upside down today. I mean, what if Fergal isn't half as interested in me?'

'Would you like to invite him over for a drink later?' Brendan suggested.

'I'm not sure. He's quite shy, really, and he has to go to work. We'll see what happens.'

Their little storm over, they settled themselves again and began eating. 'What do you think of Alfredo?' Brendan asked.

'He seems really nice. It's funny seeing his face, after all those years of seeing that picture of you, him and that soprano on the mantelpiece at Mum's.'

'You mean Marla Davis. Tell me, do you think he knows Fergal is gay?'

'I don't know. Did you know when you first met him? I mean, I had my suspicions, but I wasn't a hundred per cent sure.'

'I knew you were gay long before you told me, so I think I'm a pretty good judge. To be honest, though, I didn't really think about it with Fergal. He's sensitive, yes, but not effeminate. You know Alfredo is, don't you?'

'Is he? Well, that's no great surprise, but he's quite contained, isn't he? He doesn't give much away.'

'All I'll say is that you should be very careful with Fergal and Alfredo. Alfredo is investing an incredible amount of his time and energy into Fergal's career, and he's fiercely protective of him. Also, until this week, Alfredo and I hadn't seen each other since before you were born, so he's feeling vulnerable about all the Fiscettis.'

'Dad! You didn't have a thing with him, did you – you know, in your experimental years, before you met Mum? Were you hetero-flexible?'

'Fintan, what kind of question is that for a son to ask a father? The answer is no! And you made up that word, didn't you? Hetero-flexible, indeed! I know you think everyone is gay, but I never had any experimental years – although not for the lack of offers, I can assure you.'

'Actually, Dad, come to think of it, I don't really want to know.'

'Hey, you started it! Anyway, Alfredo and I were very close when we toured together, and, well, how can I put it? Alfredo's boundaries became a little blurred when it came to our friendship.'

'Beautifully put, Dad. You mean he fancied you rotten and couldn't have you.'

'If you must put it like that, yes.'

'Well, well. Do you think Fergal knows about any of this?'

'I'd say Alfredo has kept it close to his chest, but you never know. He seems much more relaxed these days. But he was very religious, you know – wherever we went on tour, he was always asking the theatre manager where the nearest church was – and Italy is a very Catholic country. I would imagine he's still trying to find a balance there.'

'God, look at the time! I said I'd meet Fergal. Look, I'm so glad you know about everything. Thanks for listening – and for the hug. You never know, we might see you later.'

Brendan loved seeing his son genuinely happy. He knew that no matter how well off they were financially, life hadn't been easy for their only child, what with Amelia's long illness and his constant travelling. Fintan's earlier words had torn at his heart, but he was glad that his son felt he could say them to him.

'Good luck, my darling, handsome son. Tell Fergal I send my love.'

The two young men met at Café degli Artisti again, and this time there was a new intimacy in their smiles, an intimacy that was only possible because of the previous night. They spent the afternoon wandering the piazzas. In all his time in Rome, Fergal had never explored so much of it as he had that week. They took the metro to the Colosseum, but a man dressed as a centurion was holding a sign that told them the queue was two hours long. Dumbstruck, they headed back to the Spanish Steps. A tiny man with a Polaroid camera offered to take their picture for a small fee. When they looked at the little image of themselves together, Fergal didn't know what to say. He hardly recognised his own happy, tanned face smiling back at him.

'Now we have to fight over who keeps it, eh?' Fintan laughed. 'Speaking of fights, I had a bit of a go at my dad earlier, but it was fine in the end.'

Fergal listened intently and thought about how his own da would never have backed down and said he was sorry for anything. He couldn't help feeling envious of Fintan's relationship with Brendan, and feeling a deeper and deeper loss at his own lack of any relationship with his father.

It was almost time for Fergal to leave for work, so they had one last coffee and talked about the dinner that Alfredo was planning.

'Alfredo is a man for the food, isn't he?' Fintan said. 'God, I love Italy. Hey, Fergal, you did realise Alfredo was one of us, didn't you? You know, the pink pound? Or what would they call it here, the Liza lira?'

Fergal laughed. 'Yeah, I knew Alfredo was gay. He told me a while back. I told him about me, too, but he'd already guessed. He's pretty private about himself, though.'

'Hey, you can't tell anyone, but did you know he was in love with my dad, years ago, before we were born? But with Dad being straight old Dad, the feeling wasn't mutual.'

'He told me that too. Did you ever see those old pictures of them? They weren't exactly ugly – and your da's still a fine-looking man. It must be awful to be in love with someone who doesn't want you.'

'Yeah. The scourge of unrequited love, isn't that what it's called?'

'I'll take your word for it.'

'Dad was telling me about it over breakfast – actually, I was so late getting up that it was more like brunch. You must be knackered, Fergal. We didn't half go for it last night. God, I wish you could've stayed the night!'

Fergal blushed and nodded. Then he asked, 'So…your da knows about you?'

'What? Being gay, you mean? Oh God, yes. I came out to him when I was sixteen – to them both, in fact.'

'What did they say?'

'They said they already knew. I was expecting a bit of drama, at least, but I suppose a lot of Dad's friends in the theatre world are gay, so it wasn't a big deal. I was a bit disappointed. Actually, they were lovely about it. Mum's theory is that we're like plants – there are variations within any species, and they're all equally special and in need of care. How about your parents? Did your father know? Does your mum know yet?'

'Jesus, *no*!' Fergal half shouted. He composed himself and continued, 'My ma is very Catholic, and my da was…God, it's weird talking about him in the past tense. Let's just say he was a law unto himself. I don't even think they really knew what heterosexuality was, never mind any other kind. There's four of us – the twins, me and then Ciaran – so I'd say they did it a total of three times. Jesus, I really don't want to picture my ma and da doing it!' They both laughed.

'I'm glad you've got a sense of humour about it, at least. Fergal, I should tell you that Brendan knows about us.'

'What? How?'

'Please don't be angry. He just took one look at me this morning and guessed it wasn't insomnia that kept me up. He knows I don't know anyone here but you, and he put two and two together – it wasn't hard. And I blabbed. I'm sorry. There was no point in trying to deny it. When I lie, I change colour completely. And I don't lie to my father – well, not often, anyway.'

'Oh shit, Fintan. What if he tells Alfredo?'

'Hey, calm down. You don't have to worry about my dad being discreet. Anyway, Alfredo's not the bloody Pope! It's our business.'

They looked at each other, unblinking.

'Fintan, what's happening here?'

'What do you mean?'

'I mean, I know we only met the other day, but I really feel like I can talk to you – really talk to you.' Fergal dropped his head and half whispered, 'I wish…oh, never mind.'

'Tell me, please.'

'Well, we've just met, and you're about to leave again. I just wish you weren't going, that's all.'

'Ah, Fergal. I thought about you all last night, that's why I hardly slept. I'm supposed to be thinking about where to study next. I could reapply to Paris, I could go back to London and live at Dad's. I know how privileged I am to have those choices, but you've put a spanner in the works, you really have. There, I've said it. Fergal Flynn, look what you've done to me.'

They sat with their legs interlocked like vines, not able to say any more.

Finally the church bell interrupted their thoughts, and Fergal saw that it was time to go to work. 'Even though I don't want to,' he said, 'I should probably go home tonight after work. I'll be knackered, to be honest, and Alfredo was still up when I got back last night. I couldn't do it again without him asking loads of questions.'

'You're probably right. Will you ring me at least before you leave the theatre? Or when you get home?'

Fergal smiled. 'Of course I will.'

They hugged and kissed each other on the cheek. In that crowded square, it would have been more unusual for two young men not to.

27

Alfredo's world had gone into overdrive. Not only was his diary full of private lessons – Salvatore, the singing butcher, was coming every week now – but he had been on the phone to Father Mac, making sure that Angela was definitely coming in the next few weeks. The seminary had called about publicity for the recital and he was trying to get hold of Brendan to organise the farewell dinner party. It would be a small gathering, just the four of them and Arianna. It was all too much and very stressful – just the way he liked it.

Alfredo and Brendan met for a late lunch at the Café degli Artisti. Brendan had exhausted the hotel menu some weeks earlier. Alfredo was still amazed at how things had turned around in only a week – not a word for over two decades, and now, for the third time in a few days, they were sitting down to eat and talk together.

'Brendan, forgive me for repeating myself, but it's just so good to see you so much, after all that silence.'

'Yes, it is amazing. Alfredo, I know we can't get back the time we lost, but will you come to London as soon as you can? I have a big house that hardly ever gets any visitors. Promise you will?'

'Of course. I'm delighted that you ask. Will Amelia join us? I'd love to see her.'

'You never know. After this week, I'd say anything is possible.'

They took their time over the menu, ordered plenty of food and drank a fair bit of wine. They talked about the operas they'd seen and the recordings of the newest generation of tenors that they favoured. Brendan said that as much as he had loved the performances, it was sheer luxury not to have to be aware of the clock and of whether his voice was sufficiently warmed up. The conversation was lubricated by countless glasses of wine, and over coffee and cognac the subject matter moved naturally into more personal waters.

'Alfredo, did you never fall in love, you know, after you left Venice that time?'

'Not really; not properly. If we're going to be honest, it took me a long time to get over you. I'm sure it sounds odd for you to hear this, but unrequited love has to be one of the most painful things in the world. Can you imagine if Amelia hadn't felt the same way as you? How heartbroken you would have been?'

'My God, Alfredo. I can't imagine it, I really can't.'

'I never want to go through that again. I was so jealous of Amelia, and it was made harder by the fact that she was so nice. I was poisoned by my own need, and there was no antidote in sight. I struggled for a very long time after that. I didn't even want to be gay, but it's who I truly am. It's been strange, meeting someone like Fergal.'

'What do you mean?'

'In some ways, I think I was trying to heal that part of myself that was still damaged from my time with you. Why else would I

301

go into the world and find a tenor who did need me, albeit only musically?'

'You don't fancy Fergal, do you?'

'No, no. He's handsome, of course, and that voice is to die for, but he's far too young. I prefer older men any day. The bigger and hairier, the better.'

Brendan burst out laughing. 'Good for you! Horses for courses, I suppose.'

They had had several liqueurs at this point, on top of all the wine, so Brendan was a lot less discreet than usual. 'Fergal and Fintan really seem to have hit it off, wouldn't you say?'

'Yes, I know.'

'Alfredo, did you know that my son is gay? And I think – well, I know – they've become very friendly since they first set eyes on each other in my dressing room.'

'Really?'

'You should have seen Fintan at breakfast this morning! They'd been up half the night. Too much information for any father, but I gather they're at the talking-all-night stage.'

Alfredo's eyes had widened. 'You mean they've become lovers? Are you sure?'

'Alfredo, one of the only good things about boarding school education is that Fintan grew up very fast. He's more like my friend than my son.'

'Yes, I noticed that he sometimes calls you Brendan and sometimes Dad.'

'Exactly. We're very close, and he came out to us when he was only sixteen, which was very brave, although Amelia and I knew all along.'

'That was brave. How ironic that you have a gay son, after what you and I…went through.'

'I know. I often thought of you. You could have been a great role model for him, and advised him in matters I have no experience of, but you did make it easier for me to understand him.'

'Did I? How?'

'You were the first great gay man I ever met.'

'That's such a lovely thing to say. I'm flattered, of course, but Fergal and Fintan? They've only just met! My God, it's almost like…' Alfredo's voice trailed off.

'Like what?'

'It's like seeing what could have happened, all those years ago, had you been cut from the same cloth as me. God, I feel so envious.'

'Well, we both know what it's like to be head over heels in love. I'd say they're both feeling very vulnerable and pretending they're not. We're leaving for the UK soon and they're trying to spend every spare minute with each other – and I gather there aren't many, given Fergal's schedule – and that makes it all the more romantic, in a sense.'

'Yes, I see.'

'I remember physically aching if I was apart from Amelia for more than a couple of hours, and I hadn't even known her a week. Talk about history repeating itself.'

Alfredo dropped his head.

'I hope I haven't upset you, Alfredo? I know I probably shouldn't have said that – but look how many years of our friendship are gone, and we can never get them back. I refuse to waste what precious time we have with lies.'

Alfredo looked away for a moment, then back at his friend. 'I understand what you're saying. You know, I never planned to fall in love with you, Brendan, and I remember that pain of separation all too well. But I can honestly say that seeing you again was exactly what I needed, even though at one point in my life that would have been unimaginable. It becomes clearer each time we meet.' He sighed. 'I wonder when, if at all, Fergal will tell me. I feel so responsible for him, like a surrogate father, I suppose, even though I hope I bear not the slightest resemblance to his natural father, who was quite a piece of work. Fergal did tell me he was gay, though, so he does trust me.'

'Alfredo, forgive me, but I don't think we should say anything to either of them. I shouldn't have told you, but I'm a bit drunk and it's too late now. And I trust you wholeheartedly. Promise me you won't say a word to Fergal at our farewell dinner?'

'Of course not. It's just amazing that you seem to know much more about his life than I do.'

'That's not true, Alfredo. Naturally, we saw a lot of each other when I was working at the Teatro, but our conversations were mostly about you, and I know almost nothing about his life in Ireland. He always changed the subject when it came up, so I didn't push it. I feel close to him because of his voice and the fact that he's my son's age, but Fintan was the one who told me about this. And, of course, I've already broken my promise not to tell anyone. You're an exception, though.'

That made Alfredo smile.

They spent the rest of the afternoon wandering slowly past Rome's finest vast sculptures and monuments. Alfredo was only too delighted to gossip about which ones were said to have been created by Da Vinci's apprentices, although they were attributed to the great man himself.

'You mean he subcontracted?'

'That's what they say!'

The only time he alluded to the coming dinner was to ask Brendan what his favourite food of all time was.

'Pasta, of course. What else would I say in Italy?'

'Perfect. Our family has the best sauce recipe in all of Italy – all prejudices aside. My sister will come. She treats Fergal like a son too. You know he used to live at her restaurant until he moved in with me? I suppose we have become his new family, really. I'm glad you told me about him and Fintan. You Fiscetti boys are certainly fast workers! I'm just a bit sad he didn't tell me himself.'

'Alfredo, it's only been a week. Give the boy a chance. He probably can't believe what's happening either. Let's wish them well and stand back. What do you say to another drink?'

They found a bar and spent what little was left of the afternoon drinking, until Alfredo realised he was late for a lesson with Salvatore. As he was leaving, Brendan pulled him closer and whispered drunkenly, 'We have to find someone for you, Alfredo. You're too special and too smart to be on your own. There must be someone out there right now, thinking exactly the same thing, wondering where you are.'

Alfredo went forty shades of tomato. 'Look, I'll see you for dinner tomorrow at my house – eight o'clock.' With that, he was out of the bar and hailing a taxi.

Salvatore was just leaving when Alfredo came panting up the path, shouting apologies, promising he'd make it up to him and trying not to appear too drunk. As Alfredo fished in his pocket for his front door key, he wondered whether it was the wine or whether his carcass-chopping pupil was far more attractive than he had ever realised. He opened the front door, glancing quickly at the butcher's chunky, pristinely scrubbed left hand, and thought to himself, *Well, no wedding ring – that's a good start.*

After he clocked out at the stage door, Fergal did as he had promised and dialled Fintan's hotel. When the receptionist connected him to the room, Fintan picked up immediately.

'I knew it was you, Fergal. Are you tired?'

'I'm wrecked, to be honest. Looking forward to getting to bed.'

They both laughed, and Fintan said, 'I know you have to go home, but I just wish you were here and I could kiss you goodnight.'

A few of the stagehands passed Fergal in the corridor, clapping him on the back, and the night watchman rustled his newspaper. 'Look, I can't really talk here. How about a late breakfast tomorrow morning?'

'Yes, great idea. Why don't you come over here? The food is brilliant – and we could have room service…'

Fergal felt himself hardening at the very thought, and he quickly agreed.

'Goodnight, then, Fergal. Consider yourself kissed.'

'Night, Fintan. Same to you.'

On his walk home, Fergal thought about Father Mac. He had truly believed that nobody could ever take Father Mac's place in his heart, but then Fintan had appeared and done just that. But Fergal wondered what was going to happen to their fragile new relationship. In a couple of days, Fintan would be gone. There were no guarantees. He also wondered what Father Mac would do. Would he find another lover, in time? Fergal knew how strong his faith was – but he also knew what a great kisser he was.

Distracted by the discussion in his head, he had reached Alfredo's front gate without realising it. He saw the lights on and pictured Alfredo sipping red wine and listening to music. Fergal wondered what would become of him – would he ever have a lover?

He opened the front door and, sure enough, there was Alfredo, with a new album in one hand and a glass of wine in the other, dancing around the floor in his socks with his eyes closed. He didn't even hear Fergal come in. When he opened his eyes, he nearly spat out his mouthful of wine.

'Fergal! Here, have some of this red, it's unbelievable. Look, there's a glass waiting for you, and I had an extra one, just in case we needed it.'

'Is someone else coming over?'

'No, it's just that you and Fintan seem to be seeing so much of each other that I thought he might be with you.'

Fergal panicked for a moment, then he realised that Alfredo must know or suspect something, so he decided to come clean. He felt he owed him that much.

'Alfredo, there's something I need to tell you.'

'You're falling in love with Fiscetti Junior.'

'How did you—'

'I'm not blind. And I told you his father had much the same effect on me when I was around your age. Those Fiscettis – they're unbelievable. At least Fintan is gay and you're not wasting your time.'

'I don't know. I hope he feels the way I do. He says he does, but—'

'Fergal, do you ever relax? Why wouldn't he feel the same?'

'You saw where I grew up, Alfredo. Sometimes I feel, well, that I'm not good enough, you know? Look at the life he leads with Brendan and Amelia. I can't compete. He went to public school and all—'

'Fergal, Fergal, when will you wake up? This is directly linked to your singing, too. Let go of the past. Let it go. It's only holding you back.'

Fergal nodded and drank more wine. He knew Alfredo was right, but he wished he could be sure what was in Fintan's heart.

Alfredo refilled their glasses, turned up the music and pulled him up to dance. 'Come on! We have our lives to live, while we still can – especially you, young Fergal!'

And they did the tango across the front room, throwing their heads back and laughing as if God had told them the dirtiest joke in the world.

28

The next morning, Fergal woke early, a bit dehydrated from the red wine. Alfredo had insisted that they finish it, because the ancient bottle had waited a long time to be opened. Surprisingly, it hadn't made him feel asthmatic, as red wine often did. Typical, he thought – the only red wine that didn't give him asthma was the most expensive kind.

The house was still quiet when he left, and he was glad of the walk to Fintan's hotel. He still felt a little intimidated by the grandeur of the lobby, and he walked nervously towards the reception desk, feeling as if one of the security guards might grab him by the scruff of the neck at any moment and land him on his arse in the street for not looking rich enough.

He was about to ask the receptionist to ring Fintan's room when he heard a familiar voice boom at him across the lobby, 'Fergal Flynn, is that you?'

He turned around to see Brendan at the door of the conservatory, with only a newspaper for company. 'Brendan, how are you?' he said, trying not to stammer.

'Starving, actually – and they do the most fantastic breakfast here. Are you waiting to see Fintan?'

'Well, yes, I was about to ring his room, because the lifts don't work without a room key – but of course you know that...' *Dickhead,* he said to himself, *stop babbling!*

'Yes, indeed.'

'He invited me over for breakfast.'

'Wonderful! We'll get a table and call him from the restaurant. How about that?'

'Yeah, great,' Fergal said reluctantly, and he followed Brendan in the direction of the conservatory, which was beautifully laid out for buffet breakfast.

Brendan had been a guest at the hotel for long enough to know the first names of the staff they encountered, and they treated him like visiting royalty. Fergal found a house phone and rang Fintan. He picked up, sounding sleepy but sexy.

'Fergal? Is it breakfast time already? Are you downstairs? God, I was just dreaming about you.'

Brendan had chosen a table not far from the phone, so Fergal tried to sound as delighted as possible. 'Fintan, guess what! I just bumped into your dad at reception, and he's invited us to breakfast. Isn't that lovely?'

He smiled over at Brendan and lowered his voice. 'I'm sorry, he just dragged me into the conservatory and said I could ring you from here.'

Fintan was laughing. 'Don't worry. I'll get dressed and come right down. It's not a problem – even though I'm dying to kiss you! Anyway, it's not as if we have anything to hide from him.'

Fergal hung up and went back to his seat. 'You mean he's awake?' Brendan laughed. 'You're obviously a good influence.

Usually it's impossible to get him out of bed in the morning.'
Fergal would have preferred to get him into bed, but he kept that
to himself, although he blushed badly enough that Brendan asked
if he needed a window opened.

Fintan found them at their corner table and kissed them both
good morning. Fergal couldn't get over how handsome he looked
when he was sleepy and dishevelled. They took their plates and
queued at the huge buffet. Brendan hadn't been lying about the
breakfast – there was every kind of food imaginable, and Fergal
could only stare at some of the combinations of things that the
other guests were piling on their plates, like pancakes with fresh
cream and bacon on top. He settled for scrambled eggs and tiny
sausages, croissants and coffee. Fintan and Brendan had identical
enormous appetites and kept going up for more bacon or more
toast. The waitress hovered with constant coffee refills, and by the
end of the meal the caffeine was sending a strange current
through Fergal's blood and making him talk faster than normal.
Every now and then Fintan would smile apologetically and say,
'Sorry, Fergal, my brain is still in neutral – say that again?'

Brendan was the first to leave, folding his paper under his arm
and saying he was off to read it in a nearby park. They both
watched him leave. When they were on their own, Fintan turned
back to Fergal and said, 'Well, that wasn't so bad, was it?'

'No, I suppose not. It's funny, though, he's not like your da at
all, is he?'

'What do you mean?'

'He seems more like a mate or something. I can't believe how
well youse get on.'

'There isn't much that man doesn't know about me. We have
our moments – I told you I yelled at him yesterday – but it always
blows over. And there's nothing like a hug from my dad.'

'Sounds great. My da only ever punched me, and sometimes I

felt like that was better than nothing. At least he touched me for a second.'

'God, Fergal, don't say that! It's not the same thing at all.'

'I know, I'm just saying.'

'Dad is so fond of you, you know. He thinks you have an incredible voice, and I can tell you, he's fiercely critical. I could get jealous if he's not careful.'

'Yeah, right! You jealous of me?'

'Why not? I think he'd secretly have loved me to follow in his operatic footsteps, but I haven't a note in my head.'

'Really?' Fergal had gone red in the face again, and Fintan laughed. He reached for his hand under the tablecloth, but Fergal felt too self-conscious; he pulled away.

'Hey, you don't regret the other night already, do you?'

'What? No! Are you joking? Jesus, I love being with you. I'm just not comfortable…you know, in front of people.'

Fintan tilted his head and looked at him sleepily, then he said in a fake American accent, 'So you wanna go upstairs and fool around?'

Fergal didn't need to be asked twice.

They put the 'Do Not Disturb' sign on the door handle and hardly had time to close the door before they grabbed each other and fell to the floor, heated hands undoing layers of clothes until they were naked again. Without a word, they covered every area of the room with their lovemaking – Fintan knocked over a lamp and they howled with laughter – before finally settling, breathless, on the unmade bed. Fintan pushed Fergal onto his back and straddled him, and Fergal watched, drunk at the sight of this beautiful man above him, as Fintan took hold of his thickness and lowered himself onto it, eyes shut tight. They exhaled loudly as their bodies met, then, with slow, sure movements, they found a rhythm that made them both arch their backs and call to each other in soft moans.

The thrusting grew harder and harder. They rolled over and Fintan gripped Fergal's lower back with his legs and looked him straight in the eyes. 'Oh, Fergal – oh God, yes – feels so good...' Sweat was dripping off both of them, and Fergal thrust more and more wildly. He knew he couldn't hold out much longer. He managed to say, 'Fintan, I'm close, I'm really close. Are you close?'

'Keep going – I'm nearly there...'

Fergal slid out of him and they took hold of each other, stealing kisses, until there was no going back. With one final thrust, their bodies stiffened, and Fergal collapsed on top of his lover.

After a moment he started to move off, but Fintan stopped him, murmuring, 'Don't...' So they lay there, breathless and conjoined in those blissful, vulnerable seconds. As Fergal drifted off, he felt Fintan nuzzle his ear, and he could have sworn he heard him whisper, 'I love you, Fergal,' but he wasn't sure if it was a dream.

They woke with a start to a loud knock and a call of 'House-keeping! You want your room made up?' Fintan shouted, 'Not today!' just in time, before the maid used her key.

Fergal rolled off instinctively, to the other side of the bed, and Fintan stretched out and yawned, rolling over onto his stomach. The room was hot, and they let their arms coil around each other loosely. They must have drifted off again, for the next time they woke it was because a cold breeze was blowing over them from the open window. The room was almost in darkness.

'God, what time is it?'

Fintan flicked on the lamp. Fergal jumped up – he was dying to go to the toilet – but his nakedness embarrassed him. He grabbed a T-shirt and a pair of boxer shorts from the pile on the floor and put them on behind the closed door of the bathroom. When he came out, Fintan burst out laughing and fell back on the bed. Fergal was about to ask him what he was laughing at when he looked down and saw he was wearing Fintan's underwear, back to front. He laughed and jumped onto the bed, and they kissed themselves properly awake. It wasn't long before the shorts were flung back to the pile on the floor, to tell the other clothes it was a false alarm.

'Shall we get into the shower?' Fintan suggested. Although Fergal was a bit shy because it was so bright in there, it didn't take him long to start enjoying it once they were under the water. They touched each other slowly under the hot jets, kissing and washing each other's chests. Once they were spent for the second time, they sat in the bath and let the water wash over them like a welcome shower of rain. With his face pressed against Fintan's, Fergal finally found the courage to ask, in a whisper, 'Fintan, did I hear you right earlier?'

'What?'

'Did you say...did you say that you loved me?'

Fintan unlocked himself from his dripping lover and looked into his eyes. 'You heard me right.' He kissed Fergal on both eyelids.

'I thought I was only dreaming. Just so as you know – I love you too, Fintan.'

They kissed as the water cascaded down and baptised their union, and it was impossible to tell the tears from the torrent of clean, clear water.

As they were getting dried together, Fintan looked more closely at Fergal's face. 'I've only just noticed that scar on your cheek. Where'd you get it?'

Fergal put his hand up to his face and said blankly, 'Um, my mother, when I was a kid.'

'What? How?'

'It doesn't matter.'

Fintan saw that his face had clouded over and he began to apologise for intruding, but Fergal suddenly stopped him.

'She got me with her nails. I think her nerves were really bad that day, and I wouldn't stop humming or something, I dunno, and I'd hidden the hose of the washing machine.'

'Why? So she couldn't do the washing or something?'

Fergal laughed, then stopped abruptly. 'The washing? I can't tell you how many times she beat me with that thing till I bled – across my legs, my back, anywhere. I think that day she couldn't find it, so the next best thing was her nails.'

Fintan was horrified. 'My God! What did your father say?'

'My father? Jesus, he was worse. You didn't get a warning with him. Anyway, let's not talk about any of that. It's in the past, where it belongs.'

'Fergal, I'm so sorry. I just can't imagine living like that. My dad wasn't around as much as I'd have liked, but he was good at writing to me, and my mum, well, she was always somewhere in the distance. But they never, ever hit me, not once.'

He paused for a minute and then said, in a lower voice, 'They beat you a lot, didn't they?'

Fergal nodded. For a fraction of a second, he looked about six years old.

'But what about your brothers? You said you have twin older ones and one younger one, right? Did they get beaten too? Did the older ones never try and help you?'

'Oh God, Fintan…where do I start?'

'Right at the beginning, that's where.'

'Look, if you must know, the twins enjoyed goading my ma into beating me. I used to talk like a…' Fergal stopped.

'Go on, Fergal. You can tell me anything. Please. You'll feel better.'

'I used to talk like a girl, apparently. My ma hit me in the mouth if she heard me saying girly words.'

'Like what?'

'Like "dear". I know it sounds mad, but if I finished a sentence with "dear", she would reach over and hit me in the mouth. She said it was for my own good, because it wasn't normal for a boy to talk like that.'

'Fergal, that's – that's insane.'

'Who are you telling?'

'Why would she single you out like that?'

'She did go after the twins from time to time – never Ciaran. But I just wasn't like the rest of them. And I was always in trouble in school.'

'What kind of trouble? I'm sorry if this is all too much – it's just that I want to know who you are, how you grew up. Forgive me if I've gone too far.'

'No, no. Sure, I've asked you about your childhood, haven't I? I got beaten up a lot at school, because I had a high speaking voice, my walk wasn't manly enough and I couldn't kick a football straight – in my school, that was the ultimate crime. One day I was queuing to get into the classroom, and a fella grabbed me from behind and slammed my head into the wall. The next thing I knew, I woke up in the headmaster's office, with my ma beside me wringing her hands. I got murdered all the way home because she'd lost an afternoon's wages, having to come and get me.'

'That's unbelievable.'

'Things like that happened all the time. My da used to throw his scalding tea in my face if I challenged him about anything. I finally moved into my granny's, to get away from them. But she got sick, and, well, that's another story for another day.'

Fintan was speechless. Finally he said, 'Fergal, how do you seem so together? How did you *survive*? I would never have guessed any of that was under your surface, and I'm sure it's just the tip of the iceberg. You're amazing, do you know that?'

'Ah, now.'

'No, you are. Do you speak to your family at all now?'

Fergal shrugged. 'Well, they're the only family I've got. I saw my brothers at Da's funeral. Ciaran smiled at me, but the twins acted like they hardly knew me. My mother and I – we're trying our best to start over. She's actually coming over soon, to this recital that Alfredo's organising. I wish you were going to be here for that.'

'I know. I can't wait to hear you perform, but I will soon...I hope.'

It was almost midnight when Fergal finished telling him the edited version of his life story. Fintan still couldn't take it in. 'Like I said earlier, it's a miracle you're alive to tell me the story. I can't believe they used to hit you for your voice – of all things.'

'That's what Father Mac always used to say. Even some of the teachers at school used to make fun of the way I talked. And in the end it was my voice that saved me. It's ironic, isn't it?'

They finally kissed goodnight, and Fergal reluctantly got a taxi back to Alfredo's. This time the house was in complete darkness, and he slipped in as quietly as he could and went straight to bed. Although he felt glad that he'd been able to tell Fintan about his life, he also wondered if he had told him too much and maybe put him off. It struck him that Father Mac had ultimately rejected him; his da had died, leaving no possibility of repairing their relationship; he couldn't keep living at Alfredo's forever; and now Fintan was going to leave too. Fergal felt more vulnerable than ever, and he wondered why it was that all the significant men in his life, be they good or bad, left him. Suddenly he wondered if Father Mac was all right, and he thought about getting up again to phone him, but all he really wanted to do was sleep and forget about Fintan leaving.

29

Alfredo was the first up the next morning, and he set about planning the menu for that evening's feast in honour of Brendan and Fintan's farewell. He had already persuaded Arianna to take the night off from Moretti's and let him cook for her, for a change. The first thing he did was call on his pupil, Salvatore, to order the meat for the sauce and the starters. As the sauce was an old family recipe, Alfredo wanted to choose every ingredient personally. He could have easily gone somewhere more local, but the huge man increasingly intrigued him, and this errand made a good excuse to try and find out more about him.

Alfredo wasn't prepared for the sight of Salvatore in his white apron. Daniela usually did the bulk of the shopping, and he had only seen the butcher for lessons. Salvatore was no oil painting, but he looked so unexpectedly handsome that Alfredo stared at him silently until the butcher looked up from the job in hand.

'Signore Moretti!' Salvatore cried, delighted but a little nervous

– his singing lessons were a well-kept secret from his brother. 'It is an honour to have you in my shop. How can I help you?'

'I have some very important guests coming to dinner tonight, and I need your finest ground beef for the main course and a selection of salami for the starters.'

Purely out of habit, Salvatore began humming one of the ballads that Alfredo had been teaching him. He stopped self-consciously, but Alfredo urged him to continue. He even joined in, and they stood there amongst the hanging dried meats, singing to each other across the counter. Salvatore's younger brother thought he was hearing things and popped his head in from the back, where he had been cutting up new deliveries, so they stopped abruptly and said nothing until they were alone again.

'Now, Signore Moretti, do you want the meat now, or shall I deliver it later – free of charge, of course, seeing as I know the address so well?'

'I couldn't ask you to go that trouble, Salvatore.'

'It's no trouble for our special customers, and I have to make another delivery not far from your road. Is half past four too late?'

'No, no, perfect. I have a list of shopping to do. See you at half past four.'

As Alfredo walked out the door, he looked back for a second and saw that Salvatore had begun humming again, with an enormous smile. He was glad that he'd called. Alfredo had to admit to himself that he had a sizeable crush on his sizeable pupil.

On he went, into the city centre, for just the right kind of fresh pasta, herbs, bread and oil. His final stop was the winery, where he knew exactly what he wanted: six bottles of his favourite red wine and six of white, followed by two special dessert wines. As he shopped, Alfredo wondered if Salvatore's inclinations in the ways of love were similar to his own. It was hard to tell. He did know that Salvatore was a confirmed bachelor. The week before, when

they had taken a coffee break during their lesson, he had remark-
ed that Salvatore seemed only to want to learn very romantic
material, and that his wife was a very lucky woman. Salvatore had
looked at his teacher – for a little longer than a heterosexual
man would have, Alfredo thought – and then said that he
was unmarried and would stay that way. Alfredo dearly wanted to
find out whether Salvatore shared his preference and his interest,
but he wasn't entirely ready. He just needed a little sign – anything
at all.

Brendan and Fintan spent the day walking slowly through the
market squares in an attempt to find a present for Alfredo.

'What do we get the man who has everything?' Brendan
wondered.

'I don't know, Dad – a large chocolate-coated husband,
perhaps?'

They laughed. 'Keep a lookout for that stall,' Brendan said. 'I'm
serious, though. I don't actually know too much about his tastes
these days – and before you say something filthy, I meant
something that Alfredo would love but wouldn't buy for himself.
You know, like…like…'

'Like a husband, Dad. Let's face it, Alfredo does have
everything else. All he needs is someone to share it with. Don't
you agree?'

'I suppose you're right. Does Fergal talk about him when
you're together? Has he mentioned seeing Alfredo with anyone?'

'No. I mean, Alfredo's quite private, and he's very much the
teacher and Fergal the student.'

They walked and walked all afternoon, but Fintan spent most
of the time daydreaming about his new love. By the end of the
day, he knew he had made up his mind. As they sat under the
outdoor umbrella of a café, he asked his father, 'Dad, what would

you say if I told you I was thinking of spending a lot more time in Rome? I mean, look at this place! The architecture of that fountain alone is reason enough for anyone with an ounce of artistic intent to move here. I really feel drawn to this city.'

Brendan raised his eyebrows. 'Now, Fintan, this wouldn't have anything to do with Fergal, would it?'

'Look, Brendan.' He always called his father by his first name when he was really serious. 'I won't deny that my feelings for Fergal are very powerful, and that the idea of seeing him regularly is appealing, but I need to leave Paris and expand my horizons.'

'Yes, that you do. But—'

'Dad, I've really thought about it. I'll need you to help, until I become internationally rich and famous, but I could get a job teaching English, maybe. I've heard about people doing it, and my Italian doesn't have to be that great to begin with. I've also rung the institute of art here, and they asked me to submit an application and my portfolio by the end of the month.'

'My word, you've been a busy boy.'

'What do you think, seriously? Do you think I'm mad or what?'

'I think you should do what your heart tells you. Certainly there's no denying the wealth of artistic possibility here. Why not? If you hate it, you can always leave – although preferably after you've finished the course, to which I see your mother and I are going to contribute heavily. Which, of course, is our pleasure and duty.'

Fintan smiled broadly, but Brendan raised his index finger. 'There's only one condition.'

'What's that?'

'That I can come and stay with you when I visit. We might even coax your mum into joining us, seeing as I now have two excuses to come back to Rome.'

Fintan threw his head back, laughing. 'I know one voice teacher who's going to be delighted with that news.'

'And I know one future opera star who won't exactly be complaining either.'

They hugged and had an Irish coffee to celebrate. Just as they were leaving the square, they saw a vintage wine shop, and Brendan bought a very expensive magnum of champagne. He turned to his son and said, 'When all else fails, bring bubbles and plenty of them. We have a lot to toast tonight.'

Fergal woke late and had to rush to his Italian lesson. He had agreed with Giovanni that he would start a few hours early at the theatre that day so that he could leave early. They climbed into their overalls again and set about giving one of the dressing rooms a fresh coat of paint. Fergal was distracted by the fear that Fintan would wake up and think twice about getting involved with him after what he had told him about his childhood. As he coated every crack and bump with white paint, he wished he could give his past a similar fresh covering.

Giovanni had heard about Fergal's phone calls from the stage doorkeeper, and he couldn't help asking about Fintan. 'So,' he began, 'you seemed to get on well with Brendan Fiscetti.'

'Yeah. He was incredible, wasn't he?'

'Indeed. Tell me, though, what did you think of the son – Finnan or something, wasn't it?'

'Fintan, you mean. I think he's great.' Fergal's voice trailed off for a second as a little film of their lovemaking ran through his head. 'He's…lovely, yeah.'

Giovanni forgot himself for a moment. 'Well, I'd definitely get the knees of my jeans dirty for that one! Not sure about the red hair, though – he might have to dye it!'

'What do you mean? I think his hair is beautiful.'

'Yes, but can you imagine the pubes?' Giovanni covered his mouth in mock shock.

Fergal went a pronounced deep red, heightened by the crisp white of the room, and Giovanni realised he'd gone a bit too far. He changed the subject quickly. They finished the job earlier than they had expected to, so Giovanni kindly sent Fergal home, wishing him a great evening, then giggled to himself the second the stage door closed behind him.

The Moretti household was so clean that it looked like they were expecting the pontiff himself. Daniela was famous for her tirami-su, and in true Italian style, she had made more than enough. Alfredo had been perfecting the sauce all day, and the kitchen had been out of bounds to even her until he was certain it tasted just right. He hummed approval at every room as he inspected it. 'You're sure you don't mind staying late, Daniela?'

Daniela was decanting the first of the many bottles of wine that had just arrived. 'Signore, I've been looking forward to this night all week. Do you think Signore Fiscetti or you or Fergal might sing?'

'Who knows? I can't put any pressure on Signore Fiscetti to perform – as you know, he's just finished an exhausting run at the Teatro – but you never know what magic the exquisite wine and food will work.'

That was enough to make her grin.

Just then, the doorbell rang. It was exactly half past four, and Salvatore was delivering the meat like clockwork. He handed Alfredo a beautifully wrapped white paper package, tied with string. 'I've added a few extra portions, free of charge,' he said, 'just in case of emergencies.' Then he smiled, pointing to his teacher's sauce-stained apron. 'It's nice to see you wearing one of those, for a change!'

Alfredo held his gaze for a moment. 'Do you have time for a quick glass of wine?' he asked.

Salvatore's smile broadened, but he shook his head. 'Thank you, Alfredo, but I can see you're busy, and I still have a few more orders to deliver.'

'Are you sure?'

'I'll tell you what.' Salvatore leaned closer and lowered his voice. 'If you ask me another day, I'll definitely say yes.'

Then he turned around, not waiting for an answer, and left Alfredo holding the parcel in the doorway, lost for words but sure of exactly what he wanted to do next. He was going to bite the bullet and ask Salvatore out on a proper date.

Once Alfredo had calmed down and the meat was sorted out – in the sauce, at a very low heat, under the watchful eye of Daniela – he was free to go and lounge in a lavender and rosemary bath at the top of the house. He couldn't help imagining all of the romantic possibilities with the butcher. He even allowed himself to picture what Salvatore might look like naked, and to wonder whether he would be a good kisser…

Soon there was singing coming from his room, and from Fergal's room, and even Daniela found herself making up a melody that seemed to fit in with what was coming from the upper floors as she mixed the salad dressing.

Brendan and Fintan arrived at Alfredo's gate at exactly eight o'clock, but before they got a chance to ring the bell, the man of the house flung the front door open in a cloud of lime and lavender cologne. They joined Fergal in the sitting room, where Brendan presented Alfredo with the magnum of champagne and Daniela brought in a tray of welcoming Kir Royales. This time the doorbell did get a chance to ring, and Fergal opened the door to a delighted Arianna, who was carrying an enormous box of chocolates from her favourite shop. Fergal loved the way everyone kissed so warmly – especially when he and Fintan did it.

Daniela handed round the snipes, and Alfredo raised his glass.

'My family and friends, let us drink to what I hope will be the first of many wonderful gatherings!'

A chorus of 'Hear, hear! *Salute!*' filled the room, and they took their seats for the first course. The table was meticulously set for five, and Fergal noted with delight that there was a little place card in front of every setting. He was next to Fintan, and Alfredo sat at the head of the table, with Brendan to his left and Fintan to his right. Arianna was next to Brendan, facing Fergal, and Alfredo noticed how uncharacteristically coquettish she had become in the assembled company. Brendan was asking her questions about growing up with Alfredo and listening to her answers as if his life depended on them.

Fergal was straightening his napkin on his lap when he felt Fintan's fingers tickle the back of his hand. He smiled nervously and stared straight ahead, stroking Fintan's hand in return and squeezing it under the canopy of the crisp linen, until the first layer of plates was removed and the sorbet palate-cleanser allowed them a little break before the drama of the main course.

On cue, Daniela carried in a huge, covered ceramic bowl and placed it in the centre of the table. Then came its twin, which she set down beside it.

'Oh, Alfredo!' Arianna cried. 'Grandma Moretti's pasta dishes! I haven't seen them in years.'

'I know. I haven't used them in years.'

'Do you remember the day we filled them with water and soaked our old postman from the bedroom window?' The table erupted into laughter. 'As our punishment,' Arianna finished, 'we had to dry all the envelopes in the sun and hand-deliver every last one of them!'

Alfredo stood up and placed a hand on top of each ceramic lid, and the table went quiet. 'Ladies and gentlemen, I present Grandma Moretti's secret sauce!'

He lifted the lids in a cloud of hot steam. The aroma was incredible. One of the dishes was piled to the top with ribbons of pasta and perfectly placed last-minute basil leaves, while the other contained a mountain of spicy red sauce. Arianna passed the plates forward in rotation, and her brother smothered every plate with a healthy combination of pasta and sauce. Daniela appeared again, with freshly grated bowls of pecorino and Parmesan cheese and a basket of warm bread.

'Now, this sauce has been in our family for as long as anyone can remember,' Alfredo said, 'and it has quite a kick. I hope everyone likes garlic and chillies.'

Soon the only sounds in the room were the clicking of cutlery and the soft groans of approval. It was as if the Moretti ancestors were gathered by the ceiling rose in anticipation, floating near the cornicing on a temporary visa from the other world to make sure that the family reputation lived to see another day.

'Oh, Alfredo, it's magnificent!' Arianna said. 'Grandma would be so proud!' Everyone raised a glass to the host.

Fergal was nervous that he was going to smash one of the good plates or knock over his crystal wine glass. He had been clumsy as a child, but that had been because of the cramped living space and the constant need to dodge fists and flying objects. He didn't know what had got into him over the past few days to make him so jittery. It was as if he was trying not to feel too much for Fintan, because somewhere at the back of his mind he felt he didn't deserve to be happy.

He reached for the bread and almost knocked over his glass. When he looked around the table, he realised that he had emptied his plate well ahead of everyone else. Fintan laughed. 'My God, Fergal, do they not feed you here?'

Everyone joined in the laughter, and Fergal went bright red with embarrassment. Alfredo and Arianna were always trying to get him to eat more slowly, but rushing through meals was a hard habit to break, even though he no longer had to worry about his brothers' antics or his parents' attacks. The inner Belfast voice was back: *Fintan's used to this kind of life,* it said. *He belongs in it. You've just borrowed it, so you have. You don't deserve it, not one bit.*

Fergal felt genuinely hurt that Fintan had drawn everyone's attention to him like that, and he began to fume silently. It struck him suddenly, as he looked around at the assembled company, that he had never eaten with his own family like this, around a table. The table had always been covered in damp washing as Angela waited for the rain to stop so she could hang it up on the makeshift line in their tiny back yard. They had eaten in the living room, in front of the telly. *Maybe Fintan doesn't really love me,* he thought suddenly. *Maybe he just feels sorry for me.*

The wine was strong and thick. Fergal had never tasted anything quite like it, but it made him feel more and more vulnerable. He looked around at the familiar faces and convinced himself they were all looking back at him with pity in their eyes. He felt Fintan's hand trying to take his, but he knocked it away. Ignoring Fintan's puzzled look, Fergal pushed back his chair, excused himself and went upstairs to the toilet.

Fintan followed him and tapped on the bathroom door. 'Fergal? Fergal, let me in. What's the matter?'

The door clicked open and Fergal stood there, looking furious. 'Did you have to make me feel so stupid, in front of everyone?'

'What? What are you talking about?'

'Jesus, don't pretend you don't know!'

'I don't! You mean because I teased you about eating quickly?'

'Bingo!'

'Ah, Fergal, I didn't mean anything. God, but you're over-sensitive! Come here...'

Fergal pushed him away. 'Look, I know I didn't grow up like you, with too much of everything to choose from, but—'

'Oh for fuck's sake, Fergal, I'm not going to apologise for not being poor. What are you saying, that I wanted to make you look like a fool? Jesus Christ, I don't believe it!'

'Fucking believe it, Fintan. Why on earth would you be even slightly interested in me, anyway? Are you bored or something? Are you just looking for someone to keep you amused till you get back to Paris or London or where-fucking-ever—'

'Fergal, stop it! I don't deserve this shit over a throwaway remark.'

'Is that all I am to you? Someone you can throw away?'

'Don't twist my words. Why are you being like this? Have you drunk too much, or—'

'Oh, how fucking convenient: the drunk Paddy. Sorry, sir—'

'Stop it, Fergal, stop it! You know I didn't—'

'Oh, fuck off!'

Fergal pushed past him and rejoined the supper party.

Everyone managed a second helping of the pasta, except Fergal, who was feeling more self-conscious than ever. 'With so much garlic in the sauce,' Alfredo joked, 'none of us has a hope of being kissed tonight!' He shot a little glance at Fintan and Fergal. 'Unless, of course, the kisser has also been eating it…'

Fergal looked stony-faced and Fintan coughed uncomfortably. Alfredo, realising he had touched a nerve somehow, dropped the subject and asked Fintan what he thought of Rome.

'I love it. I've been giving it a lot of thought, and the more time I spend here, the less I want to leave.' He glanced at Fergal for a second. 'I was talking to Dad today, and I've decided I want to apply for a place at the art institute here to continue my studies, concentrating on oils. My years in Paris have been incredible, but it's time to move onwards and upwards – and where better than here?'

Fergal thought his heart would come out his mouth. He felt completely stupid about the earlier fight.

'That's wonderful news, Fintan, it really is,' said Alfredo.

'Yes,' Brendan said. 'I'm delighted to think of my son spending time here – and it's yet another excuse to come back. We do have to find him somewhere to live, though, a little studio flat, somewhere as close to the institute as possible. Alfredo, do you know an agency we could approach?'

Alfredo thought for a moment, his face serious. 'Fintan, if you'll permit me, I would like to offer you the other spare room in this house, at least until you find somewhere. That way you can take your time to find the right place. The room is full of junk right now, but it could easily be ready by the time you get back.'

Fergal was stunned. 'Alfredo, that's an amazing offer,' said Fintan, shooting a look at his father to gauge his reaction, 'but I couldn't possibly expect you to go to any more trouble than you have already. Honestly, it would be too much.'

'Yes, Alfredo,' said Brendan. 'You've done so much already.'

'Brendan, Fintan…this week has been unforgettable, and I would be insulted if you came back and stayed in a hotel. Fergal, tell Fintan here that it's not such a bad house to live in, will you? The food has its moments, even if I say so myself.'

Fergal managed to nod his head. He couldn't look at Fintan.

'It's settled, then,' said Alfredo, raising his glass. 'To our new houseguest, Signore Fintan Fiscetti!'

They raised their glasses. Although Arianna was a little concerned about her brother's generosity, she knew of old that there was no point in challenging him, and she was deeply moved by the fact that he seemed genuinely happy, for the first time in a long while.

As the remains of the main course were taken away, Brendan was deep in conversation with Alfredo, and Arianna asked Fintan about Paris. He told her about St Germain and the view from the top of the steps at the Sacre Coeur. 'You can walk almost to the top of the Eiffel Tower now. There are steps all along the steel framework, and although it's steep, it's definitely worth it.'

328

When Arianna turned to talk to Brendan, Fintan leaned closer to Fergal. 'I wanted to tell you earlier, but maybe you don't care?'

The chairs were pushed back a bit, and the room seemed to breathe more easily. They decided to take a break from eating, and Alfredo warned them all jokingly about Daniela's imminent dessert – 'No pressure, of course, she only spent most of yesterday making it in our honour!'

Fergal was dying to ask Fintan about his decision to move to Rome, but he didn't know how. Luckily, Arianna asked the questions instead. 'That's great news about the art institute, Fintan.'

'Well, it will be if they accept my application. I have to go back to Paris and update my portfolio. I have to photograph the newer pieces and make slides for the institute to appraise, then I'll ship all the stuff to London or Bath for storage.'

'How long will that take?'

'It's hard to say. I'm hoping no more than a month or so. I have the apartment in Paris for another three months, but I'll see if the landlord doesn't mind me leaving earlier. Dad might even get his deposit back.'

Fergal felt smaller and smaller as he listened. While he had been living with his Granny Noreen in her wee two-up-two-down mess, Fintan had probably been ordering a latte somewhere in Paris and deciding what to paint. He couldn't help feeling jealous and inadequate, even though he knew it was hardly Fintan's fault.

Arianna lit a long cigarette by the open window, once she was sure no one minded, and Fintan looked at her enviously and then at his father. 'Look, I'll only have one. You don't have to watch. Anyway, it's all Paris's fault. I didn't smoke as much before I moved there.' He glanced at Fergal. 'But I certainly need one tonight.'

Brendan looked at Alfredo, and they both threw their eyes to the ceiling in despair.

It was ten o'clock before Alfredo gave the signal for dessert to be served. Normally Fergal would have refused the creamy concoction because of his voice, but as he wasn't singing the next day, he accepted the large portion and tried his best not to wolf it down. He ate each spoonful with exaggerated slowness, and all Fintan could do was tut in annoyance at him. Again the talking vanished, replaced by muffled sounds of approval, and when Daniela appeared with more wine they all applauded her.

They moved into the front room to take coffee and sit by the low fire listening to music. Fergal tried to sober up a little and recover some of his confidence. He was desperate to clear the air with Fintan. Finally he asked Alfredo, 'Can I show Fintan the spare room where he's going to stay?'

'Oh, but I'm sure it's a mess, Fergal...' But when Alfredo saw the look on Fergal's face, he relented, and the two young men left the room as calmly as they could.

Fergal opened the door of the spare room. Sure enough, it was full of all kinds of things, in neat enough piles. He snapped on the light and moved a few boxes so they could get in and close the door behind them. He couldn't look at Fintan.

'Well, here it is, then.'

'Fergal, you didn't bring me up here to show me the room. Why the fuck did you get so angry with me?'

'I just...I don't know. You made me feel stupid, really stupid. Do you not see that?'

'For fuck's sake! No, I don't see that. What I see is someone overreacting to a simple—'

'Simple? What? Do you know how hard it is for me to sit here and listen to all these people talking about their wonderful lives and their wonderful travels? It makes me feel...' His voice trailed off.

'What, Fergal? What? Tell me.'

'I've told you too much already. It makes me feel worthless, that's all. There you were, running about in Paris smoking your head off, while I was stuck in Belfast trying not to get shot or get my head kicked in. Jesus, Fintan, don't be coming back to Rome on my account. I'll only let you down eventually.'

This time Fintan got angry. 'Don't flatter yourself, you self-obsessed wanker! Jesus, you're just like my fucking father, do you know that? Yeah, the rich, privileged opera star sitting downstairs, who, along with my even richer mother, has bankrolled me since I was born – big fucking crime, being born wealthy. No wonder he thinks you're so good, you two are like peas in a pod. You both think everything in this world is about you. Why did I ever get involved with a bloody singer? Fuck you, Fergal Flynn – fuck you!'

He pushed Fergal out of the way, headed back downstairs and asked Arianna for another cigarette.

Fergal listened to him descend the stairs and burst out crying, feeling stupider than ever. He knew he had drunk too much, and he began to feel a bit sick. He went into the bathroom to rinse his mouth out, and when he saw his face in the mirror he wanted to punch himself. *Well done, Flynn,* he thought. *You've just driven him away. Are you fucking happy now?*

When he rejoined the dinner party, Fintan was recounting more details of his life in Paris to Arianna, who seemed fascinated. 'Tell me, if you don't mind my candour,' she asked, 'do you have a girlfriend there? They say the women in Paris are incredibly beautiful – they eat all day but remain as thin as cigarettes.'

Brendan and Fintan both laughed, and Fintan answered, 'Well, I've painted many beautiful women as part of my life studies, but to answer your question, no, I don't have a girlfriend I'm leaving behind.'

Fergal panicked for a heated second, thinking that Fintan was about to tell her he was gay, but the moment passed. There was a strange momentary silence, but Daniela's timing triumphed again: she appeared in the doorway with coffee and chocolates laid out on antique silver plates. Everyone complained loudly, but no one refused a taste of the handmade confectionery.

It was well after midnight, and well after several cognacs, when Brendan peered at his watch and stood up to say his goodbyes. He toasted the whole room and then each guest individually, leaving his host till last.

'Alfredo, my dear returned friend, what can I say? This has been an unforgettable trip to Rome. Not only have we reconnected after all these years, but my son is coming back to stay here in your beautiful home. What a host you are! I insist you come to London as soon as your timetable allows so that I can attempt to return this royal hospitality. *Salute!*'

A few tears escaped Alfredo's eyes as he smiled in gratitude and stood to receive Brendan's embrace.

Arianna and Brendan went out to the taxi and Fergal attempted to walk Fintan out, but Fintan told him it wasn't necessary, said goodbye coldly and walked off. Alfredo and Fergal waved the taxi off from the front door. When they came back in, Daniela was starting to clear away the dinner things so Fergal insisted on helping her. He knew Alfredo could see something was up, and he didn't want to talk about it.

Alfredo thanked Daniela for all her work and begged her repeatedly to leave the larger jobs till the next morning, but she wouldn't hear of it. She made a disgusted face and told him it would be a sin to leave such a mess overnight. Alfredo was a little emotional and completely exhausted, so he hugged Fergal and said goodnight, urging Daniela to take home any food she wanted. By the time he got to the top of the stairs, it was all he could do to step out of his clothes and draw his blankets up around him before he was gone into the other world, dreaming of Salvatore.

Fergal was miserable. When Daniela left, he thought about storming over to Fintan's hotel right then and there, but he knew he was in no state to make any sense. Besides, he was still angry with him. He stomped up to bed in a rage, getting angrier and angrier as he thought about what Fintan had said. It was all he could do not to cry himself to sleep. He couldn't believe everything could turn so quickly from good to bad, and the more he thought about their arguments, the less he understood them. He was convinced that Fintan wouldn't come back at all – and it was all his own fault.

30

Alfredo was worried about Fergal. He knew that he and Fintan had had some kind of a fight, but when he tried to inquire politely about it Fergal nearly bit his head off, so he stayed clear of the subject.

Alfredo was a little distracted anyway by a phone call he had decided to make. He found Salvatore's number in his book and made sure his office door was closed before he dialled slowly. As he waited for someone to answer, he absent-mindedly drew a heart beside Salvatore's name, like a schoolboy with a crush.

Salvatore's brother answered. '*Pronto,* Santamaria Brothers?'

Alfredo took a deep breath and asked nervously for Salvatore. But when Salvatore came on, he sounded terribly polite and stand-offish. Alfredo nearly lost his confidence, until he realised that his brother must still be within earshot.

'Salvatore, is your brother nearby?'

'Yes, that's right.'

'So that's why you sound a bit odd!'

'Yes, indeed.'

'Listen, would you like to come to my garden for that drink?'

'Absolutely.'

'Is tonight at seven o'clock too soon?'

'No.'

'Wonderful! I'll see you then.'

'Yes, that should be fine. I'll drop the meat over then.'

'Great.'

Alfredo put down the phone and looked at himself in the mantel mirror. Was he being ridiculous to think he could find someone, at nearly fifty years of age? He shook his head and started humming 'Que Sera Sera'.

Fergal was going out of his mind. When Father Mac phoned that morning to say that Angela's passport had come through and she could come to Rome the following month for the recital, he barely reacted.

'Fergal, what's the matter? You sound awful tired or something.'

'Ah, I'm fine. I'll be fine.'

'If you don't want to tell me, that's okay, but don't pretend you're fine when you're obviously not. Do you think I don't know when you're upset? I thought we could tell each other anything.'

Fergal sighed. 'You're right.'

He spent the next twenty minutes telling Father Mac how down he had felt when he came back from Ireland, and all about meeting Fintan. He told him how quickly they had fallen for each other and how, just when things seemed to be going brilliantly, they had turned sour. 'And now,' he finished, 'I don't know what to think.'

Father Mac had listened carefully. 'Try not to dwell on it too much,' he said gently. 'Maybe things will be better when Fintan comes back.'

'Yeah, *if* he comes back. I think I've scared him off.'

'Look, Fergal, you've got a lot of work ahead for the recital. Concentrate on that, and then see what happens. Don't think everything is so permanent all the time. It's good to fall out sometimes. Making up again can be really special, and it can bring you closer in the long run. I can't say it enough – you need to learn more about forgiveness. Even if you're completely in the right, you have something to learn from this. By the way, your mother wanted to phone you later, from here. Will you be in?'

'Really? What for?'

'I think she's just excited about coming to Rome and I'd say my hallway is the only place she can get any privacy. Every phone box on the road is busted. Maybe she wants to talk about your da. You know, she's probably reliving all kinds of memories in her head and maybe she feels she can talk to you. You are a good listener, that much I know.'

'I'll be here, but I'm working tonight, so around dinnertime would be good.' Fergal still didn't completely trust his mother, but there was a part of him that was looking forward to seeing her on her own and it made him feel good that she might think of him as someone she could talk to now that they were a bit older.

When they hung up he felt a tiny bit better, but he still thought Fintan might have at least phoned before he left for London.

Poor Brendan Fiscetti. His son was in a huff the whole way home, and when they reached their house in Highgate he went straight to bed. Brendan tried to talk to him, but Fintan ignored him. Some of what Fergal had said had really made him think, but he was too furious even to consider talking to him – at least, not yet. As he lay in the room that had been his from birth, he wondered whether he really wanted to get involved with a singer who, like his father, would probably end up being away a lot of the time. But in his quieter moments, he allowed himself to picture Fergal's face, and his heart melted just a little.

That evening, before Fergal went to work at the Teatro, the phone rang. It was Father Mac again, with Angela beside him. Fergal felt strange talking to his mother, knowing that she stood in the very hallway where he and Father Mac had practically ripped the clothes off each other in a fit of lust one night, when they couldn't wait to get up the stairs.

'Hello, Fergal? It's me.'

'Hello, Mammy. How are you?'

'Ach, you know – taking it a day at a time. I miss your da, for all his shenanigans.'

'I suppose it must be strange being on your own again, seeing as you were married for so long.'

'Oh, it is. I sometimes think he's coming in the door but it's only a neighbour over to say hello. I even made his dinner the other night and sure I had to throw it out.'

She didn't tell him that she'd also found an old pair of his socks under the bed when she was cleaning and although she'd laughed at first she ended up crying into them and then putting them under her pillow.

'Mammy, you're going to have a great time over here. I promise you'll love it.'

'Sure, a change is as good as a rest, isn't that what they say, son?'

Fergal always felt a bit awkward when she called him 'son', but deep down he was pleased too.

'You know I'm doing a wee concert while you're here?'

'Yes, Father MacManus was telling me.'

'It won't be long till you're here and we can talk properly then. I'm away to work now, so I have to go. See you, okay?'

'See you, son.'

As Fergal was leaving for work, Alfredo asked, 'How was it, talking to your mother?'

'It was good. But a bit strange, too.'

'Whatever it is that's making you so upset, I hope it gets resolved before too long.'

'Thanks, but it's not so easy.'

'It's about Fintan, isn't it? Or is it about your mother?'

'No, it's not her at all – for once. I don't really want to talk about it.'

'It's your business. But remember, I was once in love with a Fiscetti, although, mind you, we were never lovers like you and his son. Fergal, whatever has happened has happened. With a bit of time and distance, it won't seem nearly as bad as it feels right now. Just try and cheer up.'

Fergal felt like nobody understood him, but all he could do was say, 'I will' as he pulled on his coat.

After Daniela went home, Alfredo had a shower and a shave – his second that day – and then tried to find something to wear that wouldn't make him sweat too much. When the doorbell rang, he breathed into his own cupped hand and smelled his breath one last time before he opened the door. His gentle giant of a pupil, equally nervous, stood at the top of the steps, holding a bottle of Prosecco and a little bag of meat, which he'd had to bring because his brother had heard him mention it.

Salvatore Santamaria was almost fifty and had lived with his younger brother Ciro above the family butcher shop since the day he was born. He treasured music above all else and had always dreamed of singing on stage to a packed house instead of to his hanging audience of headless carcasses, but because he was the first born, he was expected to follow in his father's sawdust footsteps, and he had inherited the shop when his parents died.

'I thought we might sit in the garden?' Alfredo said. 'The weather isn't bad, and you might be glad to be outdoors after a day in your shop?'

'Yes, good idea.'

When Alfredo went to get drinks, Salvatore smelled his hands, afraid for a moment that he hadn't been able to get rid of the raw-meat odour that often accompanied him. Alfredo returned with the tray of beer and glasses and caught him, and Salvatore laughed. 'I just wanted to make sure I don't still smell of the shop. It's hard to tell.'

'Here, give me your hand.'

The butcher nervously stretched out his palm, and Alfredo inhaled the clean skin at the base of his thick fingers. Then he shook his head. 'No, they smell…great.'

They sat across from each other on the terrace and talked easily about their changing city.

'Your house is incredible, Signore Moretti. Do you live here all by yourself?'

'I did for many years, but now my Irish pupil Fergal Flynn lives here too, while he's studying with me. And an old friend's son will be coming to stay for a while. He's a painter called Fintan, Brendan Fiscetti's son.'

'You mean that incredible tenor who was just here at the opera house?'

'Why, yes. Did you go?' Alfredo loved looking at Salvatore up close, taking in the details of his blunt, handsome face.

'I did. I love to hear that kind of singing.'

Salvatore told Alfredo about his family, and that he shared the apartment above the shop with his brother. 'I thought you were married when I first came for lessons,' he said.

'Oh, you mean Daniela? She's been my housekeeper for a very long time. I don't know what I'd do without her. I thought you were married, too.'

Salvatore smiled. 'The only time I'll ever walk down the aisle is on Sundays to get Holy Communion.'

'Does your brother know?' Alfredo asked carefully. 'About you?'

'You mean that I…that I'm attracted to men? Good God, no. He's very old-fashioned, even though he's younger than me.'

Alfredo exhaled in relief. 'Oh, Salvatore, I'm glad you said it! I'm not barking up the wrong tree after all, then?'

'No, you're not.' They smiled at each other, and both of their hearts beat faster.

The two men talked on into the evening, gradually unwrapping their individual stories. When they got hungry, Alfredo unloaded the groaning fridge and found a couple of bottles of wine left over from the party.

Eventually they moved down to the hanging sofa, in the most secluded part of the garden, beside the magnolia tree. As soon as Salvatore sat his bulk down on it, it nearly touched the ground. He tried to stand up again, stumbled and had to reach for Alfredo's offered hand. But instead of pulling himself up, he pulled Alfredo down on top of him. They both laughed, then, without another word, their lips touched – once, then twice, and then they were kissing as if they had never been kissed before.

Alfredo felt faint as Salvatore held him in his firm grip. They opened their eyes at the same time, to prove to themselves that it was really happening. Salvatore whispered, 'I've been dying to do that for a long time, Alfredo.'

Alfredo leaned against him, and they held hands as the night air gossiped about them. Alfredo was dizzy, and he knew that it wasn't from the wine. Finally he said, 'Where did you come from?'

'What do you mean?'

'You've been coming to my house for so long, and I never saw you for who you are. I wonder why?'

'I've spent a lifetime covering up. But I was here all along, holding a little candle for you, but far too shy to let you see it.'

'Oh Salvatore, if only I'd known. But I suppose I wasn't ready to see.'

Before Alfredo finished speaking, he knew why he had been so blind. He had never really recovered from Brendan Fiscetti. Only when Fergal had reconnected him to his past had he been able to let go of it and let someone else in. The truth of it hit him in that moment, and he was speechless.

Salvatore looked at Alfredo and saw his eyes filling up. He raised his eyebrows, then kissed Alfredo again and again, on his lips and on his closed, damp eyes.

They didn't hear Fergal's key in the front door. Fergal was in mildly better form, even though he had spent the whole evening thinking about Fintan. Every time he passed the stage door he had glared at the phone, willing it to ring, but it had never happened.

When he saw that the house was dark, he decided he couldn't be bothered to eat and went straight up to his room to read in bed. The last thing he expected to see as he went to close his window was his teacher and the butcher on the swinging sofa, snogging for all they were worth. Fergal couldn't believe it. He thought of the first time he and Fintan had kissed, on that same sofa, and felt more depressed than ever. He lay on the bed and said to the ceiling, 'God, if that sofa could talk...'

It was after midnight when Alfredo and Salvatore reluctantly said goodnight. Although sex was very definitely on the menu, and although neither of them wanted the evening to end, they decided to take it slowly. They were from the same generation, old-fashioned in their own way, and it was only the first date, after all. They agreed to meet again very soon. Salvatore slipped out of the front door. When he was sure the street was empty, he blew a little kiss to his new love, who was waiting in the moonlit window.

Alfredo blew a kiss back. When he moved away from the window, his legs nearly gave way. In spite of his considerable bulk, he felt as light as air.

He looked at himself in the hall mirror, to see if he could see any difference now that he had allowed himself to be kissed properly by another man. His reflection's eyes sparkled with hope. He floated off to bed, unable to believe that his whole life had turned around in only a day, and that love had been so patiently close the whole time.

31

The next morning, as Fergal finally slumped into his seat at the breakfast table, Alfredo was humming and singing and practically dancing around the kitchen.

'Isn't it a gorgeous morning, Fergal?'

'If you say so.'

Alfredo screwed up his face at his pupil and poured him some orange juice. 'We have a very busy time ahead. You're going to need all the vitamin C you can get.'

Fergal wondered if he should mention the fact that he had seen Alfredo and the butcher at the bottom of the garden, but he thought better of it. Fintan's presence was like a fog in his head. It was hard to see anything clearly through it.

As the days passed with no word from England, Fergal dropped further and further into himself. He stopped shaving for a whole week, and even he was surprised at the thick, reddish beard that grew – in apparent tribute to Fintan. Alfredo told him it suited him perfectly, although it did make him look older.

Fergal felt powerless. He didn't know which way to turn. They had both said some hurtful things, but now it was all muddled up in his head, and he felt as if he had painted himself into some kind of a corner. It was bad enough that they were apart, but he realised it would be a lot worse if Fintan came back to live at Alfredo's and they were still not speaking. Alfredo went so far as to suggest that Fergal should just bite the bullet and phone Fintan instead of wasting precious time, but Fergal could be stubborn when he wanted to – and he wanted to.

The recital was only a few weeks away, and their preparatory work grew more and more intense. They had decided on a forty-five minute set of songs, to include an Irish selection, seeing as the recital was to be held at the Catholic seminary's music space, which was run by a Mayo man called Sean. Sean was on the phone every other day to discuss preparations, and the tickets were selling fast. Fergal had his photo taken by a friend of Giovanni's and Alfredo had posters made with the photo of Fergal and a tiny picture of himself, advertising the fact that he would be accompanying his protégé on piano. That alone was enough to draw the right attention to the event. Even some of the leading dignitaries of the Irish embassy had reserved tickets and said they were looking forward to the evening with great interest.

Brendan and Alfredo talked often, at night. Alfredo had broken the news that he was seeing someone, and Brendan was delighted and wanted to know everything about Salvatore. He also said that he had mentioned Fergal's name to his agent and that the agent was very keen to hear him, especially since Alfredo was teaching him.

'Really? Brendan, that's wonderful news. Maybe I should re-cord the recital. It wouldn't be that hard, and I may not even tell Fergal. He doesn't need the extra pressure.'

'Good idea. If it turns out well, and you think it would make a good introduction, then we'll play it to my agent. I know it's all a bit soon, but you have a rare gem there in Fergal – not that I need to tell you.'

Alfredo told him that Fergal was definitely getting there, but there was still something not quite right. 'Brendan, I worry about him. Once he gets into one of his moods, it's like talking to fog. He's working hard, but I'd just love to see him smile more – like he did when Fintan was here.'

They talked about Fintan too. He was drinking too much and, according to Brendan, appeared to have forgotten the route to the shower. They agreed that something had to happen, but they didn't know what.

Brendan sighed. 'What are we like, Alfredo, worrying about our boys? I'm not sure we can do anything except ride it out and be there for them. We've no other choice.'

Salvatore had started dropping off little presents for Alfredo – packets of meat with romantic notes stuffed inside – whenever he was passing with a delivery. Suddenly these two men approaching fifty felt like teenagers.

With each week that passed, their language got braver. They talked to each other on the phone every night, in the privacy of their bedrooms. Salvatore had to be careful because his brother was nosy and their flat was small, but Ciro usually spent the evenings drinking beer and watching TV with the sound up too loud, so Salvatore was safe. Alfredo was dying for him to come and spend the night, and he said he would love to, but he wasn't sure when. The truth was that he was incredibly shy about his body. Even though he wanted Alfredo, he was going to need a lot of encouragement. Little did he know that Alfredo felt exactly the same way.

Salvatore had come over for a drink a couple of times, and

Fergal liked him, even though he was jealous that his teacher was in the first throes of romance and that he no longer had Alfredo's exclusive attention. He knew he was being selfish, but he couldn't help it. He was heartbroken. Whenever he thought about Fintan, the ache was ten times worse than any hangover. Brendan had spoken to him on the phone a few times, trying to cheer him up, but he could hear the loneliness in his voice. He was beginning to regret ever introducing the two young men.

Fintan couldn't take it any longer. He got drunk and phoned the Teatro, but Fergal wasn't working that night, and Fintan was so rude to the stage doorkeeper that he never gave Fergal the message. When Fergal didn't phone back, Fintan thought it was because he wanted nothing to do with him.

Father Mac rang again, to check that Alfredo had all the right flight information. Angela was all ready to fly over that coming Friday. Her future daughters-in-law had even clubbed together to buy her a new dress, and she was genuinely touched. She would be staying until the following Monday. The recital was on Saturday night, and there were posters strategically placed around the city centre and at the Institute of Music. Daniela had transformed the spare bedroom that would be Fintan's, if he ever arrived. Angela was going to be using it for her first weekend in Rome, to visit her son who was studying to be an opera singer – as she told the immigration officers while they tried to decipher her accent.

Alfredo and a very nervous Fergal stood in the arrivals hall. They both spotted Angela, wheeling her little trolley and looking in every direction but theirs, at the same time. Fergal thought she'd lost weight since he'd last seen her, and she thought the same about him when he called to her across the hall. They hugged each other, a little awkwardly. Angela was clearly exhausted by the first international flight of her life. Fergal still couldn't get over how tiny she was.

On the way home, she talked non-stop from nerves. Alfredo asked her about Belfast and about how she was coping without her husband and she became a little tearful, but she calmed down after a pot of tea. She couldn't believe that anyone could own a house so big and so full of things.

'Jesus, I'd hate to have to clean it, Freddie, I'll tell you that.'

'It's *Alfredo*, Mother,' Fergal corrected, but Alfredo waved his hand, laughing.

Angela loved her room. Fergal couldn't help feel strange as he showed it to her; it was meant to be for his lover. His mother knew he was sad, but she thought it had something to do with her husband's death, so she unpacked her wee travel bag and handed him a package.

'What is it, Mammy?'

'Something to remember your da by. I know youse didn't see eye to eye, but he was your daddy, and you only get one of them. I was clearing out his things, and when I found it I thought you might wear it at your concert thing tomorrow.'

Fergal unwrapped a dark brown silk tie. 'That's the one he wore the morning we were married,' Angela said, 'twenty-two years ago.'

Fergal didn't know what to say, but his eyes spoke for him: they filled with tears. His mother reached up to touch his face and he flinched instinctively before realising that the days of her hitting him were over. She couldn't even reach his head now.

Angela put her arm around him, and they cried together for the first time in their lives. It was exactly what Fergal needed.

Alfredo took them to dinner at Moretti's, and Arianna made a special fuss of Fergal's mother. Angela's accent was so strong and fast that, even though she did her very best, Arianna hadn't a single clue what she was saying, so she just nodded hopefully. She noticed that Fergal looked a little more at ease than he had in a while.

In one way, the dinner was bad timing. Fintan called the house that evening, and found them gone. When Brendan asked him innocently what he wanted for dinner, Fintan muttered something rude and headed for his room.

Brendan had had enough.

'Right, Fintan – enough. I have put up with your sarcasm, your moods, your rudeness, but *no more!*' He slammed his fist down on the table. 'Do you hear me?'

Fintan was shocked. He had never seen his father lose his temper before. 'I'm sorry, Dad. It's just…Fergal. I can't get hold of him.'

'And what? There are no planes to Rome from Heathrow? You don't have a credit card with a decent limit? We Fiscettis follow our hearts. Swallow your pride and go find him. I don't want to hear another bloody word about it until you've done something. Do you understand?'

Back at Moretti's, Arianna innocently asked after Brendan and Fintan, and Fergal's mood began to plummet again. Alfredo made a face at her and then said that young Fiscetti was due to come back in a few weeks. Angela thought he'd said 'Fish-heady', and she giggled like a little girl. She'd had a fair few glasses of Prosecco, and once she got over her initial suspicion of the unfamiliar menu, she had loved everything she tasted.

By nine o'clock, though, she was exhausted, and they took her back to Alfredo's. When Alfredo asked her if she needed to phone anyone before she went to bed to tell them she had arrived safely, she thought for a second, then said, 'No, Freddie. Sure, let them worry about me for a change.'

Then she winked at Fergal and went up to bed.

Alfredo put his hand on Fergal's shoulder. 'You know how much I admire what you're doing, don't you?'

'What am I doing?'

'You're trying to forgive your mother. That's why she's here. I can't imagine how hard that is for you, in the middle of all this other heartache with Fintan.'

Fergal nodded wearily, but he felt a little comforted. At least Alfredo understood. He cleared his throat and asked, 'Is Salvatore coming to the recital?'

The tone of his voice told Alfredo that Fergal knew more than he had thought. 'Well, Fergal, you don't miss much, do you?'

'No, particularly not when I happen to look out my bedroom window in the direction of the swinging sofa.'

Alfredo's eyes widened and he blushed, delighted that for once he had something to blush about. 'It's very early days and Salvatore is incredibly shy, so it's our little secret for now, okay?'

Fergal couldn't help grinning at him. 'Okay.'

They spent the rest of the evening going over some final notes and the running order for the recital. When Fergal finally got into bed, he felt touched that Alfredo had trusted him enough to tell him about Salvatore and a little startled by the fact that his own mother was asleep in the same house, but it was Fintan he thought of as he drifted into a deep, dark sleep.

Alfredo, ever the host, woke early and had breakfast ready when the Flynns arrived downstairs. Angela was dying to see the Vatican, so Fergal agreed to take her, although he would have to be back in time for lunch, before they went to the seminary building for the last run-through before that night's recital. The nerves were multiplying in his chest. He hadn't needed his asthma inhaler in a long time, but he had to puff on it that morning before he and his mother left the house.

Alfredo watched them go, smiling. He knew they should spend what little time they had together, and he also wanted to see if Salvatore could sneak away from the shop for lunch. He almost fainted with delight when the butcher showed up with a bag of pork chops. Alfredo fried them in garlic, and they fed each other at the little table in the garden before kissing on the swinging sofa again.

Fergal and his mother wandered the piazzas and he bought them ice creams. When they finally queued in St Peter's Square to go into the basilica, she blessed herself and pulled out Noreen's little laminated mass card. She kissed it and then held it up to the basilica. 'Here, Mammy, look – me and our Fergal's in Rome! We're going to light a candle for you and for my Paddy, God rest him. I hope youse are getting on better up there than youse did down here.' Fergal smiled. She was still more concerned about dead people than she was about her own living self.

When they finally got inside the vast church, the first thing Angela did was light two candles at the altar of the Virgin Mary. Only then could she relax and take in the magnificence around her.

'Fergal,' she asked as they left the basilica, 'do you think you'll ever live in Belfast again?'

'Never say never, but…I can't see it, Mammy. I want to travel the whole world and sing.'

'Yes, I know. I'm looking forward to tonight. Are you going to wear your da's tie?'

'The strange thing is, I was going to wear my brown linen suit that Alfredo and Arianna gave me for my last birthday. Da's tie will be perfect with it.'

'Ah, good. At least a wee bit of him will be with you.'

They walked around for an hour or so and then stopped for coffee. Angela didn't have a strong back, so she was glad to take what little weight she had off her legs.

Out of the blue, at the café, she said, 'If Paddy and John get married soon, will you come?'

'Why on earth would they invite me?'

'Fergal, they're your brothers.'

'Let's not rake over all that, eh? Let's just have a good time.'

She looked at him for a silent moment and asked, 'Is that Freddie fella married?'

'No, Mammy, of course not, otherwise you would've met his wife.'

Angela nodded, and Fergal knew what was coming next. 'Fergal, do you think you'll ever get married?'

'It's not for everybody.'

'Jesus, don't say that! And us at the Vatican and all.' She blessed herself automatically.

'Tell me honestly, Mammy,' Fergal said. 'If you had your time over again, would you marry Da? Truthfully?'

She looked down at her hands and thought for a long time.

'No, I don't think I would, son.'

'At least you're honest. And by the way, I don't blame you.'

'Do you have a girlfriend coming tonight?' Angela asked. 'Someone you want me to meet?'

Fergal hadn't seen that question coming. 'What? No – no. I'm far too busy, and…oh, God.' He turned away from her.

'What? What is it?'

'I can't, Mammy. Not now – not here.'

'Jesus, Fergal, what is it? Are you sick? Is that why you've changed so much? Oh, Holy Mother and all her saints, I knew it was too good to be—'

'Mammy, stop. I'm not sick. I don't have a girlfriend because…because…'

'Because you like fellas.'

Fergal thought the sky had collapsed on top of him. 'What? Mammy, how did…? ' He was stammering badly with shock.

'Ah Jesus, Fergal. Sure, I might not have gone to school, but I'm not that stupid. Even when you were a wee boy, sure, you weren't like the rest of them.'

'You mean you always knew?'

'Well, I did and I didn't. That's not to say I agree with it, you know.'

'Ah, Mammy, don't say that.'

'So...do you have a fella here, then?'

Fergal went purple. 'I can't believe we're having this conversation. I really can't.'

'Well, I can't believe your da's dead and I'm sitting beside the Vatican, but he is and I am.'

'No, I don't have a fella here.' Fergal wanted to tell her about Fintan, but he couldn't – not while he had no idea what was going to happen.

They sat in silence for another while, until Fergal realised it was time for them to go back to Alfredo's. 'We should get back, Mammy. I'm...I'm glad you know.'

'Ah, sure, at least you won't have any kids to drive you round the bend with worry. Live and let live; we'll all be dead soon enough.'

At Alfredo's gate, Angela turned to Fergal and said, 'I suppose Freddie is a poof as well, is he?'

Fergal laughed. 'Mammy, you're unbelievable. No, he's not a poof, he's *gay*.'

She shrugged. 'Here, he's not your fella, is he?'

'What? God, no! He's far too old.'

'Aye, but he's loaded.'

Fergal just shook his head and opened the front door. Salvatore was just leaving, and when Angela saw this giant of a man coming towards her, she blessed herself. Salvatore smiled, said hello and kissed her on both cheeks. All she could say in response as she looked his bulk up and down was, 'Jesus on the cross, your poor mother – that's all I have to say! The size of you!'

Even though he didn't really understand, Salvatore laughed as he left, saying he'd see them later.

When Angela went upstairs, Alfredo asked Fergal how his day with his mother had gone. He looked at the ceiling intently and then lowered his voice, saying nonchalantly, 'Oh, you know, nothing out of the ordinary. Walked, took in the sights, told her I'm gay...'

'What? You're joking! What did she say?'

'Not too much. I couldn't believe it, but she seemed to take it in her stride, even though she doesn't really approve. She also asked if you and me were, you know, but I put her right. I didn't say anything about Fintan.'

Alfredo was wide-eyed and wondering if the day could get any stranger. 'Well, Fergal, one less thing to worry about. Well done. I would never have been so brave with my mother.'

32

Daniela volunteered to take the delighted Angela to the markets for the rest of the day while Alfredo put Fergal through his paces at the seminary building. The music hall was a long wooden structure where the seminarians' choir rehearsed, and it had a beautiful grand piano. It was warm and wide, and as Fergal and Alfredo positioned the piano and warmed up, there were several volunteers discreetly setting out chairs, as well as one man making sure Fergal didn't notice him testing the levels of the microphones. The seminary choir was regularly recorded, and their microphones, hanging from the rafters not far above Fergal's head, were the latest in technology.

As his voice took flight, Fergal was unaware of the red recording light. Alfredo quietly noticed a difference in his tone and thought that Angela's presence had been good for him, in her own way.

The day seemed to be vanishing before their very eyes, and Fergal's nerves were mounting. Back at the house, he stayed under the heat of the shower jets longer than usual. Then he climbed into his linen suit and did up his father's wedding tie as best he could. He looked in the mirror and tried to imagine what his father, Patrick Flynn, had been thinking about as he put on that tie all those years ago, when he was still single and, technically, childless. Had he had cold feet? One thing was certain – had Patrick Flynn not gone through with his wedding, Fergal wouldn't have been standing there. Somewhere in his heart, his anger towards his father dropped a degree or two.

He stroked the brown silk and headed downstairs. When Angela saw him come into the living room her eyes filled up, and Daniela gave her a little glass of wine to calm her.

They arrived at the back of the seminary hall, and all of a sudden Fergal thought about Father Mac. He wished he had been able to come, but in another way, he was glad not to have any more of Belfast in the room than there already was. They were led backstage to a little changing room, while outside the entrance doors the air began to fill with the bustle of the gathering, curious audience. Fergal paced up and down nervously, checking the clock every few minutes. He knew how important this recital was, and he wanted more than anything to obliterate the bad memory of the exam. He hoped silently that Granny Noreen could prise his da away from the sports channel in the sky, so they might be able to hear him somehow.

Alfredo looked out from behind the curtain and saw that the hall was filling quickly. He saw many familiar faces, including his sister's, and he was just in time to notice Signore Arnelli discreetly slipping into his seat. Alfredo hadn't been sure whether the legendary examiner would come, and it made him glad – and extra nervous – that he had.

Fergal's stomach was churning, and when he held out his hands to check his nerves he saw that they were trembling. Alfredo took him by the shoulders and looked him in the eyes.

'Fergal, remember that you are more than capable of this performance. I urge you to take your time, breathe properly and, above all, try to enjoy yourself.'

Fergal swallowed hard and nodded. 'I'm ready, Alfredo. I'm ready. Let's do it.'

Daniela took Angela to her special seat, and at eight o'clock precisely the house lights were dimmed and Fergal stepped into the main spotlight. The full room welcomed him with applause.

Alfredo's first chords rang out, and Fergal glanced at his music stand. Then his voice commanded the room.

Angela was looking at the boy to whom she had given birth, but she was hearing a strange man's voice come out of his throat. Fergal sang two arias and two Irish songs, then he paused. 'I'm very nervous,' he told the audience, 'for lots of reasons. One of them is that my mother is in the audience tonight.' Everyone clapped, and Daniela made the mortified Angela wave from her seat. 'I'd like to dedicate the next song to her and to my late grandmother. My grandfather, who I was named after, used to sing it for her.'

As the first few lines of 'I'll Take You Home Again, Kathleen' floated into the room, a few Irish people exhaled in bittersweet pleasure as their own memories joined the invisible queue. When Fergal finished the last line, it got the first standing ovation of the night.

He sang selections from Puccini's *La Bohème* and Verdi's *Otello* and gave them everything he had, but time and time again, thoughts of Fintan Fiscetti pulled at his heart. His grandmother's face crowded his head and his father floated there; at one point he glanced at Alfredo and saw him looking worried, holding a chord down and waiting for Fergal to come in. He realised just in time to recover well and not lose his place. Alfredo threw him a look that said, *Concentrate!*

There was a fifteen-minute interval, and when the two of them got back to the little makeshift dressing room, Alfredo grabbed Fergal by the shoulders again.

'Fergal, you have sung some pieces tonight better than you ever have, but towards the end I lost you. Where did you go?'

'It won't happen again.'

'See that it doesn't. I shouldn't tell you this, but Arnelli is in the audience. I know you can do this.'

Something inside Fergal shifted. He looked at Alfredo and said earnestly, 'I don't care who's out there. I can't wait to get back on and sing.'

Alfredo smiled. 'That's the spirit, Fergal. That's what I want to hear.'

Angela wanted to go back to the dressing room, but Daniela read the situation well and convinced her to have a glass of wine instead. As they queued for the wine, Daniela could have sworn she spotted a young man she knew, disappearing into the men's toilets, but she said nothing.

The second half, a mixture of classical pieces and traditional Irish songs, was even more intense. Alfredo had asked Fergal to find something he could sing unaccompanied, and he had chosen a lament. As he started the first verse, the whole room seemed to hold its breath.

> *I wonder what is keeping my true love tonight,*
> *I wonder what is keeping you out of my sight,*
> *For it's little you know the pain I endure,*
> *Or you wouldn't stay from me this night, I am sure.*

The hairs on the back of Alfredo's neck stood to attention.

> *Oh, love, are you coming our cause to advance,*
> *Or, love, are you waiting for a far better chance?*

You know you have my whole life placed by yours in store,
And I can't bear to think that I'll see you no more.

Fergal opened his eyes and nearly lost his balance. The unmistakable face of Fintan Fiscetti shifted at the side of the audience, where he had to stand. He had bought the very last standing-room ticket that afternoon.

For sometimes we loved lightly; ah, but more times we loved long,
And when I think about you I know where I belong.
Last time you said you loved me, and you put my world at ease;
Now you're far from me – ah, come back, darling, please.

Fergal couldn't sing any more. He broke down momentarily, turning away from the audience, but Fintan started clapping, and it spread until the whole room was wild with support. Fergal was afraid to look at Alfredo, but when he did, his teacher was crying unashamedly. He got up from the piano, went to him and hugged him. The front row stood up, clapping and calling for more, then the middle rows followed, and then the rest of the room. Some of the house lights came up and Fergal was able to see Fintan more clearly. As their eyes met, Fintan threw a rose onto the stage, and it landed at Fergal's feet.

They managed to quiet the room, and Fergal sang another lament – this one from the final act of Puccini's *Tosca*, when Cavaradossi is going to be executed. When the last note of 'E lucevan le stelle' ended, Signore Angelo Arnelli of the Institute of Music led the clapping and the standing ovation.

When Fergal finally left the stage, he thought he was going to collapse. Angela was the first into the dressing room to see him. She was beside herself. She couldn't figure out where his voice had come from. The room filled up with well-wishers and friends of Alfredo's who wanted to meet his sensational protégé. Fergal searched the room for any sign of a red bunch of curls, but none arrived.

When they finally left for home, Fergal asked Alfredo, 'Did you see Fintan?'

Alfredo looked at him as if he were mad. 'Fintan Fiscetti, here? Tonight? I didn't see him. Are you sure?'

Suddenly Daniela piped up. 'That's who I saw going into the men's room! I knew I recognised him, but I couldn't place him. Yes, the tenor's son. He was running, but I saw him.'

Fergal was glad, but he was wild with tension and excitement. Where was Fintan now?

They stayed up at Alfredo's, drinking wine. Fergal couldn't relax, but he pretended everything was fine because of his mother. She told him that her favourite part of the evening had been when he had dedicated 'Kathleen' to her. Daniela plied her with brandy, and by midnight she needed her son's strong arm to get up the stairs to bed.

Alfredo was also exhausted, but thrilled. 'You broke new ground tonight, Fergal. I'm glad I had the foresight to record the recital.'

'It was recorded? My God, I'm glad I didn't know that beforehand!'

Alfredo smiled. 'Precisely!'

They talked about Fintan's possible whereabouts, and Alfredo even phoned Brendan to see if he knew anything, but there was no answer. 'There's nothing else we can do but wait till morning,' Alfredo said at last. 'He should have this number. I wonder why he didn't let us know he was coming?'

At that moment, the phone in the hall rang. Alfredo knew to let Fergal get it.

'Fintan?'

'How did you know?'

'My God! I saw you tonight at the recital, and I thought I was seeing things.'

'I know. Sorry I didn't stay around afterwards, I just got a bit, you know…overwhelmed.'

'Where are you now?'

'Guess.'

'I've no idea.'

'The hotel. I got a good last-minute rate because of Dad. Please say you'll come over.'

'I'm on my way.'

Alfredo reassured him that it was okay as long as he promised to be back for breakfast, and he managed to get a taxi in no time. Fintan was waiting for him in reception.

They didn't embrace. All Fintan said was, 'Hey.'

'Hey.'

'That was some concert,' Fintan said in the lift.

'Do you think so? I was dying with nerves.'

'Well, I'd never have known.'

They had reached Fintan's floor. He searched for his key and Fergal was glad to see that he had a completely different room; it was like a clean start. They sat down on the sofa, and for the first time they were shy of each other.

Fergal was the first to speak. He was still so fuelled by the concert that the silence made him want to burst. 'Fintan, I'm so glad you came back. I'm sorry I've been so…so up myself. It's just…' He ran out of steam.

Fintan turned to face him. 'Just what?'

'It's just that I was so scared. I'd convinced myself I wasn't good enough for you, and so I ended up pushing you away before you had a chance to push me. I know it sounds mad, but that's how I felt, because…' Fergal ran out of breath again. His heart was making a racket in his chest. 'Because you really touched me, and then you hurt me, and my head was all upside down.'

'Oh God, Fergal, I'm so sorry. I know I can be a real insensitive wanker at times. I think I was trying to protect myself too. You know, getting involved with a singer woke up all this resentment I had about my dad always being away. I know I need to think about other people more. It's hard when you're an only child. I'm sorry – I never want us to fight again. But you hurt me too, you know.'

'I know, I can see that now. And I'm sorry too, for being so over-dramatic.'

'I think it was a good thing we didn't see each other for a bit. It really brought things into focus. I'm miserable without you.'

'And me without you.' Fergal thought he would never breathe again.

Their apologies evaporated, and they reached for each other. The heat of their kisses rose, and without another word they undressed each other quickly and fell onto the bed, making up for lost time.

'Fintan,' Fergal whispered, 'I've missed you so much. I want to feel you inside me. Will you?'

'Are you sure?'

'Be careful, won't you?'

'I will, I will.'

Fintan pushed a pillow under Fergal's lower back and positioned himself above him. As they kissed, Fintan gently pressed the stiff tip of himself against Fergal's opening and moved his whole body forward, very slowly, so he could stop at the slightest sign of resistance. Fergal looked at the man on top of him and wanted nothing more than to stay in that moment forever.

'Go on, Fintan. I want to feel you inside me.'

They exhaled together, and slowly Fintan was able to move inside him. Although it was uncomfortable at first, he began to relax into it, and it felt better and better. Fintan's rhythm sped up.

He leaned forward, supporting himself on his outstretched arms, so that he could kiss his lover as they stayed attached to each other in their slow, sure sex.

'Are you okay?' Fintan asked, but Fergal was only able to answer breathlessly, 'Don't stop.' He grabbed the back of Fintan's thighs, and their bodies pushed against each other with greater and greater urgency.

'Fergal, are you near? I'm going to…oh, God…'

With one swift movement, Fintan pulled out of him, and they exploded together.

Fintan collapsed on top of Fergal and they lay there, still drunk – drunk on the evening and on each other. Slowly, they drifted into a blurred sleep.

Fergal was the first to wake, when he heard someone shouting in a far-off piazza through the open windows. Fintan had rolled off to one side and was till unconscious. Fergal stretched his neck to see the clock on the bedside cabinet. It was 4.46 am.

He lay still for another moment, inhaling the scent of Fintan's neck. Then he began kissing and nuzzling him lightly, and gradually he began to respond. Fergal whispered into his ear, 'I want to remember this night forever, Fintan – the smell of you, the taste of you, the feel of you.'

Finally they rolled apart, and Fergal slid off the bed and dressed in the dark.

'What time is it?' Fintan managed to say from some sleepy, dark valley.

'It's early, nearly five.'

'Jesus, why are you up?'

'I should head back to Alfredo's. My mother is there and we're going to have breakfast together. Will you come?'

'Do you want me to?'

'Of course! I don't want to be apart from you again. I can't believe you came back for the recital.'

'I couldn't stay in London, I was driving Dad mad. I missed you – I really did. Can we start over?'

'Of course, of course. Oh God, Fintan, don't leave me again. I need you.'

'I need you too.'

They held hands for another silent moment. Then Fergal got up to leave, but Fintan wouldn't let his hand go, so he pulled him up and they moved to the door, kissing again.

'I love you, Fergal. I do.'

'I know. And I love you, Fintan.' And then he was out the door.

Fergal walked slowly back across the city as the morning sky began to show its true colours. He let himself into Alfredo's house as silently as he'd left and curled up in bed for a few more hours' sleep. His night with Fintan was over, but he prayed that their renewed love had just begun.

Alfredo had invited Salvatore to breakfast, and Fergal was the last to join them. By the time he reluctantly dragged himself out of bed, even Fintan had rung to say he was about to head over in a taxi. Angela was talking non-stop about the concert and how much Fergal reminded her of her own departed father. She just couldn't get used to the fact that people – strangers – were being so nice to her and handing her cups of tea and food. She'd never eaten a meal she hadn't cooked herself since her wedding day. When Fintan arrived and was introduced, she told him, 'God, love, your ginger hair is lovely – not as mad as some of them. And you with an English accent and all!'

She had no idea that she had just met her son's lover. Fergal, wisely, had decided that that information could wait.

After a perfect, slow breakfast, Angela and Fergal decided to go back to the Vatican. Angela wanted to light more candles and buy rosary beads. Fergal took Fintan aside and asked if they could meet again that night.

Fintan smiled at him. 'You should spend this time with your mum. Let's meet on Monday, after she's gone? I could sleep for a week anyway.'

Fergal reluctantly agreed.

It turned out to be a good idea. Alfredo headed off with Salvatore, and Fergal and his mother walked all day. Fintan seemed like a dream to him, now that they were apart again.

'What are you going to do with the house in Walker Street?' he asked his mother.

She looked at him as if he were mad. 'Live in it, of course. What else?'

'I don't know. How do you think you'll like living on your own?'

'Jesus, I can't wait. But I think Ciaran will be there for another wee while. Everybody grows up so quick, though. I'd say another few years and they'll all be married.'

They stopped to buy an ice cream, and Angela, in her new candour, suddenly asked, 'Is that ginger fella a poof too?'

'Fintan?'

'Yes. Jesus, I'm terrible with names. I thought it was Vincent or something. Maybe my ears are going.'

'Well, yes, he's gay too.'

'Jesus, is the whole world…gay?'

Fergal laughed. 'Not quite.'

As they were walking through St Peter's Square again, a tall woman stopped them and said she had been at the recital and had been moved to tears. She asked Fergal for his autograph, and Angela couldn't believe it. 'Jesus, Fergal, wait till I tell everybody at home!' They had their photograph taken by a little man hovering with an instant camera, and Fergal bought two copies, one for each of them to keep.

'Are you glad you came, Mammy?'

'Of course. It's been the best weekend of my life. I only wish I'd done it years ago. Mind you, we never had a bean.'

'Well, just so as you know, I'm really glad you came too.'

All Angela could do was stroke the side of his face, and this time he didn't flinch. Fergal's heart had never felt so open – he knew that had a lot to do with Fintan's return – and he realised it had taken his mother all her strength to get on that plane. He could only admire her for it. He had never imagined that he could have such an easy time with her, that he could actually enjoy seeing her. He also saw how funny she was, in her own way, now that she was out of Belfast and more able to be herself. It was as if he was seeing her for the first time. Father Mac was right, of course – forgiveness was everything, and he knew that at last he had started to forgive.

At the airport the next morning, Alfredo gave Angela a beautiful set of rosary beads that he had bought in the market. He and Fergal saw her off, and this time, when mother and son hugged it wasn't nearly as uncomfortable.

'Mammy, travel safe, won't you? And ring us if you need anything.'

'I will, of course. Fergal, will you write to me? I want to hear how you get on. I can't wait to tell everybody about the concert. I don't know where you got that voice from, son.'

'Maybe your daddy gave it to me.'

It was the best thing he could have said to her. Angela blinked away tears.

'You know you can come again, Mammy, don't you?'

'You are welcome any time,' Alfredo chimed in.

'Thanks, Freddie, love. You're awful kind.'

Then Angela turned on her wee heels and was gone, feeling more rested than she ever had in her life.

★

When they got back to the house, Fintan was on the steps. They went inside, and Alfredo vanished into the kitchen to make coffee.

'I have something for you,' Fintan said. He handed Fergal an envelope.

'What is it?'

'Open it and find out!'

Inside, Fergal found two train tickets to Florence.

'Oh my God, I've wanted to go there for ages!'

'Well, pack a bag. We're going for four days.'

'What? I can't. My job – Alfredo—'

At that moment Alfredo came back into the front room, humming, and he handed Fergal an envelope too.

'What's going on?'

Alfredo smiled at him. 'It's all been organised. Giovanni will cover for you. And this' – he tapped the other envelope – 'is some of the profit from the recital, to go towards your trip to Florence.'

It was all too much for Fergal – he burst into tears. Fintan placed careful kisses on his eyelids as the tears began to dry and told him everything would be all right.

'It's just all been so mad lately – you know, seeing my mother again and actually enjoying her company, and now you, Fintan, you're back, and I'm so relieved…'

'Me too, darling Irishman, me too. Come on, you have to pack.'

As the afternoon train pulled away from Rome's central station, it was all Fergal could do to stop shaking with excitement next to Fintan and look at the horizon coming towards them. At that moment, for the first time in his life, he felt that the past was well and truly behind him.